FOR

EVA

FOR EVA

A NOVEL

JEN DAVIS

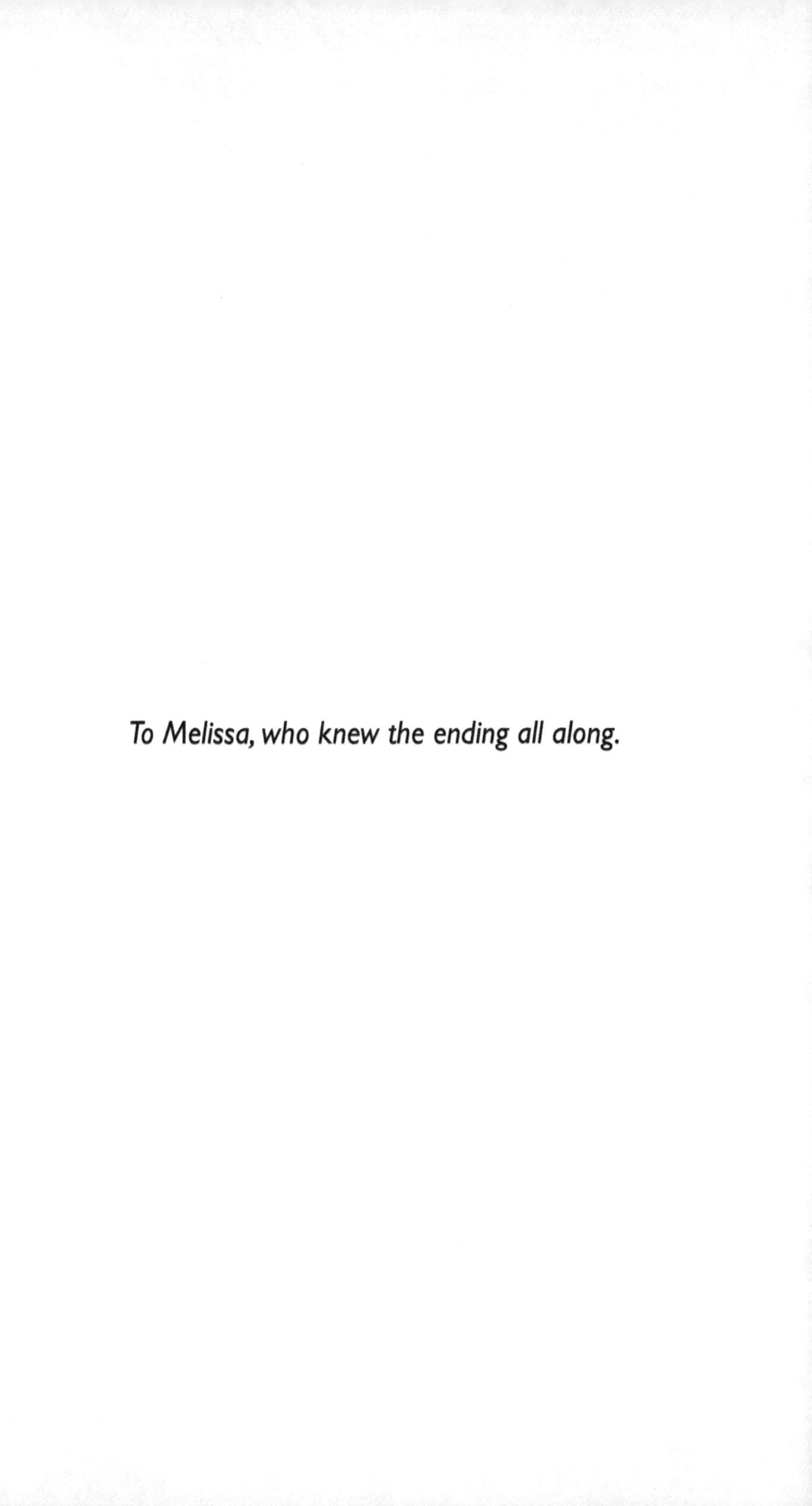

To Melissa, who knew the ending all along.

NOTE FROM THE AUTHOR

Dear Reader,

Thank you so much for choosing to read Eva's story. It's one that's been inside me for quite a while, and I cannot tell you how amazing it feels to share it with you.

I do want to let you know that this story contains topics which some readers may find triggering, such as abortion, loss of a parent, drug and alcohol addiction, and a brief mention of non-consensual sexual contact.

Your mental health is of the utmost importance, so if now is not the time for you to read this book, it is with great care and compassion that I encourage you to put it down and come back to it when and if you are ready.

All my love, always,
Jen

PART I

CHAPTER ONE
EVA
SEPTEMBER 2008

"Lucas and his girlfriend are having sex," Denise said as an orange plastic flag signaled for me to pull forward in the school pickup line.

I chuckled, sweeping my hair off my neck, silently cursing the Nashville heat. "Aw, he's growing up to be just like his mom. You must be so proud."

I heard a car door shut and the jingle of keys through the phone. "I mean, you do understand, Eva, that I found *multiple* condom wrappers in my son's bedroom?"

I stifled a laugh. I'd met my best friend when she was only a little older than Lucas, and there was no telling all the things she'd done in her own bedroom by that point.

"Denise," I began, clearing my throat. "He's seventeen. This is what boys his age do when they have an eager and willing participant. So, I think you just have to be glad they're using protection."

"I'm going to say this to you in a couple years when you find out Drew is banging some chick, and you're going to hate me as much as I hate you right now."

I gasped in feigned horror. "Drew would never! He's totally

waiting until he gets married. And you don't hate me, you love me. You always have and always will."

"You're right, I do. But you can bet your ass I *will* be repeating those exact words to you." She sighed. "When did this even become my life?"

I bit my lip. "I have no idea. But I wonder the same about my own."

"Oh my God, Eva. I am *so* sorry. This isn't even why I called. I got totally sidetracked by the whole thing with Lucas. How are you? Are things okay?"

"Yeah. I'm okay. The boys are okay. Seems crazy that it's been almost a month since things were official," I said, inching closer to the entrance of the school. "Also seems crazy that Aaron has barely seen the boys since then."

"What the hell? Wasn't he supposed to take them to that amusement park last weekend?"

"Didn't pan out. Something came up with his girlfriend. You know, the one he knocked up."

"I still can't believe she's pregnant. Jesus. When did he become such a jackass?"

"I think he's always been one. Just took me all these years to see it. But we can talk more about that later," I said as Miles burst through the doors of the building. "Got a kiddo about to get in the car."

"All right, I'll let you go. But call me tonight if you want. I'm gonna go figure out how to deal with fucking Condom-gate."

I laughed. "Will do, babe. Love you. And thanks for checking in."

"Of course." Her voice felt like a warm hug through the phone. "Love you, too."

"Hey, Mom!" Miles heaved his backpack into the SUV, then

pulled himself up into the seat as I disconnected the call.

The sight of his mussed brown hair and rumpled clothes caused a smile to tug at the corners of my mouth. "Hey, buddy. How was your day?"

"Good. Mrs. Stark actually gave us a project." He buckled his seat belt and pulled a piece of paper out of his backpack. "It's about what we wanna be when we grow up. We have to write three paragraphs and make a poster."

I craned my neck to check for oncoming traffic before making a quick left turn. "So what *do* you want to be when you grow up?"

"At first I was thinking maybe I wanna be a chef," he answered. "Like a pizza chef. Because you know I love pizza."

I chuckled. "That I do."

"And then I thought, no, I *actually* want to be a baseball player. Like a famous pitcher. Because I'm really good at pitching."

My insides turned to mush. This was one of those moments I wanted to stay with me forever. The kind I now knew to hold on to so I could remember what a sweet nine-year-old Miles had been, just in case he turned into the perpetually grumpy teenager his brother had become.

I stole another glance at him in the mirror. "So is that what you decided? Famous pitcher?"

Miles cocked his head and stared out the window. "No. I wanna be a lawyer. Like Dad."

A thousand knives stabbed my heart, and I gripped the steering wheel so tight I thought it would break. I was thankful for the red light ahead and used the time to quickly swipe my fingers under my sunglasses before Miles saw my tears.

I smiled at him in the rearview mirror. My precious boy

who looked so much like his father that it was almost too pain-ful a reminder of the life we'd had—or the life I'd hoped we'd have. "Well, I think you should do whatever makes you happy."

He shifted his gaze from the window to look at me with his blue-gray eyes—Aaron's eyes—and nodded. "Yeah. And if I get bored with that, I'll go pitch for the Braves. Atlanta isn't that far, right?"

"Four hours. Just don't make me drive down there during rush hour to watch you play."

"I'm gonna fly you in my private jet," Miles said.

I smacked my hand against my forehead. "Right. Because why *wouldn't* you have a private jet? You'll be a famous million-aire major league pitcher."

We both giggled as the light changed to green, and I turned onto the side street that connected to our cul-de-sac. I was able to laugh away the tears by the time I pulled into our drive-way and saw Drew laid out on top of the front stoop.

What the hell?

"I'm going to Max's," Miles announced before ejecting him-self from the car and running into our neighbor's yard.

I blew out a steady breath before grabbing Miles's backpack and heading for the door. I stood on the step directly below Drew and removed my sunglasses, squinting so I could zero in on his coffee-colored eyes—my eyes—which glistened in the sun.

He grinned at me. "What's up?"

I sighed. "What's up with *me*? What's up with *you*? I thought you had football practice after school."

Drew pushed himself up against the black iron railing that climbed the stairs to the house and swept his blond bangs out of his face. "It got canceled. Coach said it was too hot. Which it is because I've been out here for an hour waiting for you to get home, and I'm sweating to death."

I rolled my eyes and shoved the key into the lock on the front door, dropping my purse on the console in the foyer.

"What happened to your key?" I asked, kicking off my sandals and heading into the kitchen.

He followed behind me and pulled a Gatorade out of the fridge. "I dunno."

"What do you mean 'you dunno'? You can't go around losing house keys, Drew."

He shrugged. "I mean, it's here somewhere, I just have to find it."

"How'd you even get home?"

"This guy Jackson."

Fucking high school.

I pressed my hands into the cool granite countertop. "What? Who's Jackson? We've had this discussion multiple times. I don't want you getting into cars with people I don't know."

"Oh my God, Mom, chill out. He's a junior on the varsity team. He asked if I needed a ride when all the practices were canceled. What was I supposed to say? My mom doesn't let me get in cars with strangers?"

I ran my hands through my hair. "Look, I know that's embarrassing, but you're not even fifteen yet. I just need some time to adjust to this whole high school thing. So, for now, if this happens again, go to the office and call me."

"Might help if you'd get me a freaking cell phone since every other person I know has one."

"I've told you we'll figure that out. Just bear with me for a bit, okay?"

FOR EVA

Drew expelled an obnoxiously loud sigh and mumbled "whatever" before retreating into the living room.

"Don't 'whatever' me, Drew!"

I pulled in another deep breath and exhaled slowly, releasing my clenched fists and jaw. I couldn't count how many conscious breaths I'd taken since Aaron left. All I knew was I wanted just one day of breathing *unconsciously*. And the frustration and anger and sadness I felt not knowing if that day would ever come was almost too much to bear sometimes.

The red light on the cordless phone blinked from the alcove by the door to the patio, beckoning me to it. I trudged over and picked up the receiver, punching the button for voicemail, wondering why I even bothered to still have a landline.

Beep. "Hey, Eva, this is Haley. Haven't seen you in a while and was wondering if you wanted to make an appointment for a color and—"

I fingered the two inches of dark roots on the top of my head and grimaced as I pressed the button to skip to the next message.

Beep. "Hi there, this is Carolyn Jenkins, the room mom for Mrs. Stark's class. I was hoping you might be able to help us out with—"

Another skip. I'd figure out what Carolyn needed me to bake later.

Beep. "Hi, this is Simon Rogers with *Rolling Stone*, and I'm trying to reach Eva Mitchell—formerly Eva Holloway. We're doing a profile piece on Eric Stratton for an upcoming issue, and I understand you worked with his former band, Counting Backward. Eric mentioned you as someone who could possibly provide a bit of commentary on what, um, *happened* during that time. I'm also wondering if you might still be in touch with Danny Kincaid. He's proven quite difficult to get a hold of. Anyway, I'd love to chat with you at your earliest convenience. Please give me call me at—"

The phone slid out of my hand and crashed to the floor before I could hear the number. Not that it mattered. I wasn't going to call him back. I *couldn't*. A rush of prickly heat shot through my body, setting my chest and face on fire. My neck throbbed with my racing pulse, and I grabbed the edge of the counter to steady myself.

"Mom? Are you all right?" Drew's voice came from behind me.

I nodded and mumbled something about accidentally dropping the phone, hoping he would disappear back into the living room. I couldn't turn around. I didn't want him to see me so shaken by something that had nothing to do with him or Miles or the life I'd decided to build nineteen years ago.

That was all *before*.

It was in the past.

Or at least it had been.

CHAPTER TWO
EVA

JANUARY 1988

"Holy shit, that's strong." Denise stuck her tongue out and shook her head full of long dark curls.

"So strong we probably shouldn't do another one." My mouth curved into a grin as I slid the next round of tequila shots closer to us.

"Obviously. We wouldn't want to get drunk or anything," she quipped, her ruby lips mirroring mine. "But since we did one to celebrate the start of your LA vacay, we have to do another to celebrate the new job back in Chicago." She nodded toward my glass and picked up her own. "Welcome to the world of corporate bullshit, Eva Holloway. We're so glad you could join us."

"Well, when you put it that way." I emptied the contents with a quick toss of my head, scrunching my nose as the hard liquor attacked my taste buds.

We hadn't bothered to ask for salt and limes, settling instead on a couple of beers for chasers. The bartenders at the Rainbow already had their hands full slinging drinks to the wannabe rock stars flirting with the girls waiting to be noticed by the bona fide ones. The bar area was standing room only, but we'd managed to wedge ourselves between several occupied stools at the counter.

"You're so right about the corporate bullshit. I mean, working for a big advertising agency? Making a bunch of rich assholes even richer? I could've at least tried to find something meaningful. I'm a sellout, Denise." I sighed dramatically and dropped my head into my hands, my hair falling around my face.

She rested her hand on my shoulder. "Yeah, so correct me if I'm wrong, babe, but I thought the goal was to make more money than you did at the bar serving shit-faced frat boys bottles of Bud while they stared at your tits?"

"The goal was to make my dad shut up about me being a year and a half out of college and not having a 'real job,'" I explained, lifting my head. "Having shit-faced frat boys stare at your tits is actually quite lucrative."

"True." Denise tipped her beer bottle toward me before taking a sip. "And let's be honest. You may be serving up marketing strategies instead of cheap beer, but at the end of the day, every man in the room is just a former frat boy thinking about sticking his di—"

"Well, *I've* never been a frat boy, but I definitely still think about sticking *my* di—"

Without taking her eyes off me, she raised her hand and covered the mouth of the lanky figure who'd materialized beside us.

"What?" he asked, the muzzle she'd slapped on him garbling his voice.

"Wait, why don't I get to find out where he thinks about sticking his…whatever we're talking about." I shifted my gaze back to Denise, trying to contain my laughter.

She inhaled deeply through her nose and rolled her eyes before removing her hand from the guy's mouth. "Because I'd prefer not to relive the details of my poor decisions," she said dryly, though the tiniest smile caused the corner of her mouth to twitch.

The guy scoffed and slid his arm around Denise, pulling all five foot one of her—five foot five if you counted her spiked heels—into him. "You mean the poor decisions you've made, like, seven times?" He raised his chin in a thoughtful pose. "Or is it eight?"

She wiggled out of his grip and leaned back against the bar, the smile she'd been holding in forcing its way to the surface. "Eva, this is Matt, a seven- or eight-time poor decision. Matt, this is Eva, my best friend."

Matt nodded as we exchanged nice-to-meet-yous. He was good-looking, with messy shoulder-length blond hair. His black jeans and Sex Pistols T-shirt made him *look* like a rock star, but since Denise hadn't mentioned him even once, I placed him squarely in the wannabe category.

"What are you drinking, ladies?" he asked, reaching for his wallet.

Denise pressed her hand against her chest and gasped. "What's this? You have *money?*"

He tipped his head back and laughed slowly, pronouncing each *ha* with sarcastic clarity. "You know what, evil woman? We *do* occasionally sell tickets to our shows. Or actually, maybe you don't know since you never come to any."

"Yeah," she began, sucking in air through her teeth. "That all feels a bit too girlfriend-y. Let's just stick with the occasional drunken hookup ending with me telling you that's the last time and kinda sorta not really meaning it."

"Fine. But you're going to regret this when I'm headed off for our world tour on a private jet that's crawling with half-naked chicks who are dying to make me their next 'poor decision.'"

A laugh that sounded like a sputtering car engine escaped my lips, causing Matt to turn his attention to me. "Eva, right? You're hot. What's your deal? And why have I never met you?"

Denise slapped his arm. "You haven't met her because I don't introduce you to my friends. Regardless, she doesn't even live here, and she's not gonna fucking sleep with you, you idiot."

I flashed a wide grin and shook my head. "She's right, I'm

not. But buy me a drink, and I'll see if I can convince Denise to go for drunken hookup number eight—or is it nine—tonight."

He gestured to the bottles lined up behind the bar. "I like you, Eva. Get whatever you want. And I guess you can, too, Denise." He winked at her, and she fixed her gaze on him, a sexy smile that straddled the line between fuck *off* and fuck *me* dancing on her lips.

Matt's eyes remained on Denise as he mumbled "Jack and Coke" and handed me a twenty. I leaned against the counter, trying not to elbow the surly-looking biker beside me as I signaled for a bartender's attention. By the time the drinks were mixed, I was pinned in by the crowd, able to twist ever so slightly to hand Matt and Denise their glasses.

Matt called my name above the guitar solo screeching through the speakers just as I was finally able to break free and turn around with my vodka cran clasped in my hand. "Hey, Eva, I want you to meet my friend. This is—"

Someone squeezed in between me and the bar, and I suddenly found myself flattened against the person standing in front of me. My drink sloshed over the glass, splashing us both with pink liquid.

"Dude, what the fuck was tha—" I stopped midsentence and raised my eyes from the cranberry stains on my white tank top to see whose chest was pressed against mine. And then the room went quiet. I could no longer hear the music or the crowd, just a high-pitched hum that clogged my ears and scrambled my brain, making me feel for a moment like the floor might fall out from under me. I tried to speak, but after several attempts I realized I couldn't combine consonants and vowels to form any intelligible words.

Except one.

"*Danny?*"

CHAPTER THREE
DANNY

JANUARY 1988

*E*va?

Her name caught in my throat. Or did it? I wasn't sure, but the way she stared at me with those soft brown eyes told me that even if I had managed to speak, she hadn't heard me.

Memories I'd forced to the back of my mind surged forward—the very same ones that sometimes grew so strong they caused the wall I'd built between *before* and *after* to crack. Until that moment, I'd always found ways to fill those cracks. By landing gigs at clubs I'd only ever dreamed of playing. By going home from those gigs with chicks who were up for all kinds of crazy shit I'd only ever imagined. By reminding myself the life I was living wouldn't have been possible if I hadn't walked away from her.

But standing there, face-to-face with the person at the center of each of those memories, I knew the dam had burst. And it was going to take me turning and running out of that bar as fast as I fucking could to even have the slightest chance in hell of rebuilding it.

The strange thing was, I didn't know if I wanted to. I also didn't know what the odds were that if I stayed, I'd end up getting punched in the face. But I took a chance, leaned over her shoulder, and put my lips to her ear.

"Is this when I'm supposed to say that line about you walking into my gin joint?" Her hair smelled like vanilla, making me forget I was standing in the middle of a bar in West Hollywood rather than her parents' basement in Illinois.

Her cheek brushed against mine. "Is this when *I'm* supposed to say that you semi-remembering a quote from *Casablanca* is impressive enough that I've decided not to ask the Hells Angels-looking guy behind me to beat the shit out of you?"

I shifted my gaze to the man at the bar who was wearing a leather vest that strained across his back. "This is definitely when you're supposed to say that."

"Consider yourself safe then…for now." Her voice landed somewhere between sweet and sour, purposefully leaving me hanging.

I was still pressed against her, afraid to pull away and find out the smile I imagined on her face wasn't there, when something jabbed my arm. I turned to see the girl I'd just met standing beside me, her head cocked, eyes shifting between me and Eva.

"Hey, hi, excuse me. Do you guys know each other or something?"

Eva stepped back slightly and bit her lip, glancing at me before turning her attention to the dark-haired girl—*Deanne? Denise?* "This is…um…this is Danny."

"What?" She leaned in, straining to hear her over the music that had been cranked up.

"I said, this is Danny!"

Deanne/Denise narrowed her eyes. "Yeah, Matt just introduced me. But how do you know him?"

"Because he's *Danny*." Eva emphasized my name, her face tightening and eyes widening, as though she was trying to transmit a telepathic message.

"Yeah, but I don't—" The other chick's mouth dropped open, and she grabbed Eva's hand, yanking her past me so fast I barely had time to turn before I saw them bump into Matt, who was weaving his way back to us.

I'd been so focused on Eva I hadn't realized he'd left. The girl whose name started with a D exchanged a few words with him, while Eva glanced at me over her shoulder. And then they disappeared.

My pulse picked up, my eyes darting back and forth through the sea of people as Matt approached me. "Wait, where are they going? Did they leave? Are they leaving?"

He placed his hand on my shoulder. "Dude, calm down. They're coming back. Denise said they were going to the bathroom."

I released the breath I'd been holding. I didn't fully understand the panic I felt thinking she'd walked out the door, bidding me one final *fuck you.* After all, *I* was the one who'd left. I was the one who'd made the decision five and a half years ago that I couldn't live out my dream with her in my life.

"Come on," he said, turning to work his way through the crowd. "Nikki's working tonight, and she hooked us up with a table."

I nodded and followed behind him. Our drummer's sister escorted us to the booth, and I told her we needed two of whatever girls liked to drink, adding that I didn't care what she brought me as long as it was strong and cheap. With the unexpected turn of events, I was gonna need as much alcohol as I could afford—which, admittedly, wasn't a lot.

"What's with you and that chick, anyway?" he asked as we slid into opposite sides of the booth. "You've known her for thirty seconds, and you're acting like life as you know it will be over if you don't see her again."

More like life as I know it will be over if I do see her again.

With that thought, I should've left. Stood up and gotten the hell out of Dodge while I had the chance. But I kept thinking about how beautiful she was and how much I hadn't let myself think about missing her. And that's what kept my feet glued to the floor.

"Earth to Danny."

I startled as Matt waved his hand in front of my face. "Yeah, sorry, I, uh…This is all kinds of fucked-up, man." I shook my head and blew out a breath. "That girl, Eva. She was my girlfriend. In high school, back in Illinois."

"Are you serious? What the fuck is she doing here? How does she know Denise?"

"No idea. But I don't know what the hell to do right now."

He snorted. "What do you mean you don't know what to do? You get drunk, you fuck for old times' sake, and that's that. Denise said she doesn't even live here. This isn't a hard decision."

I lit a cigarette and leaned back against the booth, staring up at the colored lights strung overhead. "It's just that it's more…*complicated* than that."

"Dude, it was *high school*. How complicated could it have been?"

I ran my hand through my hair and shrugged. "I know it sounds stupid. But she'd been through a lot before I left for LA, and I told her we'd stay together, but I—"

He reached across the table and nudged my arm. I looked up to my left to see Eva standing there. Long blond hair, bangs swept to the side. Tight white tank top that made it impossible not to stare at the way it hugged her tits. Jeans that made it impossible not to notice the way her waist curved perfectly into her full hips.

"So, Danny Kincaid." She slid into the booth and turned to face me as she took a cigarette from her purse, placing it between her glossy pink lips. With her head cocked, she leaned toward my lighter, then pulled back and blew a stream of smoke from the corner of her mouth. "Let's start by you telling me what the fuck you've been up to for the last five and a half years."

I swallowed, sweat beginning to break through the skin above my brow, wondering when she'd break the stare that

FOR EVA

had me feeling like I was under interrogation lights being questioned by the hottest detective on the whole goddamn planet.

I tried to smile. I tried to laugh. I opened my mouth to speak, but nothing came out.

And it was then I knew I was fucked.

Totally and completely *fucked*.

CHAPTER FOUR
EVA

JANUARY 1988

"I'm just sayin', Eva…this is some pretty cosmic shit. You and Denise going to college together, Denise knowing Matt, Matt and me being in the same band. And now here *we* are." Danny leaned against the wall, his arm draped over the back of the booth, offering me an opportunity to take him in.

"People run into each other all the time, Danny." I'd been staring at him much too long, but I couldn't tear my eyes away. "I wouldn't read that much into it."

"Right," he said, dragging the word out and slowly nodding his head.

His hair was darker—dyed from brown to black—and fell to his shoulders, curling slightly at the ends. Several pieces swept across his eyes, almost down to the top of his perfectly straight nose. In his half-unbuttoned shirt with the sleeves rolled up to his elbows, and his scuffed-up boot planted on the red leather seat of the booth, he reminded me of a younger Keith Richards. Effortlessly fucking cool.

I turned my head, letting my hair fall in my face to hide the warmth spreading across my cheeks, and watched as Denise and Matt flirted without a care—without any history to complicate things. She gave me the occasional glance across the table, making sure I was okay since I'd been far from it a couple of hours earlier. By the time she'd pulled me through the bar and into the bathroom, I'd broken into a cold sweat, and my lungs were squeezed so tight I was sure all the oxygen to my brain would be cut off. All of the cool I'd initially displayed in front of Danny had evaporated.

Denise ran her hands gently along my arms, repeatedly telling me everything would be all right until I could catch my breath.

"What do you wanna do, babe? We can leave right now. We can walk out that door, and you can forget you ever saw Danny Kincaid." She scanned my face, and when I didn't answer, she squeezed my hand. "I'm calling it. We need to go."

"No, wait," I said, my hand falling from her grasp as she started to walk away. "I don't wanna go. I can do this." A shaky confidence coursed through me, and I turned to the mirror and dug in my purse. "I want to make that motherfucker regret everything he did."

Denise shook her head slowly. "Eva, I—"

"No, listen. I'll flirt like hell with him all night. Make him think I'm still madly in love with him. And then, as we're leaving—just when he's thinking *I can't believe I still get to fuck this chick after the way I treated her*—I tell him to fuck off." My hand trembled as I swiped a wand full of pink gloss across my lips. "It's a good plan, right?"

Denise sighed and leaned against the wall. "You're forgetting one thing, Eva."

"What's that?" I smacked my lips together and checked my reflection.

"You *are* still in love with him."

I paused before reaching for a paper towel to dab at the splashes of cranberry juice on my tank top. Was that true? Was I still in love with him? As many drunken late nights as Denise had listened to me lament the end of our relationship, she hadn't ever put things quite so plainly. But at that moment, the answer didn't matter. Because I'd somehow convinced myself that even if I did still love Danny Kincaid, I hated him even more, and *that* was going to give me the strength to finally get the closure I so desperately wanted.

Two hours in, things were still going according to plan. I cleared my throat and picked up my drink, raising my eyes to Danny's before taking a sip.

"So how's Lena?" I asked, deciding to further poke the bear by mentioning his mother, who had unequivocally adored me from the moment she found out her underachieving son was dating a straight A student. "Still in DeKalb? She misses me terribly, right?"

He chuckled, then took a long drag off his cigarette. "Oh, I'm sure she does. And yeah, still there and still thinks all of this is just a phase—that I'll come to my senses, move home, get a job, find a nice girl."

I narrowed my eyes and tapped a fingertip against my lips. "You know, I seem to recall you had one of those once."

"One of what?" His brows turned in, and his mouth formed into a crooked smile. "A nice girl?"

"Mm-hmm."

Danny closed one eye and raised his chin before shaking his head. "Nope, don't remember that."

"Wow," I said. "How quickly we forget."

He paused for a moment, then let out a sharp laugh. "Oh, I'm sorry. Are you saying *you* were that nice girl?"

I fingered the small jewel on my necklace. "What? You think I'm not nice?"

He leaned forward, the look in his hazel eyes so intense my stomach flipped. "I think I remember a hell of a lot more naughty than nice."

"You know, it's super creepy when guys say the word *naughty.*"

"I don't know what else to call you letting me go down on you in the school—"

"That was *one* time."

He tilted his head and smirked. "Really? Because I also remember one night when your parents were literally in the next room and you—"

"Fine," I conceded, cutting him off before my face turned the color of the red leather on the bench. "Two times."

"Pretty sure it was more than that." He stubbed his cigarette out in the glass ashtray, exhaling one final stream of smoke. "But you were nice, too, Eva. And considering you haven't gotten that biker to body slam me, I'm guessing you still are."

I shrugged as I finished off my vodka cran, trying to slow my racing pulse. "Place isn't closed yet. Still plenty of time."

Danny laughed and took a sip of his beer. "Hey, that reminds me. Remember the time we snuck into that bar over in Rockford? Summer before senior year? And I spilled my drink on that huge biker dude, and he was about to fucking flatten me?"

I brushed my hand across his knee, feeling an instant jolt of electricity that made me wish I hadn't touched him. "Oh my God, how could I forget? I thought we were both gonna die."

"He shoved me so hard I fell backward. But then you stepped in front of me and shoved him back, and he was so fucking shocked he just stood there."

I nodded. "And then you grabbed me and got us the hell out of there."

"Yep. And we went to Denny's, and I bought you that ring out of the gumball machine for saving my life."

He smiled at me. Not the grin or the smirk he'd been flashing all night, but a genuine smile that filled his eyes with warmth. I smiled back, remembering the bent gold band topped with a five carat plastic ruby. I wasn't going to tell him I'd kept that ring until it eventually got lost during one of my apartment moves in college. I supposed I'd held on to it to remind myself there was a time when things hadn't been so heavy. When almost getting my ass kicked in a bar was the scariest thing I could ever imagine happening. But even that wasn't so scary I couldn't stuff my face with pancakes and laugh about it afterward.

The corners of his mouth fell, but the tenderness in his eyes remained. "If I bought you another one, would you believe me when I say how sorry I am for what I did?"

And that was it. That was the moment the calm, cool, and collected act I'd committed to fell apart. That one memory, that one *sorry* I didn't even know if he meant, grabbed the pulls and revealed the person behind the curtain was not, in fact, the Great and Powerful Oz. Instead, she was a twenty-three-year-old woman who'd never been able to fix what had broken inside her when she was a seventeen-year-old girl.

I didn't know if he noticed. I didn't know if he saw my face soften and my body begin to melt into itself. But *something* happened. A shift between us. A moment of understanding. And then he spoke.

"Do you wanna get out of he—"

"Yes."

Denise's eyes burned into me, and the tip of her pointed heel assaulted my shin under the table.

I avoided her glare and quickly grabbed my purse, pulling out my credit card and tossing it in front of her. "We're going, everything's on me."

She shoved the card back into my hand before we both scooted out of the booth. "Eva and I need to go to the bathroom for a second."

Matt looked up at us, squinting with confusion. Danny averted his eyes and rubbed his chin.

"I don't have to go to the bathroom," I said, a tense smile plastered on my face.

"You sure about that?"

"Yep, I'm sure."

Denise wrapped her arms around me, pretending to hug me goodbye. "What the fuck are you doing, Eva?" she hissed into my ear.

"It's fine, Denise."

"This wasn't your plan."

"I know, but I came up with a new one."

"That guy's a motherfucker, Eva. Remember the conversation we had, like, two hours ago? Remember how he made you feel? What he did to you?"

"Yeah, but I can make him regret things even more if I sleep with him. Show him what he's been missing out on." This was actually not my new plan, but I decided to throw it out there anyway to see if Denise would buy it. To see if *I* would buy it.

"You're drunk, Eva."

"I'm not that drunk. It's all good, I swear."

She sighed, her shoulders dropping in defeat. "Okay, go. Do whatever the new plan is. I love you. But remember: *muh-thur-fuh-kur.*"

She released me and clenched her teeth into a fake grin as Danny worked his way out of the booth.

"Later," Matt said with a wave.

I started through the room, my head hazy and my legs a bit wobbly, then turned back to sneak a quick smile at Danny. I saw he was still with Denise, her hand clasped tight around his arm.

Fuuuuuck.

When he finally began to walk toward me, there was a tightness in his jaw that hadn't been there before. Without a word, he pulled me against him, steering us toward the exit before it even registered that I was back in his arms again.

"What did she say?" I asked, not sure I actually wanted to hear the answer.

He sucked in a deep breath and placed his hand on the door. "Just tell me one thing," he began, looking over at me before we pushed through to the swarms of people cruising Sunset. "She doesn't really own a gun…right?"

———————

"I've missed the fuck out of you, Eva."

I could barely remember how we got to his apartment. I couldn't recall any conversation, only the faint sounds of a song I'd never heard before coming from the radio of his old Ford Bronco and swirls of pink and blue lights dancing in the palm trees that lined the streets. And then, suddenly, I was stepping over guitar cases and old pizza boxes, pulling off my shirt and tossing it somewhere among the clothes strewn across his bedroom.

"Really?" I panted as I unbuttoned his shirt and pushed it off his shoulders.

He answered by crushing his lips against mine and pulling me onto the mattress on the floor. His body hovered over mine, our bare chests rising to meet one another in quick, shallow breaths.

"I mean it," he said, holding my gaze. "I've missed you more than you know."

Fuck. My plan. I'd almost forgotten, too tangled up in him and the moment that I hadn't been able to focus on anything other than how fast I could get my clothes off. But this was too easy. Too perfect. I felt like an evil genius, rubbing my hands together, relishing the imminent demise of my nemesis as a list of possible responses to his confession scrolled through my brain.

A childish yet concise *sucks to be you.*

A melodramatic yet powerful *regret is a wasted emotion.*

A crass yet straightforward *shut up and fuck me.*

But none of these made it to my lips, because a thousand stars were bursting inside of me, each one being devoured by the black holes in his eyes.

"I've missed you, too."

And that was the moment my hastily woven plan unraveled. The moment I knew it had been so poorly constructed that it was bound to come tumbling down and leave me lying in the rubble.

There wasn't one damn thing I could do to save myself. So, I closed my eyes as my misguided intentions collapsed around me, leaving only a tiny seed of hope that Danny Kincaid would finally fix what he'd broken.

CHAPTER FIVE
EVA

JANUARY 1988

A distant sound outside the bedroom window caused my eyelids to flutter. A rhythmic vibration that stopped momentarily, then started up again. The sound grew closer as I drifted over the threshold into full consciousness, and I extended my arm behind me to the other side of the bed, reaching for a pillow to cover my ears.

But rather than landing on a pile of feathers, my hand landed on someone's head.

What the...

My brain flipped through images of the night before. The Rainbow, colored lights, tequila shots...

My eyes flew open, and I gasped.

Danny.

Oh God. Oh God, oh God, oh God.

I clasped my hand over my mouth and curled my knees to my chest. He sighed and shifted, then started snoring again.

What had I done? It was a rhetorical question, of course, because I remembered everything: my stupid plan, Danny saying he was sorry and he missed me, me saying I missed him. Was that really all it had taken? A couple of meaningless lines? Did he really make me that fucking weak?

I could've laid there for hours contemplating what an idiot

I was, but there was no time to think about it. I gently peeled off the covers and crawled to the end of the mattress, which was my only means of escape since I was trapped between Danny and the wall. Thanks to the sun that had begun to peek around the black sheet hanging over the window, I was able to locate my clothes. My purse and shoes had to be in the other room, so I'd grab those on the way out, find a pay phone to call Denise, and we'd be laughing about all of this over coffee in no time. It would all be fine.

Once my bra, tank, and underwear were on, I slid one leg into my jeans and let out a small sigh of relief. I was less than a minute from hitting the sidewalk and heading for the nearest 7-Eleven. But as I attempted to step into the other leg of my pants, I tripped, tumbling sideways until I landed on the floor with a thud that quite possibly registered on the Richter scale.

It did not help that I also involuntarily shouted something along the lines of "motherfucking Jesus why."

"What the…" Danny mumbled as he propped himself up on his elbow, rubbing one eye with the base of his palm.

He looked over at me, a heap on the floor with only one-half of my jeans on. "What are you doing? Are you leaving?" There was a quietness to his voice, something that sounded almost like disappointment. It surprised me, but I quickly chalked it up to his wanting to enjoy my inability to resist him one last time before I left.

I rolled onto my back and tugged on the rest of my jeans, then blew out a breath as I stared at the ceiling.

"Denise and I have plans," I said, pushing myself up to stand. "We're, uh, going hiking. At one of those canyon places."

He narrowed his sleepy eyes at me. "You hike?"

"Yeah, I, um, just started." I bit my lip and crossed my arms over my chest, looking up, down, around the room—every-where but at him. I despised hiking, but I would've done it naked all the way down Hollywood Boulevard if it would've gotten me the hell out of his apartment.

FOR EVA

Danny sat up. "I thought you hated outdoor shit. You used to refuse to even pee in the woods at parties."

I rolled my eyes and uncrossed my arms. "Well, I'll make sure to take care of that before I go."

He ran a hand through his messy black hair and sighed. "You're telling me you guys went out drinking last night and planned a sunrise hike for this morning?"

My brows turned down, and I scoffed. "What, like that's weird?"

"Eva, seriously, what's going on?"

"Nothing's going on. I just need to go. So, yeah." I nodded and started toward the door.

He pushed himself up from the mattress, and I quickly averted my eyes while he pulled on his jeans. "Okay, but can I at least drive you home so you can make your…*hike*."

"It's fine, I'm gonna call Denise," I said, opening the door. "Is the phone out there?"

"Eva, wait." He dropped the shirt he was about to pull on and hurried over to me, placing his hand against the doorframe. "Can I see you again? You said you're here for a week, right?"

I laughed sharply and pushed past him into the dingy living room-slash-kitchen. "You mean can we have sex again? I don't think so."

He followed behind me. "Listen, can you just sit for a second?"

"I told you I have plans," I insisted, surveying the space for my purse and shoes.

"*Eva, please.*"

I closed my eyes momentarily and pressed my lips together, then whirled on him. "Fine. Here's the deal. I'm not going hiking. I fucking hate hiking. But I also hate this," I said, waving my hand back and forth between us. "So, I'm gonna leave, and then we can both forget what happened and go on with our lives."

"But I don't wanna forget what happened." He reached out and placed his hand on my arm.

I glanced down at it before jerking away. "Look, Danny. You don't have to say that. I know last night was a mistake, and I don't need you to pretend you care or try to make me feel better. Because I'm fine. And I actually *do* want to forget about it."

"I'm not trying to make you feel better about anything, Eva. I'm trying to get you to listen to me. I wasn't lying when I said I missed you. I *have* missed you. And I know you probably hate me, but if you'll give me a chance to—"

"Seriously, where the fuck is my fucking purse?" I whipped around and began digging under the cushions on the second-hand sofa.

"Eva, would you please just—"

"No." I groaned and pressed my hands against my temples. "I will not just do whatever it is you want me to do. I need to find my shit and leave."

"And then what? I never see you again?"

I turned around slowly. He stood with his hands out to his sides and a blank look on his face, like he hadn't considered the possibility that would happen.

"Isn't that what you wanted?" I asked, my voice matching my icy stare.

"Come on, Eva, I told you I—"

"Oh my God." I threw my hands over my face as a scene from the night before flashed in my brain. "Did we even use a condom? *Shit.* I can't even think about this." I sucked in a breath and stomped across the room to the kitchen, almost tripping over my shoes on the way. I reached down and swiped them off the floor.

"I...You didn't ask me to, so I thought...You're, like, on the pill or something, right?"

"Yes, Danny, I am. I learned that lesson years ago, remember?" I shot him a look, this one steeped in even more animosity, before I opened the stove to see if my purse had somehow ended up in there since it sure as hell wasn't anywhere else. "Although, I now probably have God only knows what kinds of diseases."

"I don't *have* any diseases, Eva." He paused. "At least I don't think I do."

"Oh, good, that's very comforting."

"Okay, look, if you just give me, like, five minutes—"

"No."

"But I don't understand why you can't stay so we can talk about—"

"Because you broke my heart, Danny!" I threw my shoes to the ground, five and a half years of hurt, resentment, and betrayal erupting from the deepest parts of me.

I watched as he shrank back, my anger surprising him as much as it surprised me. "What?"

"My heart, you asshole." I glared at him, my chest heaving. "You fucking broke it."

"But I—"

"My mom wasn't even dead a fucking year. My dad could barely speak to me. All I had was *you*. And you fucking lied to me, and you left." I choked on my words and shifted my eyes away from him, attempting to swallow my emotions. I couldn't believe I still had tears left to cry over him, but somehow, I did.

"I know, Eva," he said, stepping toward me. "I *was* an asshole. But I cannot count the number of times I've wanted to tell you how sorry I am for what I did. I was eighteen and stupid and selfish and—"

"And what?" I snatched the receiver from the telephone on the kitchen counter and dialed Denise's number.

"I was wrong, Eva. And seeing you again, just as fucking beautiful as you've always been, I know I fucked up. I fucked up big time, and I swear to fucking God, I would do anything to—"

"Don't. Don't say any more, Danny." I stared down at my bare feet as the phone rang for the final time and the answering machine picked up.

My hand trembled as I placed the receiver back in its cradle, then glanced over to see him sitting on the edge of an old recliner across from the sofa with his head in his hands, hair threaded through his fingers.

I cleared my throat. "Look, um…if you're really as sorry as you say you are, can you help me find my purse and drive me to Denise's?"

Danny looked up. "Yeah. Yeah, I can do that."

I nodded, then disappeared into the bedroom to see if my purse might have ended up there at some point during the night. Once I was sure he hadn't followed me, I leaned against the wall and let out a tiny sigh of relief. For as much as it pained me to ask him for anything, I knew the sooner I left, the sooner I could pretend to forget about Danny Kincaid all over again.

———

"Okay, I'm gonna need more information here, Eva." Denise handed me my coffee before settling into the chair across from where I was seated on the sofa. "But before you speak, may I say once again how sorry I am that I slept through your phone call, and I let you leave the bar without making sure you remembered my address? I should be in best friend jail."

I pulled a pillow onto my lap, resting my mug on top. "You're forgiven. Anyway, it's my fault, I barely gave you a chance to tell me anything before I left. And I knew the name of the street. Just had to drive around the block a couple times to find it."

"Okay. Good. So back to Danny. You go to his apartment, he says he misses you, you have sex, you wake up, he says he misses you again, you scream at him, you finally find your purse, he drives you here…and then what?"

I sighed before taking a sip of coffee. "And then I got out of his car and knocked on your door, and thankfully, you opened it. But I would've sat outside for five hours waiting for you rather than sit beside him for one more second. It was the most awkward car ride in the history of car rides. He tried to talk to me, but I just smoked and stared out the window, praying you didn't live far away."

"But he wasn't being a dick, right? From everything you told me, it sounds like he was apologizing and begging you to hear him out."

"He was being nice because he felt bad for me. Or guilty. Or both. I mean, I fell on the floor in my underwear trying to sneak out, for Christ's sake, and he woke up looking like some messy-haired, bare-chested rock God." I covered my face with my hand. "I can't believe I still think this about him, Denise. Why does he do this to me?"

I peeked out from between my fingers to see her shaking her head.

"I don't know, babe. This is so insane to me. I mean, what are the odds?"

I gathered my hair into a haphazard ponytail with a tie I'd stolen from Denise's bathroom. "One in five hundred forty-six billion."

"Yeah." Denise raised her mug to her lips, cocking her head before taking a sip. "But what if that means…"

"What if that means what?"

She held her hand out to me as if she was trying to stop the oncoming traffic in my brain. "Just hear me out, okay?"

I narrowed my eyes.

"What if this happened for a reason? What if you're supposed to reconnect with him for some greater purpose?"

My shoulders dropped, and I groaned. "Oh my God. You sound like Danny last night talking about fate and the cosmos and whatever. Plus, less than twelve hours ago, you were telling me not to go home with him because he's a motherfucker. So, don't think I'll be putting a lot of stock in that."

She chewed on her long red nail and nodded slowly. "I know, I know. But what I *didn't* know was that the motherfucker was gonna pour his heart out to you."

I shook my head. "You kill me, Denise. How do you always manage to be so *mushy* when these things involve other people and so *not* when they involve you?"

"One of life's great mysteries. But whatever. You said it yourself: this isn't about me. And you also said the chances of you running into him were slim to none. I mean, who knew he was even still out here?"

"I guess it did cross my mind that he could be."

That was a lie. I didn't *guess*. I knew damn well each time I'd visited Denise I'd wondered if Danny was still in LA. Just like I wondered every Thanksgiving and Christmas if I might somehow see him pumping gas at the Phillips 66 or checking out at the A&P in our hometown.

"Think about all the things that had to happen in order for *this* to happen," Denise began, counting off on her fingers. "I had to decide to go to DePaul, and we had to end up as roommates. Matt and Danny had to join the same band. I had to move back home and meet Matt and accidentally keep sleeping with him. You had to come out here, and we had to go to the exact same bar on the exact same night as Matt and Danny." She paused and tipped her mug at me. "I mean, that's some crazy shit to just be one big coincidence."

I squinted up at the ceiling, considering what she'd said. "But how come *you* never met Danny? I mean, you've known Matt for a while, right?"

"A couple months, I guess," she answered with a quick shrug. "But Danny wasn't with Matt the first night I met him, and since then, he pretty much comes here, we have sex, and I kick him out."

Her honesty never ceased to amaze me.

I opened my mouth to close the book once and for all on the supernatural speculation but pressed my lips together as the chain of events Denise had listed out settled into my brain. I had to admit it was kind of crazy. More than kind of.

A lump formed in my throat. "Why do you think he said he missed me?"

"Maybe he really does. I mean, he didn't *have* to say that. You were naked in his bed. It's not like you were going anywhere."

Outwardly, I cringed at the memory, but a white heat burned inside me as images of his head and hips between my thighs flickered behind my eyes.

Her face softened as she placed her coffee on the small side table and uncurled her legs. "Look, I don't wanna make up stories about this. Who knows what he's thinking. In my mind, he *is* still a motherfucker until he proves otherwise. But he's off to a good start based on what you told me. And what happened between you guys…You were teenagers, Eva. He's older. Potentially wiser. And there's a possibility he knows now that he actually *did* fuck up."

I swallowed and nodded, thinking about the things he'd said earlier that morning. All the things I'd repeated to Denise when I'd first gotten back to her apartment. "He, uh…he asked me to come to their show tonight."

Denise's eyes widened. "He did? At the Troubadour?"

"Yeah, how'd you—"

"Matt. He never gives up."

"Right. Anyway, I didn't tell you because I'm obviously not going." I grimaced, realizing I'd phrased my last sentence more like a question than a final decision.

"You sure about that?"

"Totally," I insisted, clearing my throat. "He just thinks I'll have sex with him again. That I'm a sure thing, which, clearly, I am, given the failure of my ridiculous plan last night. So, I need to stay away."

Denise gritted her teeth. "Eva, I mean absolutely *no* offense when I say this because you are always the most gorgeous woman in every single room you're ever in. But there are gonna be at least fifty girls at that show who Danny wouldn't even have to so much as say hello to before they had his dick in their mouths. So, you know…I don't really think he's too worried about getting laid tonight."

I stuck my tongue out. "Ew."

She shrugged and reached for her coffee. "Musicians."

"It's still gross."

"Like you haven't had his dick in your mouth five hundred times."

"*Denise.*" I tried to stifle my laughter but lost it once she sputtered and doubled over, her entire body shaking.

"Okay, okay." I wiped under my eyes as I managed to catch my breath. "I'm going outside to smoke and think about it. But I'm telling you, it's gonna be a no. One of those fifty girls can have him. In fact, they can all have him."

I grabbed my purse, pushed myself up from the couch, and headed for the small patio outside of the apartment, catching a sideways glance from Denise before I opened the door. "What?"

She held her hands up, pleading innocence, though a smug, crooked smile remained on her lips. "Nothing, Eva. Nothing at all."

"I cannot believe I'm fucking doing this," I said as Denise squeezed into a parking space. I massaged my temples, trying to relieve the tension in my head. It felt like it weighed a hundred pounds, crammed full of fear and worry that I was setting myself up for disappointment.

Denise reached into her purse and opened her compact, repainting her lips before turning to me. "Do you wanna leave? Because we can leave right now, and you will never have to see Danny Kincaid ever again."

Part of me wanted to grab the gear shift and switch it into drive myself. But a bigger part wanted to stay. The part that thought maybe I'd been too quick to uproot that tiny seed of hope from the night before. That maybe Danny was older and wiser. And that maybe Denise was right. What if I *had* run into him for a reason?

"I don't want to leave," I confessed.

"You know it's okay to want to be here, right? It doesn't

make you weak or whatever it is you're thinking. It actually makes you a normal human being." She reached over and squeezed my hand. "I had to say that since you wouldn't let me say it before."

After chain-smoking for a good twenty minutes that morning, I'd walked back inside and announced we would be going to the show, but there would be no further mention of it until we were in a moving car headed for the Troubadour. I'd picked apart Danny's every word, every move, and every expression before making my decision and didn't need any cause for further dissection.

"Thank you," I said. "And just so you know, one day *you're* gonna be a normal human being, and I'm gonna be saying all that mushy stuff to you."

"Oh, please, Eva. You know I'm immune to that shit."

We exchanged a knowing glance, and I snickered as she cut the engine to her car and opened her door.

We started up the sidewalk on Santa Monica Boulevard, the sound of our heels hitting the concrete almost as loud as the sound of my heartbeat pounding in my ears. The black spandex dress that Denise had insisted I wear felt increasingly tighter as we approached the club, and I was sure the silver concho belt around my waist was about to cut off circulation to the lower half of my body.

"That's a really long line. What if we can't even get in?" I asked, slowing my pace as I spotted the crowd gathered outside.

"You said he was gonna put us on the list. The list means we're in."

I nodded, following behind her as she led the charge past the line to the large man in a solid black T-shirt standing at the door. He held a clipboard in his hand, monitoring the crowd and occasionally waving people inside.

Denise bounced up to him and chirped our names, then grinned at me as he stepped aside and allowed us to enter.

"Hey, Eddie," he called to a man standing inside the door. "Can you take these girls backstage?"

My eyes swept around the venue which had a smaller section upstairs in addition to the downstairs; both were already packed. A thick haze of smoke hung in the air, several beams of light slicing through it from different directions. I licked my lips, my mouth feeling like a bucket of sand had been poured into it, then leaned over to Denise. "So I'm guessing his band doesn't suck?"

She raised her brows as we followed Eddie through the crowd to a door by the stage. He opened it for us, revealing a group of people mingling, drinks and cigarettes in hand.

I hesitated as Denise pressed against my side and discretely clasped my hand. It was only a matter of seconds after we stepped inside that I spotted Danny practically tripping over himself to get to us, ignoring several nearly-naked girls attempting to get his attention.

"Eva. Oh my God. You came." His shaky voice and wide-eyed expression hovered somewhere between surprise and relief.

He looked incredible in his black jeans and silky purple shirt, which was mostly unbuttoned, revealing his smooth chest. I wanted to fall into his arms, forgetting all my fears and doubts. But I remained stoic, refusing to give myself away—although I suspected that actually showing up at the gig had already done that.

"Yeah, uh, thanks for getting us in. You've got a crowd out there." I motioned to the door, my body as stiff as my voice, which sounded like I was about to engage in an official business transaction on a Monday morning rather than hang out and listen to music on a Saturday night.

What the fuck. Loosen up, Eva.

"Yeah, we do okay," he said, a humble smile appearing on his lips.

Suddenly, Denise, who was standing just off to my side sizing Danny up, let out a squeal. We turned our heads to see Matt grabbing onto her waist as she tried to wriggle out of his grip.

"This is a goddamn miracle. You *actually* came to see me play. I'm wearing you down, Denise."

"I'm here with Eva, you idiot," she said, punching him in the arm. "And no, you're not coming over after the show."

"Hey, Eva." Matt ignored Denise's insult and nodded in my direction. "Good to see you again."

I gave him a small wave as a guy with an easy smile and a sleeve of tattoos approached us.

"So is this the old friend from Illinois I heard about?" he asked, adjusting the backward baseball cap on top of his shoulder-length light brown hair and extending his hand. "I'm Will."

Danny cringed at his description of me, and I had to fight the urge to show my cards as well. I didn't know if that was what Danny had told him or if Will was just being cautious with his words. Whatever the case, being given the title *old friend* made my stomach drop, and I wasn't sure if it was because I thought I *deserved* more based on the past, or I wanted to *be* more in the present.

"Eva. Nice to meet you," I said, giving his outstretched hand a weak shake. The half-dilapidated couch pushed up against the wall had more personality than I did. I was wound up tighter than the fucking strings on one of Danny's guitars.

Will lit a cigarette and motioned to a girl with teased red hair calling for him from the other side of the room. "You, too. I'll let you guys catch up. Gotta run."

I was trying to think of what meaningless topic of conversation I could offer up when a tall, slender figure stalked into the room. Long dirty-blond hair hung over his shoulders onto his bare chest, and his black leathers rode low on his hips. He made a beeline for Danny and stopped in front of him.

"I can't get the vocals right on 'Another Night.' We gotta drop it from the set list."

Danny rolled his eyes. "Your vocals are fine, I heard them at sound check. Calm down, dude."

The other guy looked down at me, surprise flickering across his face as if he'd just noticed I was there. "Who's this?"

He continued to study me like I was the subject of some appraisal I wasn't aware I'd have to endure. It didn't feel like an assessment to determine whether I was worthy of taking home that night; it was more to decide whether I was worthy of even being in his presence.

"Eva," I answered, squaring my shoulders. "And you are?"

"Eric," he said in a voice as sharp as a razor's edge before turning his attention back to Danny. "Anyway, we're dropping the song."

"I don't care, cross it the fuck off," Danny said.

Eric nodded. "Fine." He gave me the once-over again, turned, and walked back out of the room.

I scoffed. "Wow. Nice guy."

"I'll just apologize for him and say his social skills are lacking. Hell of a singer, though."

"Ten minutes, everyone," a woman sauntering by us announced.

Danny placed his hand on my arm and my knees buckled, but I didn't recoil like I had that morning. "Listen, I gotta get ready, but I'm gonna have one of the security guys take you and Denise out to the front of the stage."

I shook my head. "This place is packed. We'll find a spot in the back and—"

"No," he said, cutting me off. "It's been five and a half years since I got to play a show for Eva Holloway. I want you down front with me."

"Yeah," I said quietly. "Okay."

He gave me a hopeful smile and turned to find someone to escort us out. A familiar tingle traveled through my body, and when it hit my lips, I finally managed a tiny smile of my own. I looked down at the ground, warmth spreading across my cheeks, but raised my head when he said my name once again.

FOR EVA

"Hey, Eva. Don't leave right after the show, okay? I wanna take you out afterward, just you and me. And I don't mean to my apartment." He paused, his eyes searching my face for any indication of what I was thinking. "Can…can we do that?"

The smile on my lips grew wider as something in his voice replanted the seed I'd dug up earlier. "Yeah. We can do that."

I hadn't had to think about my answer to his question. I'd known by the end of my conversation with Denise that morning which part of me was winning the tug-of-war happening in my head. And now the opposing team had officially been yanked face down in the mud. I still didn't know exactly what he wanted, but the way he spoke to me, the way he looked at me, gave me enough pause to not blow things off as merely an attempt to ease his conscience. I didn't know if I was kidding myself—if I was stupid, if I was weak. But the thought of not finding out why Danny wanted to see me again only guaranteed I'd spend hours…days…*months* wondering.

As soon as he disappeared, we were led back out front. Denise had swiped two beers from backstage—not nearly enough to calm my nerves but better than nothing. I downed mine quickly and was anxiously picking at the label when the house lights went down and a powerful, deep voice boomed from the speakers.

"All right, Hollywood! You wanted the best, you got the best…"

I cocked my head and raised my brows. *The KISS concert intro?* Danny *hated* KISS. I imagined him backstage, jaw clenched and eyes rolled up to the ceiling.

There was a snicker, then the voice from beyond soared up a pitch. "Nah, I'm just fuckin' with you. But these guys are pretty fuckin' good, too. Ladies and gentlemen…put your hands together for Counting Backward!"

Four shadowy figures walked onto the stage, and the crowd erupted. Will sat behind his kit, a stack of amps surrounding him, and stomped out a quick beat on the bass drum. Matt took his position stage right, bass guitar slung low across his hips, and Danny stood stage left, directly in front of Denise and me, his face illuminated by the orange glow of his cigarette as he took a drag.

My head and stomach were woozy, and my only comfort at the moment was that there were enough people around me to break my fall if I went down. Denise smiled and bumped my hip, and I leaned over to tell her I might pass out. But before I could manage, spotlights flipped on and the tall, imposing figure from earlier was standing in the middle of the stage belting out the first song.

"If I tell you that you're *craaaaay-zaaaaay*," Eric sang, forcefully grabbing onto the mic and writhing along with the rhythm as the rest of the band joined in.

Danny was right. This guy *was* a hell of a singer.

The song was driving with a catchy hook and chorus. There was a hint of blues interspersed between the heavy guitar licks, which made sense given Danny's affection for bands like the Stones and Aerosmith.

Danny lowered his gaze to me, winking between his backup vocals, and I watched in awe as his fingers moved expertly up and down the fretboard of his ebony guitar. I'd seen him play so many times before, but it was always in the storage space down the street from his house or at a backyard party when someone's parents were out of town. I'd never seen him like *this*. The gauzy scarf with metallic threading that he'd added over his loose, half-tucked shirt, and the silver hoops dangling from his ears occasionally caught one of the stage lights and sparkled against his black hair. He was rock 'n' roll personified, all eyes in the crowd focused on him, while his were focused squarely on me.

The band moved seamlessly from one song to another, Denise and I occasionally glancing at one another in disbelief at how amazing they were. The music came to a halt after a song about a girl who'd lost her way in Hollywood, and Danny grabbed a towel, wiping his face before tossing it back on the drum riser. His chest glistened, and the ends of his dark hair had separated into sweaty tendrils. My pulse quickened, but this time it wasn't from nerves.

He walked back over to his mic and leaned down to me. "You good?"

I smiled and nodded, at a loss for words.

He and Matt played a few random chords on their instruments, allowing Eric to grab a beer off the drum riser. Eric took a swig and sauntered back to the mic, his hair plastered to his shoulders with sweat.

"We're gonna mix things up a little bit tonight," he said between screams from the crowd, "and do a song for a very special guest of Mr. Danny Kincaid's." He cast a steely glance at me, then motioned over to Danny, who raised his hand in acknowledgment. "Said she'd know it from their old days in Illinois."

Denise looked over at me, wide-eyed, her jaw hanging open. I cupped my hand over my mouth as Danny began to play a haunting guitar melody to the cheers of the crowd. I wasn't sure how he had convinced Eric to play a song for me, the girl whose mere presence he'd questioned with his sharp tone and judging eyes, but at that moment, I didn't care.

"This one's by Aerosmith," Eric continued, adjusting the mic. "It's called 'Seasons of Wither.'"

Danny continued to play, with Matt and Will joining in on cue. I stood completely still in front of the stage, shocked that Danny remembered my favorite song. It was five albums old by the time I could drive, but I still played it on repeat in the Mustang my parents had bought me for my sixteenth birthday. The melancholy notes and memories of us listening to it with the windows rolled down on hazy summer nights sent an unexpected tear spilling onto my cheek.

Eric grabbed the mic with both hands, casting a sultry stare into the crowd. Danny's hazel eyes became golden pools beneath the glare of the stage lights, and I was carried away, the song swallowing me up as pieces of our past floated alongside me like driftwood. I blinked and it was nearly over, the final chords crashing over me as Danny strode across the stage, staring at me like I was the only fucking person in the room.

CHAPTER SIX
DANNY

JANUARY 1988

As soon as my pick glided through the strings on the last chord, I wondered if it had been too much. If playing her favorite song had been over the top. If it even *was* her favorite song anymore. She'd practically worn out the 8-track from listening to it on repeat in that Mustang she'd driven in high school, but that was years ago. Who knew what she liked now?

I'd learned the song when I was sixteen—mostly for Eva, though I never turned down an opportunity to pretend I was Joe Perry. But after I moved out to LA, I made the conscious decision never to play it. I knew it would bring up too many memories. Which meant I had been unconsciously messing around on my guitar when Eric strolled into our rehearsal space one afternoon several months before.

"Is that 'Seasons of Wither'?" He placed a cigarette between his lips before taking a seat on one of the amps in the old warehouse.

"Huh?" I asked, not taking my eyes off the fretboard as I moved on to the next chord.

"That song."

I stopped playing and looked up. "What? Shit. Yeah, I guess it is."

"That sounds good, man." He flicked his lighter and touched

the tip of his cigarette to the flame. "We should add it to the rotation. I'm sick of the same old shit everybody plays."

I shook my head. It made me think of *her*, and that was something I categorically tried *not* to do. "Nah, it needs two guitars. It won't sound right without them."

"Whatever, dude. Matt can make sure it doesn't sound empty, and I'll sing the shit out of it." Eric smirked. "So, I mean, we can either add this or a KISS song. Your choice."

I fucking hated KISS. Which was the main reason I'd been hesitant to bring Eric Stratton on as our singer after our first guy knocked up his hometown girlfriend and moved back to Ohio. Eric worshipped that damn band, and I wasn't about to let him turn us into some fucking clown show. But while he may have been wowed by the spectacle of bands like KISS, the pyro and makeup went out the window when it came to his own songs. The first time we sat down to write was magic; his words and my music came together so naturally, so perfectly. We both knew right then that we were each other's tickets to the next level.

Of course, I also learned early on in our relationship that I'd have to pick my battles with Eric. He was kind of...well, a *dick*. But I knew that was pretty much par for the course with lead singers, and I didn't wanna get into a bullshit argument over something so seemingly minor. And when Eva walked through the backstage door, I thanked God I'd decided to put my sword down and agreed to add that song to our list of covers.

As we moved into our last number, I could barely take my eyes off her. I couldn't tell if the gleam in her own eyes was from the lights that danced across them or if the song had really meant something to her. Regardless, their soft, velvety brown had me completely fucking hypnotized. She looked so beautiful, her long blond hair swept to the side and her hips swaying in that short black dress. God, she'd always had the best hips.

And ass.

Jesus.

FOR EVA

It was hard not to get hard just thinking about it.

But wanting her back in my life was about so much more than that. Yes, she was hot as fuck. And no, I couldn't stop thinking about fucking her the night before. But all of that was secondary. There were thousands of hot girls who were great lays in LA. But none of them were Eva. And I'd blown everything by giving up on her when she would've never given up on me. She'd believed in me when no one else had. My friends, my mom, my piece of shit dad who'd walked out when I was fifteen…none of them thought I had what it took to make it. And even though she hadn't wanted me to leave, she'd told me to go, with promises we'd stay together and plans that would never come together because they were all based on lies I'd told her. So how could I make her believe that I knew I'd made a mistake? As I searched for the magic words that would make her understand, I missed a note, and Eric shot me a look straight from the depths of hell.

Fuck.

No one in the entire audience knew I'd screwed up, but Eric was glaring at me like I'd ruined the entire fucking show. I quickly shook my head, attempting to regain my focus and finish out the set.

"All right, people! We are Counting Backward! Thank you and good fucking night," he shouted into the mic as our instruments swelled together in a frenzied crescendo.

After one last crash and choke of Will's cymbal, the music came to a hard stop, leaving only the sound of the crowd. Eric swept his wild mane out of his face and saluted the audience before heading backstage, followed by Will and Matt, who raised their hands to the sea of people illuminated by the spotlights sailing over them. I unplugged my guitar, trying not to let my gaze slip from Eva for fear she would disappear, and hurried to the front of the stage.

"Hey, can you meet me right outside the entrance? Don't come backstage, it's too crazy. I just need five minutes."

She nodded, and the corners of her mouth turned up slight-ly. But she dropped her gaze to the floor so quickly I couldn't tell if that hint of a smile meant she truly wanted to see me and hear me out, or if she was placating me until she could get me alone and go the fuck off on me. I rushed backstage, thoughts streaking through my brain in reds and oranges like taillights on the freeway at night.

You cannot fuck this up, Kincaid.

You cannot fuck this up.

You cannot—

A hand cuffed my forearm, its grip so tight that it stopped me in my tracks. I turned my head to see Eric, his eyes burning into me, and immediately jerked away from him. "What the hell?"

"What the fuck was that on the last song?"

"Dude, chill the fuck out," I said, grabbing a towel and wip-ing the sweat off my face and chest. "I missed one goddamn note. The whole two hours. *One.*" I held up my finger for em-phasis.

"What's going on with you, Danny?" he asked, his tone in-dicating it wasn't so much a question as it was an accusation.

"Nothing," I snapped back at him as I crouched to open my guitar case. "What's going on with *you*? You've been a total asshole tonight."

"And *you've* been totally distracted. I mean, fucking up that note, dude? What if there were A&R people out there?"

"Well, Eric, I can pretty much guarantee you there were at least five label reps out there, and not one of them noticed a fucking thing." I placed my guitar in the case and slapped the locks shut. "You want me to count the number of times *you've* missed a note? Forgotten a lyric? It fucking happens. Plus, I think those guys at Pitfall really want us, man. I can feel it."

"Shit like that falls apart all the time, and you fucking know it."

The tone of his voice landed somewhere between disappointment and anger, and my face softened. I hadn't forgotten we'd been down this road before only to be blindsided, and there was no denying the bitterness we both still felt about it.

I sighed, buttoning my shirt. "Look, I'm sorry, okay? But I gotta go. We can talk about it later." I scanned the area for Matt, whom I spotted across the room with his arm around a tall blond. I called his name, and he looked up from the chick's tits just long enough for me to catch his eye. "Hey, man, I'll owe you one if you make sure my shit gets in the van. I gotta run."

Eric folded his arms and pressed his lips together.

"Jesus Christ, what now?" I asked, throwing my hands into the air. "I said I'm sorry. What the fuck else do you want from me?"

"That girl. *Eva*." His face twitched as though it physically pained him to say her name. "She's the one you ditched when you came out here, isn't she? The one you were afraid was gonna get in your way…make you 'lose focus'?" He curled his fingers into quotation marks.

I scoffed and reached for my guitar case. But the truth in his words delivered an unexpected jolt to my brain, causing me to rest my fingers on the handle for a moment and hesitate before answering. "So what if she is?"

"So I don't want her becoming a problem."

"Fuck off, Eric," I said, grabbing my case and pushing past him.

"I mean it, Danny," he called after me.

I raised my left hand above my head and extended my middle finger as I headed for the door, praying Eva would be outside and I'd somehow find the right words to ask her to give me a second chance.

CHAPTER SEVEN
EVA

JANUARY 1988

A helicopter whirred around my stomach, the chopping and humming of its blades causing my entire body to vibrate. It didn't help, of course, that the temperature had dropped at least ten degrees while we'd been inside. I furiously rubbed my bare arms while smoking a cigarette to calm the search and rescue mission that circled above the rough seas inside me.

Denise squeezed my shoulder and studied my face. "You okay, babe? You don't look like you're okay."

I managed a nod, which was actually more like a shiver. "Yeah. I mean, no. I'm not. But I will be. Maybe. I just need, like, a Valium. Who do you think has a Valium?" My eyes darted around the crowd spilling out of the Troubadour. "I mean, it's almost midnight in Hollywood. Somebody here has to have drugs, right?"

Denise chuckled and shook her head. "I think the best you're gonna do is coke or weed. And we don't need you booking a midnight flight to Amsterdam or passing out and drooling in Danny's lap, so I'm not gonna allow either."

Since I couldn't say with one hundred percent certainty that those things wouldn't happen based on past experience, I expelled a heavy sigh. With my arms still crossed over my chest, I dropped my head to take a drag off my smoke.

FOR EVA

"I'm so in the dark here, Denise. I mean, what's he gonna say? What's he gonna do?" I let my cigarette fall from between my fingers and crushed it with the toe of my shoe. "For that matter, what am *I* gonna say, and what am *I* gonna do?"

Denise stepped in front of me, placing her steady hands over mine. "Deep breaths, Eva. It's gonna be all right. You're in control here. *He's* the one who fucked up. *He's* the one who's groveling. Not you."

I looked up at the starless, smoky-gray sky. "Yeah, but why is this happening? What does he want from me?"

"I think you know the answer to that, babe."

My chest tightened, and I closed my eyes for a moment before bringing my gaze back down to earth.

"I think you know what he wants," she began, fixing her chestnut eyes on mine. "Just like you know what *you* want. Otherwise, why are we even here?"

Her words sent the helicopter plummeting to the bottom of my stomach and a peculiar thrill rushing through my veins. A dangerous sense of excitement I imagined came only from jumping off cliffs, scaling treacherous mountains, or offering your poorly-reconstructed heart back up to someone who had once shattered the last remaining pieces of it.

Someone you still loved despite that.

Of course, I knew why I'd come and what I wanted. And after he'd played the song—*my* song—it was hard to keep telling myself that Danny didn't want the same thing. I wasn't scared because I was in the dark. I was scared because everything was coming to light.

"Eva!"

Danny pushed through the crowd that had gathered outside the club, offering terse smiles and thank-yous to the people who tossed compliments his way. He stopped in front of me and Denise, standing just beyond the increasingly chaotic scene at the entrance. His chest was frantically pumping up and down, and the confidence he'd displayed on stage waned into a flustered humility. And while it comforted me to know he was still human, I couldn't help but wonder why, when given the choice to spend the rest of his night with groupies or unearth the past with me, he was choosing the latter. Wasn't the allure of being young and wild and free the reason he'd left me in the first place?

"Hey. Hi," he managed, setting down his case.

He was so visibly nervous that a spurt of laughter erupted from Denise, which she tried to mask by clearing her throat.

Danny's eyes flicked back and forth between us. "What?"

I nudged Denise's arm, and she immediately covered her mouth.

"Nothing," I said. "You guys were really good. And thanks. For the song."

His breathing slowed, and his shoulders and jaw relaxed. "Yeah? That was...okay?"

Okay? Sure, it was okay—if feeling like I'd stepped into a pair of ruby slippers, clicked my heels together, and returned to the last time and place I'd felt happy and safe and loved was *okay.* But it was so much more than that. It was magical. It was beautiful. And it was terrifying because I knew all too well how quickly those feelings could be ripped away. But I didn't know how to tell him that, so I simply nodded and dropped my eyes to the ground, pressing my lips together as a stinging sensation pricked at my eyes and nose.

"All right, kids, I gotta run," Denise announced. "But you've got my address and the spare key, right?" She'd confirmed I had both on the way to the show and right after, so I knew that was her way of asking me if it was okay to leave.

"Got it," I assured her, patting my purse. "Do you want us to walk you to your car?"

"Nah, I'm fine." She touched my elbow and smiled at me before turning her attention to Danny. "Good show tonight, dude. You guys are way better than I thought you'd be. But don't tell Matt I said that."

He chuckled, a look of feigned confusion on his face. "Said what?"

"Nice." Denise twisted up one corner of her mouth before starting down the sidewalk. "Oh, and just FYI, Danny," she called over her shoulder. "I don't really have a gun. But I can totally get one."

Danny gave her a thumbs-up. "Loud and clear, Denise."

She laughed and winked, then sauntered off toward her car.

Danny reached into the front pocket of his shirt and pulled out a pack of Marlboros. "Why do I get the feeling that even though she's the size of a fucking Chihuahua she could totally kick my ass?"

He looked down as he dug into his jeans trying to find his lighter, and I tried to laugh at his comment. To act like everything was fine—normal, even. Like standing in front of him didn't make me want to fall into his arms and forget all the bad that happened in the past. Like picturing him leaving all over again didn't make me want to collapse into a heap on the sidewalk.

Danny reached around to his back pocket, finally locating the red BIC. "I mean, that chick's pretty fierce, am I right?"

My chin quivered as the flame cast a warm glow across his face, and when he brought his eyes up to mine, I lost control, sobbing into my hands.

"Shit. What'd I say?" The callused tips of his fingers grazed the sides of my shoulders, rough yet reassuring against my skin. "Was it the thing about Denise? That was just a joke."

I shook my head, then leaned into him, burying my face in his neck. The smell of smoke and sweat and cinnamon was familiar and comforting, and when he wrapped his arms around me, my body went limp. For a moment, I forgot we were standing in the middle of West Hollywood, surrounded by a throng of people who had to have been wondering if someone had died, if a boy had broken my heart, or if I was just an average twentysomething girl having a breakdown on a Saturday night.

The sad truth was, it was all three.

"Let's get outta here, okay?" Danny whispered.

I nodded as he steered me away from the crowd, the street-lights hazy blurs of yellow and white through my watery eyes. Voices echoed in the alley behind the club where Danny's car was parked. He opened the passenger's side door to the Bronco for me, then threw his guitar into the trunk before climbing inside and tucking the hair that hung in my face behind my ear.

"Are you okay?"

I swiped my fingers under my eyes. "I didn't mean to lose it. It's just that last night, this morning, the show, the song…it's so fucking much, Danny." I leaned back against the seat, teardrops rolling down the sides of my cheeks. "So fucking much."

"I feel like this is my fault. I mean, it *is* my fault, I know. But I…Fuck, I don't know what I mean."

My breath shuddered. "I think my problem is that I don't know what you mean, either."

He opened his mouth, a soft rasp escaping before he shut it.

"So what is it, Danny? What *do* you mean?" I turned and held his gaze like I held onto the hope that I hadn't miscon-strued every word, every look, and every touch over the past twenty-four hours. "You asked for a chance to tell me this morning, and I'm giving it to you now. Tell me what you mean. Tell me what you want."

His eyes glistened in the flickering light attached to the building beside us. "I…I'm not sure."

I stared at him, the wind completely knocked out of me like I'd been sucked through the window of the car and slammed against the pavement.

His brows turned down, and he shook his head. "No, that's not…*Fuck.* What I was trying to say is I'm not sure what this is." He gestured between us. "But I can't stop thinking about how amazing it feels to be with you, Eva. And what I want is a chance to tell you how sorry I am that I fucking ruined us." His voice quavered, sown with both desperation and relief, as though he'd just surrendered in a war he'd been fighting for years. "And I also wanna know if I'm crazy for thinking you might feel a little bit of what I do."

He drew in a breath and scanned my face for a reaction—the slightest indication I'd seen the white flag being waved and would have mercy on him. Or better yet, that I would lay down my weapons and admit there was no point in fighting my own feelings any longer.

I swallowed, trying to ease the ache in my chest and was about to speak when a knock on the driver's side window startled us both.

Danny groaned, muttering a "goddamnit" before cranking the lever on the door. "Hey, Mike, I'm sort of busy here."

The long-haired guy squinted and leaned into the car. "Whoa, dude, sorry to interrupt. But whenever you finish, you need to get your ass to Chrissy's. Her friends from The Seventh Veil are coming over after they get off work. Including that superhot one you fucked the other ni—"

Danny coughed and began to roll the window up. "Yeah, I'm actually good, man. I'll catch you later, though."

"Okay, I get it, dude. But if you get bored you can—"

His voice became faint as the window sealed, and Danny turned back to me, shaking his head. "That guy's high, like, twenty-four seven. Sorry. What, uh…what were you gonna say?"

I wasn't angry hearing that Danny had sex with another girl. He'd probably had sex with a hundred. I sure as hell hadn't been celibate while I was still pining away for him.

"I think if you really wanna talk," I began, "we should go someplace where I don't have to endure a recap of your sex life."

Danny's eyes widened. "I didn't…That girl he was talking about, I—"

My face softened, letting him know at that moment, I didn't care about anyone but us. "Just take me somewhere else," I said. "And we'll go from there."

———

"You sure that's all you want?" The waitress stuck her notepad in the pocket of her uniform and stretched out her hand to me.

I passed her the menu after deciding the only thing my nervous stomach could handle was a side of toast and a Diet Coke. "Yeah, I'm good. Thanks."

"This is fine, right? Or is it weird? Fuck, it's weird, isn't it? That's why you're not eating." Danny squeezed his eyes shut and ran his hand along his brow. "I really thought this would be, like, a good memory."

"Hey." I reached over and nudged the arm he'd propped on the table. "I told you it's fine."

As soon as I'd seen the bright yellow Denny's sign on the side of the road ahead of us, the soft glow of nostalgia flushed my cheeks. He'd asked me five times before we got out of the car if being there was okay. I assured him it was but couldn't deny that it felt like my heart was being wrung out like a sponge while we waited for the hostess by a gumball machine full of plastic rings.

We skirted around things with meaningless talk about high school friends and our families before ordering. I told him my father had married a woman who was only seven years older than me, and they had a kid who was three. Danny told me his father divorced the woman he'd left them for and moved to Texas.

"So I, uh, need to stop fucking around and say this," Danny mumbled, another cigarette dangling between his lips. His hand shook as he held the flame to the tip, then blew a stream of smoke from the side of his mouth. "I am so fucking sorry for lying to you, Eva. About me coming here." He swallowed so hard I could see his Adam's apple bob. "About *you* coming here."

I scraped my teeth along my bottom lip and nodded, fixing my gaze on the back of the booth beside his shoulder. There had been so many times I'd thought about him saying those words to me over the past five and a half years. I'd even had dreams where he'd confessed it had been his plan all along to call our relationship quits once he got to LA, and I remembered the sense of satisfaction that coursed through me as I slept.

But the decisive victory I'd imagined ended up feeling a lot more hollow in real life. My vision blurred with saltwater waves, and I knew if I looked into his eyes, they would break over my lids.

"Yeah. I, uh…I think that's what hurt the most." I sniffed, reaching for my own cigarettes. I flicked the lighter and shrugged as I tilted my chin up, smoke streaming from my lips. "*Still* hurts the most, actually."

Danny rubbed his forehead and sighed. "I was too scared to tell you. You know, face-to-face. After everything you'd been through, I didn't know how to do it."

The waitress reappeared with our drinks, tossed a couple of straws on the table, and let us know our food would be out in a bit. I gave her a faint smile, then stared through the filmy window at the cars rolling in and out of the parking lot.

"You know, I wasn't mad at you for leaving." I paused and tapped the tip of my cigarette into the ashtray before turning my attention back to him. "I told you to go, for Christ's sake. And when we agreed—or I *thought* we agreed—I would come here after my first semester at school, I was actually excited about leaving Illinois and everything that happened there behind me. I did all the research on how to transfer schools. I went on and on about how amazing it would be to have our own apartment, wake up late, and make French fucking toast together. I told my dad he was wrong when he said following you out here was a mistake, which only made things worse between me and him. And you let me do that, Danny. You let me do all of that even though you fucking knew what you were gonna do after you left."

My mind spiraled in a kaleidoscope of sadness and anger. But it wasn't the kind of anger that had revealed itself in his apartment that morning. It was quieter. A restrained bitterness that peppered my voice with acidity but kept it low enough so as not to garner attention from the other tables.

He extinguished his smoke and rested his head in his hands. "Eva, I—"

"Did you think it would hurt me less if I heard it over the phone? Or was that more convenient for you so you didn't have to see my heart being ripped the fuck out, you only had to hear it?" A single tear slid onto my cheek, and I brushed it away.

He scrubbed his hands down his face as he lifted his gaze to me. "Do you know how much it kills me to hear you say that?"

"Do you know how much it kills me that you *did* that?"

"I know, Eva. And if I could take it all back, I would." His eyes pleaded with me as he reached across the table and placed his hand over mine. I tensed but didn't pull away. "I know it was wrong. And for a while I thought I only regretted *how* I ended things. But somewhere along the way I began to think that deep down I regretted ending things at all."

I remembered the phone call. My back against my bedroom wall as I slid to the floor. The tears as I gripped the receiver so hard my hand hurt almost as much as my heart. He needed to focus on his music. I needed to focus on school. We would eventually end up resenting each other, and it was for the best.

I remembered wondering why it was so easy for him to un-love me. Or if he'd ever even loved me at all.

I remembered never having the chance to ask because the line went dead.

And I remembered how I'd sat against that same wall, my body shaking and my brain searching for answers and reasons, when my mother had died eight months before.

I slipped my hand out from under his, absentmindedly discarding the paper from my straw and sipping my drink, trying to swallow each and every emotion attached to the memories. "You really did break the last piece of my heart, Danny."

He sighed and slid his hand across the table when our waitress appeared, balancing a tray on her right hand, and rattled off our orders as she set our food down in front of us.

Danny pushed his plates aside as soon as she left and folded his arms on the table. "I didn't want to do that, Eva. I didn't *want* to hurt you. I was young and scared and fucking careless. And after everything with your mom, everything with…I know I made it all ten thousand times worse, and I fucking hate myself for that."

I stubbed out my cigarette and picked at the toasted white bread in front of me, trying to focus on anything but images of twisted steel and shattered glass as my quiet anger turned to grief. "My mom was my fault."

"Eva, that wasn't your fault. It was another person in another car."

"But she was driving me home from the doctor, Danny. The doctor I wouldn't have had to go to if I hadn't been so fucking stupid. Even my dad knows that. He never said it, but he knows it."

"Fuck your dad. And you weren't stupid. I was there, too, you know. I could've stopped. I could've—"

"No," I insisted, clenching my jaw. "I've been over this in my mind a thousand times. And I remember telling you it was fine. I remember thinking we were always so careful, that one time wouldn't matter."

"Yeah, and I thought the same thing. The point is, people accidentally get pregnant every day," he said, lowering his voice. "We made a mistake, and we did what we had to do to fix it. And you know it was the right thing, Eva. I know you know that."

I did know it was right. At least in theory. But in actuality, if I'd never made those decisions, my mother would've still been alive.

I looked up, rolling my lips inward to hold back my tears. "I just wanna go back and undo it, you know? That one second that seemed so fucking inconsequential but ended up being the beginning of the end of everything. But I can't." I pressed my hand to my chest. "Do you know how that feels?"

He reached for my other hand, rubbing his thumb along my fingers. "Would you believe me if I said that I do?"

I tilted my head and waited for him to explain before I answered that he couldn't possibly know how I felt.

"It's not the same, and I know that," he continued. "But I wish I could go back and walk away from that phone. Or pick it up and call you to tell you I love you instead."

Love?

Electricity sparked in my chest.

He had loved me.

And he still loves me?

Is that what he's saying?

I didn't ask for clarification because I wanted to believe it. I wanted to stop thinking about everything that could go wrong and start thinking about all the things that could go right. So, I squeezed his hand and let the tension flow from my body, the weight of all my armor disappearing as it crashed to the ground. I couldn't travel back in time and undo the things that had caused everything to unravel. But what I *could* do was not let the opportunity to regain a part of the life I'd lost pass me by.

I gently let go of his hand and ran my fingers under my eyes. "I guess neither of us should have to live our lives feeling like that. Although you deserve it way more than I do, of course."

A cautious shadow crept across his face, as though he wasn't sure if it was too presumptuous to assume there was a touch of humor in my voice. "I know I do."

"All right, then. How about I eat a piece of your bacon while you tell me how you're never going to fucking do any of that to me ever again?"

A smile spread slowly across his face. "Yeah. I can do that." He raised an eyebrow as he slid his side of extra bacon over to me. "But don't act like you don't know I ordered this just for you."

I bit into the greasy strip and chuckled softly. "I guess things are off to a good start, then."

CHAPTER EIGHT
DANNY

JANUARY 1988

Four perfect fucking days.

With the perfect fucking girl.

I'd laid down the last fifteen bucks I had at Denny's, so I'd spent several hours the next day tuning and restringing guitars at my buddy's uncle's music shop. Between that, being his fucking errand boy, and the measly amount the band saw after clubs and promoters took their cut of ticket sales from our shows, I usually managed to pay rent and eat. I never worried too much about it because I wasn't ever out to impress anyone.

But with Eva, it was different. And though she didn't care how much money I had, I at least wanted to be able to buy her dinner somewhere pancakes weren't the featured item on the menu—even though she seemed thrilled to wander around the city, eating cheap tacos and drinking cheap tequila, before falling into my bed at the end of each day looking so fucking sexy I was sure I would lose my mind before I even touched her.

That's how Eva was. How she'd always been. How *we'd* always been together, at least before she'd lost her mom. But time had passed, and I could tell she was her old self again. Things were simple. Fun. Easy.

So fucking easy I almost forgot she was going back to Chcago in less than two days.

FOR EVA

"Oh my God, he lives!"

I looked up from my guitar and saw Will smiling at me as he hauled several pieces of his drum kit into the warehouse that served as a rehearsal space we shared with a couple of other bands. His girlfriend, Angela, followed behind him, a case of cymbals in one hand and a case of beer in the other.

"Yeah, what's this I hear about you and your new lover?" she asked, sweeping her long red hair over her shoulder and setting the cymbals and beer on the floor.

She settled her eyes and sideways grin on me as Will added "you mean his *old* lover" before heading back out to his car.

"So where is this chick?" she asked, flopping beside me on the sunken-in sofa and poking my arm with a pointy pink nail. "I gotta leave in a few, but I really wanted to meet the girl Danny Kincaid is *actually* serious about."

I laughed and explained that Eva was coming by later when Eric breezed into the room, barely looking in our direction as he set his mic stand on the concrete floor. He placed a bottle of Jack Daniels on top of an old plastic crate while shrugging off his black leather jacket.

"He's not serious about her," he said, exchanging the jacket for the Jack. "He's just fucking her till she goes back to wherever the fuck she came from. Which, hopefully, is soon."

My jaw immediately tensed.

"Oh, that's nice, Eric." Angela narrowed her eyes at him. "I'm always *so* glad when you show up with all of your unwanted commentary."

"And I'm always so glad when you get a night off from dancing naked for money." Eric's lips twisted with sarcasm as he screwed the top off the fifth of Jack and took a swig. "I know that's super challenging work and all."

"Oh, fuck off, Eric," I said, tossing my guitar pick at him.

"It's fine, Danny." Angela settled back into the cushions and crossed her legs. "He's just pissed because I have money...an apartment...a car...friends. You know, a life in general."

Eric smirked and walked over to the sofa, nudging her shoulder before perching on the armrest. She smiled and elbowed him in the thigh, hard enough that he winced.

"What are we talking about?" Matt shuffled in, his bass and amp in hand, doing a doubletake when he looked over at me. "Danny, holy shit, you're alive."

I threw my hands in the air. "Jesus, do you fuckers have to know where I am twenty-four seven? I just saw you all, like, three days ago."

"Four, dude," Eric corrected me, taking a long swallow of whiskey. "And we really needed to get a practice in before now, but nobody could get a hold of you."

"Don't worry about it, Danny." A cigarette dangled from Will's lips as he assembled his kit. "That Troubadour show was killer. Gina said that guy from Pitfall called her again, asking about setting up another meeting."

"She did?" I shifted in my seat, uneasiness spreading through me like an inkblot across a piece of paper. Gina was our de facto manager and usually called *me* with news about potential meetings and deals. I silently berated myself. She'd probably tried, but I hadn't checked my machine in days.

"Yeah, she did." Eric pushed himself up from the sofa. "So, we should probably get our shit together. Which means you should probably stop acting like you don't give a fuck about this band anymore."

I leaned my guitar against the front of the couch. "Dude, I was fucking *working*." Not a total lie. "You know that thing you do when you don't have some bored Beverly Hills housewife funding your entire existence?"

Eric snickered. "I can't help it if I fuck her better than her husband does."

A laugh sputtered from between Matt's lips as he hooked up his amp across the room, and Angela made a gagging sound.

"Hey, we wouldn't have been able to print those flyers for the last show if Eric's sugar mama wasn't around." Will screwed the last piece of his kit together and stood, brushing his palms against his jeans. "And Danny's allowed to take a fuckin' break once in a while. So, how about both of you shut the fuck up so we can practice?"

Matt adjusted the knobs on his amp, then plucked a loud note on his bass and grinned. "Yeah. What Will said."

"Fine." Eric rolled his eyes and handed me the bottle of Jack as a peace offering.

I nodded and took two long pulls before pushing myself up from my seat. I grabbed my guitar and glanced over at him before heading to hook up my gear, still pissed, but knowing he was partially right.

I needed to get my head back in the game.

But I had to figure out what was happening with Eva and me first.

CHAPTER NINE
EVA

JANUARY 1988

" *T*his, Eva. This right here is why I don't date Matt," Denise proclaimed as she teetered through the gravel parking lot in a pair of red pumps.

I skipped ahead in my slouched black boots. "We're getting to experience a band on the verge of greatness, Denise. This is exciting!" I twirled to the music wafting from inside the building in front of us, raising my arms in the air. "I *live* for this!"

"Oh my God, I should've never let you wash down that tiny little salad with that huge bottle of wine at dinner." She squealed as her ankle rolled under her, steadying herself before she went down. "And I should've cut myself off after rum and Coke number two."

I stopped, waiting for her to catch up. "You deserve a million rum and Cokes. You spent the last three days in the office, and you weren't even supposed to be working this week."

"If only financing deals on the verge of collapse had more respect for my personal life." She sighed before waving her free hand in the air. "But at least now I get to stare at your gorgeous face instead of having to look at Marcos for thirteen hours a day."

"Marcos...he's the one I met when we brought you lunch the other day?" She nodded, and my eyes widened as I fanned myself. "*Latin lover alert*, Denise. That guy's hot as shit. Why aren't you all over that? Or under that? Whatever position you wanna be in with that."

"Not. Interested."

"Well, he seemed pretty interested in you."

"Ugh, enough, Eva. Not happening." Denise grabbed the handle of the warehouse door and grinned. "Anyway, you obviously found other things to occupy your time while I was working."

I giggled like a twelve-year-old girl as we stepped onto the concrete floor of the rehearsal space. The band was in the middle of a song which I gathered from the lyrics was the one Eric had refused to do at the Troubadour.

> *"Another cigarette, another drink.*
> *Tellin' myself it's better not to think.*
> *Hours turn to days, how long has it been?*
> *Just another night without her again."*

His voice stopped me in my tracks, the perfect mix of soul and grit weaving in and out of the sultry groove flowing from Danny's guitar. Danny tossed his hair out of his eyes and raised his brows, flashing me a suggestive grin and holding my gaze. He finally broke our stare to remove the cigarette woven through the strings at the end of his guitar, and I gasped, snapping out of my trance as Denise yanked me farther into the room.

The song ended, and Eric grabbed a bottle of Jack Daniels, practically turning it upside down, the muscles in his throat working overtime to swallow the continuous pour. He wiped his mouth with the back of his hand and gestured in our direction. "What the fuck are they doing here?" He was staring at me and Denise, but clearly addressing Danny.

A pit formed in my stomach, and red heat scorched my skin. All eyes in the room were on me, and I froze. Had Danny not told them I was coming? And why was Eric once again acting like I should apologize for daring to enter his presence? My eyes darted to Danny, who quickly pulled his guitar over his head and set it in the stand beside him.

"Man, shut the hell up." He strode across the room toward me, shooting Eric daggers the entire way. "You invite people here all the time."

Eric's hair spilled over his arms as he crossed them in front of his chest. "Yeah, people who can comment on our sound. Not chicks who cause you to miss notes during shows."

"Look, so, Eric, is it?" Denise cleared her throat. "If this is a problem"—she circled her finger between us and him—"we can go find some other band to hang out with. One whose lead singer isn't an asshole."

Eric's eyes burned into us, his fists squeezed at his sides and nostrils flared.

"Calm down, dude," Matt said, cracking open a beer from the case beside the drum kit where Will sat resting his head in his hands. "I've been trying to get Denise over here for months. She's not leaving. Eva, either."

Eric narrowed his eyes at Matt. "Who's Denise?"

"Jesus Christ. This is Denise"—I shoved my thumb out to the left before pointing to myself—"and I'm Eva. The one you have some huge fucking issue with for reasons you're just gonna have to get the fuck over because I'm not leaving." My eyes widened, even though I was trying my hardest to appear unfazed by the volume of my own voice.

Denise snickered and took a seat on the couch, punctuating the fact that we weren't going anywhere. Eric's jaw clenched as he studied my face. I squared my shoulders and raised my chin, refusing to look away. He finally rolled his eyes to the side and uncrossed his arms, muttering a "whatever" before taking another long pull off his bottle of whiskey.

I blew out a breath and rested my forehead on Danny's shoulder.

"Holy shit, can you yell at me like that sometime just for fun?" he whispered as he ran his fingers along my arm, causing a soft chuckle to escape my lips. "But seriously, I'll talk to him, okay? He's not gonna treat you like that."

I nodded, then sank into the sofa beside Denise, thanking Will as he brought us each a beer. Danny walked back to his guitar and slipped the strap over his shoulder. Eric turned to look at him, hesitating for a moment before mumbling the title of a song.

As they moved through the next several numbers, the tension visibly lessened among the band. Danny and Eric occasionally glanced over at one another, communicating in some sort of unspoken language, nodding and pointing in ways I could only assume meant something worked or didn't. Their partnership was clearly important to the group, which made me wonder why they were so at odds when they weren't playing.

Besides the fact that Eric was a dick, of course.

At the end of a song about a relationship gone wrong, Eric held a note a bit too long, and his voice cracked like a pubescent Peter in the episode where the Brady kids decided to cut a record. I slapped my hand over my mouth in an attempt to stifle the alcohol-soaked laughter that so desperately wanted to escape. Of course, I failed miserably and the air that vibrated against my palm produced a cacophony of *pfffts* and snorts.

"Something funny, Eva from Illinois?" Eric asked into the mic.

"No." I pressed my lips together, trying to regain my composure. "Sorry. Not funny."

"Are you sure? Because it sounds like you think something is absolutely fucking hilarious." The defensive tone in his voice sparked a sense of satisfaction in me, like the tables had turned and *he* was now having to endure the pain of unwanted scrutiny.

Denise leaned her head on my shoulder, the laughter ripping through her body causing me to giggle and spill some of my drink on my jeans.

Eric glared at Danny, who shrugged, holding his hands up to indicate he wasn't my handler.

"It's just that you were giving Danny shit for missing a note and your voice cracked like Peter fucking Brady," I spurted through my laughter.

Will played a quick rim shot on his drums, and Danny nearly choked on the beer he'd just taken a sip of. Matt cocked his head and creased his brow like he'd never seen an episode of *The Brady Bunch* in his life.

"You know what? Fuck this." Eric threw his mic to the ground. "I'll be back when those two"—he pointed at me and Denise—"are gone." He stormed out of the warehouse, slamming the door behind him.

I looked at Danny, who was shaking his head at Matt, and pressed my hand against my chest. "Oh my God. I'm sorry, I didn't mean to—"

Danny laughed. "Don't apologize, he does this at least once a rehearsal. He'll be back in three, two—"

Before Danny could finish his countdown, the door swung open, and Eric stomped back inside.

"Fine," he said, looking straight ahead. "Let's do that one again."

"Fuuuuuck," Danny groaned, his breath warm against my cheek. "How do you feel so fucking good?"

My legs stretched along the mattress as the weight of his body pressed against me, and I smiled, fingering the damp curls that had formed on the nape of his neck. He rolled onto his back, and I watched as his heart pumped furiously inside his chest, gradually slowing along with his breaths.

It was past eleven the night of the band rehearsal, and after days of living in a story woven from every hope and dream I'd ever had about us, I was starting to wonder how it would end.

I pulled the thin blanket crumpled at the foot of the mattress over us and curled against him. "It's so much better now that we know what we're doing, isn't it?"

His lips quirked, and he turned to face me. "Are you implying I haven't always been the sexual master I am today?"

"Maybe." I chuckled. "We were such kids. I sure as hell didn't know what I was doing half the time."

He smiled and brushed my hair off my forehead. "Well, you definitely do now."

"I had a lot of practice after high school." I winked, laughing as his mouth fell open. "*That* was for me having to hear the stoner guy from the alley talking about you fucking Chrissy's or Candy's or whoever's stripper friend."

Danny buried his face in my neck. "I'm sorry I had sex with Chrissy's stripper friend," he mumbled like a child issuing a forced apology.

His breath tickled my skin, and I giggled, attempting to wriggle out of his arms. "You're forgiven, you're forgiven!"

He lifted his head. "Am I?"

"Oh, please, you know I don't care about that."

"No, Eva," he said, his eyes searching mine. "I mean, am I… *forgiven?*"

I swallowed, considering his question for only a second before realizing I'd spent the last four days simply assuming he was. I hadn't consciously made the decision, but it had been made, nonetheless. I loved him. I always had, and there was no way around that. And while it scared me to open my heart back up, I couldn't shake the feeling that I would ultimately be the one ripping it out this time if I didn't give us another chance.

I threaded my fingers through the black strands hanging over his eyes and brushed them back, admiring how beautiful he was. "You're forgiven."

He cupped my chin and pressed his lips against mine. It wasn't a desperate, passionate kiss, nor an invitation to do what we'd just done all over again. There was a calmness, a sense of relief, cased inside it.

Danny pulled away, rubbing his thumb along the top of my cheek. "You know, this whole week I kinda forgot you didn't live here. And now that I remember, I wish you did."

I smiled, not elaborating on the fact that *I* hadn't forgotten. "I wish I did, too."

"Then move here." His eyes widened, as if he was surprised by what he said, but the tone of his voice told me he was serious.

I furrowed my brow, his words slowly reeling one corner of my mouth upward. "Really?"

"I know this apartment is shitty," he continued. "But I'll get a better one. You can get any job here that you would in Chicago, and you won't even have to have it that long if you don't want to because I swear, the band's gonna make it."

I looked into his eyes, the gold in them shimmering with hope, and I wondered if the moment should have been a bit more complex. I pictured my mouth and eyes turning down. Saying something along the lines of *I need time to think* or *it's not that simple.* But none of those things felt authentic, because I knew the answer, and it wasn't complicated at all.

"Okay."

"Did you say okay?"

"I said okay."

His face relaxed, and he dropped his head to my chest, my skin warming as his mouth spread into a smile. "I love you, Eva. You know that, right?"

My stomach fizzed and tingled, and I nodded. "I do. But give me a minute before I say it back."

He cocked his head, a twitch of tension reappearing in his jaw.

"I feel like I've made all of this incredibly easy on you, and I wanna see you sweat just a little bit."

"You're killing me, Eva," he groaned.

I looked up at the ceiling, counting to five through spurts of laughter, then tilted my head back down. "Okay, now I can say it." I pulled him closer, my lips brushing over his. "I love you, too."

CHAPTER TEN
EVA

APRIL 1988

I stood at the beer cooler, trying to decide whether I needed to make the effort to haul more cases of Miller Lite from the back or if I could wait until Ronnie, the owner, showed up like he did every Tuesday to do payroll. He was perpetually grumpy but a good guy, so I knew he'd help me even though he'd complain about it the entire time.

I'd been at the bar, a no-frills joint off Melrose, for two months; it was nearly always busy, the pay was good, and the tips were even better. It wasn't the corporate advertising job I'd had lined up in Chicago, but the only person who was disappointed by that was my father, who I thought would wind up in the hospital when I told him I was moving to LA.

I could've spared him at least some of the chest pain by simply saying I needed to get out of Illinois, and Denise needed a roommate. I *had* moved in with her, so that wasn't a total lie. But something inside me wanted to prove to him that Danny really did love me after all, so I told him the truth, and he told me I was making a horrible mistake.

Eric hadn't been exactly thrilled with my decision either. In a move which nearly led to our first post-reunion blowup, Danny had chosen not to mention it to him until the night of a gig in Long Beach, two days after I got back into town and right before I showed up at the club.

"Jesus, Danny, you didn't tell him?" I'd hissed, pulling him away from the crowd that had gathered backstage. "I was gone for a week packing my shit in Chicago. You could've mentioned it *sometime* in there."

"We were just busy, it didn't come up," Danny said, running his hands along my arms. "And he doesn't hate *you*. He hates *everyone*. He's had a shit life, so he's pissed at the world."

He explained something about a mother who blamed him for ruining her life and a stepfather who kicked him out of the house, but I was too rattled to take much of it in. Thankfully, besides shooting the occasional dagger or offhand remark my way, Eric had backed off a bit over the past couple of months. The precarious cease-fire commenced when I told him I liked his KISS T-shirt. He snickered, asking me what my favorite song was.

"You realize that's impossible."

Eric rolled his lips inward, like he'd caught me in some sort of lame attempt to bond with him. "Mm-hmm."

"Fine. It's probably 'Got to Choose,'" I said. "The original off *Hotter than Hell*. Even though the *Alive!* version is killer, too, of course."

He opened his mouth, then closed it quickly before mumbling a perplexed "right on."

The bell on the bar door clanged. Sure it was Ronnie, I remained focused on the beer, opening another cooler. "Hey, will you help me get some of the beer from the back? I think the guy dropped a pallet off yesterday."

"Eva...right?" asked a voice which was clearly not Ronnie's.

"Huh?" I looked up and wiped my hands along the front of my jeans, blowing my bangs out of my eyes.

The petite blond walked closer. She was wearing tight leather pants and a Ramones T-shirt, and her Kewpie doll face looked vaguely familiar. "I'm Mandy. From last night. You helped get that guy who wouldn't leave me alone thrown out, and I wanted to thank you." She lifted the white paper bag she was carrying and placed it on the counter. "I remembered you saying something about how you had to open today, and all you wanted was a bottle of Tylenol and a pastrami Reuben from Canter's. I figured you probably had the Tylenol covered but wasn't sure about the Reuben."

"Oh, right. Glad I could help. But you didn't have to do this," I said as I peeked in the bag.

She smiled. "Oh, it's no problem."

"Do you want a drink or something?" I asked, motioning to the bottle and taps behind me.

Mandy bit her bottom lip and looked at her watch. "Yeah, sure, why not. I've got a work meeting in a bit, but I have time." She hopped onto one of the stools in front of me and told me a vodka tonic would be fine.

I poured a generous amount of alcohol into two glasses so she wouldn't have to drink alone, topping them off with a spray of tonic and a lime. "So where do you work?"

She raised the glass to her lips. "Perfect Circle Records. I'm in A&R. Well, trying to be in A&R. That's the group that signs bands. I'm still technically a secretary, but my boss finally realized I have a decent ear and can do more than make coffee and answer phones."

My breath caught in my throat at the letters A and R. I took a long swallow of my drink, then chuckled nervously. "My boyfriend's in a band, so I hear the term A&R at least five times a day."

It felt incredibly opportunistic, but I had to slip it in. I'd learned the wheels never stopped turning when your boyfriend was in a band that was trying to get signed. And those wheels had just picked up some serious speed.

"Oh, yeah? What band?"

"Counting Backward," I said, my chest squeezing as I waited for a reaction.

Mandy's eyes turned to saucers as the last sip of vodka

she'd taken pulsed its way down her throat. "You're fucking kidding me."

I shook my head, unsure if she meant *you're fucking kidding me, they're amazing* or *you're fucking kidding me, they shouldn't even be allowed to own instruments.*

She pulled a small notepad and pen out of her purse. "When's their next show?"

"Uh, Friday night, actually."

"Eva. I *love* them," she stressed, her dollface turning serious as she placed her hand on the bar. "The first time I saw them I knew they were gonna be huge. The singer is Eric, right? Is he your boyfriend?"

"No, my boyfriend plays guitar."

"Anyway, that Eric dude is larger than fucking *life*. And their whole sound, it's got this rawness to it, but it also totally hooks you. I've been telling my boss this for *months*, and all I keep hearing is that Eric seems difficult, and glam metal is what everyone wants. He won't even go see them, and none of the reps will back me up because they're idiots." She paused and rolled her eyes. "I know a couple of other labels have been jerking them around, which is insane, because whoever finally does grow some balls and sign them is gonna make a lot of fucking money."

So. Sweet Mandy is also tough Mandy. Smart Mandy.
Holy shit.

I picked up my pack of cigarettes from the counter behind me and fumbled with my lighter. "So, then, you know them?"

Mandy let out a sharp laugh. "Oh, I know them. And meeting you is a sign. This is the push I needed to do whatever it takes to convince Alan—that's my boss—that he's basically cutting off his own dick if he doesn't bring them on."

I choked on the smoke I'd just inhaled, amused by Mandy's intensity.

"Well, okay, then. Thanks so much," I finally managed. She smiled and I paused, considering the words on the tip of my tongue, wondering if I could sprinkle in a kernel of truth to make them easier to say. "And you're right, Eric's crazy talented. I think he comes off as difficult because he cares so much about the band. But he's really a great guy."

I wondered if my nonexistent poker face had given me away, but she didn't seem to notice.

"Just consider this an extra thank you for last night. Plus, it shows the boys' club at the label I know what the hell I'm doing." She winked and scribbled information about the show in her notepad, then sucked down the rest of her vodka. "But there's one thing I need from you, Eva."

I nodded. "Yeah, sure, anything."

Mandy leaned forward, pushing her finger onto the wooden bar top. "I need you to make sure those fuckers play the best show of their fucking lives."

CHAPTER ELEVEN
DANNY

APRIL 1988

"What if we change the key from C to D?" Eric tossed his worn notebook beside him on the couch. "It works better with the lyrics."

"And we slow the tempo down. Not a lot, though. I don't wanna lose too much of that aggression," I said, glancing up from my guitar.

Eric nodded. "Exactly."

I played a slower chord progression in D. "Yeah, I dig that. And then I can start the solo after that line about 'you couldn't drag me down.'"

"Yep." He turned up his bottle of Jack before offering it to me.

I gave the guitar a final strum then propped it against the sofa and took a drink. "Damn, this is gonna be good. Really good."

"I don't wanna get all fuckin' weird, but we make a good team, Kincaid." He leaned back and lit a cigarette. "Which is why I don't know about that chick of yours."

My head dropped as I set the whiskey on the coffee table.

Here we fucking go again.

Eric hadn't been thrilled about Eva moving to LA. Pissed the fuck off was more like it. I'd put off telling him until the last minute, tacking it onto the end of a conversation about the set list right before she showed up at the Long Beach gig. I knew I should've told him before then, but in my defense, he *had* ended up singing the shit out of every song during that show, his anger masking itself as passion to anyone who didn't know better.

I rested my elbows on my knees and scrubbed my hands over my face. "Dude, I don't get it. You have *zero* issues with Angela. Matt and I have both had girls come and go, and it's never been a big deal until now."

Eric turned toward me. "None of those girls besides Angela were ever serious. She was around before I was. Will and her are gonna grow old together and all that shit. But…"

I narrowed my eyes. "But what?"

"But the main thing is Matt and Will aren't *you*." He reached for the bottle on the table. "You and me write the songs. Yeah, they're a big part of our sound, and they bring in ideas. It's not that they *can't* do it. It's just that we're better at it. You know that, and so do they."

I bobbed my head in agreement. It was true. We all had our roles, and the dynamic worked. But that wasn't gonna change with Eva around.

"Look, I know that week she was visiting I wasn't around as much as I should've been," I admitted, pulling my pack of Marlboros from my shirt pocket. "But it's not like I've missed gigs or writing sessions or rehearsals. I call Gina every fucking day to find out who she's talking to and who wants to talk to us. So, I don't understand why you're being so fucking dramatic about this."

He arched an eyebrow. "Because you said it yourself. You ditched her because you thought she was gonna hold you back."

"Man, that was over two fucking years ago when you first joined the band," I mumbled, lighting my cigarette. "We were drunk and talking shit about how we couldn't let anything stand in our way. You don't know the whole story with Eva and me."

He took a long pull of the whiskey. "So tell me."

"I mean, I dunno. I came to LA to make it, and I was afraid she'd get in the way of that. She was pretty fragile back then and would've been out here with no one else to lean on but me while I was trying to focus on music."

"And you think that's different now because…"

I threw my hands up. "Because that was nearly six years ago, dude. We're not kids anymore. Now her best friend is here, she's got a job, she's got her own shit going on."

Eric dropped his cigarette into a beer can and set the Jack beside it. "I'm just sayin' you need to think real fuckin' hard about getting into a relationship when we're on the verge, man. Making an album, touring…that's serious shit. I don't wanna be in fucking Tokyo or something and have you bail on everything we've worked for because you've got some chick on the phone crying about how much she misses you."

I rolled my eyes. "Oh, come on, man. Do you seriously think I'd bail on this band? After everything I've put into it? Don't forget I was here before you showed up."

He scoffed. "Like I haven't paid my dues? I was fucking hustling just as much as you were."

I couldn't argue with that. Eric may have been an asshole ninety-five percent of the time, but he was a hardworking one. "Whatever, man. Just back off the Eva thing. It's a nonissue."

"Fine," he conceded, slumping back against the couch. "Who knows how long she'll be around, anyway."

My hand clasped the bottle I'd just reached for, and I whipped my head around to him. "What the fuck did you say?"

"Let's be honest, Danny. You always find something wrong with every girl you meet, date, fuck…whatever. I was worried things might be different with her, but probably not."

I wanted to punch him. Knock that smug look right off his fucking face. But I didn't. Because he could think that all he wanted if it would get him to drop the whole goddamn thing. Eva *was* different, but she wasn't gonna get in the way. She supported me and the band, and eventually Eric would see he was wrong about who she was. Having her around wasn't going to change my commitment to what Eric, Matt, Will and I had created. It wasn't going to change one goddamn thing.

"Holy fucking shit!"

The door to my apartment swung open, bouncing off the wall just as Eva flew past it. She stopped in the middle of the room, face flushed and chest heaving underneath her tank top.

Eric startled and muttered "Jesus Christ" as a shot of adrenaline sent me to the edge of the couch. "What's wrong? Are you okay?"

She nodded, a wide grin spreading across her face.

I exhaled, my body relaxing into the cushion. "Okay, so did something, like, monumental happen, or did you just have a really good day at work?"

"Monu-fucking-mental, babe." Eva hopped onto the recliner, pulling her legs up in the seat. "Well, it *could* be monumental. It's definitely a huge opportunity. Like, *huge*." She held her hands up, palms facing us, for emphasis.

Eric flopped against the back of the couch. "Oh man, did Angela convince you to start stripping? Because you've probably got a good enough body and all, and the money is great, but that whole scene would chew you up and spit you out."

"What? No." Eva scrunched up her nose and sucked in a deep breath before continuing. "I actually met someone from Perfect Circle Records today. She's in A&R. And I mentioned you guys and she said she loves you and you're gonna be huge and she's willing to do whatever it takes to get her boss to sign you and oh my God, I'm freaking *out*." She steepled her hands over her nose and squealed.

Eric and I exchanged a quick glance before he shifted his gaze back to Eva. "What does that mean? Like, she's gonna suck his dick or something and poof, we're signed?"

Eva huffed. "Eric, can you please imagine for one second that women have skills beyond sucking dick?"

"Did I say sucking dick was a bad thing? I mean, sometimes

you gotta do what you gotta—"

I sat up, slapping my arm across Eric's chest. "Who cares what the fuck she has to do. What's the deal, how did you meet her, and what do *we* have to do?"

Eva recounted the entire story while Eric and I listened, stopping her occasionally to ask for specifics. What exactly did the girl say? Did she sound sincere or was she just making conversation? Did it seem like she knew what she was talking about or was she full of shit? Our hopes got higher with every answer Eva gave us. And though we knew better than to let them get *too* high, we had to take this seriously because *what fucking if?* Perfect Circle was the real fucking deal. So, when she stood and dug a piece of paper out of her jeans with the girl's number on it, I hopped up and threw my arms around her so tight she had to tell me to stop, that she couldn't breathe. I laughed and kissed her pink cheeks and lips and thanked her a million times before I stumbled over myself to get to the phone to call Gina. My stomach twisted and my hand shook as I held the receiver, partially from excitement and partially because Eric and Eva were exchanging words which I couldn't quite filter out from the ring of the phone and the sound of my heartbeat in my ears. It didn't appear heated, but God only knew what he was saying to her. It was always a crapshoot with Eric.

"I left a message for Gina to call me ASAP," I said, returning to my seat on the couch and lighting a smoke to calm my nerves. "But what's with you two? Are you actually being civil and shit?"

I flashed Eric a sideways grin. I'd told him Eva cared about the band, and she'd just handed him the fucking proof. He pretended to ignore me and flicked his eyes away.

Eva smiled and crossed her arms over her chest, scuffing the toe of her high-top against the floor. "I, uh, *confessed* to Eric that I think he's talented. Way talented. And he deserves all of this if it, you know, works out."

I blinked in disbelief, then glanced over at Eric, whose eyes were fixed on the wall across the room. There was a subtle concentration in them, as if he was trying to make sense of what Eva had told him. Finally, he cleared his throat and shook his head.

"Yeah, uh, okay," he muttered, picking up his notebook and flipping through the pages. "We should call Will and Matt and work on the new song. See if we can get it ready by Friday. 'Cause that motherfucker has to be our first single."

PART II

CHAPTER TWELVE
EVA

SEPTEMBER 2008

"**W**hat?" Denise exclaimed. "I think I misunderstood. I thought you said someone from *Rolling Stone* called you yesterday, but I'm clearly delusional and need caffeine."

"No, you are actually completely...*lusional*." My mouth quirked before the corners turned back down. "It was a reporter who said he's doing a piece on Eric." I sucked in a quick breath. "Eric Stratton. And apparently, Eric mentioned my name as someone the guy should talk to."

Denise gasped. "Oh my God, Eva. You haven't spoken to Eric in what...almost twenty years?"

"Yeah." The guilt that had settled somewhere inside me over those years bubbled up, and I attempted to force the thoughts to the unreachable depths of my mind where they belonged. "Anyway, the reporter also wanted to know if I was still in touch with Danny."

"*Danny Kincaid?*"

"That would be the one."

"Wow." I could practically see her standing wide-eyed in the middle of her kitchen. "So did he say anything else?"

"Not really. Just asked me to call him back." I rubbed the tips of my fingers along the creases in my brow.

I hadn't called Denise immediately after getting the message because it had taken me all night to get over the initial shock. I fumbled through fixing dinner and helping with homework. When I climbed into bed, I was beginning to think maybe it was all some weird joke. And after waking up and dropping the kids at school, the shock had morphed into such an insatiable curiosity that I typed *Simon Rogers* into every search engine in existence, coming up with the same result each time. The guy had written for more publications than I knew existed and worked for *Rolling Stone* since 2000. Every image showed him wearing a T-shirt with some obscure band logo, horn-rimmed glasses, and messy hair, leaving no question in my mind that he was, indeed, a legitimate music journalist.

"Well, you obviously have to call him."

I scrubbed my hand over my face. "I don't know if I can do that. I mean, with everything else…it's just so much."

"I get it, babe. I do." Her voice softened. "But aren't you at least a little bit curious about what Eric said?"

Of course, I was. More curious than she knew, and I wanted to tell her that. But it required more thought…more explanation than I was able to give at that moment. Or quite possibly ever.

I pushed myself off the sofa, the midcentury hardwoods squeaking as I paced them with my bare feet. "He said Eric mentioned I might be able to provide commentary on what happened back then. But why would I wanna relive that? I left all that shit behind me for a reason." I grabbed a pair of Drew's dirty socks off the floor and tossed them down the hall toward the laundry room. "I am a forty-four-year-old stay-at-home mother, Denise. I'm on the goddamn PTA. I coordinate carpools and make brownies for bake sales."

"Eva. You're more than those things, and you know it," she said.

"I just mean that I packed that part of my life away a long time ago." I sighed and pushed my hand through my hair, resting it on top of my head. "He doesn't need me to help tell his story."

"Well, he may not *need* you to, but he clearly *wants* you to."

I nodded. This was obviously important to Eric, and he wanted me to be a part of it. I didn't know why, but calling the reporter was the only way to find out. Besides, I didn't have to rehash every detail. I would just tell Simon that I'd seen Eric overcome tremendous odds, and I was glad he'd been able to turn things around. The end.

"Okay, fine," I conceded. "I'll call the guy now. He's got a LA area code, and it's, what, 8 a.m. out there? So, he probably won't even answer, and I can at least say I tried."

Denise snickered. "You think he's not gonna call you back?"

"Whatever. I'm hanging up. Love-you-bye." The words spilled out of my mouth in one breath, and I dug the piece of paper I'd written Simon's number on out of my pocket. I shifted my cell from my ear and tapped on the digits. My insides felt simultaneously frozen and on fire as my thumb hovered over the call button. I muttered a quick "fuck it," then shut my eyes and pressed it.

Of course, he picked up on the first fucking ring.

"Hi, Simon. This is Eva Mitchell." I paused and swallowed, my mouth suddenly stuffed full of cotton balls. "Uh, Eva Holloway."

"Ms. Mitchell! I was about to fire up the computer to get going on this Eric Stratton piece, and here you are calling me." His Australian twang was warm and charming, and he sounded much less serious than he had on the message.

"Call me Eva. And sorry it's early, I just have a busy day and wanted to try to squeeze this in." A total lie. I was doing laundry and maybe organizing the pantry.

"No worries. I have a newborn, so I don't sleep. Wife's got him now, though. Plenty of time to chat."

"Oh, congrats." I remembered those days all too well and also wanted to offer my sympathies. But I settled back into the sofa and cut to the chase, deciding small talk was unnecessary. "So how can I help with the article? Do you just need a comment about Eric or something?"

"You know, he thinks very highly of you," Simon offered instead of answering my question.

My stomach tied itself into a knot of nostalgia, tightening with every memory that flashed in my mind. "I, um…I mean, that's nice of him, but we haven't spoken in a really long time."

"Well, then, you may not know he's opening a counseling center for underserved youth here in Los Angeles at the beginning of the year."

My heart constricted. "Oh. Wow. That's amazing. Truly. But I—"

"This is the first time he's ever really agreed to sit down and talk about his own past struggles, no-holds-barred," Simon interrupted. "And I don't think my piece would be complete if I didn't talk to the person who was there from the time the band took off to when it, you know…*ended*."

I closed my eyes, listening to the sound of my breath, unsure what to say.

"But first things first. Danny Kincaid. Do you ever speak to him? Seems the guy doesn't want to call me back."

"No," I answered, clearing my throat to free my voice. "I don't. But I have to say, I'm surprised Eric even wants you to talk to him."

"He's game for it. Danny was an important part of the band," he said, clacking away at the keyboard. "But all right, never mind him for now. Tell me about your relationship with Eric."

I chewed my lip and stared across the room at the pictures of Drew and Miles decorating the fireplace mantel. Why was I doing this? Why was I on the phone with this man I didn't know, talking about people who weren't in my life anymore?

"It was, uh, fine," I said, remembering the line I'd rehearsed. "Eric overcame tremendous odds, and I'm glad he was able to turn things around."

Simon chuckled. "That's it? That's all you're gonna give me?

Because Eric seems to think you two were a lot closer than that."

I looked down at my chest, sure I would see blood seeping from where the bullet Simon just fired had penetrated it. "What did he say to make you think that?"

"Well, I guess we can jump right to that, then." He paused and sucked in a breath. "He said you saved his life."

My mind went numb, and I swallowed hard, the lump in my throat threatening to choke me. I blinked, my vision blurred by fresh tears, and I shook my head, as though I could physically shake the scene from my brain.

"Eva? You still there?"

"Uh, yeah, hang on." I hurried to the kitchen, flung open one of the cabinets, and strained to reach the very top where I hid my cigarettes and lighter. Aaron had hated my occasional vice, and I could still hear him saying *you know those things will kill you* anytime I snuck outside.

Fuck him.

"Did I lose you for a sec? *Eric told me you saved him,*" Simon stressed as I opened the back door to the patio and took a long drag from my cigarette. "So, maybe we could start there?"

"Okay," I said, sitting on one of the brick steps and brushing away a tear. "But we should probably begin before that."

CHAPTER THIRTEEN
EVA

Mandy refused to divulge the details of exactly what she'd said or done to convince Alan Gerson, head of A&R at Perfect Circle Records, to show up at the Roxy that Friday night in April. Even after I pulled her aside before the band took the stage and asked how she'd managed it.

"You don't wanna know, Eva," she'd said, laughing and casually swirling her vodka on the rocks.

My eyes widened, my mouth forming into a naive little O as a devious grin spread across her face. This was my official initiation into Hollywood. I'd fallen down the rabbit hole, landed smack-dab in the middle of Wonderland, and *oh my God, she'd sucked his dick.*

"But before you go thinking I sucked his dick," Mandy added, leaning closer, "I didn't." She winked and downed her drink. "Now that Alan's here, though, the guys have to do their thing. I could only get him to agree to come to the show, no other promises. And no matter what I do, he's not gonna ink any deal if he doesn't see dollar signs up there on that stage. Lots of 'em."

Fortunately, Alan's eyes lit up like a Vegas slot machine. I could almost see the thoughts in his brain rearranging themselves as he watched Eric work the stage. Difficult personality be damned. This kid was gonna make him rich.

Within a week, there was a signed contract and an advance check I stared at for ten straight minutes, wondering if there were really supposed to be five zeros after the four. But knowing none of them would drop a dime of their share on anything remotely practical, Mandy, whom Alan had officially promoted out of her secretarial role, found the guys a small rental in Laurel Canyon and made sure someone brought them groceries every couple of weeks to soak up all the alcohol.

They still played all the local clubs through the summer but were also booked on a string of gigs up and down the coast—an introduction to a wider market while keeping them close enough to home to work with publicists, stylists, photographers, and all the people tasked with ensuring the band would deliver everything the label was banking on.

Fortunately, they'd found someone to advocate on their behalf when visions didn't jive and the label got pushy. Gina had gotten them a solid deal but had her sights set on opening her own club in town, not keeping a bunch of twentysomething punks in line so they didn't lose their record deal—a task which was on Keith Martin's daily to-do list. She knew him from her days as a booking agent and was convinced he was the man for the job.

Keith, however, wasn't so sure. He already had a roster full of wildly successful, badly behaved bands and no need to add to it. But after four meetings and Eric promising not to be an asshole, he finally agreed to take them on.

By September, Counting Backward was officially in the studio. Time moved at warp speed between working at the bar and hanging out in the smoke-filled confines of Sunset Sound. I was careful not to be intrusive, simply showing up with Angela in our roles as the loyal girlfriends bearing takeout and booze. Angela would get antsy and leave, but I found myself lingering, melding into one of the plush velvet couches. I listened intently, learning how each instrument was so uniquely important to the creation of a song. That the seemingly tiniest tweaks to the timing or pitch or volume could change the entire feel of it. It was endlessly fascinating to me.

The recording process went quickly. There were several fine-tuned originals the label had pegged as singles, and the guys had all agreed to tone down the partying in favor of getting down to business. So, even when Danny wasn't physically at the studio rerecording tracks or listening to playbacks, he was going over every detail in his head.

I understood his focus. That didn't stop me from draping myself half-naked over his bed, attempting to ignite some spark of interest, but I understood. I was just glad that by mid-November the tracks were finally being mixed, and we'd have at least some time together before everything that came next.

I got off early from my shift at the bar and headed straight to the Laurel Canyon house in hopes of making any sort of contact with Danny which ended with me having an orgasm. But instead of discovering him poised to grab me and rip my clothes off, I'd found him crumpled in the recliner while Eric paced the floor.

It was only out of sheer desperation I decided to stay, praying Eric would quickly grow annoyed by my presence and leave.

"Something's off," Eric said, leaning against the wall and gnawing on his thumbnail nearly thirty minutes later.

Danny sighed, running his hands through his hair. "I know, dude. It's killing me."

I was sprawled on the sofa, half-heartedly reading the copy of *Guitar World* I'd dug out from the cushions, considering locking myself in Danny's bedroom and embarking on a solo sex mission when Eric said my name.

"What do you think? I mean, from what you've heard...do you think it's good?"

I blinked. "You mean the album?"

I deserved every bit of the what-the-fuck-do-you-think-we're-talking-about look Eric gave me. But the fact he'd asked for my opinion shocked the shit out of me.

"You know I love it. I've said that since I heard the first cuts."

"Yeah, but since all the engineers got a hold of them," Danny clarified. "Like those couple songs I played for you the other day. Do they sound like *us*?"

I cocked my head and considered the question. It *was* them, so how could it not sound like them? There was a yes poised on the tip of my tongue, but I held it in as I remembered the first time I'd seen them play. And all the times after. The passion. The rawness. The energy.

"Um, okay," I began, closing the magazine. "It's *really* good. It is. But did those songs sound like you? I mean, yes and no."

"Explain." Eric crossed his arms. It wasn't a defensive move—more like he was settling in to hear me out.

"Yes, the songs sound like your songs. Because they're your words put to your music. But..." I paused, working my thoughts out in my head. "It's almost like someone took a Brillo pad to them and scrubbed till there wasn't one speck of dirt left. Like, there's no...*grit*."

My eyes darted between Danny and Eric, waiting for one of them to speak. But neither did. Danny slumped down farther in his seat, lighting a cigarette, while Eric chewed his lip and stared past me.

"But maybe that's just the ones I heard," I added, afraid I'd overstepped.

"No, keep going," Eric said, not taking his squinted eyes off the wall behind me.

I shook my head. "I don't...I'm not sure..." My gaze flicked to my lap, the glossy picture of Ace Frehley posing with his Cherry Sunburst Les Paul guitar causing my head to jerk up with such force I thought it might snap off. "It's like KISS."

Danny groaned and covered his face. "Eva, I love you, but you cannot tell me we sound like KISS without expecting me to jump out the goddamn window."

"No, I don't mean you *sound* like KISS." I sat up against the back of the couch and cleared my throat. "Eric, tell me this. When did KISS really take off?"

He shrugged. "I guess when *Alive!* came out."

"Exactly. The self-titled, *Hotter Than Hell, Dressed to Kill*"—I ticked each album off on my fingers—"pretty much considered commercial failures. But then they released *Alive!* and bam— fucking gangbusters."

"Babe." Danny pursed his lips. "We can't just go record a live album."

"And I'm not saying you should, *babe*," I stated, slightly miffed by his patronizing tone. "Everyone knows they doctored the live recordings in the studio, anyway. But the energy— the power and the rawness in their live shows—it still came through."

He raised his brows, bobbing his head side to side. "Yeah, maybe."

"Not maybe," Eric said, finally releasing his bottom lip and nodding slowly. "She's right. She's exactly right. It's too pol- ished."

"I don't know, man. I want it to be clean, I just…" Danny trailed off, taking a long drag off his smoke before sighing and pushing himself out of the chair. "Fuck. All right, I'm calling Mandy. And Keith. Maybe they can toss those tapes in the trash and let some of the dirt settle back on 'em."

"Make sure they leave them in there for a while," I called after him.

Eric drew in a deep breath as he walked the few paces across the room and flopped onto the couch beside me. "Good call, Eva from Illinois." He held up the magazine and chuckled. "Glad I picked this up the other day."

"I sure as hell knew it wasn't Danny's." I paused, reaching down to grab my cigarettes from my purse. "And listen, I didn't mean to cross any lines. But you asked, and I wanted to be hon- est because you know I believe in you guys, and I really think this album can be the one to blow the fucking roof off the—"

"Shut up, Eva," Eric said, pulling out his lighter and flicking it at the tip of my smoke. "I *did* ask. And the reason I asked is because I've seen you sitting there in the studio, looking like the wheels in your head were turning so fucking hard they were gonna spin out. So, I wanted your…*opinion*, I guess."

A smile spread across my face, so wide it caused my jaw to drop. "Oh my God, you like me."

"I didn't say that."

"But you do."

"I don't." He cleared his throat. "But uh, while we're at it, Mandy told me what you said. About me."

My brow creased. "What do you mean?"

"When you first met her. Some bullshit about me being a great guy."

"Oh, right. Well, I was lying, of course, but now that we've gotten so close." My lips rolled inward to stifle my laughter.

"Yeah, we're not close," he said as he dug in his jeans pocket. "But are you and Mandy?"

I lifted my chin, looking at him from the corner of my eye. "Why?"

He lit the Marlboro between his lips. "Because she keeps telling me she has this rule about not getting involved with anyone she works with. But I don't wanna get *involved*. I just wanna fuck the chick. So, can you, like, remind her what a *great guy* I am so she'll—"

"Gross, Eric." I rolled my eyes as I forced a stream of smoke from the side of my mouth. "And no."

CHAPTER FOURTEEN
EVA

MARCH 1989

I swept into El Compadre, taking a moment to steady myself while my eyes adjusted to the soft glow of the sconces adorning the wood-paneled walls. Traffic had been particularly hellish, even by LA standards, and I was nearly thirty minutes late. I'd been looking forward to my plans with Danny all week and prayed he wasn't on his way home thinking I'd forgotten.

I frantically searched the red leather booths in the dimly-lit space, my shoulders falling along with my hopes when I finally spotted him at the back of the room in a large, round booth with the rest of the band and Keith. Their meeting was scheduled to be over by five, at which point Danny and I were supposed to have been eating fajitas and drinking flaming margaritas.

Maybe the meeting was just running late, like I'd been. Maybe Danny told them they'd have to wrap things up as soon as I arrived, and they were all about to leave. Or maybe there were important band decisions still to be made, and I'd end up stuck in another traffic jam on the way home to watch *Cheers* and eat popcorn for dinner.

Things were fine. We were fine. But with the album scheduled to drop the next week, the label's promotional machine was running full steam ahead. The first single and video had been released in February to give the public a glimpse of what was to come, and it garnered enough attention to secure the band the opening slot on Hott Blood's North American tour starting in May. Then in the fall, they'd headline their own gigs at smaller clubs across the country before hopping back onto an arena tour with some other supergroup.

During the holidays, we'd taken advantage of the brief calm before the next storm rolled in. Rather than heading back home and numbing myself with mimosas as my father and his wife *oohed* and *aahed* over each present their daughter opened, Danny and I had driven down to Baja, spending the week of Christmas at the cheapest oceanfront hotel we could find. I got him a black leather guitar strap with turquoise conchos and silver rivets. He got me a tattoo.

My skin was still burning from the needle when we sat on the deserted beach the night before we left, smoking a joint, drinking tequila from the bottle, and talking about how our next vacation would be in Hawaii where women in coconut shell bras and hula skirts would serve us mai tais in real glasses. I'd tell him to stop staring at their tits, but they'd be so amazing I'd be staring at them, too.

We'd stay there for two weeks.

Or a month.

Or maybe we'd stay there forever.

At some point, we decided not having sex on an actual beach would be a wasted opportunity, but I kept tipping over on top of him, and we couldn't stop laughing about how we were too hammered to come. So, we eventually gave up and melted into the soft, cool sand. I dreamed that my mother was the brightest star in the sky, looking down, telling me in her gentle Italian lilt that I was still her *topolina*—her little mouse— and she didn't blame me for what had happened. It felt real enough that the tiniest splinters of guilt worked their way out of my heart each time I caught a glimpse of the scrolled letters on the back of my shoulder.

But the holidays were long gone and a subtle sadness settled over me as I walked across the dining room of El Compadre. I was fully prepared to say a quick hello, then turn around and head back to my car, when Keith slammed his fist on the table.

Christ, what's Eric done now?

I approached them and offered a weak wave, which only Will acknowledged. Eric sat with his arms crossed over his chest, glaring at Danny, whose elbows were propped on the table, head resting in his hands.

"I gotta go, but you're being insane, Danny." Matt popped up from the end of the booth, almost knocking me over. "Shit. Sorry, Eva. Didn't see you. But maybe *you* can talk some sense into your fucking boyfriend."

Danny startled and brought his head up, the look on his face leaving no doubt he was surprised by my appearance. Heat crept from my chest up my neck.

Why did I spend a single second fretting about being late, worrying he'd think I'd be the one to forget?

"Fuck, I'm sorry," he muttered. "We were supposed to be done by now." His eyes flickered around the booth. "Look, can we just talk about this tomorrow?"

Eric snorted. "Are you out of your goddamn mind?"

"No, we cannot talk about this tomorrow." Keith leaned into the table, pointing his finger at Danny. "I called in favors and put my ass on the line to get you this gig, and you're not gonna give me some bullshit reason about not doing it."

So this isn't about Eric?

Keith retreated, his eye catching mine as he reached for his drink. "Hey, Eva."

I drew in a deep breath. "Hi. And bye. Obviously, there's important business going on here, so I'll just…" I motioned to the exit with my thumb.

"No, sit," Keith insisted, scooting closer to Will, who was silently sipping a beer but looking as if he might explode at any moment. "Maybe Matt was right. Maybe you *can* talk some sense into this guy."

Danny huffed and reached for his pack of Marlboros. "Oh, come on, man. Don't drag her into this."

Keith ignored him, smiling at me in a way only people skilled at getting *what* they wanted, exactly *when* they wanted, could. "No, we're obviously interrupting your plans, so we'll just work through this little issue, then clear out."

My eyes darted to Danny, who lit his cigarette before mouthing *sorry* and waving me into the circle.

"Uh, okay," I said, sliding into the booth beside Keith. "What's going on?"

Will finally spoke. "Keith got us the opening slot on Black Widow Rising's tour."

My eyes widened, and I threw my hand over my mouth to contain the piercing squeal that came from it. Black Widow Rising had been one of my favorite bands growing up and their lead singer, Jesse Trainor, the subject of all my ridiculous teenage fantasies. "What? That's amazing. But they're on the road right now, so is this, like, later?"

"They need us in ten days. And yes, it *is* amazing, isn't it?" Eric said, shooting Danny a look that had *you're a fucking idiot* written all over it.

I blinked. "Wait, ten days? You're going on tour in ten days?"

"Their current opening band is rolling off unexpectedly, and they need a replacement ASAP," Keith explained.

"Wow. Okay, well, it's short notice and all, but you've gotta do it." I looked at Danny, who chewed his lip and picked at the label on his beer bottle. "Right?"

I rubbed my chest, trying to ease the heaviness that settled over the initial excitement as I thought about him leaving sooner than expected. But I reminded myself this was part of the deal. I'd understood from the get-go this would happen. That this is what Danny *wanted* to happen.

What I *didn't* understand, though, was why Danny was

slumped in his seat, looking like a kid whose balloon had just popped.

"It's *too* short notice," he answered, stubbing out his cigarette. "We need time to make sure we've got our shit together. The album isn't even out yet, and there's already so much buzz. I don't wanna do anything to ruin that."

"Look, Danny," Keith began, his tone sharpening. "I'm not sure if something got lost in translation, but debut albums don't just sell themselves. You may be the band everyone's talking about here in LA, but you need to be that in fucking Iowa and Indiana and North Carolina. And you know how you do that? You go on tour. As soon as you fucking can."

"We're going on the road. In *May*. That was the plan so we could have time to make sure things are tight. I don't wanna get out there and give shitty live performances."

Keith scoffed. "You're acting like you have a choice here. And I guess you do. But I'm not sticking around, and neither will the label, if you make the wrong one."

I stared at Danny, willing him to look at me, my eyes pleading with him once he finally did. He'd become even more of a perfectionist about his music since they started making the record, but Matt was right. He was being insane. This was everything they'd dreamed of, everything they'd worked for.

"We don't know what we're doing on this scale," Danny said, the quaver in his voice tugging at my heart. It was clear his nerves had taken over, and he needed a pep talk. Stat.

"But you *do* know what you're doing," I said, putting on my game face. "You've been rehearsing your asses off for months. So, you're gonna go play whatever-fucking-arena in whatever-fucking-city just like you play the Whisky or the Roxy or the Troubadour. And you're gonna blow the whole fucking audience away because Counting Backward is the best goddamn band on the planet. We all know it, and the sooner you start playing to those crowds Black Widow Rising draws, the sooner everyone else will know it."

Danny inhaled, his eyes and shoulders relaxing with his breath, and he nodded. I glanced at Keith, the thin, angry line of his lips curling into a faint smile.

Eric bobbed his head. "See, that's what we've been trying to tell you, man. Listen to your chick."

"Seriously, dude," Will chimed in.

Danny bristled at their comments, so I quickly dismissed them. We'd come a long way, baby, and all that jazz, but I knew full well that two guys telling another his girlfriend was right and he was wrong still pushed all the wrong primal male buttons.

"All I'm saying is you know how to play," I explained. "You guys just need someone to tell you where to be when and those sorts of things. And Keith will be there to do all that."

"Well, I'll be there when I can. I've got some prior commitments I've gotta deal with. Plus, Cherie's, like, eleven months pregnant." He paused and looked at his watch as if his wife could be giving birth on the floor of their house in Encino while he was dealing with a bunch of jackasses at a Mexican restaurant in Hollywood. "But you're gonna have a tour manager and an entire crew of people who know the ropes. And I'm sending one of my best guys in my place."

Eric jerked his head in Keith's direction. "Wait, what? Our first real tour and you're leaving us hanging? When the fuck were you gonna tell us this?"

"I didn't mention it because it's not a big deal," Keith said. "And I'm not leaving you hanging. Like I said, I'm sending someone from my company, and I'll fly out for shows when I can get away."

Danny squeezed his eyes shut and massaged his forehead.

"Great, so now you're *both* gonna freak out about this?" Will threw back his beer, slammed the bottle on the table, and pushed his shoulder against Keith's. We both stood to let him out of the booth. "I'm done with this stupid fucking conversation. Call me and let me know what time the bus pulls out.

Because we're *going* on this fucking tour."

We sat back down, and Keith grinned. "See, it's as simple as that. You're going on this fucking tour."

Danny threw his hands up. "I mean, fuck, I know we've gotta go, but I—"

"Obviously, we're going," Eric interrupted. "But we don't want *someone from your company*. We want someone we know. Someone who knows *us*."

Keith nodded. "I'm sending Bryan. You guys met Bryan."

"Bryan's a dumbass."

Keith shook his head and laughed. "Actually, Eric, *you're* the dumbass for not comprehending how fucking close I am to walking out of here right now."

My stomach dropped as he polished off his drink and pushed it aside. The coolness in his voice signaled he wouldn't consider this a rash decision, and that scared the hell out of me.

"I took you guys on because you're good, okay? *Really* good. But I have all the work I need without you. I also have a severely moody wife at home right now, along with a toddler who still shits his pants, yet is somehow more fucking mature than any of you. So, the last thing I need in my life is this extra fucking stress."

I closed my eyes and tried to think of something—*anything*—I could say to keep the train from jumping the tracks.

Eric sucked in a deep breath, and I peeked out of one lid, praying he wasn't going to derail it, with everything they'd all worked so hard for winding up a pile of smoking metal.

"Fine," he said. "Bryan it is. But what if you send someone with him? Like an assistant we choose?"

I allowed my other lid to open. I wasn't sure where he was going with this, but at least he was being semi-agreeable.

Keith sighed. "Eric, there are budgets, and I can't just pay people to—"

"Come on, man. We don't know Bryan, and he doesn't know us. We need to be sure someone's there who has our same vision…someone who gets us." He lit a smoke and leaned back, extending his arm along the top of the booth. "And you can sit there and say you don't *need* us till you're blue in the fucking face, but you *want* us. I know you do, because we're gonna make you a lot of fucking money."

"I'm not paying for it." Keith paused, wincing, as if whatever he was about to say was going to cause him an undue amount of pain. "But…*Fuck*. I'll ask the label to do it."

Eric flashed him a victorious grin. "Which they will. Because we're gonna make them a lot of fucking money, too." He turned to Danny. "You good with that?"

Danny nodded like he was psyching himself up. "Yeah, we're doing this, man. We have to do this."

"All right, problem solved. And Keith, you should probably go ahead and introduce Eva to Bryan."

Eric's words were met with furrowed brows and tilted heads.

"And *why* is that, exactly?" Keith asked, reaching for the wallet in his back pocket.

Eric drained his beer and burped before twisting his mouth into a smug smile. "Because I'm sure he'd like to meet his new assistant as soon as possible."

CHAPTER FIFTEEN
DANNY

MARCH 1989

"Hey, babe." A soft wisp of air skimmed my cheek, and I slowly peeled my heavy lids back to see Eva leaning over me.

"Hey." My voice sounded like I'd downed a glass of gravel, and my head felt like it was in fucking blender. "What time is it?"

She sat on the edge of the bed, fully dressed with a cute little crooked smile on her lips. "Almost noon. And in case you're wondering, I think it was flaming margarita *numero diez* that did you in."

I groaned and ran my palm over my face. "Oh, fuck. Right." My brain throbbed in sequence with the events of the night before. Stumbling out of El Compadre—had I knocked over the bowl of mints on the hostess stand or had I knocked over the actual hostess? Laughing as Eva folded me into her car. Watching my cigarette fly back in the window as we wound up the canyon. Trying to climb into the back seat to find it as Eva grabbed my leg and told me to sit the fuck down.

I swallowed, shuddering as the taste of sour mix settled at the back of my throat. "Remind me to order something else next time."

Eva smirked. "Only hurts when you drink ten, babe. Anyway, I told you to switch to beer, but you said that wasn't as much fun."

"What? Why?"

"Because you couldn't set it on fire."

"Oh, yeah." I tried to laugh but ended up coughing, which made my head hurt even worse. "It's weird how I like pyro on drinks but think it's stupid on stage."

She rolled her eyes. "You're weird, period."

"*You're* weird." I pulled her on top of me and wrapped my arms around her, smiling through the pain of my hangover as her thick blond hair fell over my face.

She giggled and wriggled away, kissing my cheek before hopping up. "Okay, we're both weird, but I gotta go. I need to shower and run a couple errands before work. I told Ronnie I'd help him with some stuff before my shift starts."

"Shit, Eva. As much as you do there, he should give you a raise and make you the manager."

She shrugged, flinging her purse over her shoulder. "Yeah, maybe. But first I need to talk to him to make sure I'll even have a job when I get back."

I shifted my head against the pillow. "Get back from what?"

"From the tour." Her face fell slightly. "The Black Widow Rising tour?"

Fuck.

I shot up in the bed much too quickly and winced. "Ow. Shit." I rubbed my forehead and cleared my throat, hoping my voice wouldn't sound as shaky as my body felt. "Yeah, the tour. Right. Sorry."

"I can't believe I get to do this. That *we* get to do this," Eva said, her eyes lighting up like two sparklers on the Fourth of July. "I mean, I know it's kinda crazy. Like, who am I to be some band manager's assistant? But think of how much fun we'll have and…" Her brows turned down, her eyes searching mine. "You're okay with me coming, right? I mean, you seemed happy about it last night, but if you think it's not a good idea or something…"

I shook my head, sharp steel blades attacking it from every angle. "Yeah, no, it's good. It'll be good," I said, trying to convince her—and myself—that I believed it would be.

She nodded slowly, the corners of her mouth turning up cautiously.

"So yeah, uh, do your stuff and call me later," I said. "I don't know how late we'll be rehearsing."

"I'll see you when I see you. Go rehearse till your fingers bleed. Or maybe not that much. Anyway, Denise and I have plans tomorrow, so I'm gonna crash at home tonight." She tilted her head and studied my face again. "But, um…" She held onto her words, but the way she looked at me told me she felt uneasy.

"Love you, babe," I blurted out, hoping that would squash her doubts, no matter how valid they were.

Her forehead creased. "Yeah, I, uh…I love you, too. But if…"

I forced a grin so wide my face hurt, hoping that would end the conversation so she would leave and I could fucking think.

"Okay. I just…never mind. I'll let you know once I talk to Keith and get everything figured out." She smiled, then pulled her keys from her bag and squeezed her shoulders together like a little kid who'd just found out she was going to Disney World. When she reached for the doorknob, her hand rested there for a moment, and she turned back to me.

Shit.

My muscles tensed, and I began to feel like the cornered rat I'd been the night before when Eric came up with his stupid fucking idea. Like a trapped animal that might do something crazy to escape. Like gnaw its own foot off. Or ruin a really good thing for the second fucking time.

"Oh, just FYI," Eva said. "All those damn mints you knocked over last night are in the kitchen. I tried to get you to leave them, but you kept crawling around, picking them up, saying you were probably gonna be hungry later."

She chuckled and winked, and I worked a laugh into the

long sigh of relief that streamed from my lips. I fell back against the mattress as she closed the door, squeezing my eyes shut and tracing circles on my temples.

Fuck me.

I didn't want her on that fucking tour.

Things had been so good since she'd moved to LA. She had her job, I had my music, we had our own friends, our own separate worlds outside of the one we had together. And the idea that she would be so fucking tangled up in this part of *mine*... It was exactly what I'd worried about before. The reason I'd called her that night and told her it was over.

It wasn't like I didn't want her around. Of course I did. We'd even talked about getting a place together once the money started rolling in. But she was supposed to be back at home decorating the damn thing, not glued to my ass while I was on the road.

I laid there for thirty minutes, staring at the ceiling and lighting one cigarette off another before flinging myself out of bed, throwing on whatever clothes I could find on the floor, and marching down the hall to Eric's room. I pushed through the door, not bothering to knock, and found him propped up in bed—jeans, no shirt, smoking and flipping through a copy of *Rolling Stone*. Beside him was a tangle of blond hair and tan limbs and lace-covered asses.

"What's up, man?" he said, barely taking his eyes off the magazine resting on his lap.

I glared at him, sure my face was as red as Chick Number One's underwear. I didn't know why the girls made me extra pissed. Maybe because Eric had so obviously proceeded to go about his night without a care in the world, while I was crawling around on the floor of a Mexican restaurant and throwing up sour mix in my mouth. All because I needed to forget what he'd done until I could make him fix it.

"I don't know, *man*. Just trying to figure out why you think you can make decisions for this band without consulting me first."

"What are you talking about?" he asked, his tone annoyingly casual as he stubbed out his cigarette.

I pushed my hands through my hair, a frustrated laugh forcing its way out of my lungs. "Are you fucking serious? Eva coming on tour? The whole *assistant* bullshit?"

"Dude, keep it down." He finally looked up at me as he bobbed his head at the bodies next to him.

"You don't even know their fucking names, so don't act like you give a shit if I wake them up."

"Look how fucking cute they are, though." He grinned as one of the girls sighed and stretched her arm, letting it fall lazily over the other. "Like, they shoulda been gone *hours* ago, but I can't do it. I think I'm gettin' soft or somethin'."

I clenched my jaw so tight I thought I might stroke out. "If you don't get your ass up right now so we can discuss what the fuck you did, I will find a way to kick you out of this band, I swear to fucking God."

He snickered. "Yeah, okay, dude. Like we don't have a contract with all our names on it."

"Get the fuck up, Eric," I demanded, my heart pounding in concert with my head. "Or I *will* kill you and cross your name off that fucking thing myself."

A blond head popped up and squinted at me before groaning and dropping back onto the pillow.

"Jesus Christ, Danny," he mumbled, swinging his legs off the bed. He nudged the chick beside him, then stood and grabbed his smokes from the nightstand. "Hey, super fun night and all, but you girls gotta go. So, just, like, get dressed, and don't take any of my shit."

He rolled his eyes as he pushed past me, and I slammed the door behind us.

Eric flopped on the couch in the living room, swept his hair out of his face, and lit another cigarette. "Okay, so why the fuck are you freaking out about this? I mean, you get to have your woman on the road with us. The one who almost got away or whatever." He pursed his lips as if that sentiment was too sappy for him to stomach. "You should be thanking me, man, not riding my ass."

I paced the floor in front of him, trying to massage the ache out of my head. "You cannot do this shit without talking to me, Eric. This isn't *your* band."

"And it's not *yours* either, Danny."

"Exactly. Which means we make decisions together. And this…this is not cool."

"It's *Eva*, dude. It's not like I picked some random person off the street."

"You're not fucking getting my point."

"What *is* your point?"

"My point is, you fucking overstepped, and I don't want her—"

I paused as the two blonds shuffled into the living room in their rumpled spandex dresses, high heels swinging off the tips of their fingers.

Eric raised his hand. "Later, ladies. Good times."

The front door shut, and Eric continued. "You don't want her…what?"

I shook my head, trying to focus on the situation at hand rather than the fact Eric had banged not one but *two* ridiculously hot chicks the night before. "I don't want her on the tour."

"Look, if she's gonna get in the way of you fucking around, then by all means, let's forget it. I just thought you two were solid."

"It's not…" *Fuck.* I stalled, pulling my cigarettes from my pocket while trying to think of how to explain where my head was at. It wasn't like I actually wanted to sleep with anyone else. But I also didn't wanna have to act like a fucking choirboy while everyone else was having the times of their goddamn lives. "It's not that, it's just…she's not *supposed* to be there. This is *my* thing, man." I waved my hand between us. "*Our* thing."

FOR EVA

Eric sighed and scrubbed his hands along his face. "Do you even realize what she's done for *our* thing, dude?"

I ignored him and lit my smoke. "I mean, what's she even gonna do while she's there? Sit around and wait for Bryan to tell her to go get him coffee and shit?"

"She's smart, man," Eric said as I stopped pacing and landed in the recliner across from him. "She knows what works and what doesn't. She gets what we're about."

I closed my eyes and pinched the bridge of my nose. "But she's not part of the band, so I don't…"

"No, she's not, but let me just go ahead and list out what she's done *for* the band since you seem to have forgotten." He leaned forward and pressed his cigarette into the ashtray on the coffee table. "*One*, she's a big part of the reason why we even have a fucking tour to go on. I mean, yeah, we earned the record deal, but she saw an opportunity, and she ran with it. *Two*, she told us what to wear for every single photo shoot and was so right that the actual stylists on set didn't even understand why they were there. *Three*, she saved our album from sounding and looking like an overproduced piece of shit."

"Yeah, but —"

"But nothing. Do I seriously need to remind you that if it wasn't for Eva, the picture on our album cover would be a woman in a chain mail bikini walking a goddamn tiger down Hollywood Boulevard? *She's* the one who told us to push back on the label if we wanted to sell the fucking thing to anyone other than thirteen-year-old boys. Once she stopped laughing, of course." He sat back against the cushions, a look of satisfaction settling on his face. "So, you know…I'm pretty sure she'll find some shit to do."

"I'm not saying she's not smart. But what the fuck, Eric? You don't even like her, so why the hell do you want her on this tour?" I narrowed my eyes at him. "Something else is going on, man, and you need to tell me."

He shrugged. "Eh, she's a good kid. Not what I thought.

But fine. I also figured if she was there you couldn't freak out. You couldn't worry about being away from her, lose focus, and wanna come home. But I clearly misjudged how much you're gonna miss her."

"I'm not…Just shut the fuck up about that. I *am* gonna miss her. Stop trying to get in my head, dude. You don't know what I'm thinking."

"You're right, Danny. I really fucking don't." He studied my face and shook his head before pulling another cigarette from its pack. "But whatever, man. It's a done deal. Keith got Alan on the phone last night, and the label's on board. So, if *you* don't want Eva to come, then *you* can tell her."

My face tightened as I stared across the room, past Eric, at an invisible spot on the wall. I was cornered once again, with no means of escape. There was no way I could tell her not to come. No fucking way.

I launched myself out of the chair and stalked down the hall without saying a word. I sat on the edge of my bed, elbows on my knees, working my palms into my forehead, hoping it would help get my head on straight.

What the fuck was wrong with me, anyway? She was my girlfriend, the one who almost got away, just like Eric said. And the tour was only six weeks. Six weeks wasn't forever. I'd have to find a way to be okay with it. I didn't have a choice. Because I wasn't gonna be the bad guy. And I sure as hell wasn't gonna lose Eva all over again.

CHAPTER SIXTEEN
EVA

APRIL 1989

"You guys are supposed to be at sound check at one. Then there's press stuff back at the hotel before the show, so it would be awesome if some level of coherence could be maintained for that." I looked around the bus and sighed, fairly certain that *gained* would've been the more appropriate word since there wasn't a sober—or at least non-hungover—person in sight, with the exception of our driver and Bryan, who was cursing and furiously adjusting the antenna on his Sony Watchman. "This is a *big* deal, okay? Black Widow Rising got their start here, so please, please, *please* Eric, remember what city we're in when you do the outro."

Eric flung his head up from the lines of white powder on the table in front of him. The hair that hung in his face was dark and slick with grease, and I wondered when he'd last bothered to wash it.

I pressed the heel of my palm into my forehead to soothe the mounting tension behind my eyes. "Yeah, see, this is what I'm requesting you *not* do."

He sniffed and rubbed his fingers under his nose. "Chill out, woman. This *makes* me coherent. And clearly we're in"—he squinted out the window as the bus rambled down I-20—"whatever city is really...flat." He turned to the sofa across the aisle, where Danny sat snickering behind a pair of mirrored aviators as he took a sip from the red plastic cup at his lips. "Where in this country is really flat, dude?"

Liquid sprayed out of Danny's mouth, and both he and Eric doubled over with laughter.

"Dallas, you dumbass." I slapped my tour binder shut and tossed it on the table beside me. "We're in Dallas."

"How the fuck are we in Dallas? We were just in fucking Alabama, like, an hour ago." Will groaned from the other side of the couch, his baseball cap planted strategically over his face to keep the light from assaulting his eyes.

I sighed and flopped onto the seat across from Eric. Maybe I did need to loosen up a bit. But rocking and rolling all night and partying every day for the first week of the tour had made me antsy for something to do other than suck down vodka and run menial errands for Bryan. So, I'd started to hang around after fetching his coffee to see if I could help with some of his actual work.

"Aren't you just here because you're Danny's girlfriend?" he'd asked one morning in Miami, not bothering with a nod or smile or *thanks for the coffee* as he'd flipped through several pieces of paper on his hotel room desk.

My teeth clicked as I locked my jaw. "No, I'm supposed to help. I *want* to help," I answered in the sweetest tone I could muster, channeling my frustration into the fists tightened at my sides.

"All right, then. Does Danny play Gibsons?"

I peeked around him, my eyes darting through the type to see if I could find any key words to clue me in on what he was reading. Bryan finally turned and looked up at me, and I quickly averted my gaze to the ceiling. "Hmm?"

"Danny. What does he play?"

"Oh, um, mostly Gibsons."

He stared blankly past me, his forehead creased. "Huh. Why did I think Fenders?"

FOR EVA

I knew exactly why, but I wasn't going to tell Bryan he didn't pay attention to details, and he hadn't taken a single minute to get to know any of the guys individually—what brands they played, what made each of them tick, where they saw their music going. They were simply *the band*, and he rarely spoke to them outside of that context. Bryan also didn't seem to work particularly hard but most definitely enjoyed giving the appearance he did, and I was certain I could use that to my advantage.

"Eh, it's hard to keep up," I said. "But is that one of those endorsement deal things?" I bobbed my head at the papers on the desk and innocently raised my brows. I knew what it was, but I also knew playing the dumb blond, while not something I relished, served its purpose from time to time.

He cleared his throat. "Uh, yeah. Just something kinda minor. They wanna give him a few guitars, maybe some gear. I mean, he's got to use them, of course."

Really, Bryan? I had no clue that's how an endorsement deal worked.

"Well, if you think it's solid, I'll get him to sign it," I offered. "And I could maybe call their entertainment relations department and set up a time for him to go by when he's back in LA?"

Bryan titled his head, and I thought for a moment he might ask me how the hell I knew what entertainment relations was. I wanted to tell him I didn't get a degree in marketing for nothing. To announce I hadn't realized until the band almost ended up with a fucking tiger on their album cover that I'd been using it for the past year without a title and a paycheck. But I just smiled at him until he handed me the proposal and mumbled, "Okay, sure."

Not only had I called the ER department later that day, but I'd been able to get them to agree it was a fantastic idea to do a photo shoot for ad placements.

After I delivered the news to Bryan, he decided I could handle everything his job entailed, with the exception of telling Keith how well *he* was handling it all. So, he mostly hung back, tried to tune into Lakers games on his stupid Watchman, and told me what he wanted for lunch.

"Oh, hey, Eva." Bryan took his headphones off as the bus lurched to a halt at the back of the arena. "Did you get everyone to sign those NDAs for the after-party tonight?"

I nodded and pointed to the binder I'd left on the counter. "I think Eric signed his *fuck off*, but yeah, that's done."

Eric smirked, tapping the short straw he'd used to vacuum up what I hoped was the last of his stash. "I don't understand why they're so fucking paranoid."

"Because this is their comeback tour with their brand new clean and sober image, man." Danny lit a smoke and flipped his sunglasses on top of his head. "So, they don't want you running your fucking mouth to anyone about the fact that you watched them snort coke off some naked chick's ass."

Will chuckled from behind his hat. "I'm surprised we even got invited."

To be honest, I was, too. Black Widow Rising had been around since the '70s, crashed and burned in the early '80s, then somewhere around '86 managed to take the needles out of their arms long enough to realize there was still money to be made. But rehab hadn't exactly stuck. They were simply more discreet, their tastes were more discriminating, and their interests most definitely did not include associating with a bunch of kids who'd just been handed the keys to the candy store.

Not that I blamed them. For Black Widow Rising, Counting Backward was there to sell tickets to a younger crowd, period. Danny and Will were half-drunk half the time and mostly drunk the other. Matt was right there with them, until he got bored and his focus shifted to how many chicks he could bag on any given day (after I'd assured him the chances of anything serious with Denise were slimmer than none). And Eric had fallen into a pattern of getting hammered and snorting himself awake. Rinse and repeat. Danny had said the coke wasn't anything new for him, he just didn't have to rely on his Beverly Hills housewife to get it anymore.

"I mean, I know it's probably not a big deal, but do you think he's maybe, like, a little *too* into it?" I'd asked as I sat cross-legged on the hotel bed after the show in Raleigh several nights before.

Danny walked out of the bathroom, one towel wrapped around his waist as he mussed his hair, damp from the shower, with another. "He's out there killin' it on stage every damn night. What does it matter?"

The corners of my mouth turned down. "Wow, way to care, Danny."

He rolled his eyes and sighed, dropping the towel from his hand and flopping on the end of the bed. "I'm just saying he's fine. And it's not your job to worry about what he's doing."

I wrinkled my nose. "Well, I mean, it kinda is."

"It's not, Eva," he said, pulling me on top of him. "You're only here for two more weeks to get Bryan his lunch or whatever, and then you'll be home. We'll get back out on the road, and you won't have to deal with any of this."

I raised my head and studied his face. "You think that's all I do?"

"What?"

"You think all I do is get Bryan his lunch?"

"No, I just meant—"

"Whatever, Danny." I pressed my hands into the mattress and pushed myself off him, but he gripped my shoulders.

"No, babe, I know you do other shit. Stuff." He paused and sucked in a breath. "*Work*, I mean. I was just trying to say you don't need to worry about him. You need to focus on your *work* until you get back home. And then you can focus on picking out a place for us to live." He smiled and trailed his fingertips along my arms.

"Say you're sorry," I demanded, sliding my hands along the sheets so my face was within inches of his.

He reached around and grabbed my ass, pressing me against

him. "I'm obviously very, very sorry." And like the lovesick teenager I still was on the inside, I covered his grin with my mouth, forgetting what he'd said, until later that night when I lay in bed wondering why I'd let him off the hook so easily.

———

Black Widow Rising's homecoming party was ramping up by the time we arrived around eleven thirty. Counting Backward were greeted with a modest amount of fanfare as newly anointed members of the rock 'n' roll aristocracy before the crowd went back to sipping their cocktails, awaiting the appearance of bona fide royalty.

I couldn't take my eyes off the view from the penthouse, the city lights guiding me like stars to the floor-to-ceiling windows encasing the room. I glanced behind me to make sure no one was watching and placed my hand on the cool glass, my eyes caught between my watery reflection and the buildings which bobbed in the sea below me. My short, strapless leather dress, kohl-lined eyes, and burgundy lips gave me the appearance of belonging, but I felt like the girl on the other side of the window, wondering if I really did.

"Champagne?"

"Huh?" My hand slid down the glass, and I gasped as another image melted into my own. "Oh, yes, thanks."

I turned to the woman behind me dressed in a black bandeau and miniskirt and lifted one of the delicate flutes off the tray perched on her lace-gloved hand. She nodded and drifted past me as a woman who could've been her twin approached, smiling and offering me a silver platter full of neatly cut white powder.

"Interested?"

I took a long sip of my drink and let out a nervous laugh. Maybe I really was outside the window looking in on someone else's life. "I'd better not. Last time I did coke, I got it in my head that I wanted to go to Amsterdam, like, *right then*, and ended up trying to hail a cab to O'Hare at midnight. I didn't go, of course, but my best friend always reminds me of that every time I—"

"Okay," the woman said, her tone turning flat before she sauntered off.

I blew out a long breath, wishing I'd opted for a *no thanks* rather than a silly explanation. Surely, I wasn't the only person at the party turning down free drugs.

"Holy shit, Eva. Did you know they're serving cocaine off silver fucking platters?" I teetered on my spiked heels as Matt bounced up to me, nearly knocking me over.

"And I see you've had some." I chuckled at the childlike excitement dancing across his face.

"Like anyone's gonna turn down free drugs?"

Okay, maybe I am the only person.

Danny slid beside me and snaked his arm around my waist. "Babe, did you know they've got coke on fucking plat—"

"Yeah, uh-huh." I cut him off as the crowd erupted at the arrival of the guests of honor. My eyes were needles threading through leather and leopard print, and my pulse picked up as they landed on Jesse Trainor, Black Widow Rising's lead singer.

He was dressed in black jeans and a silky white shirt, unbuttoned to reveal his smooth, tanned chest. Long dark-blond waves fell over his shoulders, and my teenage heart fluttered. I'd occasionally seen him backstage but had always averted my eyes, not wanting to bother him or humiliate myself. But now that he was off the clock, could I say hello? Could I tell him I'd hoped and prayed my first time would be with him on a waterbed in Tahiti, but instead it had ended up being with Danny in his twin bed while his mom was at work?

"Dude, I think Eva's got a crush." Matt jabbed his elbow into my arm.

"Oh my God, I do not," I insisted, shoving my own elbow into his ribs. I flicked my eyes to the ivory carpet, forcing myself to stop staring at Jesse.

"She's been in love with him since she was fourteen," Danny said. "Do you know how weird it was trying to make out with her while that dude was looking at me from all angles on her bedroom walls?"

He laughed and tickled my side, causing me to writhe as I attempted to pry his hands from my waist. "Stop! I'm just…a fan."

He leaned into me, his lips brushing my ear. "Then, strictly as a fan, of course, I'm sure you'll be excited to know he's coming over here now."

"Wait, what?" I brought my gaze up to see Jesse approaching us, holding a glass of wine the color of my lips in one hand and a flute full of bubbly gold in the other.

"What are we talking about over here, and who is this vision?" He offered me the champagne, which I took, shoving my empty glass at Danny.

"Oh my God," I squeaked.

Matt threw his hand over his mouth, a series of sputtering noises escaping as he attempted to excuse himself before spewing his beer all over Jesse.

"I'm, uh…I'm…"

Oh my God, I can't remember my name. What is my fucking name?

Danny cleared his throat. "This is my girlfriend, Eva."

Jesse reached for my free hand, placing a gentle kiss on top.

"Yes. Right. I'm Eva. Sorry, I think I must have had too much champagne." I raised the glass he'd given me and took a long swallow. "Oops, there I go again."

Jesse laughed, and I joined in much too loudly, but he kept smiling, so I assumed he found my display at least somewhat charming.

"And it's Danny, right?" Jesse tipped his wine glass, and Danny nodded. "Your band is really good. Thanks for getting the crowd ready for us every night."

I didn't know if Jesse was being intentionally aloof or if he really wasn't sure of Danny's name. What I *did* know was his

FOR EVA

Texas drawl made me feel like I was back in Illinois, squealing in front of the television as he chatted with Dick Clark on *American Bandstand* in 1978.

Danny grinned. "Oh, man, thank *you* for having us here. It's such an honor, really." He paused and acknowledged Bryan, who waved him over to where he stood with Will and a guy in a gray suit who looked like he'd just stepped out of a boardroom. "I think our manager needs me. But thank you. Again."

Jesse smiled and nodded as I searched my brain for something to say to him that wasn't ridiculous. My teenage fantasies about losing my virginity to him hadn't exactly included any conversational elements.

He swirled his wine, and I watched as burgundy droplets formed on the inside of the glass. "So, gorgeous girl, what's the deal with you and the guitarist? Is it serious, or can you have a little fun?"

I coughed as Jesse's words caused my last sip of champagne to catch in my throat. A server offered me another glass, but I shook my head and handed her the empty flute. "Sorry. I, uh… What?"

"I'm asking if you're fucking him because he's in a band, and if he's fucking you because he can."

"I…" My eyes widened as I shifted them to the floor. Surely, I was just starstruck, and words weren't making sense. "I, uh…Well, yeah, it's a serious thing. Is that what you asked?"

"I did. Not that it really matters, I suppose."

I managed an uncomfortable laugh, and Jesse tilted his head and looked at me in a way that made me feel like my dress had fallen off, and I was standing stark-fucking-naked in front of him. A pit formed in my stomach, and I instinctively crossed my arms over my chest. This wasn't how things were supposed to go. I was supposed to act like a bashful fan and tell him how much I loved Black Widow Rising. Then he was supposed to tell me how grateful he was for the support and offer to introduce me to the rest of the band. Not treat me like I was just some disposable girl to fuck.

He slid his arm around my waist and pulled me into him, moving his hand down my ass to the top of my thigh. I gasped and pressed my hand against his chest, scanning the room for Danny, whose back was to me while he was deep in conversation. "Danny and I are actually very serious, so I should—"

"What the fuck is going on over here?" I whipped my head to the right to find Eric standing beside us. His blue eyes had darkened to an angry gray, wild and streaked with lighting, like a storm was raging inside them.

The thunder in his voice caused Jesse to pull back, and a few people close by lowered their voices and glanced in our direction. I wriggled out of Jesse's grip, smoothing my hand over my dress. "Nothing. Just meeting Jesse. That's all."

"Really?" Eric cocked his head to the side, studying my face. "'Cause it looked like he had his fucking hand on your ass."

"It's fine, Eric." My voice shook, and my eyes burned into Danny, desperately willing him to turn around.

Eric shoved his finger in Jesse's face. "Don't fucking touch her again."

"I thought she was your guitarist's girl," Jesse drawled. "Certainly are protective of her, aren't you?"

Eric drew in a deep breath. "Do it again and I'll kick your fucking ass, I swear to God."

His voice rose to a level that caused the loud chatter in the room to come to a dead halt, and Danny finally turned around. I locked eyes with him, pleading for help, but he stood motionless, staring at the three of us.

Jesse snickered and raised his glass to Eric. "Well, congrats, kid. You're off this goddamn tour. So take your band and get the fuck out of here."

"Fuck you *and* your tour, man. Just leave *her* the fuck alone." Eric turned and pushed through the crowd, disappearing inside the private elevator.

Gasps and whispers rippled through the crowd until Jesse

smiled and waved and told them everything was fine. He took a long sip of wine and pursed his lips before turning to walk away. "Too bad that didn't work out, sweetheart."

My skin burned, and the girl outside the window screamed at me, telling me to leave—to break through the glass and disappear into the darkness. But I couldn't. I couldn't let the band get kicked off the tour. Not on my watch and most certainly not *because* of me.

"No, wait," I said, grabbing his arm. "Eric just misunderstood. He didn't mean what he said, and I'm sorry I didn't, uh... *Shit.* I'm just sorry, okay? I'll fix this. I'll find him and explain everything."

"You're very loyal." Jesse leaned into me, and I shivered as he whispered into my ear. "I like that." He pulled back, wearing a smirk which made my stomach turn. "How about you tell Eric to come talk to me tomorrow, and we'll see what happens?"

I nodded, wondering exactly whom I was being loyal to, as I rushed for the elevator and jabbed the call button. I dabbed the corners of my eyes, trying my damndest not to cry. I prayed Danny would sprint to my side, hold me, and whisper that everything would be okay. But I stepped into the dimly lit box alone, casting one last glance at him, still wide-eyed and paralyzed. Hot tears trickled down my cheeks as the door closed, and I collapsed against the wall, shame swallowing me whole.

CHAPTER SEVENTEEN
DANNY

APRIL 1989

"Come the fuck on," I hissed as I punched the gold button on repeat, waiting for the elevator to make its slow climb up to the penthouse.

Over my shoulder, I spotted Bryan buzzing nervously around Jesse, who finally turned his back, ending the discussion with a flick of his hand. Bryan searched the room, his eyes landing on me, and he bolted in my direction as I stepped inside.

"What the fuck happened, man?"

I could barely hear him over the blood pounding in my ears, so I shook my head and pressed the button for the eighth floor, allowing the door to slide shut despite his panicked protests. I leaned against the cool metal, my thoughts shifting like pieces of a puzzle I was desperately trying to put together. What the hell had caused Eric to blow up at Jesse? And what did Eva have to do with any of it?

The elevator lurched to a halt, and I shot out into the hallway. I rounded the corner and spotted her sitting on the emerald carpet, hands buried in a nest of blond hair.

"What the *fuck* did Eric do?" I pointed to the door behind her. "Is he in there?"

"No." She grabbed her shoes and scrambled to her bare feet, pushing past me and entering our room.

"What the hell?" I said, catching the door before it slammed shut. "I'm not the one who lost my shit up there. Why are you pissed at *me*?"

She tossed her purse on the bed and reached for the zipper on the back of her dress. "I can't fucking talk to you right now, Danny."

"What? Eva, you *have* to talk to me. Are we off this tour? Is that what Jesse said?" I raked my hands through my hair, gripping my scalp.

She stepped out of the black leather into a pair of jeans, then frantically pulled a T-shirt over her head. "I don't know. I mean, *no*. I'm gonna fix this."

She rushed past me, and the water turned on in the bathroom.

"Eva, you can't fucking fix Eric publicly humiliating the lead singer of the band we're opening for," I insisted, following her. "I mean, I know you think you can make this better, but you have to tell me what happened so I can—"

She ran a towel over her freshly scrubbed face, and I stared at her reflection in the mirror.

Her eyes were rimmed in red, and her cheeks were blotchy and pink. "Wait, are you crying?"

She sniffed as she squeezed between me and the doorway and began rifling through her luggage.

I crouched down beside her and closed the lid on the suitcase. "Enough, Eva. Tell me what the fuck Eric did before I go beat the shit out of him."

She looked up at me, her nostrils flared. "He was doing what *you* should've been doing, Danny."

"*What?*" I blinked and jerked my head back. Was I losing my fucking mind?

"You heard me. Now move your hand so I can get my fucking shoes."

Now *I* was pissed. I pressed my hand hard onto the top of the suitcase. "Fuck this. My goddamn career is on the line here.

My band could get thrown off our first big tour. Do you have any idea how bad this is? And now you're defending Eric when I still don't know what the fuck happened!"

She glared at me before springing from her knees and retrieving her cigarettes from her purse. "Fine. You wanna know what happened? Jesse Trainor asked if you'd mind if he fucked me. And then he proceeded to feel me up in the middle of the goddamn party."

"He did *what?*"

She flopped on the bed and lit her smoke. "And what I don't understand is why Eric saw it all, and you couldn't be bothered to so much as glance in my direction until everything exploded. And even *then* you just stood there like a fucking statue."

Fuck. Me.

I sighed and pushed myself up. "Are you sure he…Was he joking around, or did you, like, say something that made him think…anything?"

Her eyes narrowed. "Are you fucking serious right now?"

"I just know he's used to chicks throwing themselves at him, so maybe he misunderstood."

"Oh my God, I'm not on trial here, okay? I told Jesse you and I were serious, and he still did what he did. He's an asshole, and if we weren't in this crazy fucking world we're in, Eric would be fucking Superman. But he's not because saving me could cost you this tour." She paused, taking a long drag off her cigarette. "Do you realize how fucked up this is? Like, *hey, thanks, Eric, for doing what my boyfriend didn't, but now you gotta go say you're sorry.*"

"Babe, stop saying I didn't do anything! I didn't know what the fuck was going on."

"Because you weren't even paying attention to me, Danny! You were so fucking involved in whatever conversation you were having that you didn't even look back once to check on me. *Not once.*" She tossed her half-smoked cigarette in the ashtray, not bothering to put it out. "Shit, how did this even happen?"

I bit my tongue to stop the words I wanted to say from flying out of my mouth. If she'd stayed in LA, it *wouldn't* have happened. Our spot on the tour wouldn't be in jeopardy, and I'd be snorting cocaine off one of those silver fucking platters instead of sitting in a goddamn hotel room trying to figure out how to undo the drama *she* was at the center of. This proved what I'd known from the beginning—that it was a terrible fucking idea for her to be here. But I couldn't tell her those things because I didn't want her to leave *me*. I just wanted her to leave the fucking tour.

I sat beside her, trying to pull her into me, but she resisted, her eyes fixed on the wall. "Look, I'm sorry I wasn't paying attention. The industry guy Bryan introduced me to kept saying how he saw all these big things ahead for us. I got wrapped up in it all and…Fuck, never mind, it doesn't matter. I'm gonna go find Eric and take care of this myself."

She shook her head. "No, you guys are gonna end up in some huge fight, and that isn't what we need. We just need to—"

There was a loud knock at the door, and Eva gasped. "Maybe that's him."

My fists clenched at the thought, but I tried to maintain some semblance of cool as I walked toward the door and opened it, praying it wouldn't be him so she wouldn't see me lose my mind on the motherfucker. Yeah, he'd stood up for Eva, but he could've done it in a way that didn't leave our future up in the fucking air.

"Am I gonna have to call Keith and tell him we're off this tour?" Bryan's voice was panicked and breathless, like he'd just run laps around the hotel.

"No, I'm taking care of it," I said. "Don't call Keith."

"But I'm—"

I shut the door and rubbed my eyes, running my hands up to my forehead, then walked back to the bed. "Stay here, okay?

I'll go find him."

Eva sucked in a breath and threw her hands in the air. "Whatever. But Jesse wants to talk to Eric, and I'm leaving a message for their manager to make sure that happens."

I nodded and headed for the door knowing full well that I'd be the one in that meeting with Jesse. Because even if Eric wanted to go, there was no way in hell I was letting him fuck things up even more than he already had.

I didn't have to go far to find him. I was walking toward the revolving door to search the bar across the street when I saw him in the lobby, a brunette with legs almost as long as his sitting on his lap, twirling her hair. She whispered in his ear, no doubt something about how she gave the best blow jobs in the city, and he grinned, smacking her ass as they stood.

No fucking way. He wasn't gonna get his dick sucked while I was trying to save our collective asses.

"Hold the fuck up, Eric," I said.

He threw his head back and sighed. "Dude, I'm busy. What the fuck do you want?"

I didn't know whether to punch his face or laugh in it.

"What the fuck do you think I want?"

"Oh my God, you're Danny!" The girl squealed and pressed her hands into my chest. "You *have* to meet my best friend. I told her we'd find y'all, but she gave up and went across the street. She's so into you, she's gonna freakin' *die.* You like blonds, right?"

I cleared my throat, forcing the corners of my mouth down as I tried not to let my ego get the better of me.

Eric snickered. "Yeah, his girlfriend's a blond, actually."

She opened her mouth and started to smile until Eric's words clicked, causing her to let out a nervous giggle. "Oh, well, she doesn't care if you have a girlfriend."

I shook my head, hoping to blur the image my brain conjured up. "Yeah, I really gotta talk to Eric."

"So talk," he said, crossing his arms over his chest.

"I'm not having this conversation here."

He drew in a breath and rolled his eyes, letting his arms fall to his sides. "Fine. Look, Stacey—"

"Stephanie." The girl's brows sloped downward, a tiny pout forming on her frosty pink lips.

"Right," he continued, unfazed. "How about you go find your friend and come back in fifteen?"

"But what if—"

"If I'm not here, I'll catch you next time we're in…wherever we are," he said over his shoulder as we headed for the elevators.

"Dallas," she called from behind us.

We stared straight ahead the entire ride to our floor, not speaking until Eric opened the door to his room, grabbed his Jack, and guzzled what seemed like half the bottle.

"So go ahead," he said, wiping the back of his hand across his mouth. "Tell me why you're pissed that I stopped Jesse Trainor from fucking Eva in the middle of the goddamn party."

My jaw instantly tightened, and I shoved my finger in his face. "Shut the fuck up, Eric. Shut your fucking mouth right now. Do you have any idea what you've done? Any idea at all?"

He slapped my hand away as he pushed past me, sat on the bed, and lit a cigarette. "Fuck off, dude."

"You're fucking crazy, you know that?" I said. "There are ways to fucking talk to people that don't get you thrown off tours!"

"He's not throwing us off the tour. We have a fucking top ten album right now. People are coming to the shows to see *us*." He leaned against the headboard and stretched his legs along the mattress. "What's really important here is that I saved Eva from getting fucking molested by him. So, you know…*you're welcome*."

I shook my head. "You don't even fucking get it."

"What do I not get? That *is* important…isn't it?" He tilted his chin up and blew a stream of smoke from his lips.

"Of course, it's important. But you could've come and told me, and I would've handled it."

He snorted. "Really? What would you have done, Danny? Asked if he'd mind taking his hand off her ass—pretty please and thank you?"

I tightened my fists and pressed them against my forehead to keep from hitting him. "This is *your* goddamn fault, Eric. Not only because you lost your shit, but because it would've never even happened if you hadn't had the stupid fucking idea for Eva to come with us in the first place."

"You need to get the fuck over that, man. I'd think that if anyone could recognize everything she does for us, it'd be you." He threw his legs over the side of the bed and twisted his cigarette into the ashtray on the nightstand.

"I don't need to get the fuck over anything. What I need to do is talk to Jesse and tell him you're sorry. Tell him I'm sorry—we're *all* sorry. And then, if he doesn't tell me to fucking beat it, we're gonna finish out this tour, and you're gonna smile at that motherfucker every time you see him."

"No, I'm not. But do what you want. Go grovel at his feet and tell him it's fine to hit on your girlfriend." He paused and retrieved a small amber vial from his shirt pocket, tapping a small line of coke on the side of his fist and snorting it. "I'm going downstairs to see if what's-her-name decided to stick around, because I'm assuming Eva's pissed the fuck off at you, and I think at least one of us should be getting laid tonight."

"Fuck you, Eric." I kicked the wooden dresser beside me so hard my foot throbbed inside my boot as I turned and threw open the door, letting it slam behind me.

I stalked through the hall and leaned against the wall just outside our room, my back sliding down it until I was sitting on the floor. I lit a cigarette, and my eyes snaked along one of the gold scrolls in the carpet like it was the fucking yellow brick road. I took a long drag and squinted through the smoke, wondering if I followed it long enough, there'd be another world at the end.

One where Eric wasn't so goddamn irrational.

One where Eva wasn't so goddamn *involved*.

One where people didn't keep complicating my goddamn life.

————

"So, kid," Keith began as he turned the sugar dispenser upside down and a million white crystals streamed into his coffee. "How's it feel to be famous?"

"It feels fuckin' good, man." I flicked my lighter at the tip of my Marlboro and tilted my head back, sending a puff of smoke toward the ceiling. "Really fuckin' good. Glad you made me agree to this tour."

"It's cute you think you had a choice." He chuckled, clanking his spoon against the ceramic mug before setting it on the table. "You ready to do it all again in a couple weeks?"

I nodded, taking a long pull off my orange-tinted vodka. The Black Widow Rising tour was coming to an end that night in Phoenix, and Keith had flown out earlier in the week for our final four shows. I'd been too wired to sleep, anxious to get to sound check to make sure everything was perfect for the grand finale, so I'd headed down to the hotel restaurant where I'd found Keith finishing breakfast.

"I'm psyched, man," I said, pointing to my drink and smiling at the waitress who glanced over at us a couple of tables away. "Those shows have to be sold out or close to it. Even if I don't get that whole over-the-top glam shit, Hott Blood is huge."

"For now they are, so we gotta ride that wave. The big hair and makeup aren't gonna last forever. The good thing is Counting Backward straddles the line. Your image is important, but not too important. And your music's fun, but not too fun." He bobbed his head at the waitress who topped off his coffee and told us she'd be back with my drink. "What I'm saying is you guys could be around a long time if you want to be."

I grinned, imagining rows of framed platinum albums lining the walls of the house I'd buy up in the Hills, where my close, personal friends The Rolling Stones and Aerosmith would stop by for impromptu jam sessions.

"What's got you smiling like that?"

I startled and flicked my eyes to the left where Eva was standing, head tilted and mouth twisted.

"Hey. Hi." I ran my hand along my jaw and cleared my throat. "Keith and I were just talking about the, uh, future. Future things."

"Big things, right?"

I nodded and slid my hand along the side of her hip as I ground my cigarette into the ashtray. "Big things, babe."

She sucked in a tiny breath, and I was relieved to see her lips and chocolate eyes melt into a soft smile. Things had been a little tense between us since the Jesse Trainor incident the week before. I'd managed to talk to him the day after it happened, smoothing things over with shaky promises that Eric would keep his mouth shut the rest of the tour and false assurances that I understood Eva was a hot chick who was maybe giving off mixed signals because she was such a big fan.

I had added the *maybe* in an attempt to not feel like a total fucking coward, but it only half-worked. I tried to erase the rest of the gutless feeling by telling myself Eva had wanted me to do whatever was necessary to stay on the tour. But I didn't totally believe that. Every time I allowed myself to think about it, I got tangled up in some mathematical guilt equation my conscience couldn't solve. I only knew telling her what I'd said wasn't the answer, and I thanked God she didn't press me on it. It seemed as if she was doing her best to forget about it, and as I looked up at her and matched her smile, I hoped it meant we'd reached an unspoken agreement that we were both moving on from the whole episode.

"Good," she said, releasing me from her gaze and turning her attention to Keith. "Anyway, I just came down to get Bryan a cup of coffee before the meeting. You almost ready?"

"Yeah," he said, reaching for the wallet in his back pocket. "I'll be right there."

Eva leaned down, her lips gently touching mine as my fingers instinctively traveled under the bottom of her T-shirt, brushing against her soft skin.

When she pulled away and winked at me, my dick shifted against my jeans, sensing the truce had been officially called. I hoped we'd be able to celebrate in more ways than one after the show. We'd had sex only once since Eric had blown up on Jesse, and she'd kept her shirt on and stared at the ceiling the entire time.

"All right. I'll see you up there, Keith." She turned and headed for the coffee station near the entrance of the restaurant.

My brow crinkled. "Wait, is she, like, *in* your meeting?"

"Yep," Keith said, tossing a twenty on the table. "And I actually wanna talk to you about that."

I thanked the waitress as she slid a fresh screwdriver in front of me. "What's up?"

Keith took a sip of his coffee and let out a contented sigh. "Now that I'm freed up, my plan is to be out on the road with you guys more."

"Yeah, man, we'd love that."

"I'll send Bryan home, of course," he said, massaging his chin with his thumb and forefinger. "But I wanna keep Eva here to help me."

I swallowed hard and gripped my drink until my hand slipped against the sweat. "You what?"

"Eva. I want her to come back out on the road with us. I wanna hire her."

Fuck me.

"Oh." I rubbed my lips together, then tossed back half of my drink, buying myself some time as I thought about what I should say—what I *could* say—to discourage Keith's plan without sounding like a terrible fucking person. "I, uh…I mean, she probably wants to stay in LA. She talks about how much she misses her roommate and stuff."

The latter wasn't a total lie, but I knew she wouldn't turn down the chance to work for Keith. Not in a million fucking years. Her eyes lit up every time she talked about the band… every time she got us the cover of a magazine…every time she dreamed up some promotion that sent our album sales soaring even higher.

He grinned and patted his wallet. "I'll make it worth her while."

Fuck me again.

"I don't know, man." I ground my teeth on an ice cube. "Is it a good idea for her to work for you when me and her are together?"

"Has it been a problem so far?"

"I don't think you know, but there was this thing with Jesse Trainor and—"

He waved me off. "I know everything, Danny. Including the fact Jesse Trainor is an asshole who likes to talk big but never backs it up."

"Yeah, but…" I trailed off, drumming my fingers on the table and tapping my foot against the floor. How was I once again in this fucking position? Could I not have this one fucking thing to my fucking self? "Maybe she could work with one of your other bands?"

"My plan is for her to work with all my bands, but I want her with me for now. She's learned a lot on her own, but I can really show her the ropes. Plus, she—" He paused and cocked his head to the side, studying my face, which had lost all the poker it had left. "What's going on, Danny?"

I shook my head and shrugged. "I just think it might get tough…working together constantly."

"It won't be forever. I just wanna take her under my wing for a bit, then I'll set her up in my offices back in LA so she can work on marketing plans, handle press, those sorts of things."

FOR EVA

Keith pulled in a deep breath and crossed his arms over his chest, leaning back in his chair. "Look, I know Bryan tries to take a lot of credit for the success you guys have had since you've been on the road, but I'm not stupid. That girl has major potential in this business, and I think everyone in this band knows it."

Christ, had Eric given him the same speech he'd given me a million fucking times about how much she did for us? Did he have it fucking written down in a notebook and whip it out for anyone who would listen?

"Yeah, she's smart, but…"

"But what? Any other issues I need to know about?" His eyes narrowed from behind the mug as he took a final sip of coffee.

I fumbled with another cigarette, nearly dropping it as I brought it to my lips. Yeah, there were fucking issues. And they involved me wanting her back in LA picking out the fucking house where the platinum albums would go. But I couldn't tell him that without sounding like an asshole. So, I shook my head, lit my smoke, and sucked the things I wanted to say deep inside.

He stood and clapped my shoulder. "This is gonna be good for her. And the band."

I nodded and gulped the rest of my drink as he headed out of the restaurant to the meeting where he'd tell Eva she had a new job. A job she'd say she wanted. A job I couldn't deny her because it would break us if I did.

CHAPTER EIGHTEEN
EVA

APRIL 1989

"This is insane." I fell back onto the mattress, chirping and flapping my arms against the palm leaf bedspread like some sort of hyperactive bird. "I never imagined…I never thought…Can you believe this?"

Danny sat in the chair between the bed and the long row of hotel room windows, plucking out the chords of a Led Zeppelin tune on his acoustic. "You must've really impressed Keith… or whatever."

"You really think so?"

He nodded, not taking his eyes off his fingers as they moved along the fretboard. "Mm-hmm."

I sat up and hugged my knees to my chest. "Are you sure you're ok with this?"

"I said I was." His foot, propped on his opposite leg, bobbed slowly as he blew several dark strands of hair from face.

"Actually, you didn't."

He sighed and leaned his guitar against the arm of the chair. "What do you want me to say, Eva? You came in here, told me you took the job, and *then* asked for my opinion."

His words bore into me like a screw, twisting and tightening my insides. Heat blossomed on my cheeks, but I didn't know whether it was because I was ashamed I hadn't consulted him beforehand or pissed that he'd expected me to.

"Look, I just don't want you making some major decision without thinking it through." He fell back in the chair and lit a cigarette. "I know you miss Denise and your friends from the bar. And what about wanting to find us a place of our own? You shouldn't have to put all those things on the back burner because you wanna help the band."

My brow creased, and I opened my mouth to tell him none of those things had to fall by the wayside—which was the truth, but not the whole truth. So, I rubbed my lips together and stared past him as I thought. "But I'm not doing this for you or the band," I said, finally, shifting my eyes to his. "I'm doing it for me."

He took a long drag off his cigarette. "Oh."

I held out one hand, the other clutched to my chest. "I mean, it's great that I get to help you guys. But this is so much more than that. It's a whole *career* for me. One that involves using my degree for something I really enjoy doing. Something I never imagined as a possibility, but here it is in front of me."

He cleared his throat and rubbed his hand along his jaw. "Well, then, I guess you gotta do it. If it means that much to you."

A cautious smile crept across my face. "So you're happy for me?"

He nodded and flicked his cigarette into the amber ashtray on the nightstand. "Sure."

He looked sexy—his lean frame relaxed against the chair, messy black hair grazing his shoulders, smoke streaming from his lips—and for the first time since the incident with Jesse, I wanted him. *Really* wanted him.

I sank my teeth into my bottom lip and cocked my head. "So...how happy are you, exactly?"

He raised an eyebrow, and his lips twisted into a tiny smirk. "Is that an invitation to show you?"

I hadn't deliberately tried to punish him by not having sex

with him. It was just that whenever he touched me, all I could feel was Jesse's rough hands against my skin, and all I could see was Danny's back turned to me. I'd let those feelings construct a wall between us, but as he looked at me, the bricks fell away one by one.

"What do you think?"

He stubbed his cigarette out before standing and moving to the edge of the bed. I ran my hand along the front of his jeans and unfastened his belt. I gazed up at him, the gold shining in his hazel eyes, and he gently brushed my hair away from my face, making me feel like I mattered.

———

"They're good, Eva. They're really fucking good." Keith tipped his beer bottle toward the stage where Eric was running from one end to the other, a streak of hair, leather, and sweat glistening in the pulsing white lights. Danny stood stage left, head down, deep in concentration, making the crowd feel every single note he played. He'd occasionally glance over at us to gauge the sound, and we'd give him a quick nod or thumbs up.

"They're gonna be huge…*boss*," I said with a wink.

"They already *are* huge. Did you see the latest charts? The single is—"

"Number three, album is number five. It'll be certified gold within the week, and once they're on the road with Hott Blood, it's going platinum, no question."

"Wow. I should hire you." He looked at me from the side of his eye and gave me a knowing smile.

I laughed and nudged his shoulder.

"All right, Phoenix! We are Counting Backward from Hollywood! Good fucking night!"

Eric's voice echoed throughout the arena, and with one last crash of Will's cymbals, the stage went dark and dueling spotlights followed the loud roar of the crowd as they chanted the band's name, begging for an encore—an impossibility for an opening band but something that was becoming a nightly occurrence, nonetheless. Eric swiped his bottle of Jack off the drum riser, and the band filed offstage.

"That was amazing," Matt said, running a towel over his face. "Fucking amazing."

"I swear, half the crowd was here just for us," Will chimed in, shaking his head in disbelief.

"More than half, and I hope those fuckers in Black Widow Rising know it," Eric added, taking a long pull of the Jack before handing it to Matt.

Danny rolled his eyes, grabbing the beer I'd opened for him. "Dude, that's over and done. Let's move the fuck on."

Eric shrugged and pushed through us to head backstage. We all followed, the rest of the guys clapping each other on the back and congratulating one another on a job well done. The revelry came to an abrupt halt as Jesse Trainor rounded the corner.

Fuck.

My pulse quickened, but time slowed as I realized he and Eric were about to directly cross each other's paths for the first time since the party. Jesse looked straight ahead, his face pinched as if he'd swallowed something sour. But he didn't acknowledge anyone, so I assumed the crisis was averted.

Until Eric acknowledged *him.*

"What's up, cocksucker?"

Oh my God.

Jesse came to a dead stop and slowly turned around. "What the fuck did you just say?"

Eric crossed his arms and walked back toward him, bringing them face-to-face. "I called you a *cocksucker.*"

Oh my fucking God.

Jesse snorted, his eyes shifting to us, then back to Eric. "Do you wanna take that back before I completely ruin you?"

"No, I fucking don't. In fact, I wanna do this." He cocked his fist, thrusting it forward, so it landed squarely on Jesse's jaw.

The impact sent Jesse reeling backward as Eric turned and stalked around the corner toward the dressing room.

Jesse pushed himself off the wall, rubbing the side of face. "That guy's fucking finished," he spat, glaring at Keith.

"Sorry about that, man. Won't happen again." Keith flashed me a conspiratorial grin as Jesse told him to fuck off and stormed past us.

Keith shook his head and laughed. "I suppose I should go smooth this over. Not that he stands a chance in hell of ruining anyone's career, but you know, burning bridges and all that shit."

He followed behind Jesse as the rest of the guys stood motionless, mouths gaping open. My eyes darted back and forth between them. "I'll, uh…I'll go talk to Eric. Maybe give me just a minute before you head to the dressing room."

I hurried down the hallway and opened the door to find him sitting on the black vinyl couch, hunched over several white lines on the glass top of the coffee table.

"I know, I know. I fucked up out there," he said, putting the straw to the table and vacuuming up one of the lines. He raised his head and rubbed his nose before attacking the second. "But that guy *is* a cocksucker."

"I didn't come to yell at you, Eric."

He pressed his hands onto his leather-clad thighs and stood, massaging his fist. "Huh?"

"I think I'm *supposed* to yell at you. But how do I do that when I haven't even said thank you for saving me from that asshole?"

He blinked, and before I knew what I was doing, I threw my arms around him. He cautiously moved his hands to my back, his chest expanding against mine as he pulled me closer—just for a second—before breaking away and shifting his eyes to the side. "You're, uh, welcome…I guess."

I cleared my throat. "But as part of my job, I'm pretty sure I'm supposed to tell you not to punch the lead singer of the band you're opening for ever again."

He snorted. "Yeah, okay. Congratulations on that, by the way. You, uh…you really deserve it."

"You think so?"

"Yeah, Eva." He lit a cigarette, leaning back against the wall and sending a stream of smoke to the ceiling. "I don't think you have any idea how much you fucking do."

I cocked my head, his words pulling the corners of my mouth upward. "Well, thanks."

"What's with your face?"

"I just didn't know—" I paused as voices echoed in the hallway. My mind switched gears, and I grinned. "I didn't know you had such a good right hook, dude. Last show of the tour, and Jesse's gonna sound like he just got a fucking root canal."

CHAPTER NINETEEN
EVA

JULY 1989

"Platinum, fuckers!" Matt raised his shot glass before throwing back the contents and refilling it from the bottle in his other hand. "*Pla-ti-num!*"

Will caught him as he teetered on his barstool and propped him back up so he could pour them both another shot.

"We sold a million fucking records, babe." Danny pulled me into his arms, pressing his whiskey-soaked lips to mine, and I chuckled as I wiped the back of my hand across my mouth.

"I know, I'm so exci—"

"Hey, Matt, gimme another one of those shots," he called, bouncing away before I could finish my sentence.

We'd found out earlier that day the album had gone platinum. And the party that popped up during sound check had raged on during the show, then backstage, then at the hotel restaurant, which I had reserved to continue the celebration. Of course, it had quickly turned into a full-on fiesta with the band and the entire crew filling up the place, while fans gathered in the lobby, hoping to talk their way past the ropes. The successful ones usually had tits, but by the time Matt had taken over as unofficial bartender, no one really cared who was there. All that mattered was the drinks were flowing and Counting Backward had a platinum fucking record.

FOR EVA

"Eva! You don't look like you're having fun. Why aren't you having fun?" Keith breezed by me as Will called him over to where a girl with teased blond hair lay on the bar, her tanned stomach exposed as Matt poured a stream of Jägermeister into her navel.

"I'm having fun," I shouted over the music as I looked down at the watery remnants of my vodka cranberry. "I'm going to get a refill after they finish up with the whole body shot situation."

He was long gone before he could hear what I said, but I figured I'd let myself finish at least one sentence since I hadn't had the opportunity to say much that night. When he wasn't throwing back shots, Danny had been involved in conversations with his tech about some vintage guitars they were drooling over—something about which I had nothing to offer. I was unbelievably happy for the guys, but everywhere I turned, I was a little out of place, and I wished my own friends—Denise, everyone from back at the bar—were there.

The two week break we'd had in LA after the Black Widow Rising tour felt like two seconds. Danny and I were both so exhausted that we decided to put off looking for a new place until we had more time and energy. We hadn't talked any more about the new job, and I got on the bus as planned for the Hott Blood tour once the break was over.

I sighed and looked toward the crowd cheering as the blond girl swung her legs over the bar and raised her arms in the air, squealing with delight. Matt grabbed her around the waist and whisked her through the throng of people who had gathered at the bar in hopes of partaking in the next round. I chuckled to myself, my eyes following them across the room before landing on a booth in the back corner. Eric sat in the center, strands of hair falling into his face. His eyes were covered by dark sunglasses as a girl wearing a tiny jean skirt and crop top shrugged and walked away from him.

I weaved my way over, stopping for a fresh drink, then slid

into the booth and bumped his shoulder. "What's up with you? You look like a guy who found out his dog got run over, not a guy whose album went fucking *platinum*."

"Just taking it all in, I guess," he mumbled, before grinding his cigarette into the ashtray in front of him.

"You should be celebrating." I raised my glass toward the space full of revelers. "Go over there with Danny and watch people suck Jäger off chicks' stomachs. I think there's actually some girl-on-girl action happening now."

"Yeah, I'm not in the mood."

"Not in the mood? Eric, your album officially sold a million copies." I smiled and put my hand on his arm, gently shaking him. "What's your problem, dude?"

He cleared his throat and removed my hand. "My problem is that I was sitting here, enjoying my night, and now you've showed up and won't stop talking."

I rolled my eyes and dug my cigarettes and lighter out of my pocket, tossing them on the table. "Oh, come on, Eric. You weren't enjoying *anything*."

He flipped his hair from his face and grabbed my vodka cran, downing it in one swallow before slamming it back on the table. "There. Are you happy? Am I partying enough for you now? Woo-fucking-hoo."

"Actually, you're not." I popped a Marlboro Light in between my lips and lit it. "And now you have to get me another drink."

"I don't."

"Fine. You're not having fun, and I'm not *really* having fun. So, let's get out of here, and you can buy me dinner instead of a drink. I'm fucking starving."

He pushed his sunglasses onto his head. His eyes were bloodshot and tired, the skin around them looking almost bruised. "You want me to take you to dinner?"

"I want you to come with me to the Chinese place I saw down the street earlier today."

"I'm not hungry."

"I'm sure you aren't, considering you snort half of Colombia on a daily basis." I bit my lip as soon as the words were out. "But you'll be hungry after you help me smoke this." I pulled a joint from my pack of cigarettes.

He rubbed his thumb along his jawline.

I raised my brows and grinned. "Tempting?"

"Tempting."

I swiped my smokes off the table and nudged his arm as I scooted along the seat. "Then let's go."

––––––––

The hands on my watch were doubled up on the twelve as I snuck the last crab rangoon from its paper carton and shoved it in my mouth. I wasn't sure why we'd gone so feral over creamy imitation crab meat, but we both swore it was the best thing we'd ever eaten. How the last fried wonton had escaped our attention was a mystery.

Eric gasped at my attempt to chew discreetly. "Dude, did you find another crab rangoon?"

"No," I said, my voice garbled by the dumpling.

He leaned over and punched my arm. "I can't believe you didn't fucking split that with me."

I rubbed my skin and instinctively opened my mouth, creamy crab on full display. "Ow."

He recoiled against the concrete perimeter of the roof where we'd gone to smoke our joint and polish off nearly every item on the menu from Top China in Cleveland, Ohio.

"Fucking gross, Eva."

I forced the food down my throat and chuckled. "You shouldn't have hit me then, jackass."

"You owe me a fucking crab rangoon." He flicked his lighter against the tip of a Marlboro. "Whatever city we're in next, you're buying."

"Ooh, that's Columbus. They're totally out of rangoon.

Massive shortage. Don't you watch the news?" I pinched my lips together to keep from laughing. "Hmm…as angry as you look, I can tell this is the first you're hearing of it."

I kept my eyes locked on his as the muscles in his cheeks twitched, and we both doubled over with laughter until a tap on my back caused me to jerk my head up. "What?"

Eric sucked on his cigarette, exhaling a stream of smoke into the warm night air. "What's that tattoo on your back? What's it mean?"

"Oh," I said, turning my chin against my collarbone to glance back at the ink peeking around the strap of my tank top. "It says *topolina*. Little mouse in *inglese*. My mom…she used to call me that."

"A mouse?" The wind whipped a piece of hair in front of his face, and he flicked it away. "That's a weird thing to call a kid."

"In Italian it's, like, a term of endearment. She would say '*Aaaaava, tu sei la mia topolina*.' That's actually how you're supposed to pronounce my name, but Americans kept saying *Eeee-eva*, so we just gave up."

"Your mom's Italian?"

I pressed the heels of my hands into my eyes, a kaleidoscope of fuzzy shapes hurtling through my brain.

"Earth to Eva."

I let my hands fall to my lap, and the wave of green triangles slowly fizzled into Eric's face. "Well, she *was* Italian."

"Is she all of a sudden not Italian anymore? Did she come down with a sudden case of German? Or French?" He sputtered and collapsed onto himself once again.

I twisted my lips and titled my head back to the sky. All the stars had been blotted out by the lights from the city. "More like a sudden case of dead."

"Oh shit, Eva."

I squinted at the hazy gray above me, searching for at least one tiny ball of light to remind me of the beach in Mexico where I'd last dreamed of her. A plane roared overhead, the lights on the tips of its wings blinking at me, and I decided that would have to do. "It's okay. It was a long time ago."

Was it, though? Was nearly eight years a long time when it came to someone disappearing from your life? From this world?

Eric cleared his throat. "How'd she…"

"Car wreck," I said, bringing my gaze to him. "Some guy ran a red light and crashed into us. Then she died. And I didn't."

"*Fuck*, you were with her?"

"Yeah. I was the reason we were driving on that street. At that time. At all, really."

He leaned back and stretched his denim-covered legs, crossing them at the ankles. "What do you mean 'the reason'?"

I drew in a deep breath. "I was knocked up, and I didn't wanna be. She was driving me home from the doctor and then…*crash*."

"Shit. Was it Danny's?"

"Yeah." My eyes flicked across his face as he chewed his lip and nodded.

"Well," he said finally. "You shouldn't think it was your fault. Because it wasn't."

"I don't know. Maybe a part of me will always believe it was." I placed a cigarette between my lips, and Eric flicked his lighter in front of me. "I know a part of me will always believe my dad thinks it was."

"Did he *say* it was your fault?"

"No, I just get a feeling."

"Why don't you ask him?"

"Because what if I'm right?"

"But what if you're wrong? You don't know till you ask."

I shrugged. "I guess that's true."

"I don't have to wonder what my parents think. My dad left right after I was born, and my mom made it clear she didn't give a fuck when she let her husband kick me out when I was sixteen."

"Jesus."

"Yeah, I've always known *exactly* what she thinks of me." Eric shook the ice in his Styrofoam cup and drained the last of his Pepsi. "The first thing I ever remember her telling me was that I ruined her life. It's also the last thing I remember her telling me, so kind of a fun full circle moment." He laughed, but it was tinged with a sadness I could tell made him uncomfortable.

"You don't talk to her anymore?" I realized that was a stupid question after what he'd just told me, and I waited for him to say something sarcastic. But he didn't.

"Nah." He took one last drag off his cigarette and tossed it in the cup. "Not since her husband told me to beat it."

"Christ, I'm sorry."

"I'm not. She's a fucking bitch. I'm better off without her in my life." Another plane flew overhead, and he turned his eyes upward, following it through the sky. "Anyway, new topic."

"Okay, new topic."

"How's your job?"

I cocked my head and raised an eyebrow. "You really wanna know?"

"I really wanna know."

"Okay, well"—I took a long drag off my cigarette, then watched as the plume of smoke dissolved into the air—"I fucking love it. It's, like, of all the things in the world I could do, I was meant to do *this*. And I think…Is it weird to say I think I'm really fucking good at it?"

He shrugged. "Maybe. But *I* can say you're good at it, and it's not weird."

I laughed. "Oh, you saying it is even weirder, dude."

"What? Why?"

"No reason. I'm just gonna take what you said and know that Eric fucking Stratton thinks I'm good at my job—the job he recommended me for, which is something I'm still trying to figure out, by the way."

"You saved our album, Eva."

"Oh, I didn't *save* it, I just told you not to put a fucking tiger on it. It still would've sold…maybe."

Eric rolled his eyes. "Now you sound like Danny."

"What do you mean?" I asked, sweeping the hair stuck to the back of my neck over my shoulder.

"Nothing."

"No, come on. What do you mean?"

"Nothing. I…Fuck," he said, throwing his hands in the air. "Fine. What I meant was, I wish he'd give you more credit. He *knows* you're good at what you do, I just wish he'd *say it*."

"Yeah. Me, too." My stomach dropped, and I took a breath. It was the truth, even if I hadn't allowed myself to think about it much. I also hadn't expected the words to ever come out of my mouth, much less in front of Eric, so I quickly tried to stuff them back in. "I didn't mean it like that. Like you said, he knows. What I do. What I've done. He's excited for me, he's just…Danny."

Eric pursed his lips. "Yeah. He's Danny, all right."

"Anyway, new topic," I said, grinding out my cigarette.

"Okay, new topic."

I reached into my pocket and pulled out a folded piece of paper. "I got this fax today. Mandy's assistant at the label says this person won't stop calling for you."

He grinned and snatched the paper from my hand. "Ooh, do I have a secret admirer?"

"Not sure. Do you know a Steve Anderson?"

Eric's gaze fell flat as he studied the fax. He blinked slowly, covering his mouth with his hand. "I, uh—"

"Oh my God, there you are! I've been looking *all over* for you."

The girl in the tiny jean skirt whom I'd seen at his table earlier that night stood at the door, narrowing her eyes at me. I could've sworn she was about to raise her claws and hiss, but Eric spoke first.

"Fuck." He wadded the piece of paper into a tight ball and

stuffed it in his pocket, springing up from the concrete. "I, uh…I gotta go."

"What? Who's Steve?"

"He's no one. You should go find Danny."

I scrambled to my feet and tossed my hands in the air. "Eric, what did I say?"

"Nothing, Eva. I just gotta go." He looked around at the empty Chinese take-out cartons, ran his hand through his hair, and sighed before heading through the door with the girl.

CHAPTER TWENTY
DANNY

JULY 1989

I sank into one of the plush chairs in the lounge outside the hotel restaurant and watched as Will and a few roadies polished off a bottle of something or another at the bar. The party had died down, sending people scattering out onto the street or off in pairs, heading up to rooms to have a hell of a lot more fun than I was having.

I'd searched around for Eva earlier but assumed she was tired and had called it an early night, and honestly, I was glad for the reprieve. I remembered when I thought being a rock star would be a carefree, endless party. But it turned out the fastest way to kill that vibe was to have your girlfriend on tour.

"Aaaand you're an asshole," I mumbled, taking a sip of my beer.

"Who's an asshole?"

"Huh?" I turned my head as a woman in white jeans and a tight off-the-shoulder shirt appeared from behind me and brushed her hand against my arm.

She giggled, rolling a cigarette between her red-tipped fingers. "Sorry, was just gonna ask you for a light, and I heard what you said."

"Oh. Ha. Well, *I'm* the asshole, but I will offer you a light." I held up my BIC as she flipped her long honey-colored curls

148

behind her shoulder and bent down, her dark green eyes meeting mine.

"Mind if I sit?" she asked, exhaling smoke through her full lips and motioning to the chair beside me. "And mind if I ask why you're an asshole?"

"No reason. And yeah, have a seat." My voice quavered a bit as she melted into the chair and crossed her legs. I'd seen some gorgeous girls on tour, but this one was a total knockout.

"I'm Shawna," she said, extending her hand to me.

"Danny," I said, taking it into mine. God, it was so soft.

Her smile spread slowly across her lips, and her eyes narrowed in a way that told me she knew exactly who I was. "Nice to meet you. And congratulations on your album."

"Thanks," I said, running my hand around the back of my neck, which was suddenly damp with sweat. "So, uh, how do you know this crowd?" I motioned to the few people left mingling about.

"Oh, you know," she said, waving her cigarette. "A friend of a friend of a friend." My eyes traveled down her delicate neck to her tits which looked damn near perfect in her tight shirt.

I nodded, shifting in my seat. "So you're from here?"

"Born and raised," she said, flicking her cigarette into the ashtray between us.

"Nice. You'll have to tell me what to do on my day off tomorrow, then. We don't leave for Columbus till Monday."

"I mean, I have an idea." She twirled one of her loose curls around her finger and flicked her tongue over her lips. "If you're up for it, of course."

Her stare caused me to blush, and I let out a nervous laugh. "Oh, yeah? What's that?"

I knew exactly what she was talking about, and normally I would've told her I was flattered, but she should meet Matt or Eric. Neither was anywhere to be found, though, and I didn't want to stop playing this game. The girl was insanely hot. Besides, it wasn't like I was doing anything wrong. It was just a little harmless flirting, and talking with fans was good for business.

Shawna extinguished her cigarette, exhaling the last of her smoke over her shoulder. "Oh, I think you know what I'm talking about." She leaned forward, her cleavage exposed, setting off all kinds of dirty thoughts in my head.

I took a deep breath and shifted in my seat again, trying to keep my dick in check. "That's, um…that's tempting."

"Shall we?" She raised her eyebrows and extended her hand.

I looked down at it, then at my own in disbelief as my fingers reached for hers.

"Hey, man, what's going on?"

Will's voice startled me, and I quickly retracted my hand and took a long swallow of my beer.

He offered a half-hearted wave to Shawna. "I'm Will."

"Hi," she said, the corners of her mouth turning downward.

"I, uh, need to get some sleep." I put my drink on the table between us and rose to my feet. "Nice to meet you, though."

She pursed her lips at Will before looking back at me. "You, too."

I shoved my hands in my pockets so I wouldn't have to touch her soft hands again and walked off with Will toward the elevator.

"That chick was smokin'," he said, looking back at her before pushing the call button.

I ran my hand through my hair and took a deep breath. "Fucking tell me about it."

He hiccuped and stepped into the elevator. "Did I, uh, interrupt something?"

His eyes burned into me, trying to extract my thoughts, so I diverted my gaze to a corner of the ceiling. "Nah, man, just some girl looking for a guy in a band. You know how it goes."

"Eva's a good woman," he slurred. "You don't wanna fuck that up."

The elevator came to a stop, and we exited onto our floor.

He gave me a squeeze on the shoulder and a quick "night, man" before heading down the hallway in the opposite direction. I trudged to my room and fumbled for the key, Will's words echoing in my head. He was right. Eva *was* a good woman. She believed in me and the band, and she'd never give up on any of us. But she was around *all the fucking time.* At sound check, in band meetings, on the bus…*everywhere.* It was getting to be too much, and even though I kept telling myself it would be over soon, things were getting dicey. Because I knew damn well I'd be with that chick if Will hadn't shown up.

And I didn't want that.

At least I didn't *think* I wanted that.

I dropped my chin to my chest as I inserted the key into the door. "You really are an asshole, dude."

CHAPTER TWENTY-ONE
EVA

AUGUST 1989

I woke to the sound of raindrops pinging the hotel window and watched as water snaked down the glass from a gap on the side of the thick curtain that covered the length of the wall. Thunder from the mid-August storm rattled the walls, but it was the ring of the phone that startled me, and I reached carefully over Danny to pick up the receiver from the nightstand.

"Hello?" I whispered.

"Eva, it's Keith. Come down to my room as soon as you can. We need to talk."

"Yeah." I wiped a strand of hair from my face and peered at the alarm clock by the phone. Eight a.m. I grimaced as the pit in my stomach from the night before was awakened. "I'll be right there."

I slipped from under the covers and pulled on yesterday's clothes. After a quick check of my hair, I grabbed my tour binder and stepped into the hallway, my stomach churning as I headed for Keith's room. I was certain he wanted to talk about last night's show, but I didn't know how bad the news would be. Had the press somehow managed to trash us already? What rumors had begun to spread overnight that we needed to squash?

He looked like hell when he opened the door, his hair tousled and his collared shirt rumpled. The rims of his eyes were red like he hadn't slept, and the corners of his mouth were turned downward.

"Hey," I said, stepping into the room.

"Have a seat." He motioned to a set of chairs in the suite.

I nodded as Keith padded barefoot across the carpet behind me.

He flopped in the chair beside me and exhaled, running his hands down his face. "We need to talk about Eric."

I sucked in a breath, my suspicion about why he'd called an 8 a.m. meeting confirmed. For the past month, Eric had been acting more and more erratically. Late for gigs, doing the outro with the wrong city names. But the night before, he'd barely made it through the show, forgetting half the lyrics, not following the set list, and hanging onto the microphone like it was the only thing holding him up.

It was no secret that Eric was drunk or high the majority of the time. But until recently, he'd always managed to get himself together to put on killer performances. When I really thought about it, it seemed things had gotten worse after that night on the rooftop when I'd given him the fax—the one that said someone had been trying to get in touch with him. I'd tried to talk to him about it, but he'd blown me off each time.

"It's nothing, Eva," he'd insisted after sound check in Tampa as he tapped out several lines of powder onto the table in front of him and snorted them. "Just some guy I used to know."

I crossed my arms over my chest and pursed my lips. "But you've been off since I gave you that fax. You don't look good, and I'm worried about—"

"I'm fine. So fucking drop it, okay?" He brought his head up, staring past me with vacant eyes.

Keith cleared his throat, and I shook the thought from my head. "Last night was a fucking disaster. I don't even know if I can bring myself to read the goddamn reviews today. And the guys in Hott Blood aren't happy *at all*."

It had been more than a disaster. After the show, Danny had stormed off the stage and not said a word until we got back to the hotel room where he ranted about Eric's performance while lighting one cigarette off the other. "Between the fucking fifth of Jack he drinks every day and all the shit he puts up his nose, I never know whether he's gonna pass out on stage or swing from the fucking rafters."

I sat forward, my eyes focused squarely on Keith. "What do we need to do?"

"What we *need* to do is to lock him in a room and let him dry the fuck out. But that can't happen right now. He's gonna have to straighten up and finish out this tour, so I want you to tell Joe to be up his ass night and day. Get him to back off the booze and coke. Distract him somehow." Keith waved his hand in the air, indicating he didn't know what that would involve, but that was for me and Joe to figure out.

I hesitated before nodding, hoping our head of security was up to the task.

"Okay, I'll take care of that, no problem," I assured him, my voice sounding a hell of a lot more confident than I was.

Keith stood, and I followed him to the door, folding my arms around the binder.

"Anything else I can do?" I asked.

He breathed deeply as he placed his hand on the knob. "Yeah," he said, opening the door for me. "You can tell Eric to shape the fuck up before his antics cost us this tour."

"Are Hott Blood that pissed?"

Keith frowned. "Let's just say I had to do a lot of ass-kissing last night."

"Miss?"

I murmured a "huh?" before realizing there was a person standing over me and bolting upright in my seat.

"Sorry, miss," the waitress apologized, holding out a silver carafe. "Just wanted to see if you needed more coffee?"

I smiled weakly and nodded. "Sure. Thanks."

She filled my cup before heading off to the next table. I doused the coffee with cream and sugar and watched the liquid swirl as I moved a spoon through it.

I'd been settled into the booth at the hotel restaurant for a good while, trying to wrap my head around how to tell Eric he had to get his shit together. Not only because we were in danger of losing the tour, but because I was genuinely concerned about him.

Out of the corner of my eye, I saw a figure approaching the booth. My heart quickened, and my first instinct was to attempt to casually turn my head toward the wall and let my hair fall over the side of my face.

"Eva?"

Fuck.

I swept my hair behind my shoulder and turned to face him, staring up into a pair of eyes that looked like the life had been drained out of them. Dark circles, made even more prominent by the paleness of his skin, framed his lids. I swallowed and glanced back down at the table.

"Hey," I said.

Eric slid into the seat across from me, his long legs brushing mine underneath the table.

"So. Who spiked the punch last night?" He cracked an emotionless smile and motioned for the waitress.

My face tightened as she returned to the table, her cheeks tinted pink. She clearly recognized Eric and was starstruck, even though he looked like shit.

"Can I get a Bloody Mary—heavy on the vodka, light on all the other shit that goes in it?" He winked and shot her sly grin.

"Of course." She giggled and shifted her wide blue eyes from side to side, as she pulled a napkin and pen out of the apron tied around her waist. "And would you mind giving me an autograph?"

He smirked, picked up the pen, and scribbled his signature on the napkin. She smiled and swiped it from the table, stuffing it back into her apron.

"Thank you," she said, her cheeks still flushed.

"Anytime…Kristi," he said, studying the name tag pinned over her ample right breast.

She let out a little squeal of excitement and hurried away to put his order in at the bar.

I ran my hand through my hair and let out an incredulous laugh.

He looked across the table and shrugged. "What?"

I pressed my lips together. "Eric, you fucked up last night's show beyond all recognition. And now you're ordering a drink at nine in the fucking morning? Have you even been to sleep?"

Eric rolled his eyes. "Oh, please. I forgot some lyrics. So what?"

"Forgot the entire set list is more like it."

"You're being dramatic."

I sighed and shook my head. "No, I'm not. You're just not taking this seriously."

Kristi returned to the table with his drink and placed it in front of him. "Heavy on the vodka," she said, her voice shaking with excitement.

"Thanks, doll," Eric said, bringing the glass to his lips and taking a large sip. His hand shook as he set it back down. "It's perfect."

"Let me know if you need *anything* else."

Eric's eyes scanned her body. "Will do."

I sucked in a deep breath. "We need to talk about this, and I need you to listen."

"Okay, Eva." He leaned back against the seat and folded his arms behind his head. "What do you want to tell me? That I fucked up some words? That I missed some cues? Big fucking deal."

"It was beyond that, Eric, and you know it. Or maybe you don't. You've been so messed up lately, and I—"

He threw his head back and blew out a breath before I

could finish my sentence. "Are you fucking serious right now?"

"Yes, I'm serious. You could barely stand up last night. You didn't know what city we're in—maybe you still don't know."

"Does it *matter* what city we're in?"

"Actually, it does." I leaned forward and tried to look him in the eyes, but he shifted his gaze. "You need to back off the booze and the coke, okay?"

He unfolded his arms and crossed them over his chest. "And *you* need to back the fuck off in general. *Okay?*"

I pressed my finger onto the table. "Look, I know you don't wanna talk about this, but you've been severely fucked-up since I gave you that fax, and I don't know why you won't tell me—"

"Would you shut the fuck up about that already?"

"But I don't understand who it was and why it made you so—"

"I said, *shut the fuck up.*"

I reached across the table to touch his arm, which he immediately pulled away. "Eric, I'm worried about you."

"Yeah, well, I don't know why the fuck you are. It's not like we're friends, Eva."

My face fell, and I swallowed hard.

Eric's lips twisted into a smirk. "Oh, wow. You actually thought we were friends, didn't you? That's super cute. But we're not, Eva. We've never been friends."

I jerked back as the sword entered my chest. I looked down in disbelief at the point of impact, my mind churning. I had two choices. I could run off and bleed alone, letting Eric know he'd wounded me to the point where I could no longer fight. Or I could pull out the sword and turn it around on him. Both were painful options, but I knew what I had to do.

"Fine then," I spat back at him. "We're not friends. So, I'm gonna tell you straight up. Lay off the shit, Eric, or you're gonna lose this tour. The guys in Hott Blood are pissed, our guys are pissed, and—"

"You mean *Danny's* pissed," he interrupted. "Did he put

you up to this? Did he tell you to talk to me because he's too fucking scared to do it himself?"

I squeezed my hands into fists, insulted he didn't think I could form my own fucking opinions. "No, he didn't. Anyone with two fucking eyes can see you're spiraling out of control. So, until we finish this tour, Joe will be by your side twenty-four seven to make sure you don't spiral any further."

He narrowed his eyes at me. "*What?*"

"You heard me."

Eric snorted and shook his head. "Fuck that. You're fucking crazy if you think that's gonna happen."

"Oh, it's happening," I assured him. "Keith and I met this morning. I'm about to go talk to Joe and—"

His lip curled into a snarl. "You act like you're so concerned, like it's such a big goddamn deal. But you know what? You're just Keith's fucking mouthpiece. And you wouldn't even be that if I hadn't told him to hire you." He jumped up from the booth, knocking his drink over in the process, spilling ice and red-tinted liquid across the table. "So don't fucking forget that I'm the only reason you're here."

He stormed off through the restaurant and lobby, then burst through the doors to the outside. Kristi hurried over to me, wiping at the table with a rag as the remains of his Bloody Mary dripped onto my lap and hot tears pricked at the corners of my eyes.

CHAPTER TWENTY-TWO
DANNY

AUGUST 1989

"Hey. Eva. Wake up."

She moaned and turned over, opening one eye. "What's going on?"

"I woke up and found you over here."

She lifted her head from the spare bed and flicked her eyes around the dim room, her gaze finally settling on my face. "What time is it?"

"Eleven thirty."

Eva gasped and bolted upright. "Holy shit."

"What?"

"Shit, shit, *shit*."

"What?"

She pressed her hand to her forehead. "I...*Fuck*. Keith called me earlier this morning and asked me to tell Joe to stay close to Eric after what happened last night. But I ran into Eric first and tried to talk to him about it. He flipped out on me and took off, so I came up here to regroup before talking to Joe. I must've fallen asleep and—"

A knock at the door silenced her. I trudged over to open it, and there was Keith standing in front of me, his brow creased and mouth turned down. "Have you seen Eric?"

"No, man, I haven't."

FOR EVA

"Is Eva here?"

He didn't wait for my answer before pushing past me.

"Keith, hey, I was just going to talk to Joe," Eva said, flipping on the nightstand lamp, bathing the room in a soft yellow glow.

"You haven't spoken to him yet? I thought you were going right after our—" He threw his hands in the air. "Whatever, doesn't matter. Eric isn't in his room. Not in the lobby or the restaurant. You have any idea where he is?"

Eva's face twitched as she fingered the ends of her hair. "I saw him earlier. I told him about Joe and he, uh…he wasn't happy."

Keith pursed his lips. "What does that mean, *not happy?*"

"He took off. Outside. I'm not sure where he—"

"You let him leave this fucking hotel, Eva? We pull out of here in two hours."

Eva started to tremble as she wrung her hands together. "I'm sorry, this is all my fault."

He sucked in a deep breath and clenched his fists. "I honestly don't give a shit whose fault it is. We're going to find him. *Now.*"

"There's, um, a bar—a few bars—down the street," Eva said, her voice quavering.

Keith nodded. "Fine, let's go."

We rode the elevator down to the lobby in silence and were immediately hit with a gust of wind and a spray of rain as we opened the double doors leading to the sidewalk. We headed down the block to a lit sign jutting out from a brick building, but the place was closed. The next joint was also a bust, and by the time Keith swung the door open at the third bar, I was beginning to worry we'd have to go on stage the next two nights in Denver without a lead singer.

We rushed in, damp from the rain, and I squinted my eyes in an attempt to adjust my vision to the low lighting. To my left was a dark wooden bar where a few patrons were seated. As we made our way farther into the bar, I spotted Eric. He was seated between a man and woman, all of them laughing as they slammed shot glasses on the bar.

I motioned for Keith and Eva to stay back as I continued forward and placed my hand on Eric's shoulder. I wanted to turn him around and beat the shit out of him, but I had to keep my cool if I was going to get him out of there.

"Hey, man," I said.

"Danny!" He shifted in his seat and patted me on the back, attempting to pull me closer to the bar. "Get in here and drink with us!"

"Tempting, dude. But we gotta go. Bus is heading out soon."

"You gotta meet my new friends," he slurred, motioning to the people on either side of him. "This is, um…" He trailed off as he pointed at the brunette to his right.

"Tracey," she said, offering me her hand. "And that's Vince." She motioned to the man on Eric's left, who nodded in acknowledgment and turned back to the bar.

Eric smiled, the alcohol seeming to have erased the anger Eva had endured earlier that morning. "Yeah, Tracey and Vince."

The bartender placed another round of shots in front of them, and Eric knocked his back quickly, wiping his mouth with the back of his hand.

I reached into my back pocket and pulled out my wallet, tossing a hundred dollar bill on the bar.

"Come on, Eric, let's head out. Hopefully this covers the tab," I said to Tracey, whose eyes grew wide as she grabbed for the money.

Eric pushed himself back from the bar. "Duty calls, friends." He lost his footing as he attempted to stand, and I caught him as he stumbled forward. I motioned for Keith to come over, and we placed his arms over our shoulders before guiding him toward the door. Eric eyed Keith, confused, but didn't question why he was there. Eva hung her head and walked ahead of us.

Fortunately, the rain had stopped, as it proved challenging to haul Eric's semi-limp body along the sidewalk. His head wobbled back and forth between me and Keith, until he caught sight of Eva and managed to steady it.

"Aw, Danny, that's so sweet. You brought your girl along to rescue me. Although, she wasn't very nice to me this morning." He paused, then expelled a laugh so bitter I could almost taste it. "Danny and Eva foreva!" he yelled as we stopped at a crosswalk, cars whizzing past us, whipping Eric's long hair into his face.

I exchanged a look with Keith, then glanced over at Eva, who stood with her arms folded across her chest. Her jaw tightened as she stared impatiently across the street at the flashing light signaling it would soon be safe to cross.

"Foreva! For Eva! Get it?" Eric leaned forward and cackled, nearly causing us to stumble out into the road. We took a step back from the oncoming traffic, and he lifted his head. "But you wouldn't get that, would you, Danny?"

"What the fuck are you talking about, Eric?" I asked.

The signal on the other side of the street changed, allowing us to cross. Eva walked ahead, creating as much distance as possible between her and the scene Eric was causing.

"I'm talking about *you*," Eric slurred loudly. "'Cause you've never really been *for* Eva, have you? You didn't even want her on this tour with us. You wanted to keep her back in LA, stuck in some shitty bar job." He raised his head and called out to her. "Did you know that, Eva? *Did you?*"

Fuck.

Eva stopped abruptly and turned to us, stray pieces of hair darting around her face in the wind. "What did you say?"

"Danny doesn't fucking want you here," Eric announced as we approached her.

She shifted her eyes to me, her piercing stare slicing through my heart. Without another word, she twisted on her heels and started toward the hotel, quickening her pace until she was running.

"Eva, wait!" I slipped out from under Eric's arm and jogged

ahead, but she only sprinted farther and farther away.

I scrubbed my hands over my face and blew out a long breath before heading back down the sidewalk, where Keith was struggling to keep Eric upright against the side of a building.

Motherfucker. I wanted to fucking pummel him, but that would cause even more of a scene, and the look on Keith's face told me he was done. So, I grabbed Eric's arm, threw it over my shoulder, and slogged toward the hotel as he mumbled incoherently, then passed the fuck out.

———

After depositing Eric with Keith, I trudged down the hallway to our room, where I rested my hand on the cold silver handle and leaned my forehead against the door. Inside, there was loud music and the sound of drawers slamming shut. I took a deep breath and turned the knob, bracing myself for the worst.

Eva was in a flurry, her hair flying wildly as she threw clothes into the open suitcase on the bed. Joan Jett blasted from the boom box on the dresser, drowning out my entrance. As she walked over to empty out a drawer, she caught sight of me and stopped in her tracks, her stare freezing my insides. Then, just as suddenly as she had stopped, she released me from her spell, and began tossing more clothes into the suitcase.

I took a deep breath and walked over to the boom box, turning the volume down. Eva immediately pushed past me and adjusted it back up.

"Can we talk about this?" I asked, raising my voice above the music.

She ignored me, zipping the suitcase and lugging it off the bed onto the floor. As she attempted to push past me toward the bathroom, I grabbed her arm and turned her around to face me.

"Hey! Can you fucking listen for one second?"

Eva yanked her arm away and shoved her hand into my chest, sending me backward into the dresser. "Don't fucking touch me."

As she stomped off, I turned around and fumbled for the stop button on the boom box. Without a word, she stalked back over and pressed play on the tape, the sound of Joan Jett singing about hating herself for loving someone once again blasting from the speakers.

I turned and punched the eject button. "Fucking stop this already!"

Eva's chest heaved as she looked up at the ceiling and pressed her lips together.

"Can we please talk?" I asked again.

"What, Danny? What do you want to say?"

"What Eric said," I began, inching closer to her. "It's not what you think. He's a goddamn addict, Eva. He just wanted to start some shit because he's fucking miserable and wants everyone else to be miserable, too."

Her nostrils flared, and rage crept up her neck, painting her cheeks bright red as she dropped her gaze to me. "Seriously, Danny? You expect me to believe you? Why the fuck would Eric make that up?"

I shifted my eyes to the floor before bringing them back up to her. "Look, I may have expressed some…*reservations* about you coming on tour. But we had just gotten the gig with Black Widow Rising, and I was freaking out about *everything*."

"Uh-huh."

I ran my hand along my face and groaned. "Fuck, Eva. It's not the way he made it sound."

An incredulous laugh escaped her lips. "I'm not stupid, Danny. I always knew deep down you were hesitant about having me work with the band. But what I didn't know is that you expressed that to Eric and Keith and whoever else would fucking listen."

I sighed and flopped on the end of bed, resting my hand on my chin as I tried to think of the words I could say to make things right. But none came to me.

"I suggest you pack your shit if you'd like to come to Denver," Eva said, picking up her suitcase and flinging her backpack over one shoulder. "And yes, I *am* saying that as part of the band's management. Because personally, I couldn't give a fuck if you come or not."

CHAPTER TWENTY-THREE
EVA

AUGUST 1989

I tapped my nails on the rail of the elevator and ground my teeth, waiting for the signal that I'd reached the tenth floor. Keith had asked me to round up the guys for a band meeting before our show that evening, and I dreaded having to speak to both Eric and Danny. Eric because he'd been an asshole every time he saw me. And Danny because we still hadn't made up after our fight two days prior.

I didn't know what to say to him. Was he being honest when he said he'd only had reservations at the beginning?

What if he didn't want me here now? What if he didn't want me here ever?

Sure, I'd be done traveling with them full-time once the Hott Blood gig was over, but I'd still be around. I'd still be working for Keith. It made me question everything about our relationship, and I couldn't figure out how to have that conversation while we were just trying to make it through the last several weeks of the tour. So, I'd tried to keep things all business since we'd gotten on the bus for Denver that rainy afternoon. But it was going to be impossible to keep that up until the tour ended. Something would have to give, I just didn't know how or when.

I reached Eric's room, giving the door a quick knock as I stared down at the gold vines weaving through the burgundy carpet in the hallway.

"Eric," I said, knocking again. I leaned my ear against the door to see if I could hear anyone stirring in the room. "It's Eva. Open up."

I tried the handle, but as expected, it was locked. I groaned, twisting my wrist to look at my watch, then pounded the door with my fist.

"Come on, Eric! Keith wants everyone in his room for a meeting in fifteen minutes."

The sound of shuffling came from the other side of the door, and I thanked God I wasn't going to have to figure out how to execute a break-in.

The door opened, and I breathed a sigh of relief. "Oh good, I was—"

I cut myself off, my jaw dropping when my eyes settled on Joe, head of security, in nothing but a pair of striped boxer shorts.

He tousled his hair and yawned, squinting his eyes in an attempt to focus on me. "Eva?"

I furrowed my brow and cocked my head. "I, um…Never mind. Where's Eric?"

Joe ran his hand through his short dark hair and blinked slowly. "Uh," he muttered as he turned around and looked back into the room.

I peered over his shoulder to see a pair of bare feet hanging off the end of the bed. Narrowing my eyes, I pushed past him into the room to find a woman face down on the bed, her ass barely covered by a pair of lacy underwear.

"Really, Joe?" I said, rolling my eyes as I walked into the living room of the suite, expecting to find another half-naked woman along with a half-naked Eric.

But there was no woman and there was no Eric. Taking a deep breath, I walked back into the bedroom.

"Okay, so what's all this, and where the hell is Eric?" I asked, pointing to the woman on the bed.

Joe's face flushed as he pressed his lips together, and his eyes fell to the floor. "Fuck."

The woman stirred, moving her hand up to a mess of tangled blond hair and propping herself up on one elbow. Her eyes, smeared with mascara, struggled to focus. "What's going on?"

I crossed my arms over my chest and stared at the ceiling to avoid looking at her bare tits.

Joe darted in front of me to the chair where the woman's crumpled red dress lay and handed it to her. "You have to go now," he said as he grabbed his own clothes and pulled on his jeans, nearly tumbling over in the process.

I stepped to the side as she made her way to the dresser and picked up her purse, along with the stack of money beside it.

"Tell Eric thanks for the tip," she said, raising her eyebrows at Joe as her faded red lips curled into a seductive smile.

Joe nodded quickly as she sauntered out of the room.

"Tip?" I asked, unfolding my arms and placing my hands on my hips.

Joe sat in the chair where the woman's dress had been and ran his hands down his face.

"Fuck, Eva. I did *not* mean for this to happen."

"Didn't mean for *what* to happen?"

He sighed and ran his hand around the back of his neck. "Eric, he, uh…he was bored sitting in the hotel room and suggested we call up some girls."

I clenched my jaw. "Girls…as in ones you *pay for?*"

He nodded slowly, chewing his lip.

I threw my hands in the air. "What the fuck, Joe? You were supposed to be watching out for him!"

"I thought it was totally harmless," he said, his voice shaking. "It would keep him in the room, out of trouble…but they had some pills and I took one like a fucking idiot. Next thing I know, you're knocking on the door, and Eric's gone."

"Christ," I grumbled, closing my eyes and rubbing my temples.

"I am *so* sorry, Eva. Tell Keith and the guys I'll turn the city upside down looking for him."

"The show is *tonight*, Joe. There are over a million people in this city. You think you can just go find him and have him back here in time to get him on stage?"

He closed his eyes and shook his head. "Fuck me. I'm so fucking fired."

I dropped my arms to my sides and sighed. "Look, I don't know what Keith will do, but I've got to go tell him Eric's taken off to…*somewhere*. So, put your shirt on and go look for him if you want. I'll be in Keith's room if you find him," I added, opening the door.

"Excuse me, are you with Counting Backward?"

The voice practically caused me to jump out of my skin as the door shut behind me. I turned my head to see a tall brunette standing beside me holding a notepad and pen in her hand.

"What? Why?"

She poised the pen over the pad. "I'm with *Insider* magazine, and we'd love to get some commentary on the accusations Eric Stratton's stepfather is leveling."

I squeezed my eyes shut and shook my head. "What are you talking about? I can't…I'm not commenting on anything to do with Eric's family." I stepped around her and started down the hallway toward Keith's room.

"Are you sure?" she asked, following on my heels. "Because this is pretty serious. Steve Anderson is saying he reached out to Eric multiple times asking for help with Eric's mother's cancer treatments, but he refused, and she passed away in July."

I stopped abruptly and turned my head. "Eric's mother's not—Wait, what name did you say?"

"Steve Anderson."

My stomach dropped as I stared past the reporter. The

name from the fax the label had sent me. The one I'd given Eric on the rooftop in Cleveland.

"I, uh…I'm not commenting on that," I said.

Her eyes widened, sensing she had roused something inside of me. I quickly turned and continued down the hall.

"Did Eric refuse to pay for his mother's lifesaving chemotherapy? Is that why she died?"

Her words pierced me from behind, but I kept going until I turned the corner and was out of her sight. No wonder Eric had gotten so out of control after I'd given him that fax. His mother had *died*. Even if he didn't have a relationship with her, it still had to be painful. But had he denied her money for treatment? He wouldn't do that…would he? My brain was a muddy river, thoughts trying to swim their way through it to some sort of clarity. I let my body sink into the wall and buried my head in my hands as I fought my way through the murkiness, trying to figure out what the fuck to do.

CHAPTER TWENTY-FOUR
DANNY

AUGUST 1989

"I think we're gonna have to call it," Keith said, walking over to the makeshift bar backstage. He filled a tumbler halfway with Jack Daniels, throwing it back in one swallow.

I looked at my watch for the twentieth time in the last ten minutes. Seven fifty-five p.m. Eva sat on the leather couch, rubbing her hand along her forehead. Matt stood by her, plucking an occasional note on his bass, and Will leaned against the wall, staring off into space while spinning a drumstick through his fingers. Silence hung thick in the air, broken only by the sound of the drumstick slipping from his hand and hitting the floor.

Will sighed as he scrambled to pick it up. "I agree. Eric didn't show up for sound check, and he hasn't done any warm-ups. Even if he does somehow magically appear, he's gonna sound like shit."

I kicked the coffee table in front of me, sending it screeching across the floor. "I fucking *hate* doing this to fans! Especially at the eleventh fucking hour."

Matt shook his head. "It's bullshit, man."

Eva looked up, studying Keith's face. "What should I do?"

"Make an announcement," Keith said. "Tell them Eric's voice went out while he was warming up. And let the Hott Blood camp know. Maybe they can go on earlier." He paused and

171

slammed his hand on the table. "Goddamnit."

I glanced at Eva, who bit her lip and looked back at me with dull eyes. We'd barely spoken since our fight. I'd given up trying to explain myself. Everything that came out of my mouth was a lie, anyway. And now, on top of my personal life being in the shitter, the band was in serious fucking trouble.

"What's up, fuckers?" Eric exclaimed as he burst into the room in his leathers and a sleeveless Harley-Davidson T-shirt like he'd been down the hall doing warm-ups rather than MIA for the last eight hours.

What the fuck.

I stormed across the room and pushed him against the door, grabbing a fistful of his shirt. His eyes widened, his pupils two large dark orbs. Beads of sweat lined his brow and upper lip. "You motherfucker!"

Will darted across the room and pulled me off him as Eric adjusted his shirt.

"Jesus, Danny. Calm the fuck down." He laughed as he bounced up to the bar and took a swig directly from the bottle of Jack, his eyes flickering around the room. "Why is everyone so fucking sober? Who fucking died?"

I scowled at him, my chest heaving beneath my shirt.

Eva flinched, then stood and cleared her throat. "It's five after. Are we going on?"

"I'm here, man!" Eric took another long swallow from the bottle. "Let's fucking do it!"

I sighed and shook my head. He was high as a fucking kite. But I supposed that was better than drunk and unable to stand up straight, so I swiped my cigarettes and lighter off the coffee table and nodded at Matt and Will. "All right, let's go."

We filed out of the room and headed down the hallway to the stage while "Crazy Train" played over the PA. The crew cut the house lights, and the crowd erupted as darkness fell across the venue.

As my tech hooked the wireless amp system to my guitar

strap, I narrowed my eyes at Eric. "Don't forget there's a set list taped to the stage. Fucking follow it."

Eric snorted. "I'm the fucking front man, Danny. *You* follow *me*."

I squeezed my hands into fists as I stomped onto the stage, which was hidden from the audience by a billowing black curtain. Will followed, hopping onto the drum riser, and Matt took his place stage right. The curtain dropped and beams of lights attacked the stage as I played the first notes of the opening song, and Eric bounded out to the roar of the crowd. Will and Matt joined in on drums and bass as Eric grabbed the mic stand and began to belt out the lyrics.

They were the right ones. And he sounded *good*, giving it his all for the first time in a fucking month. A wave of relief washed over me, and I relaxed into the music. We sailed through the next several numbers, and by the end of the fourth song, I was confident we were going to make it to the end of the show without incident.

Eric headed to the drum riser to towel off and take a swig of Jack. He stumbled, his long hair falling over his face as he regained his footing and placed his hands on his knees. I held my breath until he popped back up and strode over to the microphone stand.

"Denver! How you all doing out there?" he screamed into the mic, and the audience erupted once again.

"All right," he said, working to catch his breath as he grabbed the mic off the stand. "So we've got some more songs for you all, but I just wanted to take a minute to thank Hott Blood for have…for having…"

His voice faded and the mic fell on the floor, sending a shriek of feedback through the venue as his body began to sway. I charged toward him to tell him to get his fucking shit together. That he wasn't going to take me down with his goddamn sinking ship. But when I opened my mouth to speak, his head slumped forward, and he clutched his chest. An eerie

FOR EVA

silence fell over the crowd as Eric staggered, his eyes meeting mine for a fraction of a second before he collapsed onto the stage. The thud of his body hitting the ground echoed like a gunshot, and my blood went cold as a single agonizing scream pierced my brain.

CHAPTER TWENTY-FIVE
EVA

AUGUST 1989

"Eric!" A force gripped my lungs and squeezed all the air out of me. I gasped for breath, staring at his body crumpled on the floor, as the band and crew hurried over to him.

People called his name. Shook him. Cried for help. But I'd gone silent. I was underwater, my vision blurry and the sounds muffled. Keith pushed past me, bringing me to the surface, and my eyes darted to the audience, surfers in a rough sea, struggling to keep their own heads above water as a wave of confusion crashed over them.

No. They can't see him like this. He wouldn't want this.

"Hide him," I said, my voice shaky and small. I cleared my throat. "Keith, tell them to hide him."

Keith turned to me, his chest heaving.

"I can help," I shrieked out in a voice I almost didn't recognize as my own.

He barked orders at the people standing around, who shuffled to form a human shield, blocking Eric from the crowd.

I pushed my way behind the blockade and looked down at Eric's body. His eyes were closed, and he was still. *So still.* I knelt beside him, my entire body trembling. I hadn't done this in forever, and it wasn't even on a real person. Did I remember? Was summer lifeguard training really enough to save someone?

FOR EVA

I tossed my hair over my shoulder and put my ear to Eric's lips, hoping to feel his breath against them. But there was nothing. I placed two fingers under his jaw and pressed them into his neck, moving them along his skin, checking unsuccessfully for the thumping of a pulse. "Someone get the paramedics."

"Is he okay, Eva?" Matt asked. "What's going on?"

"Just fucking get them!"

"They're coming," someone said from above me.

I nodded my head, trying my damndest to focus. *Fuck.* Was it compressions first? I searched the furthest corners of my mind, attempting to remember what our instructor had told us. *Yes. Fifteen compressions, then two breaths.*

I centered my shaking hands, one on top of the other, over his chest and locked my elbows. *Come on, Eva, you can do this.* I pressed down with the force of my body weight and began to count. *One, two, three...*

Sweat formed on my brow as I tried to block out the chatter of the people around me. Someone shouted for the rest of the group to be quiet, and soon there was just the breathy sound of my voice. *Thirteen, fourteen, fifteen... What's next?*

I tilted Eric's head back and pinched his nose, sealing my mouth over his, tasting the whiskey on his lips before blowing a puff of air into him.

Do it again.

I leaned down to see if he was breathing and felt for a pulse. But the only sound I could hear was my heart pounding in my ears.

No. No, no, no.

"You can't die, Eric," I choked out. "Please don't die."

Tears spilled over my lids as I began compressions again, the numbers getting caught in my throat, my arms aching. I repeated the breaths, then the compressions, then the breaths. I wiped at my eyes before placing my ear to his mouth once again and pressing two fingers to his neck.

The salt from my tears stung my dry lips as I bore down

on his chest. I'd lost all concept of time, but it didn't matter. All that mattered was that I didn't stop.

Through my watery vision, I saw my mother lying crooked like a broken mannequin on the pavement. A thick, dark pool formed beside her, staining her golden hair crimson. I was trying to stand, to tell the men I knew CPR and I could save her. But they kept pushing me down, holding my arms as I cried for them to let me help her.

"That isn't what she needs," they said. "You can't save her."

Four, five, six…

"Let go of me, I want my mom," I begged.

Eight, nine, ten…

"You can't save her, honey. No one can save her."

You're not going to die on me, Eric. You're not going to die on me, too.

Breaths, compressions, breaths, compressions.

"Everyone out of the way. Move!"

Elbows hooked under my arms and lifted me to my feet. I steadied myself and pushed my hair out of my face to see a man in a dark blue uniform had taken my place beside Eric. He checked Eric's breath and pulse.

"Everybody back up, now!" he instructed as he took over the chest compressions.

We did as we were told while another man dressed in the same uniform kneeled, placing an orange box on the ground. "Did he take anything? Drugs of any kind?"

My gaze flickered among the band and crew, whose eyes were wide and lips were sealed tight, then to Keith, who ran his hand along his brow. "Alcohol. And coke, I think."

The man nodded as he inserted a needle into Eric's arm and attached a syringe to it. I steepled my hands over my mouth as the man pushed down on the top of the syringe, then moved his fingers to Eric's neck. I remembered that morning several days ago in the hotel restaurant when Eric had told me we weren't friends, and I'd lashed out. If only I hadn't been so hard on him. If only I'd been more understanding. If only I'd known his mom had died.

"I have a pulse," the paramedic announced. "We need to intubate."

I sucked in a shaky breath, closing my eyes and pressing my palm into my chest as I let it out. I opened them to see one of the paramedics attaching a balloon to a tube extending from Eric's mouth as they lifted him onto the stretcher two other men in the crew had carried onto the stage.

"Let's get him out of here."

I laced my fingers together and whispered a "thank you" into the universe.

"Eva, let's go."

Keith placed his hand on my shoulder, and I nodded, letting him quickly steer me backstage. He put his arm around me, whispering that I'd done good, that everything would be okay. The words floated past me, my head too heavy to absorb them.

Will and Matt followed at our heels, but Keith put his hand out to stop them. "I know you're worried, but let Eva and I handle this right now. Too many people at the hospital would create a feeding frenzy for the press. We'll let you know what's going on as soon as we get there and have some information."

Their protests became muffled as my eyes caught a spark of orange light over Will's shoulder. I squinted to see Danny leaning against the drum riser, smoking a cigarette. He glanced up as if he felt my stare and held my gaze for a moment. I opened my mouth to call his name, but he dropped his head and turned, walking off the other side of the stage.

For a moment, I thought he'd come back. But as he disappeared from my sight, it felt like a boot landed against my stomach, bruising my insides, and stealing my breath. I gasped, placing my fingers over my mouth, and my lips trembled as Keith took my arm.

"We need to go *now*, Eva."

I stumbled as he gave me a gentle tug toward the exit, and

I turned my head once more, hopeful I'd see Danny appear around the corner. But he wasn't there, and my chest and my stomach ached so badly I wanted to curl into myself. But I couldn't. And so, I moved forward, left to wonder why the person who was supposed to care about me more than anyone in the world had walked away just when I needed him most.

CHAPTER TWENTY-SIX
DANNY

AUGUST 1989

My heart pounded throughout every inch of my body as I hurried down the backstage corridor.

What was I doing? What the fuck was I doing?

Thoughts raced in blurry laps around my brain, and there was no explanation for how or why my feet continued to move forward. My pace quickened as voices echoed somewhere behind me, and I jogged toward the alcove ahead and ducked inside. I pressed myself into the cinder block wall, my limbs stiff and lips sealed tightly in an attempt to quiet my breathing.

What was I hiding from? Was it Matt and Will coming to find me? How could I possibly explain to them I didn't want to be here? That I didn't want any part of what was happening with Eric? I fucking hated him for destroying our dream—*my* dream—and for ruining everything I'd worked so goddamn hard for. The early years we'd spent playing our fucking hearts out in shady clubs for ten people like it was a fucking arena. Busting our asses, passing out fliers on the Strip every night, begging booking agents to give us a chance. All that time, all that energy, fucking *wasted*. Our stint on the tour was done, and as far as I was concerned, so was the band. I couldn't go on with just Matt and Will. They were musicians, not songwriters. Partnering with Eric had taken us to the next level, and that was fucking over. Because he would wake up and go right fucking back to being Eric. Nothing would change, and I wasn't going to put up with his bullshit anymore. I *couldn't*.

I slid down the wall, blowing out a long breath, and dropped my head into my hands as images of Eva flickered through it. The way she had looked at me. It was a look I remembered seeing in my rearview mirror when I pulled away from the curb all those years ago with my guitar, two duffel bags, and a crazy fucking dream. But this time, the look was devoid of hope. Her eyes pleaded with me on that stage to do something—*anything*. But I'd walked away, without hesitation, without a second thought, knowing she needed me. Knowing she was still hurt from finding out I never wanted her on the tour. Knowing she'd probably never forgive me. And knowing that was probably for the best because everything was fucking over anyway.

It had to be. Because when it came down to it, if I had to make a choice between having what I wanted, the way I wanted it, or having Eva, I'd choose me, every time.

I should've known that. I should've fucking known that no matter how much I'd thought I'd missed her after seeing her at the Rainbow, I'd done the right thing by letting her go all those years ago. And now was my chance to fix my mistake. To make a clean break with no one to answer to and no one to worry about except myself.

Footsteps clicked against the floor, and my muscles tensed. I raised my head to see a guy in a worn pair of jeans and long hair that fell down the back of his T-shirt. I didn't recognize him as one of our roadies, so I figured he had to work at the venue.

"Hey man," I said, pushing myself up to stand.

He startled and turned around, his eyes wide.

"Sorry, didn't mean to scare you."

He blinked and walked back toward me. "What, uh…Is Eric okay? What happened out there?"

"Yeah, he's gonna be fine." I paused for a second, unsure if that was true, but I shook the thought out of my head as I reached into my back pocket for my wallet. "But I need, uh…I need a favor. Do you have a car here?"

He cocked his head and narrowed his eyes. "Yeah, but why do you—"

"Because I'll give you a hundred bucks to get me out of here," I said. "And another hundred to pretend you never saw me."

CHAPTER TWENTY-SEVEN
EVA

AUGUST 1989

"**Y**ou doing okay?"

I heard Keith's voice, but it didn't register that he was talking to me. The city lights blurred as we whizzed past them on our way back to the hotel. My mind was focused squarely on Eric, whom we'd just left at the hospital. I didn't want to go, but there were rules the nurses kept repeating about no visitors in the ICU, and I was too tired to fight about it.

"Eva?"

I blinked and turned my head, looking over at him through the dim ceiling lights of the limousine. "Hmm?"

"Are you okay?" he asked again, leaning forward in his seat.

"Yeah. I'm okay," I answered, not really sure if I was.

"They're gonna take good care of him," he assured me. "And we'll get him back out to California as soon as we can and into the best rehab facility in the country."

I nodded again and turned my attention back to the window, pressing my forehead against the cool glass and closing my eyes.

I'd seen only pieces of Eric, doctors and nurses buzzing around like flies, as he was rushed into the hospital. A worn boot, strands of hair falling over the stretcher, a glimpse of the tube they'd placed down his throat. Finally, one of the doctors

183

had taken Keith and me aside, letting us know Eric had been sedated and it would take time for his body to recover. The doctor couldn't say how long, but because CPR had been started immediately, it was possible no permanent damage was done. I was sure he was doing the best he could with his statistics and explanations, but I could only stare past him, my watery eyes focused on the tiniest scratch on the stark white wall, waiting for him to say we could unhook Eric from the machines and walk out of the building with him. But he never did.

The limo rounded a corner and approached the hotel, bringing a crowd of people gathered outside the entrance into view. Several vans lined the street and bright lights beamed from the sidewalk.

Keith groaned, running his hand along his forehead.

"Is that…Are those *more* news crews?"

He sighed and nodded. The phone handset buzzed—the driver calling us from the front of the car—and Keith picked it up.

"Yeah, go ahead and stop," he said, placing the handset back down.

He looked over at me and slapped his hands on his knees. "All right. I know you know this, but don't say anything. We're gonna bust through there, heads down, like we did at the hospital. Okay?"

I nodded and took a deep breath as we came to a stop. The chatter of the crowd, filled with fans and reporters, bled through the windows. Our driver opened the door, and I stepped out, catapulted into a frenzy of activity. I squinted and attempted to shield myself from the camera lights that shined in my face.

A flurry of questions and microphones were thrust at us as Keith put his arm around my shoulder and guided me through the crowd.

"Where's Eric?"

"Is Eric alive?"

"Are you Eric's girlfriend?"

"Can you tell us what happened tonight?"

"Did he really let his mother die?"

We pushed through the revolving door, leaving the mob behind us. Two doormen stood watch to ensure no one followed us as we hurried to the elevators at the back of the lobby.

Keith let out a long breath as the doors clicked shut.

"I…I don't know what to do," I said, my voice shaky. "What do you need me to do?"

He turned to me, his eyes softening as he put his hand on my arm. "I'll handle it. I'll talk to Matt and Will and make all the calls. You need to get some rest."

"No," I managed, shaking my head. "It's my job. I want to help. Tell me who to call, what to do, where to—"

"Look, kid," he said, his face turning to stone. "You saved Eric's life tonight. He's alive because of *you*."

The words hit me like a ton of bricks, and I gripped the silver handrail on the wall to steady myself.

"But I need to—"

"That wasn't a suggestion, Eva. As your boss, I'm telling you. Get some rest. We'll go to the hospital tomorrow."

I sighed and nodded.

"And fill Danny in, okay?" he added as the elevator came to a stop and we stepped into the hallway.

My mouth went dry, and I licked my lips. *Danny.* In all the chaos of the past several hours, I'd forgotten what awaited me in the hotel room. How could I even look at him after he'd walked away like that?

"Okay," I said, staring down at the carpet.

"You were brave tonight, Eva. Don't forget that."

I brought my eyes up to him and managed a weak smile. "Thank you, Keith. For everything."

He nodded as we turned and headed to our rooms. I held my breath as I inserted the key into the lock and turned the knob. The room was dark, so I flipped on the light and made my way into the suite, expecting to find Danny, sitting on the bed, stewing over the events of the night and chain-smoking. But he wasn't there.

"Danny?" I called, though it was clear no one was in the room. Maybe he'd gone to find a bar, which was fine with me since I didn't particularly want to talk to him. I needed to lie down and process everything that had happened.

I moved to the dresser to pull out an old T-shirt to throw on for bed, and out of the corner of my eye, I noticed an empty space where Danny's suitcase had been earlier in the day. He never unpacked his suitcase, except to hang up some of his stage clothes. My stomach dropped as I dashed to the closet and threw open the doors.

I stepped back and swallowed hard, my breath quickening when I saw it was empty. My eyes darted around the room, looking for a sign he was still at the hotel, but only spotted a piece of paper on the nightstand. I froze in place, my chest rising and falling. When I finally managed to make it to the table, I picked up the note and read the words scribbled in Danny's handwriting.

I can't do this anymore. The band. Us. I'm so sorry, Eva. This isn't what I thought it would be.

My body dropped to the bed, and I covered my mouth with my hand as I choked on the tears that fell and blurred the ink on the paper. After all the promises…after everything we'd been through…Danny Kincaid had left me.

Again.

———

"That motherfucking *asshole!*" Denise screamed, slamming the apartment door so hard the room vibrated as I hauled the last of my luggage into my bedroom.

I caught a glimpse of myself in the full-length mirror hanging on the wall when I walked out to the living room. No makeup, tired eyes, my hair in a mess of a ponytail. I looked like shit. I *felt* like shit. I'd spent four days in Denver. Four days in the hospital, hoping they'd let me see Eric once they'd taken him off the machines, and he'd begun the detox process. But his withdrawal symptoms were too severe, so eventually, Keith, Matt, Will, and I had decided it was time to get on the bus and head home.

Without a word, I trudged over to the couch and flopped down, curling into a ball, my head resting on the arm.

"He *cannot* fucking do this to you, Eva," Denise continued, collapsing into the chair across from me. "This isn't fucking high school. He can't break up with you in a goddamn note."

I stared blankly at the wall across from me and snorted. "Should've learned my lesson from high school."

"I'm so fucking mad," she said, hitting the pillow beside her. "I'm calling him! I'm calling him right now. What's his fucking phone number?" She sprang from the chair and picked up the phone on the end table.

"Don't bother. I've only tried about two hundred times."

Denise looked over at me and put a hand on her hip. "Well, can I at least leave him a message telling him to go fuck himself?"

"It won't matter," I said. "The answering machine is full. It's done. Over. Once a-fucking-gain."

She plunked down the receiver and sat beside me, placing her hand on my leg. "I'm so sorry, babe. But it's like I don't even know what to do. I'm so fucking pissed he did this to you." She leaned forward, trying to see my face, which was partially covered by a mop of hair that had fallen over it. "Should we drive over to his house?"

I sighed, pushing myself up so I was sitting cross-legged. I then freed the rest of my hair from what was left of my ragged ponytail and shook my head. "He's probably moved out. It doesn't matter. He doesn't want to see me. He called Keith and left him a message at the hotel that he was quitting the band. Not me. *Keith.*"

I paused and cleared my throat, tears pricking the corners

of my eyes once again. "He made it clear all he cared about was getting his gear back and whatever money was owed him."

"God. When did he become such a *dick?*"

I shrugged, my mouth turning down. "I guess he's always been one. I should've never trusted him again. I was so fucking stupid." I fought back the emotions that continued to form behind my eyes.

"No. You weren't," she insisted, turning to face me. "He said all the right things. He *did* all the right things. Anybody would've believed him. He fucked you over, Eva. You couldn't have seen it coming."

I dropped my head into my hands. "But I knew it was a mistake going on the road with them. He needed his time without me always hanging around. I should've just quit."

"But you *love* your job," Denise said, squeezing my shoulder. "You couldn't give that up."

"I could've told Keith I needed to work with his other bands, that I couldn't work with Counting Backward." I took a deep breath. "But the thing is, Denise, I *wanted* to be with Danny. I actually *wanted* to be there."

"I know." She reached over and wiped a tear from my cheek. "So what's gonna happen to Eric? What about Matt and Will?"

I licked my dry lips. "Eric's apparently having some pretty bad withdrawal symptoms, but like I told you on the phone, no permanent damage, thank God. Matt and Will...I don't know. Our stint on the tour's over, obviously. Not sure if the band will get back together after Eric gets out of rehab or not. Minus Danny, of course." I paused and shrugged. "Keith told me to take a few days, then we'll get together and sort through things. He wants me to keep working with him."

"Well, that's good news, right?" Denise said, tucking a piece of my hair behind my ear.

"I don't know." I closed my eyes and shook my head. "I don't know if I can do it."

"Fuck, yes, you can do it! You're *great* at your job. I know it,

Keith knows it, everyone knows it."

I looked down and picked at my cuticles. "I'm just so fucking hurt right now." I buried my face in my hands again as my body began to shake.

She pulled me into her arms, and I rested my head on her shoulder. "I know, sweet girl. I know. But you're gonna get through this. You are."

"I wanna go home, Denise," I choked out through my sobs. "I just wanna go home."

"You are home, babe."

I sank deeper into her, my heart breaking even harder because she didn't understand what I meant.

I needed to leave her.

I needed to leave LA.

I needed to go back to Chicago.

CHAPTER TWENTY-EIGHT
EVA

AUGUST 1989

"So you're sure about this, Eva? There's no changing your mind?" Keith stared at me over the steaming cup of coffee in front of him.

I nodded, taking a sip from my own mug. "I'm sure."

We were settled into a booth at Canter's on Fairfax. I'd dodged his calls for several days, but when I finally reached out to see how Eric was doing, he'd insisted we meet up. I knew it was best to tell him my news face-to-face, so I'd agreed to join him for breakfast.

"Damn," he said, disappointment in his eyes.

"I'm sorry, Keith. I've got to get away from LA. So much of it reminds me of—" I swallowed, Danny's name stuck in my throat. "Well, you know. I just can't be here right now."

"I know, kiddo." He squeezed my hand across the table. "You didn't deserve that."

I nodded, averting my eyes so he wouldn't see them start to glisten.

He slid his hand back and picked up his mug. "So have you told everyone? Will and Matt?"

"No. I need to call them, I guess. I've really only told my roommate."

"How'd she take it?"

I sighed and shrugged. "She wishes I'd stay. But she gets it."

"This life's not for everyone, so I get it, too. It can be hard. Especially with everything that happened."

"How's he doing?" I asked, ashamed I'd waited to reach out to Keith about Eric. I knew a phone call to him would lead to a conversation about the future, and I hadn't been ready to talk about that until now.

"I'm flying out to Denver tomorrow to bring him back. The doctor said he's ready for rehab. It's all set up, so I'll take him straight there."

"You're amazing to be there for him like this," I said as the waitress refilled our cups. "I wish there was something I could do."

Keith looked across the table at me. "There is, Eva. Don't leave until you see him."

I chewed my bottom lip and stared down at the table.

"Look, I don't know if you know this, but he was your biggest champion. In his sober moments, he'd tell me all the time how amazing you were, how good you were for the band." He reached over and touched my arm, causing me to lift my eyes. "And he always wanted to make sure you were taken care of. *Always.*"

My chest tightened as I tried to swallow the lump that had formed in my throat. I thought about the day he insisted Keith hire me...the time he stopped Jesse Trainor from harassing me...the night we sat on the rooftop in Cleveland eating Chinese food.

"Did you, um...did you tell him about Danny yet?"

Keith shook his head. "I wasn't able to speak to him while he was detoxing. But I'm sure he'll ask when I see him."

I licked my lips, my mouth suddenly dry. "What are you gonna tell him?"

Keith shrugged, taking a deep breath. "I guess the truth, as fucking tragic as it is. To be honest, Eva, I don't know if the band's gonna survive without Danny. You know he and Eric were magic when it came to songwriting. Will and Matt are good musicians, but they can't fill those shoes."

I nodded, knowing he was right. "So how do I see him? I mean, when can he have visitors at rehab?"

"The admissions counselor said to give it a couple weeks. Let him settle in and get acclimated to the facility."

"Okay." I placed my elbows on the table, resting my chin in my hands. "Just, um…just call me when you find out the details."

"I will. First thing."

I looked across the table into his kind eyes. I was gonna miss the hell out of him. "Thank you, Keith," I said, trying to stop my chin from quivering. "For everything you've done for me…for Eric. You truly are one of the good guys in this fucked-up business."

He smiled and averted his eyes, which had begun to glisten. "Enough with that. You're gonna ruin my reputation as a hard-ass manager. I've worked tirelessly to get that distinction, you know."

I chuckled and swiped my fingers under my own eyes. "Okay, no crying."

He winked at me as he pulled his wallet out of his back pocket and handed me his business card. "Do me a favor and keep this. Because if you ever wanna come back to LA, all you gotta do is call me."

"Deal." I held the card tight in my hand. "And whenever you're on tour in Chicago, you better look me up. And score me the best seats in the house."

"There will always be a spot beside me backstage for Eva Holloway," he said, his smile reaching his eyes for the first time since we'd sat down. "*Always.*"

CHAPTER TWENTY-NINE
EVA

SEPTEMBER 1989

The rain splattered in large drops on the windshield as I pulled into a parking space at the rehab facility. I shifted the car into park and inhaled deeply, gripping the steering wheel and closing my eyes. The breath did little to stop the pounding in my chest. My nerves had been on fire since the night before when I realized I was going to see Eric for the first time since he'd collapsed on stage.

I'd talked to him briefly on the phone a week after Keith checked him into the center. He spoke softly, almost mumbling at times, his voice tinged with sadness. I promised I'd see him the next Sunday and immediately burst into tears after I hung up the phone, unable to erase the memory of that night from my mind.

Taking one last deep breath, I opened the car door and hurried to the front of the building. The lobby was far less institutional than I expected. Modern furniture and tall plants were placed throughout the expansive space, reminding me more of a spa than what I'd imagined for a rehab center. It smelled faintly of lemon and peppermint.

I fumbled with my car keys, trying to shove them in my purse as I walked toward the woman at the reception desk. "Hi, I'm here to see Eric Stratton. I'm Eva Holloway."

FOR EVA

She flipped through several papers on her desk, then smiled up at me.

"No problem. They'll take everyone back to the community room in a few minutes." She pointed to my purse. "I'll just need your handbag. We'll keep it locked away up here while you're visiting."

"Of course," I said, passing it to her.

"Feel free to wait over there," she said, motioning to a small group of other visitors, some standing, some seated in the area to my left.

I nodded and walked over to an empty spot on one of the off-white leather couches and chewed on my thumbnail as I watched water droplets race down the large glass windowpane, wondering how in the hell I'd ended up here.

I'm just Eva from Illinois, I thought to myself, remembering what Eric had called me my very first time at band rehearsal.

My stomach churned as the double doors behind me clicked open, and I turned my head to see a man in jeans and a polo shirt walking toward the group.

"You guys ready to go back?" he asked, clapping his hands together in front of him.

We all filed toward him, as he led us through the doors. My mouth was dry, and the churning in my stomach ramped up as we walked down a brightly lit hallway. I swallowed hard, trying to contain the emotion building behind my eyes.

We turned the corner and entered a large room with a couple of couches, tables, and chairs scattered throughout. A giant TV playing the Rams game sat against one of the walls, and there was a kitchenette with a refrigerator along another. As I scanned the room, my eyes landed on long dark-blond hair partially hanging over the couch in front of the television. Eric turned his head and surveyed the room, his gaze finally landing on me. His lips slowly shifted into a smile, and I pressed mine together to keep them from trembling.

He pushed himself up from the couch and started toward

me. He was wearing jeans and a plain white T-shirt, and for the first time in a long time, there was color in his face and life in his eyes. I threw my hand over my mouth, a wave of relief washing over me. My shaky legs carried me across the room, and I crashed into his chest, throwing my arms around him as the floodgates I'd fought so hard to keep closed broke open.

He held me close, placing his chin on my head and chuckled softly. "Good to see you, too."

I choked out a small laugh and wiped my cheeks.

"Sorry," I managed, rolling my eyes. "I promised myself I wouldn't do that."

"It's okay," Eric said, looking down at me. "We feel a lot of shit in here."

He winked and gave me a tender smile as I brushed at the damp spots my tears had left on his shirt.

"Sorry again."

"You're forgiven," he said, laughing and motioning to a glass door across the room. "You wanna go outside? There's a covered patio."

I brought my eyes up to his and nodded. "Yeah, that'd be good."

"Hang on, I have to get a light from the staff," he said, pulling a pack of Marlboros out of his pocket and placing a cigarette between his lips. "You want one?"

"I'm okay. You know I can't smoke those Reds that you and Dan—" I cut myself off as I started to mention Danny's name. It was so instinctual to talk about him, like he was still part of my life. "That *you* smoke," I continued.

A twinge of uneasiness flashed across Eric's face before he nodded and called over to the man who'd led us back to the room. Eric motioned to his cigarette, and the man followed us outside, allowing Eric to light his smoke.

The patio was decorated with cushioned wrought iron furniture, large hanging baskets of ferns, and several large ceramic planters filled with colorful flowers. There was an earthy scent in the air as the rain continued to fall. I sat sideways on the small couch, tucking one leg under the other, and Eric sat beside me, his long legs spread apart.

"So," I began, running my fingers under my eyes "I don't really know what to say. I guess 'how are you' is a good start?"

I laughed nervously, and Eric smiled, taking a drag off his cigarette.

"Besides *really* fucking wanting a drink and a few lines, I'm doing okay. What about you?" he asked, gently touching my arm.

My face flushed, and a spark of electricity traveled through me. It caught me off guard, and I looked away quickly. "Oh, I'm, uh, fine." I looked down, picking at the frayed denim around the hole in the knee of my jeans. "How was the hospital in Denver?"

He glanced up at the corrugated metal roof of the pergola covering the patio, smoke streaming from his lips. "Imagine having the worst case of the flu you've ever had. But you also can't sleep, your heart won't stop racing, and you think everyone is out to get you."

"Christ." I winced, then poked his knee with my finger. "But hey, you did it. You made it through."

"Yeah. Now to make it through my time here. And then somehow stay sober once I get out."

"So what's the plan while you're here?"

He shrugged. "I mean, everyday there's group therapy and individual therapy. They put me on meds to help with the mental…stuff." He took another drag off his smoke and looked over at me. "Fun times, right?"

We were silent for a moment, listening to the rain drumming on the tin roof, and I studied his face. I watched as the corners of his mouth turned downward, and his eyes flickered to the ground. "You know that stuff with my, um…my mom? It wasn't true. I didn't know she was sick. Her husband made all that shit up about trying to contact me. And having to call him to find out she'd died…it made me so fucking angry…so fucking *hurt*. I didn't know what to do except whatever I could to numb that pain." He paused and took a drag off his cigarette. "I know you guys killed the story, but I need you to believe I would've helped her, Eva. Even after all the shit she said and did to me…I would've helped."

"I knew it wasn't true. You're not that person, Eric."

"And I know you're hurt, too," he said, sighing. "Keith told me what happened with Danny."

My chest tightened at the mention of his name, and I swallowed, trying to relieve the tension. "Yeah, he…Well, he's just not the person I thought he was."

Eric snorted. "He's a fucking asshole, is what he is."

I raised my eyebrows and nodded, a loud sigh escaping my lips. "Yeah. That, too."

"You were too good for him, Eva."

His sky blue eyes met mine in a stare that sent a strange rush of warmth through my body. I broke our connection when the door opened behind me and two people stepped outside, settling in at a table on the far end of the patio. I looked back at Eric, his gaze still focused on me. My stomach fluttered and I cast my eyes downward, picking at the dark polish on my nails.

"Eva, I—" He cut himself off as he ran his hand along the back of his neck and closed his eyes. "I wanna say thank you. You know…for everything you did for me. They told me I'm alive because of the CPR. Because of you."

I opened my mouth to speak but closed it when he placed his hand on my knee. "I know I said some really shitty things to you. Things I didn't mean and I wish I could take back. But you still saved me, even after all that."

I paused and looked down, trying to swallow the lump in my throat. "I, um…I couldn't let you…well, you know. This world needs you, Eric. We all need you."

"Maybe that's true." He ground his cigarette into the ashtray on the table beside him. "Maybe we've got a lot more ahead of us."

"I know you do," I said, my mouth turning dry again as I thought about what I had to tell him. "But I'm, uh…I'm going back to Chicago."

Eric furrowed his brow and shook his head. "What did you say?"

"I just…I can't be in LA anymore."

"Because of Danny?" He narrowed his eyes. "*Fuck Danny.*"

I closed my eyes and sighed. "It was a mistake for me to come out here."

Eric winced, and I corrected myself. "I mean, not a mistake meeting you and Matt and Will and Keith. I'm so grateful for all of you," I assured him, reaching out to touch his arm. "It's just better that I go back home. Get a normal job. Live a normal life. I got so caught up seeing Danny again, and I need to figure shit out, away from LA and this crazy business."

He leaned forward, placing his elbows on his knees and resting his head in his hands as his hair fell around his face. "I don't know what to say." He paused and brought his head up to look at me. "Is it *just* because of Danny? Or is it because of what happened with *me*? Because you're so fucking good at what you do, Eva. Are sure you even wanna be *normal*—whatever that means?"

"It's Danny, it's this city, it's the business. I didn't know what I was getting into, and I don't think I'm cut out for it. I'm not…I don't know what the word is…*tough* enough, I guess? But I promise we'll stay in touch. And I'll be back out to visit Denise and I'll see you then and…"

My voice trailed off as Eric scrubbed his hands along his face and sat back with a sharp inhale. "I guess I thought Will and Matt and I would get the band back together eventually and you would, you know, *be there with us.*" He looked over at me. "And by the way, don't ever say you're not tough. You're one of the toughest people I've ever met."

I lowered my eyes and smiled, thinking of the good times

we'd all had together—when the band got signed, the first time we heard the finished album, the excitement of going on tour, and anticipation about what the future held. I remembered the shock of Eric telling Keith to hire me. As the pictures fluttered through my mind, I looked up at Eric to see his mouth was turned down.

"I'll never forget my time with you guys," I promised. "And I *know* you'll get through all this and be an even bigger success than you already are. So big, in fact, you won't even remember Eva from Illinois."

He locked eyes with me. "Trust me when I say there is absolutely no chance of me ever forgetting you, Eva."

The strange tingling sensation returned, this time settling in my stomach. "I just want to be happy, Eric. And I don't think I can do that here."

A look of resignation swept over his face, as he leaned back and stared at the metal roof, still resonating with the sound of raindrops. He swallowed so hard I could see the muscles in his neck strain. I opened my mouth to speak, to tell him how much he meant to me, but his words came first.

"I don't know quite how to say this, so I'm sure I'm gonna screw it up," he began, taking a deep breath and turning his head to me. "But for as long as I can remember, I didn't feel like I deserved happiness. I acted like I deserved the whole goddamn world because it felt a whole lot better than trying to deal with all the shit, you know? But I didn't believe it. I believed my mom and the fucking assholes she brought around who told me I was a pain in the ass. I believed the people at school who told me I was a fuckup. I believed I was nothing more than an... *inconvenience*. But that day you met Mandy and came running into the apartment screaming about the potential record deal, you told me I deserved good things. And I've never forgotten that."

His words crashed into me, fracturing my insides. He leaned over and ran his thumb along my cheek as a single tear fell from my eye.

"Now it's my turn to tell you that *you* deserve happiness, too, Eva," he said, our eyes locking as he cupped my face with his hand. "So will going back to Chicago make you happy?"

I felt like he was staring straight into the saddest parts of me, trying to find a way to heal them. I leaned into his hand, the sensation that had settled in my stomach racing to my brain, spinning a tangled web of thoughts and feelings that didn't make sense because they couldn't possibly be real. Surely, I was confused. I missed Danny and was searching for something to ease the pain. But Eric's touch was so warm...so comforting.

He leaned forward, searching my eyes, almost as if he was waiting for something he knew existed deep inside me to finally break through to the surface. My pulse quickened as he began to close the distance between us.

No, Eva. No. You know what you need to do. You've made up your mind.

A soft gasp escaped my lips as I quickly turned my head downward, and his hand slipped from my cheek. I peered cautiously back up at him, knowing if I looked directly into his eyes again, the confusion would only grow stronger. He turned his gaze to the falling rain.

"Yeah," I said. "I need to go back."

He pressed his lips together and nodded, still focused on the steady stream of water pouring from the sky. "Then you should go," he said, reaching for my hand and squeezing it gently. "Go home, Eva, and be happy."

CHAPTER THIRTY

OCTOBER 1989 - APRIL 1990

October 29, 1989

Eva,

I'm now officially sprung! Keith picked me up yesterday morning, and I'm getting settled into his guest house. His son has already decided I was brought here for the sole purpose of being his new best friend. We just finished our third water gun fight in the twenty-four hours since I moved in. Not the same as the wet T-shirt contests I'm used to, but fun, nonetheless. Keith's wife tried to tell him to cool his jets, but hell, I don't mind. I never got to do much of that stuff when I was a kid, so it's almost like I get a do-over.

I hope everything worked out with the apartment you were looking at and you've been having fun hanging with your old friends up there. Matt and Will came to visit a couple weeks ago. We talked about putting the band back together, but who knows if it'll happen. Matt's doing studio work, and Will got an offer to play with a band out of Seattle who just fired their drummer. I can't remember their name, but they're supposed to be the next big thing. I don't wanna hold him back, so I told him to do what he needed to do.

I had a lot of time to write in rehab. It was good to get shit out, and I think there are some potential songs in there. I wonder if they'll ever be heard or just remain words on the pages of a notebook. I wonder what I want them to be. I wonder what I want, period.

FOR EVA

Keith told me I could stay here as long as I needed, so I guess I'll take it one day at a time, as they say in NA. Yes, I have officially become a twelve-stepper (ha ha).

Speaking of, I've got a meeting in thirty minutes, so I should head out. Lemme know how you're doing, and take care of yourself, Eva from Illinois.

Eric

———

November 20, 1989
Eric,

So sorry, I feel like it's taken me a million years to write back! I am so fucking proud of you! I hope you celebrated properly when you got out—and by that I mean went to El Compadre and stuffed your face with chimichangas…sans the flaming margaritas, of course (ha ha)! As for me, the original apartment fell through, but I found an even better one (yay!) and have been trying to get settled. I just got back from an interview with an advertising agency downtown, and I think it went really well. Not sure if it's what I wanna do for the rest of my life, but I really liked the person I met with and got a good vibe about the company. Keep your fingers crossed for me.

Anyway, things are good, but I miss everyone. Well, not everyone. But you know what I mean. Denise is flying in for Thanksgiving with my family and will likely freeze her ass off in this fucking ridiculous weather. Middle of November and we've already had snow! Speaking of my family, I was surprised I didn't get a chorus of I told you so's from my dad when I moved back. I think he might actually be glad to have me here, which feels weird and good at the same time. Maybe we can finally talk about my mom. Or maybe not. I don't know…do you think I should tell him how I feel? Show him my tattoo? I'm scared of what he'll say. Or won't say.

Anyway, enough about me. Tell me more about what's going on with you. Have you made any decisions on future plans? What am I missing in LA besides reasonable weather?

Eva

———

December 15, 1989
Eva,

I cannot believe I'm sending someone an actual fucking Christmas card, but I saw this in a shop off Melrose the other day and couldn't resist. Because what's not funny about a card with George Michael on it saying "Wake Me Up Before You Ho Ho"?

My sense of humor is off, isn't it? You can tell me.

Anyway...

So remember I told you I was looking back at what I'd written in rehab? I finally picked up an old acoustic of Keith's the other day and put some of the words to music. I had him listen to a few things I'm working on, and he really dug them. Matt's talking about moving back home to San Francisco, and Will's with that other band, but I've been thinking about trying to put together something new. I don't know if it's a whole new group, or if I'll do solo shit or what, but I miss being on stage. I really do. I need a purpose, I guess. My days are filled with twelve-step meetings and writing (oh, and water gun fights—still), but I need more. I gotta be honest and say that going back into the music scene scares the shit out of me, though. So many opportunities for...well, you know. I'm gonna talk to my sponsor and see what he thinks. I just miss it so much, Eva. So much.

I know when we talked on the phone last you said you were gonna talk to your dad. Did you do it? I've been thinking about that and wondering but didn't want to call and bring it up if it didn't go like you hoped. Let me know.

I guess this is where I sign off and say Merry Christmas and shit. Ha ha. Seriously, though, I hope you have a good one. Let's talk soon, OK?

Eric

———

FOR EVA

January 10, 1990
Eric,

HAPPY NEW YEAR!!! And new decade! How the hell is it 1990?

I'm sorry I've missed your calls. The holidays and my job have had me crazy. I'm calling this weekend though, I promise! Of course, you'll probably get my call before this letter. :) I'll keep this one short since we're definitely talking soon, but I can't wait for you to tell me more about the new music. It needs to be heard, Eric. YOU need to be heard. And I know it's scary to think about re-entering that world, but I know you'll stay strong. Think of all the musicians who've gotten sober and continued their careers with even more success than they had before. If they can do it, you sure as hell can. Because you are Eric Fucking Stratton. And don't you ever forget it.

Last thing—I did talk to my dad. I'll tell you more on the phone, but it was so good, Eric. So good. He actually cried when he saw the tattoo and hugged me like he hadn't hugged me since I was a little girl. Thank you for encouraging me to talk to him.

OK, enough before I start to cry myself! But I hope you had a good holiday with Keith and his family...and that his son didn't get any new water guns for Christmas. :)

Talk soon!
Eva

February 25, 1990
Eva,

So I did it. I fucking did it. I went into the studio, and I recorded two of the songs I wrote. After hearing about you talking to your dad...about how brave you were to do that...I decided I could be brave, too. So, I rounded up some of the guys I knew from the old days and sang my fucking heart out. I gave the demo to Mandy, and she fucking loved it. She actually fucking loved it, and the label wants to talk with me and Keith about a solo deal. Can you fucking believe this? I'm, like, happy and scared and freaking out all at once. I don't even know what the fuck to do. I mean, I want the deal...I wanna be back on stage, you know? But I'm terrified of what that means.

Keith told the guys I recorded with absolutely no booze or drugs in the studio. But you know once I get back out there, it's gonna be all around me. I mean, if I can actually put a band together, are they gonna be cool with keeping that shit under wraps? I really fucking hope so because it felt so goddamn good to be in the studio again. To hear the songs really come to life. To know I can still write and sing and do what I love to do. But it also felt different without you there. Like, I kept looking over and expecting to see you sitting on the couch, your eyes closed, your head swaying back and forth, like you did when we recorded the first album. I miss seeing that.

Anyway, I'll send you the demo if you wanna hear it. I know you'll tell me if you think it's shit because you never were one to hold back. :)

Talk to you soon, I hope.

Eric

————

March 30, 1990

Eric,

You're right. Demo's shit. Hang it up, man.

But seriously…what the fuck did you send me? Because I'm pretty sure it's one fourth of a multiplatinum album. It's good, Eric. It's soooo good. Please, please, PLEASE tell me the label is offering you a deal because I need this to happen. YOU need this to happen. THE WORLD needs this to happen!

I don't even know what to say about what's happening with me because I'm so excited for you! The job's fine. Might go to the grocery store later, then get a drink afterward with a friend if I'm feeling crazy. :) But hey, I said I wanted normal, right?

It's still cold here, and I'm so ready for warm weather. Maybe I should think about coming out to visit soon. I'll call Denise and see what we can figure out. Just promise me if I do I'll get to hear these songs live. Because they're amazing…and I really fucking mean that.

So yeah, while I'm waiting for the sun to come out and the

FOR EVA

flowers to bloom, talk to me about what it's like to see a ball of light in the sky every day. And palm trees. I miss them. Especially those really tall ones on Sunset. I sound like such a tourist, I know, but they never ceased to amaze me.

Write or call me soon!

Eva

—————

April 30, 1990

Eva,

I just left a message on your machine, but I'm writing anyway because I'm so fucking excited I can't stand it. They offered me a deal. The label actually offered me a solo deal. I can't believe they wanna take another chance on me after everything that happened. I dunno if Mandy or Keith somehow talked them into it, or if the songs are really that good or what, but holy shit! This is happening! I'm going down there to sign all the papers tomorrow.

Eight months sober and a new record deal. I should be as happy as a fucking pig in shit…or whatever it is they say. And I am happy. Trust me, I know how lucky I am to be where I'm at right now. But I'd be a hell of a lot happier if you were here. I miss fighting over the last crab rangoon with you. I miss you yelling at me when I'm being an asshole. I miss singing every song KISS ever made and annoying the shit out of everyone else in the room. I miss…I miss your smile, Eva. You have no idea how much I miss that smile.

But I guess I'm telling you now, huh?

Love,

Eric

CHAPTER THIRTY-ONE
EVA

MAY 1990

You have no idea how much I miss that smile.

I stared at the letter, the paper shaking slightly in my hands. The black ink began to blur, and my lips parted, leaving just enough room for a tiny "huh" to escape. I placed my thumbnail between my front teeth and looked up from the letter, out the window, to the sidewalk below. A couple strolled along hand in hand, and Eric's words kneaded at my heart as thoughts coursed through my brain.

Does that mean…what if…does he…

No. Don't be silly, Eva. You're friends. Friends miss each other.

But did friends' stomachs flutter at the thought of being missed? And did their minds take flight when they got a letter with a signature that read *love*?

I blinked and shook my head, my platinum bob brushing my flushed cheeks as I folded the paper and placed it on the small dining table beside me. I was already running late. No time to overthink.

I grabbed my satchel bag, swung it over my shoulder, and plucked at my freshly cut bangs in the mirror before heading out the door and down the stairs to my old VW Rabbit parked up the street. I hopped in and immediately rolled the window down. It was a warm Saturday afternoon, and I didn't have to think twice when one of my college girlfriends called and asked me to meet her for lunch and cocktails on the patio at one of our favorite spots.

As I made my way down Clark Street, traffic picked up, and I wondered if I should've taken the "L" even though driving with the windows down and tunes cranked up had sounded like a much better idea. I twisted the knob on my car stereo, bits of songs blipping from the speakers, until I settled on one of the local college stations. I turned up the volume on the Jane's Addiction tune playing as the sun beamed in on my shoulders, covered only by the thin straps of my short flowered sundress. I reached over and dug through my bag for my cigarettes. My attempts to quit since I'd moved back to Chicago had failed repeatedly, though I promised myself one of my top New Year's resolutions for 1991 would be to stop for good. But I had eight months left with my Marlboro Lights, and I intended to spend some quality time with them.

I pushed in the car's lighter, singing along with the radio while I waited for it to pop. As I reached down to retrieve it, my eyes flickered from the road for a second, and before I knew what was happening, my body was thrown forward against my seat belt, and there was a loud thud. I looked directly in front of me to see I was bumper to bumper with a black BMW at a red light.

Fuck. Double fuck.

The driver raised his head to look back at me in his rearview mirror. I scrubbed my hands over my face and sighed as the light turned green, and he signaled out the window that he was going to pull over to the side of the street. I parked behind him, muttering a "goddamnit," and turned off the radio as a tall athletic figure stepped out of the BMW and surveyed the back of the car for damage. He was dressed in long gym shorts, a T-shirt, and a baseball cap.

Great. A sporty asshole in a Beamer. Just what I need.

I hung my head and opened my door, dragging myself out of

the car as the owner of the luxury vehicle walked toward me. The accident was clearly my fault, so I decided to fess up.

"Shit, I'm so sorry," I blurted out. "I was reaching down to light my cigarette, and I wasn't paying attention. Totally my fault. Full admission of guilt." I laughed nervously as I swept my sunglasses onto the top of my head.

All of what had to be six foot two of him stopped in front of me.

"Cigarette?" he said, narrowing his eyes at me. "You shouldn't smoke. It's bad for you."

I nodded. "Yeah, so I can give you my insurance info or whatever and—Wait, what?"

"Smoking. It's bad for you."

I looked up at him, tilting my head and squinting. "Oh, yeah, I know. I'm quitting next year." I turned and opened my car door, reaching into the passenger's seat for my bag. I pulled it out and began to dig through my wallet.

"Fuck, I know it's here somewhere," I mumbled as I rifled through old receipts and credit cards, dropping several that bounced off my Doc Martens onto the street.

He reached down and picked them up, handing them to me as a smile spread across his face.

"Thanks. Can't ever find anything when you need it, huh?" Another nervous laugh escaped my lips as I gave up the search, plopping my wallet into my bag and leaning against my car door.

He took off his ball cap and rubbed his hand along his dark brown hair before placing it back on his head, the smile still planted firmly on his lips.

Damn. Is he kinda hot? Like in an I-play-sports-and-drink-beer-with-my-old-frat-brothers kind of way?

"It's okay," he said, chuckling at my frenzied attempt to find the insurance card. "Really. I don't think it even did any damage."

"Seriously?" I asked, pushing myself off my car and heading over to assess the situation as he followed. "I mean, I don't care about my car, but there's definitely some missing paint on yours."

"Eh, that's easy," he said, brushing my fingers as we touched the chipped spots.

A wave of red heat rose to my face as I instinctively pulled back my hand and tucked it away, crossing my arms over my chest.

"Anyway," I said, clearing my throat and standing upright. "I'll give you my number, and you can call me if you want that insurance info. I'm sure it's at home."

He cocked his head for a moment as if he were considering something, then nodded. "Yeah, okay." He paused and stuck his hand out. "I'm Aaron, by the way."

"Eva," I said, grasping his strong hand and smiling. I was taken in by his big blue-gray eyes and continued to hold his grip until I realized I was in a complete daze. I shook my head and blinked. "Yeah, so, let me give you that." Once again, I dug through my bag, finally producing a pen and random gum wrapper on which I scribbled my name and phone number.

"Thanks, Eva…Holloway," he said, examining the wrapper and grinning.

"You're welcome, Aaron…"

"Mitchell."

I nodded, sneaking another peek at him before averting my gaze. "Well, I'm supposed to meet my friend, so…"

"Yeah, I've got a softball game to get to," Aaron said, motioning down the street.

"Okay, well, please call me, and I'll give you all my info. Seriously. I feel like an idiot."

He laughed. "Don't feel like an idiot. But *do* stop smoking. Those things'll kill you."

"1991. It's my year, I can feel it." I raised my fist and chuckled as he stepped backward, then turned and headed toward his car.

Aaron looked back at me once more and smiled before

getting in his BMW and pulling out into traffic. I took a deep breath and leaned against the hood of my Rabbit. I watched as he disappeared down Clark Street, putting my hand to my head and wondering if it was woozy from the impact of the crash or the guy I'd crashed into.

———

I dropped my keys on the small table by my apartment door and walked into the kitchen to grab a glass of water. Lunch had extended late into the afternoon and involved several large margaritas which had me absolutely parched and a little sleepy. I guzzled the liquid as I pressed the blinking red button on my answering machine and plopped on the couch.

"Hey, it's me." Eric's voice flowed from the speaker. "Sorry I missed your call last night. I was at a meeting, then Keith and I went out to dinner to talk about the solo project. Give me a call, I'll fill you in. Good stuff happening soon. Talk to you later."

I smiled and rested my head on the back on the couch. He missed me. I missed him. Because we were friends.

But what if…

"Hey, Eva," the next caller began as the tape continued to play. I jerked my head up and looked over at the machine. "It's Aaron. You know, from the car thing earlier. Don't worry, I haven't decided to sue," he added with a laugh.

I gasped and scooted to the edge of the cushion.

"So I was just thinking, maybe you could take me to dinner to make up for the accident instead of going through all the insurance crap. Or actually, maybe I should take you to dinner. Unless you have a boyfriend or a husband, in which case this is completely inappropriate." He paused, and I stared at the machine with wide eyes. "So, long story short, if boyfriend-slash-husband doesn't exist and you wanna do something, give me a call at 555-6431. Hopefully, I'll talk to you soon."

I leaned forward, my elbows on my knees and my hands covering my mouth.

FOR EVA

Holy shit. Is this for real?

I reached over and pressed the rewind button to play the message again and heard the same words from just a minute before.

I couldn't imagine I was in any way Aaron's type. And though he was much too preppy for me, there was something about him that intrigued me. By all standards, he was a good-looking guy. *Really* good-looking. But his hair was short and he played sports, not instruments, so naturally, I was confused about the instant attraction. Because as much as I'd craved a normal life when I left LA, old habits still died hard.

I retrieved a pen and piece of paper from the junk drawer in the kitchen and played the message once more, this time jotting down the digits of his phone number. I sat back on the couch and stared at them for a good five minutes before picking up the cordless receiver. As the line started to ring, I closed my eyes, took a deep breath, and prayed this wasn't a bad decision.

"Hello?"

"Um, hey, this is Eva. Is this Aaron?" I clenched my teeth and opened one eye.

"Eva Holloway!"

I laughed and relaxed my jaw a bit. "Yep, it's me. From the gum wrapper."

"Am I to assume that you calling me means there is no boyfriend-slash-husband who heard my message and now wants to kill me?"

"Your assumption is correct." I crossed my leg, bobbing it up and down to release the nervous energy flowing through my body.

"Good. Also, is it weird that you hit my car, and I immediately called and asked you out? I don't think I've ever done this before. But then again, you've never hit my car before. So, first time for everything."

My God, he's charming. And funny. And seriously, what is going on here? Am I really attracted to a guy who probably belongs to the

Chicago Sport & Social Club and wears a suit and tie to work every day?

Well, you did say you wanted normal. And here it is being served up on a silver platter.

"I don't think it's weird." I paused and titled my head. "I think I'm actually glad you called."

"You *think?*"

I laughed. "I *am* glad you called. I'm surprised, that's all."

"What? Guys don't usually just randomly call you up and ask you out?"

"Ha! No. Not at all." I paused, letting the truth of that sink in. I'd turned down the two dates I'd been asked out on since moving back to the city. It had taken me months to get over Danny, and it still hurt to think about what he'd done.

I cleared my throat and changed the subject. "So did you win your softball game?"

"We did. I even hit a home run. Does that impress you?"

"I think I'm ready to come over to your place right now, forget dinner," I joked.

He chuckled. "Speaking of dinner, does next Saturday work for you?"

"Sounds amazing."

My eyes widened, and I folded my lips inward, unable to believe those words had actually come out of my mouth.

"Great. I'll call you this week to firm up plans."

"I guess it's a date, then," I said, still in awe of what was happening.

"You *guess?*"

"I'm doing it again, aren't I? It absolutely *is* a date." I laughed, finally allowing a grin to spread across my face.

I swore I could almost hear his smile through the phone before he spoke. "Believe me when I say I cannot wait."

CHAPTER THIRTY-TWO

MAY 1990

May 27, 1990

Denise,

I miss you. I love you. I ADORE you. And I may be buttering you up because you're going to kill me for not telling you this sooner. But last time I called, I ran up a ridiculously high long-distance phone bill, and I'm but a poor junior marketing associate. Plus, I kinda wanted to wait to see how things played out. So here's the deal: I met someone. A couple weeks ago. And I know you hate me right now, but I promise I'll tell you everything!

His name is Aaron. He's 29 and an attorney with a big law firm in the city. He has short hair, no tattoos, and wears polo shirts. I'll let you go ahead and freak out now.

(Pause)

OK, hopefully, you're done. I know he doesn't sound anything like my type, but I'm into him, Denise. I really am. I rear-ended him on Clark St., and he was so nice about it, and he called me afterward and asked me out. And for some reason—I don't know if it was his eyes or his smile or what—I said yes. And we've pretty much been hanging out every night since, even though he works a ton. Sometimes we meet for a late dinner out, or he'll come over and I'll order takeout or cook. Me cooking—what the hell?! But it all feels so… normal. So…how life is supposed to be…right?

It sounds crazy, like we're complete opposites, but something about it works. I think. Who knows, it's only been a few weeks, maybe it'll fizzle out. Maybe by the time you get this and call to yell at me for not telling you sooner, I'll be dating some long-suffering musician and hanging out at underground clubs every night, pining away for him while he pines away for his career.

The more things change, the more they stay the same, I guess.

All right, I'm signing off, but I'll talk to you soon. Use that big, fat finance salary to call me! :)

Love you!

Eva

CHAPTER THIRTY-THREE

JUNE 1990

June 6, 1990

Eric,

So sorry it's been a while since we've talked/I've written! Things have been so busy at work I've barely had time to breathe. But I've been thinking about you and wondering how the solo project is going. You're probably recording as I'm writing this. Didn't you say the album was scheduled for a September release?

I know you mentioned on the phone last month that you were looking at a place to rent in Studio City. Just close enough to Hollywood without actually being in Hollywood—smart thinking. :) Have you moved out of Keith's yet? Or are you still dodging water bullets from his son?

Let me know how you're doing!

Eva

CHAPTER THIRTY-FOUR
EVA

JUNE 1990

"**I**'m just saying, Eva," Aaron explained as he stepped into my apartment, shutting the door behind him. "How hard is it to cook a fucking steak medium rare?"

I sighed and tossed my purse onto the dining table. "I know, babe, but it wasn't the waiter's fault."

Aaron slipped off his shoes and flopped onto the couch, aiming the remote at the television. "Do you want me to go back and apologize?" he asked as the TV sprang to life. "I still left him a decent tip."

"I just think that—" I yelped as he grabbed my waist and pulled me onto his lap.

"You just think what?" he said, warming my insides with his blue-gray eyes.

I inhaled the scent of his cologne—cedar with a hint of spice—and ran my thumb along his jaw. "I just think you could've gone a little easier on him."

He cupped my chin in his hand and kissed me softly. "I'm sorry. It was a long day at work."

My cheek brushed against his, a hint of stubble scratching my skin as I whispered into his ear. "Well, in that case, we should probably go into the bedroom and—"

The trill of the phone on the table next to us startled me,

217

and I pulled away, reaching for the receiver. Aaron grabbed my hand and placed it back on his shoulder as his lips moved down my neck. "Let the machine get it."

I smiled, giggling and throwing my head back as his mouth made its way to my chest, and he began to unbutton the front of my dress. I barely heard the outgoing message and beep that followed, lost in the anticipation of what was to come.

"Eva Alessandra Holloway! Pick up the fucking phone right now, or I'm never fucking speaking to you again!" Denise's voice bellowed out of the answering machine.

Aaron slumped against the couch as I popped up to grab the cordless receiver from its base.

"Babe, I love you so much, but can you call me back tomorrow? I—"

"I will *not* call you back tomorrow because I checked my mail for the first time in a week, and all of a sudden, I'm standing here with a letter in my hand telling me you're dating some hotshot attorney!"

"Okay, I can talk for a second." I bit my lip and slipped Aaron an apologetic glance. He huffed, rolling his eyes and flipping the television to ESPN. I mouthed a quick *sorry* before retrieving my cigarettes from my purse and stepping out on the small deck off my apartment.

"What the *fuck*, Eva? Why didn't you call me?"

I cradled the receiver between my ear and shoulder as I lit my cigarette. "Because long-distance charges are killing me! It isn't my fault you didn't check your mail for a week. Or that you haven't called me in ages, by the way."

"What can I say, work has been nuts. And this is *phone* news! You could've called, and I would've called you back." She paused, and I could practically hear her grinning through the phone. "Is he there now? Were you guys about to get it on?"

I chuckled and took a long drag off my smoke. "Maybe."

"Oh my God, I cannot believe this," she squealed. "I need to know everything. And I mean, *everything*. Size, shape, technique…"

"Denise!" I leaned against the brick wall, crossing my feet. "I'm not just fucking him. I think it's kinda…I don't know… serious, I guess?"

"Well, obviously, if you're *cooking* for him," she said. "Who are you, and what has this man done to you?"

I smiled, goose bumps popping up on my arms. "I don't know. It's crazy because we're so outwardly different, but I think that's what we dig about each other. It's *exciting.*"

"I assume he's seen your tattoo?"

"He loves my tattoo."

"He knows you wear combat boots?"

"I was wearing them when I met him."

"And he's aware you don't typically date men who wear shirts with collars?"

"He knows about Danny, if that's what you're asking."

A long exhale traveled from Los Angeles to Chicago. "Well, then. I am speechless. Except to say, once again, *oh my fucking God, I cannot believe this.*"

I flicked the tip of my cigarette into the ashtray on the railing. "I know it's nuts. But he's great, Denise. He's gorgeous, he's got a stable job, he's originally from Nashville, and his family sounds so close and amazing."

"Nashville? Who's *from* Nashville?"

"He is."

"Fine. But what's he like?"

"I just told you."

"No, I mean what's he *like*? Personality-wise?"

"He's…I don't know. He's a nice guy." I shrugged, taking another drag off my cigarette before stubbing it out. The scene from dinner where he scolded the waiter over the temperature of his steak flickered in my mind but quickly disappeared. "He sent me flowers after our first date. Can you imagine Danny *ever* sending me flowers?"

"Are we still saying his name?"

"That was the last time."

"Good," Denise said. "So I guess I'll let you get back to your attorney. *But* I'm calling you tomorrow for more information. Deal?"

"Deal," I agreed.

"I'm happy for you, babe."

"Thanks. I love you."

"Love you, too. Now go get fucked."

I smiled and clicked the button on the receiver as I peeked through the glass panes on the door. Aaron's head was turned to the side, his eyes closed, remote still in his hand. I screwed up my face and carefully opened the door so as not to wake him. "I think that ship has sailed, actually," I muttered to myself.

CHAPTER THIRTY-FIVE

JULY 1990

July 16, 1990
Eva,

Saw this postcard and remembered how much you said you missed the palms along Sunset, so I'm sending them to you. Left a couple messages on your machine, but I know you said the job has been keeping you busy. Things are sounding great with the songs for the album. Spin is doing a short article about my "comeback" (crazy, huh?) so if you see next month's issue, pick it up and tell me if I said anything dumb during the interview. You were always good for that. :)

Miss you,
Eric

CHAPTER THIRTY-SIX
EVA

AUGUST 1990

*A*ll in all, sobriety looks—and sounds—good on Eric Stratton. Album release date scheduled for September 25.

I ran my fingers along the glossy page adorned with a picture of Eric sitting on a green velvet couch, leaning forward with his long legs spread wide and arms draped across them. He was dressed in faded blue jeans and a loose white shirt that was unbuttoned halfway down his chest. The sleeves were rolled up, exposing his forearms, and I noticed a new tattoo. His expression was stoic, a deep stare into the camera, and I wondered what he was thinking as the photographer captured his image. Was he imagining what might have been had he not gotten sober? Was he still shocked the label had offered him a solo deal? Was he missing the days before the drugs and alcohol had taken over, thinking about what could've become of the band? Was he missing…*me?*

I shook my head and let out a sharp laugh. *Don't be ridiculous, Eva. The man has a highly fucking anticipated album coming out, and that's all he's thinking about.*

I placed the magazine on the coffee table, grabbed a pen, and flipped over the postcard of the Navy Pier that I picked up at the drugstore.

Thanks for the palm trees. Here's a Ferris

wheel that has nothing to do with anything (ha ha), but it was the best postcard I could find. You nailed the interview. Can't wait to hear the whole album—only one more month! Eva

A loud knock startled me, and I quickly shoved the postcard under the magazine. I stood and smoothed my hand over my sundress, then hurried to the door to find Aaron holding a bouquet of white roses in one hand and a gift box in the other.

I tilted my head and smiled. "You're early."

He leaned forward and placed a quick kiss on my lips. "Is that bad?" he asked as he stepped inside and handed me the flowers and present. "Happy Birthday, baby."

I placed the gifts on the dining table and wrapped my arms around his neck. "Thank you. You know I love white roses."

"I do," he said, the corners of his mouth turning upward as I leaned in to kiss him.

I pulled away and ran my hand along his chest. "I should go put them in water."

"Wait." He gently tugged me back to him. "I want you to open your present first."

I narrowed my eyes, a smile creeping across my face. "Is it that good?"

"Open it and see."

I picked up the gift, my eyes flicking back and forth between it and Aaron as I peeled off the silver foil wrapping paper to reveal a black velvet box. I flipped open the top and saw a string of white beads resting on a silky cushion, along with a pair of matching earrings pinned in the middle.

Pearls? He got me pearls?

Heat traveled from my chest to my cheeks as I tried to think of what to say.

I've never worn pearls in my life.

Needles pricked at my body, but I managed to lift my head and fake a smile. "They're…I don't know what to say. They're so…pretty."

Aaron grinned. "I figured you could wear them next weekend."

I raised my eyebrows. "Next weekend?"

"My parents decided to come into town. I want you to meet them."

I blinked, and my false smile turned sincere. "You do?"

He nodded. "I do."

I snapped the box shut and set it on the table, then steepled my hands over my mouth. "Are you sure?"

He laughed and folded me into his arms. "Yes, I'm sure."

My heart and stomach fluttered, and I leaned into his chest, feeling his breath on my hair as he held me close. "I saw the pearls and thought they'd look beautiful on you. Every classic woman should have them."

"Thank you." I pulled back and gazed into his eyes. The gift may not have been my style, *but he wanted me to meet his parents.* I'd known things were getting serious, but this was a huge step. One I was ready to take, even if it meant wearing pearls. Aaron made me feel safe. Stable. Secure. He was everything Danny wasn't. "And I'd love to meet your parents."

"Good," he said. "I'd love it, too. Because I love *you,* Eva."

I gasped, air catching in my throat. We'd danced around the words for what felt like forever but hadn't said them... until now.

I finally forced the air into my lungs and swallowed. "I love you, too." I chuckled as I wiped at a tear that trickled down my cheek. "So, why am I crying?"

He laughed and pulled me close again. "Because you're crazy, Eva Holloway. And that's one of the things I love so much about you."

CHAPTER THIRTY-SEVEN
EVA

SEPTEMBER 1990

I squeezed my way onto the "L", grasping one of the silver poles as the train pulled away from its stop. Rush hour was never fun, but after a year of being back in Chicago, I was used to being crammed shoulder to shoulder with every other person leaving downtown at six o'clock.

I reached into my satchel and pulled out my Walkman, placing the headphones on before pressing play. I'd picked up Eric's new album the night before at the record store around the corner from my apartment but had only been able to make it halfway through before Aaron had come over.

The songs I'd heard so far were amazing, a few of them deeper and darker than those he'd written with Counting Backward, and the music fit them perfectly. With Danny's influence gone, they were less guitar-driven but still heavy in all the right places.

As sound streamed through the headphones, I closed my eyes, letting Eric's powerful voice envelop me. I was so immersed in the music that the lyrics didn't quite register, the way it often was when I listened to a new album. It always took a few times through before they really sank in. Something about a rooftop...a late night talk...

Wait, what?

My heart lurched along with the train, which came to a

stop. I stared out the window, my cheeks growing warm and my breath picking up as my body swayed in different directions each time a person pushed past me.

What did he say?

As the new crowd of commuters settled into their spots and the train pulled away once again, I pushed the rewind button, then play.

> *"Sitting on the rooftop*
> *A long late night talk*
> *Wondering if I'm falling for her*
> *Wondering if I should walk*
> *'Cause she's not mine to love"*

I rewound the cassette three more times to make sure I'd heard the lyrics correctly.

Was there another girl he sat on a rooftop with? Surely, there was. All those girls on the tour…there were so many of them. And he didn't mention any specifics…no Chinese food, no talking about our families. It has to be someone else. It has to be.

I clicked the stop button and spent the rest of the ride home listening through my headphones to the muffled ramble of the train on its tracks. My eyes and nose prickled with that familiar sting. The one that happened when you felt like you might cry but weren't quite sure. Because I *wasn't* quite sure. I wasn't sure if the song was about me. I wasn't sure if I *wanted* it to be about me.

One thing I did know was that I would never ask. Because that part of my life was over. And I couldn't go back. I could never, ever go back.

CHAPTER THIRTY-EIGHT

OCTOBER - NOVEMBER 1990

October 15, 1990

Eva,

Holy shit. Holy, HOLY shit. Keith just called and told me when the Billboard Charts are released tomorrow, my first single is gonna break the top ten. I've been trying to get in touch with you, but guess you're swamped with work, so I had to sit down and write you because I can't fucking believe it. I never thought I could do this on my own. Hell, I didn't even think I could stay sober. But it's happening. How is this fucking real?

We're putting together a tour to start next year, and I'm sure Chicago will be a stop. As soon as I get the dates, I'll let you know. Tickets, backstage passes for you, your friends…whatever you want. Or I don't know…maybe I can come visit before then? Beg you in person to move back to LA and work for Keith? You know he'd take you back in a fucking heartbeat. He asks about you all the time. You can live in his guest house since I've finally settled into my new apartment. Or if you don't feel like water gun fights with a four year old, I've got an extra room.

Anyway, speaking of Keith, he wants to take me and the guys in the band out to dinner to celebrate, so gotta run. Let's talk soon—I miss hearing your voice.

Love,

Eric

PS—What do you think of the album?

PPS—Are you getting my messages on your machine? Starting to get paranoid—ha ha. :)

———

October 24, 1990
Eric,

Yes, I've gotten your messages, and I'm so sorry I haven't called you back! We have this huge project going on at work. But I wanted to sit down and write while I have a minute to breathe. I AM SO FUCKING PROUD OF YOU!!! I know I suck as a friend lately, but I'm totally losing track of time. I got promoted, which is great, except it means there's more shit to do, so maybe I should come back to work for Keith (ha ha). Sometimes I wish I could, honestly, but there's just too much…well, you know what I mean. Please tell him I said hello, though!

I will try to call next weekend. I know I'm gonna have lots of late nights at the office this coming week.

Eva

PS—Did I mention the album is AMAZING? :)

———

November 7, 1990
Denise,

So my dad and step-whatever-she-is finally found time to drive to the city and meet Aaron last Saturday! You know I met his parents back in August, so it was way overdue, but there was always some reason—they couldn't get a babysitter, their kid had a gymnastics something or another and they had to watch her do fucking cartwheels…blah, blah, blah. Anyway, we went to dinner and of course, they love him. Because what's not to love? My dad was practically doing cartwheels himself when he found out Aaron's an attorney and not a musician. Now I just need YOU to meet him! So…when's that gonna happen? COME SEE ME!

Speaking of visits, I'll have you know I wasn't acting "weird" (as you called it) on the phone about Eric wanting to come to Chicago. I'm just, like, what's he gonna do? Sleep on the pullout couch while Aaron and I sleep in my bed? And before you say that's exactly what you would do, please remember you are my best friend and female. Of course, you're probably much too busy with your lover to come to Chicago. Why so secretive about that, by the way?

Write me ASAP!

XOXO,

Eva

CHAPTER THIRTY-NINE
EVA

"**L**adies and gentlemen, welcome aboard American Flight 734, nonstop from Nashville to Chicago. We'll be pulling back from the gate shortly, so please buckle your seat belts, ensure all items are stowed properly under the seat in front of you, and your tray tables and seats are in an upright position."

I flipped up my tray in accordance with the flight attendant's instructions, placing the *Rolling Stone* I'd picked up in the airport gift shop on my lap. I flipped mindlessly through the pages until I spotted a picture of Eric holding a framed gold record, Keith and the rest of his band surrounding him. I smiled and let out a tiny squeak.

"Hey, isn't that the guy from the band you used to work for?" Aaron pointed to the picture, and I startled, clearing my throat.

"Huh? Oh yeah, I guess it is," I said, bringing the magazine closer to my face, pretending to examine the photo. "Looks like he got a gold record or something."

Aaron nodded. "That's cool."

"Yeah." I closed the magazine and shoved it in the seat pocket in front of me.

"You ever talk to those people anymore?"

"No," I said quickly, the hairs on my arms standing on end

as if I'd shocked myself.

Why did I lie to him? Why do I turn down the volume on the machine whenever he comes over just in case Eric calls? Why do I erase Eric's messages so there's no chance of him ever hearing them?

He motioned toward the magazine. "Yeah, that scene was no good for you. I know that guy's supposed to be sober now or whatever, but let's be real—how long is that gonna last?"

His words pricked at my heart, and I tightened my fists. I wanted to tell him how hard Eric had worked. That he went to 12-step meetings almost every day. But instead, I shrugged and stared out the window.

Aaron is my life now. Not Eric.

"So," he said, lacing his fingers through mine. "Our first Thanksgiving together was good, yeah? My sister said she was impressed at how her kids took to you."

"Well, they're cool kids," I said, shifting my eyes from the tarmac. "I think your niece might grow up to be a punk rock girl. She kept wanting to try on my Doc Martens."

"Laura really liked you, too."

"Your sister is so nice, she probably likes everyone."

"Not true," he said, squeezing my hand. "I mean, yes, she's nice, but she doesn't like *everyone*. She did think it was funny you didn't understand grits, though."

"Sorry. Never had a true Southern breakfast before, I guess." I chuckled. "I'm kinda surprised she said good things about me, honestly. I didn't know if I quite...*fit in* with your family. I mean, it was one thing to meet your parents in Chicago, but to be with them in your hometown..."

He furrowed his brow. "What do you mean?"

I sighed and turned toward him as the plane lurched, pulling back from the gate. "I mean, your mom and sister took me to the nail salon, and the first color I reached for was dark purple. But I put it back because they both chose light pinks. And then when we went shopping, they bought cardigans at these really nice stores, and all I wanted to do was find the thrift shop to see if anyone had donated any cool old band T-shirts."

"I've seen you wear a cardigan to work."

"I have two that I rotate," I answered, resting my forehead on his shoulder.

He tucked his finger under my chin, tilting my head up and forcing me to look into his eyes. "They adore you, Eva. They're just older and have a different style. I mean, I'm sure you won't wear ripped jeans and band T-shirts *forever*. You barely even wore them this weekend."

"I just want your family to like me."

"They do." Aaron cupped my face, gently running his thumb along my cheek.

I swallowed and nodded before giving him a quick kiss and turning forward in my seat. They may have liked the me they'd met, but was that the *real* me? What if I *had* gotten the purple nail polish or asked to go to the thrift store? Would they have liked me then?

"Hey." Aaron pressed his mouth against my ear so I could hear him over the roar of the plane. "Look at that family over there."

I peered around him to the other side of the aisle where a young child was nestled in the seat between his mother and father, holding both their hands.

"That could be us soon," he said.

My chest squeezed, but I wasn't sure if it was because his comment made me happy or nervous. Maybe a bit of both.

"Just not *too* soon on the kid," I said, trying to laugh off the unease.

"Huh?" he said as the plane picked up speed.

"Never mind."

I sighed and gripped the armrest as the plane's engine whirred, ready to take me back home, where I could finally relax and be myself again.

CHAPTER FORTY

DECEMBER 1990

December 2, 1990
Eva,

Now I'm the one who needs to apologize for not being in touch. Things have been so hectic with promoting the album, I haven't had time to do anything except pose for a million fucking pictures and go to my NA meetings. Still keeping up with those at least!

Wanted to let you know we're kicking off the tour next week in Miami and will be in Chicago March 23rd. Lemme know if you can make it to the show, and I'll get you tickets and passes. And we have a day off on the 24th, so we should hang out…get some crab rangoon or somethin'. :)

Love,
Eric

———

December 16, 1990
Eric,

I can't believe how amazing the album is doing! I mean, I CAN, obviously, but I'm just so happy for you! I saw your picture in Rolling Stone with your gold record, which is clearly going platinum in no time.

I'm super bummed, but I'll actually be out of town when you're

FOR EVA

in Chicago! Some of my college friends and I are going to Florida that weekend for one of their birthdays. We planned it before I knew you'd be coming to town. I feel so bad I'm missing this! But I can still tell you where to get the best crab rangoon if you want. :)

Hope the tour goes great—I know it will!
Eva

CHAPTER FORTY-ONE
EVA

DECEMBER 1990

"So what do you think? This place is pretty swank, huh?" I took a sip of champagne from the delicate flute a server had just handed me.

Denise nodded, surveying the room of the restaurant Aaron's friends had rented out for their New Year's Eve bash. There were glittering gold streamers and warm white twinkle lights draped along the ceiling. Tall bouquets full of lush greenery and white flowers sat in the center of each table covered in a crisp black cloth.

"Way better than the seedy clubs I've been hanging out at...for way too long," she said, shaking her head.

I ran my hand along her arm. "Sorry that didn't work out, babe."

She rolled her eyes and took a long swallow of her drink before placing it on the table beside us. "Well, when you're stuck in Reseda because your boyfriend nodded off in the bathroom with a shoelace tied around his arm, you know it's time to cut your losses. Fucking junkie."

"Well, Aaron's friend, Mark, was asking about you, so I thought maybe I could intro—"

Denise held her hand up. "Nope. Not happening. I'm done with men for the foreseeable fut—"

"Eva! I've been looking for you all night."

A tall dark-haired man dressed in a light blue button-down slid up to me, and I shot Denise a nervous glance indicating I may have already told Mark I would introduce them.

"You look stunning, per usual," he said, standing back to appraise my black sequined A-line before shifting his gaze to Denise, who was tightly wrapped in a strapless red satin dress. "And is this gorgeous creature the friend from LA you were talking about?"

I opened my mouth to answer his question but shut it as soon as Denise stuck her hand out, which he took into his.

"Hi, I *am* that friend from LA, but my drink is empty, so I need to go get a fresh one." She unclasped his hand and grabbed mine before turning and yanking me in the direction of the bar.

"Wait, I can get that for you," he called.

"No, I'm good, but thanks!"

Denise pulled me into a corner of the room and leaned against the wall, running her hand along her forehead. "Sorry, I just...I don't want to meet anyone."

"Okay, you don't have to. We can just go to the bar and get you another vodka cran." I nodded and squeezed her hand.

Concern crept like a shadow over her face as she smoothed her hands over her dress. "We can't do that, either."

"Why not?"

Her jaw tightened, and her eyes turned up toward the glittery ceiling. "Because I'm fucking pregnant, Eva."

"You're what?" My eyes widened as my hand slid slowly from hers.

"Pregnant," she repeated in a hushed tone as her eyes settled back on me. "I've been drinking straight cranberry juice all night."

The champagne flute nearly slipped from my grasp before I caught it and set it onto a table beside us. "What the hell? How...When?"

"It was an accident, obviously," she said, brushing her dark hair from her face. "And yes, it's his. There was one day when he came to my door, swearing he'd never touch the shit ever again, and I believed him. Like an idiot."

I swallowed hard. "So are you gonna get an—"

"I don't know. I just found out a few days ago." She sucked in a shaky breath. "I should've called you, but then I thought I should tell you in person, but I also didn't want to ruin your New Year's Eve, and I—"

"Hush," I commanded, placing my hands on her shoulders. "You haven't ruined anything. Do you wanna leave and talk about it? I can tell Aaron I'm not feeling well."

"Eva!" A male voice called from behind me. "Aaron needs you for a sec."

I turned my head to see Mark motioning me over to him. "Yeah, just a minute, I'll be right there."

"He said he needs you *now*."

I let out a heavy sigh and gave Denise's arm a quick squeeze. "I'll be right back, okay?"

She nodded. "Go on. We're not leaving. We can talk about it tomorrow. Nothing's gonna change between now and then."

I offered her a half-hearted smile and headed toward Mark. "What's so important that he needs me *right now?*"

Mark swept his hand to a sea of people who parted as I approached them. "See for yourself."

"I—" My words caught in my throat, and I blinked, sure the scene in front of me was a mirage...an illusion...a side effect of too much champagne.

Aaron was down on one knee, black box in hand, with a grin stretching wide across his face.

Jesus fucking Christ.

I threw my hand over my mouth and inched my way to him, my eyes darting around the room to the crowd that circled us. The music that had been playing came to an abrupt halt, and the DJ's voice boomed over the speakers. "Will everyone please turn their attention to the center of the room for a moment? I believe something very special is about to happen."

I stopped in front of Aaron, flames burning my cheeks. Thoughts raced around my brain like they were trying to win the Kentucky Derby.

Is it too soon? Do I want this? I think I do, but not this way. It's so…public. But I love him. And Denise is pregnant. What the hell. Am I pregnant? No, I'm not pregnant. Oh my God, what do I say? What do I do?

My eyes met Aaron's for a moment before he flipped open the box, revealing a sparkling stone bigger than I'd ever seen. Bigger than I'd ever wanted.

"Eva Holloway," he said, his eyes shining like the diamond he was holding, "I have loved you since the moment I laid eyes on you. Even if it was because you hit my car."

A chorus of laughter streamed from what seemed like a hundred people gathered around us.

"Will you do me the honor of becoming my wife?"

My hand slid from my mouth, falling limply to my side. He looked so handsome, so vulnerable, that the racehorses in my brain passed the finish line and slowed their pace. This was what I wanted…*right?* Even if it wasn't exactly the way I'd imagined it happening. Even if the ring wasn't exactly my style.

I nodded slowly, but no words came. He cocked his head, and I immediately cleared my throat.

"Yes." A nervous chuckle escaped my lips as Aaron slipped the ring onto my trembling finger, and the partygoers cheered. "Yes, I will."

Aaron stood and wrapped me up in his arms, covering me like a blanket, and I was reminded of how safe he made me feel. It was everything I'd ever wanted but never had. Until now. When he let his arms slide down to my waist, I turned to see Denise standing at the front of the crowd. I wiped a tear from my cheek before holding up my left hand, wiggling my fingers. She flashed a grin, walked toward me, and gave me a hug.

"Are you okay?" she whispered into my ear.

Her question caught me off guard, and I pulled back as Aaron's friends gathered around to congratulate him.

"Of course, I'm okay," I said, smiling and dabbing my fingers under my eyelashes. "I'm better than okay. This is incredible, right?"

"Right," she said, the grin turning into a tight smile. "Right."

CHAPTER FORTY-TWO

JANUARY - MARCH 1991

January 12, 1991
Eva,

Happy New Year from Miami! Just wanted to send a postcard from the road and say sorry we couldn't catch up over the phone before I left. The show went amazing last night—it was scary and exciting and crazy. Keith had to (literally) give me a push onto the stage, but once I got out there, it was like I was fucking home again. It helped that it was a smaller venue (not big enough for an arena tour just yet—ha ha), so I could really see the crowd smiling and singing. It felt fucking amazing. Wish you'd been watching from the side of the stage like old times, though. I'll try to call you soon. Maybe I can fly you out to a show since you'll be out of town when I'm in Chicago?

Love,
Eric

February 5, 1991
Eva,

I wanted to find an exciting postcard to send, but apparently everything in this state says Virginia is for Lovers, so, hey, here you go. :) Hope you're doing okay. I've called a couple times and gotten the machine. I know it's impossible to call me back, so I'll keep try-ing and hopefully catch you soon. The shows have been insane so far—sellout crowds, can you believe it?! Not the same without you here, though.

Love,
Eric

March 22, 1991

Eva,

On the road to Chicago and thinking about you. Picked up this postcard in Cleveland—the skyline at night made me think about the time we ate Chinese on that hotel rooftop. I know we were both high as fucking kites, but do you remember it? You stole the last crab rangoon and told me about your tattoo. I miss that night. I miss you.

Love,
Eric

CHAPTER FORTY-THREE
EVA

JUNE 1991

"**S**orry I can't help you pack," Denise said from the couch where she laid with her feet propped up, cradling her belly. "But you know…doctor's orders."

I snorted from the kitchen as I wrapped dinner plates in newspaper. "The doctor said you couldn't put dishes into a box?"

"She *specifically* said that. It was the weirdest thing."

"I'm questioning our friendship," I called, pulling down another plate.

Denise scoffed. "Hey, I was cooped up on an airplane for over four hours in order to be here for your wedding week. And I'm sure you don't need to be reminded I did this nearly *seven months preggers*. My feet are no longer feet, Eva. They're fucking sausages." She paused as I crouched to dig pots and pans out of a cabinet. "It's crazy you're packing this week, anyway. Shouldn't we be getting spa treatments?"

"We absolutely will do that. I've made appointments for Thursday. But we close on the house tomorrow, and my landlord has someone moving in here literally the day after we get back from our honeymoon. So, I need to have everything ready to go."

"A new house and a wedding in one week. You're a machine, babe."

I closed the box I'd been working on and wiped beads of sweat from my forehead as I padded into the living room. "I know it's crazy and definitely not something we planned. But when we saw the place was for sale, we knew we had to move fast. It's the most perfect brownstone right in Lincoln Park, Denise. I can't wait for you to see it."

I plopped on the end of the couch and began to massage her feet, which had, indeed, swollen to the size of sausages.

"Oh my God, please don't ever stop doing that," she moaned.

"I'm not the only crazy one here, you know," I began. "You got married to someone two weeks after he asked you. Good thing I like him."

"I didn't want to be ridiculously pregnant in my wedding dress. Plus, that was a strategic business decision, Eva. My father didn't work his ass off to build one of the most successful independent film financing companies in the country for nothing. When he retires, the plan is for me to take over. And I need Marcos by my side. He's the sharpest person we've got. Besides me, of course," she added with a wink.

"That guy has been in love with you since your father hired him," I said. "Plus, he worships the ground you walk on. I think you've just been fighting the idea of being with him because he wasn't *exciting* enough for you. But now you see how wonderful a nice, stable man can be."

"Speaking of…"

I gave her foot a final squeeze. "What?"

Denise hoisted herself up so her back was against the armrest. "Everything's good with Aaron?"

I blinked. "What do you mean, 'good'? Of course, it's good. I'm marrying him in five days."

"But you're marrying him because you love him. Not because he's not, you know, *Danny*." She said his name in a hushed tone, the way one might whisper the word *hemorrhoid* or *can-*

cer.

I gave her an are-you-fucking-crazy look, and she held her hands up in defense.

"Okay, sorry, I'm just asking."

"And *I* could ask *you* the same thing about Marcos."

"I told you, it was a business decision." She paused and rolled her eyes. "And *fine*, he's a good guy and will be a great dad and blah, blah, blah."

"I knew it."

"Whatever," she retorted. "I just want to make sure you're happy. Like, really happy. Because even though you're my best friend in the whole entire world and will be forever, you and I are different when it comes to these things. I don't need that mushy kind of love. But you do, Eva. And I just...I don't know, maybe I'm crazy, but have you heard Eric Stratton's latest single? Have you actually *listened* to the lyrics?"

A pit formed in my stomach. "Yeah, I have. But what does that have to do with anything?"

"Eva," she said, looking me dead in the eye. "They're obviously about you."

Fuck.

I remembered the postcard he'd sent me from Cleveland. That evening in late September on the "L", coming home from work, listening to my Walkman. And the past week when the song had come on over the speakers as I was picking out lettuce in the grocery store. I'd been so rattled that I put my basket down and ran out of the store, leaving everything I was buying for dinner in the middle of the produce section. I ended up making up something about leaving work late when I'd called Aaron to pick up takeout on his way over that night.

Sitting on the rooftop
A long late night talk
Wondering if I'm falling for her
Wondering if I should walk
'Cause she's not mine to love

"You told me about that night on the rooftop. When you gave him the fax about his stepdad, and everything started going downhill."

My eyes darted to my lap, and I picked at the threads on the tear in my jeans. "There were so many girls on those tours, Denise. It could've been any one of them."

"Then why is your face getting all red?"

"It's not getting red," I insisted, wishing my hair was still long enough to hide my cheeks behind it.

She raised her eyebrows and tilted her head. "Um, yeah, it is. You need to admit that he was—and maybe still *is*—in love with you."

"He is not, Denise. And even if he was, which I'm sure he *wasn't*, he's over it by now. That was a lifetime ago."

"Hardly."

My shoulders dropped. "Well, it seems like a lifetime ago. And I'm getting married in *five days*. To someone I love. To someone my dad loves. To someone who's successful and stable and not gonna fuck me over."

Denise pressed her lips together and nodded. "Okay, I get it. I'm sorry, I shouldn't have brought it up."

I blew out a breath. "It's fine. I just…I can't think about that part of my life anymore. I can't think about *him*." I paused and leaned my head against the back of the couch. "I lied to him about not being able to come to the show when he was in Chicago. Told him I was gonna be out of town."

Denise's brows turned inward. "He was here, and you didn't see him?"

I swallowed hard and nodded. "In March. But I couldn't do it."

"Eva, you saved the guy's life, for Christ's sake. You could've gone to see him. Even taken Aaron. Made it clear his friendship is still important to you."

"He doesn't know about Aaron, and there's no point in telling him. I have to let that part of my life go."

FOR EVA

"Because of Danny?" she asked. "Eric isn't like him, Eva. You told me how close you two had gotten over the phone and through letters. Until Aaron came along, I thought maybe you—"

"It's because of everything, Denise. Everything to do with that whole time in LA and on tour. I realized I want something solid. Something safe."

"So do you guys still talk, then? Or write?"

I shook my head as a heaviness settled in my chest. "Not really. He sends me postcards from the road sometimes. But that's about it. He used to call a lot, but I kinda stopped picking up the phone. So, I guess he senses things are…*different* now."

Denise gave me a wistful smile. "Okay, then. I won't bring it up again. But I *will* go take a nap, and then I promise to help you with the packing. I think it'll be okay if I put *one* dish in a box."

"Wow, thanks so much." I chuckled as she swung her feet onto the floor and waddled into my bedroom.

Once the door closed, I pushed myself up from the couch and hurried over to the dining table, picking up one of the several envelopes scattered across it. I held it in my hand, watching as it shook from the adrenaline coursing through my body. I hadn't exactly told Denise the truth. Eric *had* sent postcards, but a letter had arrived from him a week ago. The first I'd received in months. My hand glided over the seal, my finger poised to slip through it, but it stopped as the words I'd just said to my best friend echoed through my mind.

I have to let that part of my life go.

I turned and headed for the trash can in the kitchen, but an invisible force stopped me in my tracks. I walked back to the open box in the corner of the living room and retrieved a worn shoebox from it before sitting down and crossing my legs. Inside, there were laminates with pictures of me with my long hair teased and sprayed high, along with a few old candid photos of the band, folded pages ripped from music magazines, and a cassette tape with *Eric Stratton—Demo* scrawled across it. I stuffed the letter underneath the remnants of my past and placed the top back on the shoebox.

I hadn't been totally honest with Denise about letting go, either. There were pieces I couldn't surrender, even if they were tucked away—out of sight, but never completely out of mind.

CHAPTER FORTY-FOUR
EVA

I stared down at the two lines on the white stick as my back slid down the wall and my tailbone hit the tile floor. I hadn't even had to wait the whole time noted in the instructions before the second line appeared.

Does that mean the test is faulty? Or does it mean I'm absolutely, without a doubt, one hundred percent...

"Pregnant," I whispered.

I remembered the last time I'd muttered that word to myself when I was seventeen, and the doctor confirmed I hadn't missed my period because of stress. When I confessed to my mother that I wasn't the good girl she'd thought I was. When she cried and I cried until we both decided I was much too young and had too bright a future ahead of me. When the truck crashed into us and shattered my entire world like the glass from the windows on her car.

But I was twenty-eight this time. And married. So why were tears starting to cloud my vision? Was it the memory from all those years ago? Was I still wondering if I was too young, and how I would learn to be a mother without my own to guide me? Or was I happy I would be starting a family with a man I loved, who wanted this more than anything in the world?

It wasn't like it was an accident. I'd gone off the pill two months prior but assumed I'd have more time to let the idea of it all sink in. Aaron and I had talked about giving ourselves a while before we started trying, but when our first anniversary arrived, he immediately began to point out families pushing strollers through the park and dads and their young sons on Saturday afternoons at Wrigley Field. I'd told him I'd be ready soon, but I didn't know if that was the truth. And it scared me that I still didn't know, even though I was staring down at lines telling me that ready or not, it was happening.

The familiar creak of the front door opening signaled that Aaron was home from work. I pushed myself up from the floor, sucking in a deep breath before placing my hand on the doorknob, letting it rest there for a moment.

Once I tell him, it's real.

I turned the knob and walked down the hallway to the kitchen where he was grabbing a beer out of the fridge.

"Hey, babe," he said, the light from the refrigerator illuminating his handsome face. "You want one?"

I managed a "no thanks" as he closed the door and popped the top of the amber bottle. The house was dark except for the warm glow from the light in the foyer. I'd hastily flipped it on before darting to the bathroom with the Walgreens bag gripped tightly in my hand earlier that evening.

"Did you just get home?" he asked, switching on the fixture over the sink. "It's so dark in he—"

Aaron turned, his eyes landing on the white stick in my hand. "Is that what I think it is? Are you…"

I nodded, the tears I'd tried to swallow slipping down my cheeks. He slid his beer on the counter, a wide grin spreading across his face as he walked the few steps toward me and pulled me into his arms.

"I can't believe it," he murmured into my hair. "It's really happening." He let out a hardy laugh, squeezing me tighter. "I'm gonna be a dad."

A small burst of laughter broke through my tears, the feeling of his body close to mine slowly reassuring me everything would be okay. "Yes, you are."

He pulled back, cupping my face in his hands, his thumbs wiping away the dampness on my cheeks. "This is real, right? I'm not dreaming?"

I chuckled through a shaky breath and nodded. "I think we're awake, though I couldn't swear to it."

His grin looked as if it would remain permanently stretched across his face. "This is such amazing timing, Eva."

I sniffed and titled my head. "What do you mean?"

He reached for his beer and took a long swig. "My buddy down in Nashville—you know Kevin, he was at the wedding. Anyway, his dad is retiring from their law firm, and he's looking for someone to partner with him when he takes over."

My brows turned down. "What? Does he want…"

Aaron's head bobbed with excitement. "He wants me to come down there. Can you believe it? My own firm—well, sort of my own firm—at thirty-two?"

I ran my hands down my face, swiping underneath my eyes. "I don't…Is that a good idea? I mean, moving and a new job with a baby on the way?"

"It's the *best* idea." He beamed. "His dad's firm does well. *Really* well. And we'll be close to my family, so they can watch our kids grow up and truly be a part of their lives."

I tried to think of all the things I could counter with, without saying what I really thought. That I didn't want to leave Chicago. I didn't want to leave my friends and my job. And that I was afraid of what this would mean for the relationship with my own father—one I'd built after worrying all those years that he blamed me for what had happened with my mom.

I crossed my arms over my chest. "But can you practice law in Tennessee? You passed the bar in Illinois."

"I need to look into the whole reciprocity thing, but it should work out. Or I'll take the damn thing again in Tennessee," he explained, like it was no big deal. "This is just all so amazing. So amazing."

I swayed, pressing my hand against the fridge to steady myself. What the fuck was happening? It was as if I'd entered a whole new world, completely different from the one I'd woken up in that morning.

Aaron rushed to my side. "Whoa, you okay?"

I squeezed my eyes shut, then opened them to make sure Aaron's theory about dreaming hadn't been correct. "Yeah, it… it's just a lot to take in right now."

He gripped my hand and steered me toward the living room. "I know, I'm sorry, I should've waited to tell you. I just got so excited. You need to lie down, and we'll talk about it later. I'll get you some water."

I nodded and stretched my legs along the couch, my fingers kneading my forehead. Maybe he was right. Maybe this *was* amazing. But there was something inside me that didn't want to talk about it later. That didn't want to talk about it *ever*. That wanted to go to sleep and wake up and realize this all *had* been just a dream.

CHAPTER FORTY-FIVE
EVA

NOVEMBER 1996

"No, Drew. Listen to Mama and put that back." I took the can of corn he'd swiped off the shelf while I was scanning the aisle for French-style green beans, which had apparently sold out in the Thanksgiving rush.

I'd taken the Wednesday before the holiday off from work. Drew's preschool was closed, and I'd packed him in the car to go shopping for the side dishes I promised to bring to Aaron's sister's house the next day. And as if I wasn't already busy enough dealing with a three-year-old and trying to remember what ingredients I needed for two casseroles, I'd now have to run to another store to find the damn green beans.

"I want it," Drew cried, snot dripping from his nose. I let out a heavy sigh as I pushed the shopping cart to the front of the store, stopping in a line three people deep and digging in my purse for a tissue. He squirmed in the front of the cart as I wiped away the glob of mucus teetering on the edge of his top lip, his little legs kicking my thighs.

"Stop that, Drew," I said, balling the tissue into a wad, which I stuffed into the pocket of my jeans. "We're almost done, and then we'll go home and see Daddy."

I'd already decided I wasn't going to another store with him in tow. Aaron had told me he was calling it a day at noon, so he could deal with getting Drew fed and down for a nap while I ran back out.

Drew miraculously stopped sobbing when he heard the word *daddy*, and I smiled and ran my hand through his silky blond hair before pushing the cart forward. "Who's my best boy?"

He giggled and blew me a kiss, which I pretended to catch before I blew one back at him. As I went in to give him a real kiss on his forehead, one of the gossip magazines at the end of the checkout counter caught my eye. On its cover was a picture of Hollywood's latest "It" girl, holding hands and smiling at a tall figure dressed in jeans and a T-shirt.

Christina Hanson: How She Healed and Found Love with Eric Stratton

Pins and needles pricked at my body, and my face grew warm. It wasn't anything new to see Eric's face on a magazine at the store. He'd become one of the biggest rock stars in the world since his solo debut. We'd lost track of each other after Aaron and I had moved to Lincoln Park. More like he'd lost track of *me*. I hadn't left a forwarding address with the post office or written him with my new phone number. For all he knew, I was still somewhere in Chicago, not living in Nashville with a husband and a kid. But this blond starlet was surprising. She had to be ten years younger than him. They couldn't possibly have anything in common...could they?

"Eva? Is that you?"

"Huh?" I shook my head and turned to see one of the moms from Drew's preschool. "Julie. Hey. How are you?"

She threw her hands up. "Oh, you know, like everyone else. Just trying to make it through the start of the holidays."

I laughed politely, hoping the person in front of me would hurry up so I wouldn't be stuck making small talk for too long. The mothers at Drew's preschool were nice enough, but I hadn't found any I'd particularly bonded with. Julie was a stay-at-home mom, and while that was a choice I could've made, I'd found a dream job in marketing for a music label in town.

"I thought that was you, but I'm so used to seeing you in your work clothes," Julie continued. "I've never seen you dressed like…*this*. And I didn't realize you had a *tattoo*."

I pulled my off-the-shoulder sweatshirt up to hide the ink and managed a weak smile. "Oh, something I got a long time ago. I was just a kid."

I loved that tattoo and hated her making me feel self-conscious with the way she whispered the word while she judged my baggy jeans and Converse.

"I guess we all do crazy things when we're young," she chirped.

My smile was tight-lipped this time. "I guess we do." I paused as the conveyor belt freed up, and I moved forward to check out. "Well, it was good seeing you. Have a nice Thanksgiving."

She wiggled her fingers in a tiny wave and pushed her cart past us. I looked down at Drew, who was reaching for the candy bars stacked on the shelves beside us, and grabbed a Hershey's bar for him and two Snickers for me. As I silently cursed Julie in her pink blouse and khakis for making me want to eat chocolate, I stole one last glance at the magazine, longing to let Eric know how much I despised her, certain he'd insist I tell her to go fuck herself.

Or since I'd disappeared on him, maybe that's what he'd say to me.

———

"God, Aaron, she was such a bitch," I lamented, unpacking the groceries after I'd gone back out for the green beans. He'd gotten Drew down for his nap and opened a bottle of red for us because he said I looked like I needed it.

He was right.

"She was judging me up and down, tattoo and everything." I yanked my sweatshirt farther off my shoulder in defiance. "Like she's somehow better than me."

"I doubt she meant anything by it." Aaron poured the cabernet into two stemmed glasses and placed one on the counter beside me. "She's just used to seeing you a little more...put together."

I planted a hand on my hip. "What's that supposed to mean?"

"I mean, she sees you when you're on your way to work, that's all."

"Sorry I didn't feel like putting on a goddamn ball gown to go to the fucking Kroger."

He threw his head back and set his drink down. "Now you're getting mad at me for what *she* did."

"I'm not, Aaron. I'm just letting you know this is who you married." I swept my hands along my clothes. "This is me."

"I know, babe," he said, his tone softening. "And I love you. I'm just saying she was probably surprised to see you dressed down. You always look so nice for work."

"Implying I don't look nice the rest of the time?" I snapped back.

"I didn't say that, Eva."

"Whatever. She may have been surprised, but she's still a bitch," I insisted. "She's mentioned to me more than once at school that I look exhausted and maybe I should take some time off work to be with Drew. And I'm not dissing all the stay-at-home moms. It's just her."

"Well," he said, dragging out the word before taking a sip of his wine. "You could be a stay-at-home mom, too. I mean, we'd have to make some sacrifices, but it could work."

I shook my head, swallowing down half of my glass. "Absolutely not. I love Drew more than anything in the world, but I am not cut out to be with him twenty-four seven. Plus, I like my job."

"But what about when we have number two?"

"Are you seriously going to start with this when I'm stressed about casseroles and have already eaten two candy bars?"

He smiled and waggled his eyebrows. "Come on. Drew's sleeping, so we can at least practice. I think we may have forgotten how to do it."

A chuckle escaped through the steam that had been building inside of me. "Is it possible to forget?"

"I dunno, but I'm starting to wonder."

I blew my bangs out of my face and gave him a sympathetic smile. "I know. But I *am* exhausted. Shit, maybe Julie *is* right. Fucking bitch."

"Forget about her," he said, moving toward me and sliding his arms around my waist. "But we really should give Drew a brother or a sister. And we really should have sex."

I squeezed his arms. "Tonight. I promise. But I'm *not* getting off the pill yet."

"Just think about it," he pleaded, pulling me closer and kissing my neck. "That's all I'm asking."

"How about you stop asking and let me make this shit to take to your sister's," I said as I wiggled out of his grip.

He twisted his mouth into a sly grin and picked up his wine before disappearing into the living room.

I sighed, examining the back of the can of green beans, trying to figure out how to make good on my promise of side dishes for Thanksgiving dinner. As I dug through the bottom cabinets for a mixing bowl, I wondered if a certain Hollywood actress was making a casserole for her boyfriend. Or if they were in bed, having the sex I may or may not have forgotten how to have.

CHAPTER FORTY-SIX
FEBRUARY 1998

From: Eva Mitchell
To: Denise Abbott
Date: February 16, 1998 8:05PM
Subject: Miss You

Hi, My Very Best Friend in the Entire World.

Just got Drew out of the bath. Aaron is putting him to bed, and I'm sitting here wishing you lived next door so I could sneak over and have a glass of wine and cigarette before I crash. Afraid if I whip out a smoke in front of my current neighbor, she'd never let our kids play together again.

Kidding. Kind of.

Although I probably shouldn't do that at all. Because I sort of think I'm pregnant again. I mean, I guess I know I am. I missed my period, my boobs hurt, and I cried at lunch today because the lady at McDonald's told me the milkshake machine was broken. I should know by now that fucking thing is always broken, but I peeled away from the drive-thru, drove ten miles to Sonic, and sobbed in the parking lot while I scarfed down a large order of tots AND a strawberry shake. Which I immediately regretted because I almost threw up when I got back to work.

FOR EVA

God, Denise. Can I do this again? You know Aaron has been nonstop about having another since Drew turned two, and I somehow managed to put it off until now. I mean, it's not that I'm not happy. I am, but I'm also worried. How do I manage my job, a kid who'll be five this year, and a newborn? I literally just got promoted to VP of the whole damn marketing department, and now I have to go confess to my boss that I'm knocked up. You have to tell me before I flip my shit and go get more tots.

Love you.

——————

From: Denise Abbott
To: Eva Mitchell
Date: February 17, 1998 12:46PM
Subject: Re: Miss You

Eva! How have you not learned to call with news like this?! I just left a voicemail on your home phone yelling at you even though I know you're at work. And I'm not calling you there because we don't need you bawling your eyes out while trying to run an entire marketing department (congrats, big shot :).

So first off, take a deep breath. If I can do this, anyone can—because, as you know, I despise children, yet have had three. I suppose I agreed to the second and third at some point, but I don't really recall. It's all a blur. I also really don't understand how we ended up with men who seem to enjoy the little shits so much.

Did I write that out loud?

OK, but seriously, this is happy news. They may be shits, but they're cute shits. And they're our shits. Drew will love having a brother or sister, and once you see that baby, you know you're gonna fall completely and totally in love. Work will take care of itself. YOU ARE A TOTAL BADASS, AND YOU'VE GOT THIS!

Speaking of work, I have to run across town to a meeting.

But go pee on a stick and call me tonight.
    XOXO

CHAPTER FORTY-SEVEN
EVA

JUNE 2003

I shut the car door with my hip, my arms weighed down with two bags of groceries, and my laptop bag and purse slung over my shoulder. Drew and Miles ran ahead to the front door, shoving each other in a race to see who could get there first. I teetered on my heels up the brick walkway, trying to balance the load I was carrying, yelling for the boys to stop pushing.

I let out a long sigh as I got to the door and realized my keys were in my purse.

"Drew, will you reach in my purse and get the key to the house, please?"

He unfastened the snap and dug around in the bag, producing a tampon in a hot pink wrapper. "What's this?"

"I'll tell you when you're older. Can you just get the keys?" I asked, my voice sharp as I shifted the bags that were beginning to slip from my grip.

He shrugged and plopped the tampon back in my purse, finally producing the ring of keys.

"Okay, now take the gold one and put it in the lock on the door, then turn it."

"Mama, can we have pizza for dinner?" Miles asked, dropping his little Spiderman backpack into the row of boxwoods beside us.

I closed my eyes, my patience wearing thin at Drew's fourth attempt at fitting the key into the lock. "No, we're having chicken. It's better for you. And what are you doing? Pick up your backpack and bring it inside."

Drew finally managed to open the door, and I hurried to the kitchen, plopping the groceries on the counter and letting my laptop and purse slide off my shoulder onto the floor with a loud thud. I kicked off my heels and rested my elbows on the island, threading my fingers through my hair as the boys darted down the hallway to play video games.

I closed my eyes and slowly circled my fingers over my temples, trying to relieve the dull ache pulsing in my head. The day had, to put it plainly, fucking sucked. One of our artists was being a complete diva and threatening to walk unless we "stepped up our game," as if helping her sell a million fucking records in two months wasn't enough. To top that off, my two junior associates had managed to create an HR nightmare when they were caught having sex in one of the vacant offices. And because of the massive amount of paperwork and red tape that event entailed, I was late picking up the kids from camp.

I sighed and looked to my right at the bottle of pinot noir sitting on the counter, shining brightly and beckoning me toward my salvation like the star of Bethlehem. I slid my elbows off the smooth black granite on the island, shoved the perishable groceries into the refrigerator, and popped the cork, pouring an extremely generous portion into a globe-shaped glass. I leaned against the counter, taking a long sip, then let out an equally long exhale. At least all I had to do for dinner was boil pasta and throw some marinara sauce and mozzarella on the chicken.

I chewed my lip and narrowed my eyes as a thought popped into my head. I turned around, scanning the counter. Hadn't I put the chicken out to thaw by the wine that morning?

"What the fuck?" I whispered to myself.

I stepped over to the refrigerator and tugged the freezer

drawer open. And there it was. My package of four chicken breasts, completely frozen. I closed my eyes and took in a deep breath as the cold air flowed over my body. I slammed the drawer and went to swipe my wine glass off the counter, missing my target and sending it crashing onto the hardwood floor.

"Motherfucker," I spat, stepping back from the shards of glass scattered in front of me.

I grabbed the broom, keeping my distance so as to avoid the additional chaos of a flesh wound. I gathered the mess into the dustpan and tossed it into the trash before setting to work on sopping up the liquid with a wad of paper towels.

"Look at you on your hands and knees scrubbing the floor before your very important husband comes home from his very important job. Where's my Tom Collins and pack of Pall Malls?"

I turned my head to the side, tossing my hair out of my face, to see Aaron standing at the entrance to the kitchen in his navy blue suit pants and white button-down shirt. I'd been so frazzled by the chicken and the wine I hadn't heard him come in.

"I need a goddamn Pall Mall," I grumbled, going back to work on soaking up the last of the wine. I tossed the ball of paper towels to the side and slumped against the cabinet, my legs splayed out in front of me.

He placed his keys on the island, a lopsided grin on his face as he walked toward me and extended his arms. I grabbed onto them, huffing and pulling myself up.

"So you had a good day?" he joked, squeezing my hands before letting them fall to my sides as he walked to the fridge and popped open a beer.

"Best day of my fucking life," I said, retrieving another glass and pouring the remaining wine. "And I forgot the chicken."

"Huh?" he asked, taking a swallow from the bottle in his hand.

"The stupid chicken for dinner. I forgot to leave it out to thaw."

He shrugged. "Just stick it in the microwave. Or better yet, let's order pizza."

"I guess you really are Miles's father." I rolled my eyes and wriggled out of my black blazer, flinging it onto the island across from me.

He laughed and set his beer down, sliding in behind me and rubbing my knotted shoulders.

I dropped my head forward and moaned. "Oh my God, do that forever, please."

"Wanna talk about your day or no?"

I sighed. "Oh, just one of our biggest artists is being totally unreasonable and two of my employees got caught fucking on a desk. No big deal."

His hands stopped kneading my neck. "Two of your employees fucked on a desk?"

"Oh, yes. So now I'm two people down, and I'm sure I won't be able to replace them since we're already over budget for the year. And I was late to get the kids from camp, and I forgot the damn chicken. But it's fine," I muttered, digging through our junk drawer for pizza coupons.

Out of the corner of my eye, I saw him studying my face. "I don't think it's fine, Eva."

"What do you mean?"

"I've been telling you to quit since Miles was born. Maybe it's time you listened?"

I abruptly stopped rummaging through loose change, old flyers, and ketchup packets, and looked over at him. "Seriously, Aaron? Are we doing this right now?"

He threw his hands up. "What? What's so wrong with that? Why do you get so fucking worked up when I mention it?"

"Because I can't just quit my job. We have a mortgage, car payments, and two kids who are gonna go to college one day. And we enjoy, you know, *things*." I waved my hand around our remodeled kitchen, complete with sparkling granite, a Sub-Zero refrigerator, and an espresso machine that cost more than I cared to think about.

"Eva, we'll be fine. The firm does well enough that you don't have to worry about any of that."

I scrubbed my hands over my face, pressing my hands into my forehead to stop the throbbing. Aaron made enough on his own to support us. But I never could quite admit to him that I didn't want to quit because I *wanted* to work. Even on the worst days, I still remembered how much satisfaction it brought me. How lucky I felt to merge my background in marketing with my passion for music. It reminded me of the good times I'd had working for Keith and the band. Sure, some of the memories from that period of my life were painful, but I'd loved that job. And I loved the one I had now, too.

But that gnawed at my insides and made me feel like my priorities were out of whack. Drew and Miles were my world, but my career was important to me, too. Why did Aaron have to make me feel like that was so wrong?

I let my hands fall from my face. "I just…I don't want to quit."

He threw his head back and sighed. "I don't understand this. Think of all the time you'll be able to spend with the kids. We won't have to rearrange our days when they're sick. You won't forget to take the stupid chicken out of the freezer."

I shot him a look. "Really, Aaron?"

"I'm just saying, Eva. Look at Allison. The most stressful part of her day is whether or not she wins her fucking tennis match." He ran his hands through his hair before tossing them into the air. "Don't you want that?"

I bristled at the mention of his law partner's wife.

"Why do you look like that?"

I reached for my glass and took a long swallow of wine. "Because I'm fucking sick of being compared to her. I'm sick of you wanting me to *be* her."

"I don't…" He trailed off and pinched the bridge of his nose. "I don't want you to be her, I just don't understand why you don't want to quit. I'm offering you the fucking *dream*, Eva, and you're telling me I'm an asshole for doing it."

"My job *is* my dream, and I don't want to be a stay-at-home mom, okay?" The words tumbled out of my mouth before I was able to stop them. It was the first time I'd said it so plainly. There had always been other reasons. Money for vacations, saving for retirement, having a backup income in case the firm ever went under.

I gripped the counter, feeling the heightened rise and fall of my chest. Aaron's jaw tightened as his eyes flicked to the right, staring past me, out of the window over the kitchen sink. I opened my mouth several times to speak, but nothing came out.

"Well, then," he finally said, grabbing his car keys. "Since your fucking job is more important than this family, *I'll* go pick up the goddamn pizza."

CHAPTER FORTY-EIGHT

AUGUST 2003

From: Eva Mitchell
To: Denise Abbott
Date: August 25, 2003 9:56PM
Subject: News

Well, I did it, Denise. I turned in my resignation. In one month, I will officially be a stay-at-home mom.

Me. Eva Holloway. Mitchell. Whatever.

I didn't tell you I was definitely gonna do it because I was afraid of…well, disappointing you, I guess, and you talking me out of it. Or maybe I was afraid of talking myself out of it. I still don't know if it's the best decision for me, but I have to think about my marriage and our family. I mean, Aaron was right about things being easier. And I'll have so much more time with the kids, especially Miles. I have some of the best memories of being with my mom when I was little—maybe we can make those memories, too.

I guess I'll figure it out as I go. Not sure if all of a sudden I'm supposed to start baking and making Halloween costumes? Sign up for tennis lessons? God, all of those things sound so not me. But maybe they are, and I just don't know it. Maybe I have to give them a chance. All except the Halloween costumes, of course, because that's just crazy talk.

Aaron wants another kid, but I told him no on that. You know I love Drew and Miles more than anything, but I can't handle three. He was mopey about it but is so happy I'll be at home now, I think he decided to let that one go.

I don't know…I just had to do it, I guess. I didn't want our family to fall apart. And with me so focused on my job, I was afraid that's what was gonna happen.

Don't hate me, OK?

Love and miss you.

From: Denise Abbott
To: Eva Mitchell
Date: August 26, 2003 9:16AM
Subject: Re: News

As if I could ever hate you, babe.

I do have to say I'm a little…surprised. I mean, I know it was causing some issues between you and Aaron, but I figured he'd back off at some point.

I just worry, Eva, because you love that job and I…You know what, I'm going to shut the fuck up because you did what you needed to do, and that's what's important. All I want is for you to be happy. And if this is gonna make you happy, then it's the right decision.

Gotta run, but I'm calling you tonight.
XOXO

PART III

CHAPTER FORTY-NINE

SEPTEMBER 2008

From: Eva Mitchell
To: Denise Abbott
Date: September 16, 2008 11:14AM
Subject: Reporter Guy / Holy Shit

Holy shit. I just talked to the *Rolling Stone* reporter for an hour. I swear those guys must have some sort of magic spell they cast on people to get them to talk. Everything started spilling out—how I ran into Danny and moved to LA, how Eric hated me but then told Keith to hire me. I told him Eric and I eventually became friends and stayed in touch for a while after he went to rehab. And of course, he asked about that night in Denver when Eric…you know. It was almost like I was right there on the stage again, Denise—my hands on his chest, the medics pulling me back, Danny walking away.

Fucking Danny.

I think I need some time to come down from all of this, but I promise I'll call later. Strange what trips down memory lane can do to you.

Love you.

CHAPTER FIFTY
DANNY

OCTOBER 2008

I pulled my BlackBerry from the inside pocket of my jacket, checking to see if I had any missed calls before placing it on the bar top and sinking onto the leather-cushioned stool with a sigh. It had been a long day of meetings at the label's satellite office after a long flight out from LA the day before, and I was ready for a drink. One of my reps had been singing the praises of a young band out of Nashville for months and had finally convinced me to come hear them play a gig. He was right. They sounded even better live than they did on the demo I'd listened to in my office at least twenty times, wondering if there was a place in today's market for old-school rock 'n' roll. The kind I used to play before I'd walked off the stage that night.

A cute young blond with her hair up in a twist smiled and placed a white cocktail napkin in front of me.

"What can I get you?"

"Um, just a beer. What's that local pale ale? Zoo something? I can't ever remember."

She chuckled and nodded over to the line of taps behind her. "Yazoo Pale?"

"That would be it." I flashed her a grin, startling as my Black-Berry vibrated against the bar. I picked it up to see Jade's name displayed on the screen. I ran my hand along my brow, clicking

272

the button to send the call to voicemail. I wasn't in the mood to hear about her day spent lounging poolside at the Beverly Hilton or how one of her twentysomething friends-slash-enemies had stolen some modeling gig from her. I was pretty sure she was fucking someone wealthier than me, anyway.

While I did well as head of A&R for the label, it was obvious Jade had her sights set much higher. I wasn't upset about it. I'd known for months that I'd let my dick do way too much of the thinking when getting involved with her. And it was clear she'd come to realize that dating an ex-guitarist with one hit album in the '80s wasn't going to buy her the mansion in Beverly Hills with five luxury cars parked in the driveway. But for some reason, she kept coming around, and I kept letting her.

The red light on my BlackBerry blinked again.

Jade: *WHERE R U?*

I tapped out a quick reply that read *in a meeting* and turned the phone off.

The bartender set my beer down on the napkin. "Not from around here?"

"No," I said, slipping the device back into my pocket. "Los Angeles. Just in town for work."

She cocked her head, giving me the once-over. "Music biz?"

I chuckled. "Yeah, how'd you know?"

"It's that sort-of-messy-but-not hair, black blazer, shirt with the three top buttons undone kind of thing," she said, waving her hand in front of me.

I raised my chin and looked at her out of the side of my eye, half smiling. "That obvious?"

"Totally. But don't worry," she added, winking. "It's a good look on you."

"Ha," I managed as I took a sip of my beer. "I'm gonna leave a good tip, regardless. You don't have to flatter an old man."

She bit her lip flirtatiously while studying my face. "Is… thirty-five…old?"

I laughed as I placed my beer back on the napkin. "No, but

forty-four is."

She smiled and glanced to her left, nodding to a customer trying to get her attention. "My name's Rain. Let me know if you need anything else," she said, her hand trailing along the smooth wood as she walked toward the other end of the bar.

I shook my head, chuckling to myself. I really needed to meet some women my own age. Maybe someone who wasn't named after a gemstone or a weather event.

I took another swallow of my beer and ran my finger around the edge of the pint glass. Why *hadn't* I found someone to settle down with? For the past fifteen years, my relationships—if you could call them that—had been with a string of younger women who were primarily interested in which bands I knew and how much money I made. I'd only had one girlfriend whom I actually considered to be serious, and she'd walked out after several years of arguments about my inability to commit to marriage. And before that...Well, I didn't allow myself to think about before that very much.

I sighed and pulled out my phone, debating whether or not to text Jade. As soon as it flipped on, I saw I had three texts, all pictures of her with my German shepherd, Jade's full lips pouting for the camera.

Jade: *Come home.*

Jade: *We miss you.*

Jade: *Bridget is such a bitch. Slept with the photographer from the swimsuit shoot and got a bigger spread than I did. We hate her.*

I rolled my eyes, feeling bad that I'd left my dog in the care of such an exhausting human being. My fingers moved over the keys, typing something meaningless, when I heard the laugh. I looked up from the phone and scanned the open dining space across from my seat at the circular bar in the center of the restaurant. It was early and only a few tables were filled. A young couple at one. A group of women in business attire toasting around a larger table.

I shook my head and looked back at my text to Jade when

I heard it again.

I shifted my head to the left, this time certain of the direction from which it came. There was a woman with blond hair standing at the front of the restaurant, talking with the hostess. She turned around, extending her hand in a wave to Rain the bartender before taking a seat at a four-top table.

My breath caught in my throat and a rush of adrenaline surged through my body. It had been nearly twenty years, but I knew that laugh. I knew that face. What I didn't know is how the hell I'd ended up in the same restaurant in the same city at the same time as Eva Holloway.

I quickly averted my eyes, pretending to look at my phone while a flurry of thoughts blew through my mind.

Maybe it isn't her.

Why would she be in Nashville?

They say everyone has a doppelgänger…right?

I peered up from my BlackBerry, and she pulled her own phone from her purse, checked it quickly, then snapped it shut. She ran her hand through her hair and glanced over at the bar before turning her attention to the menu. If she'd seen me, she didn't recognize me. Why the hell would she? The way I'd treated her, she'd probably completely erased me from her memory.

"You doing okay over here?"

The sound of Rain's voice startled me, and I dropped my phone on the bar top.

"Huh? Sorry. Work email."

She raised an eyebrow. "Seems serious. You might need something stronger than a beer."

"Yeah, probably," I muttered, taking a long swallow of my drink. I set the nearly empty pint glass back on the napkin with a long sigh.

She smiled and turned to the shelves behind her, grabbing a bottle of bourbon and pouring two fingers into a rocks glass, which she slid over to me. "On the house."

I tipped my glass toward her before taking a sip. "Thanks."

She nodded and headed to the other end of the bar.

My hand shook as I set the glass back down, and my pulse pounded below my jaw as I snuck another glance across the room. Her hair was a little darker, a more natural shade of blond, and the hard angles of her body had softened. She wore faded jeans and a plain white T-shirt under a long black cardigan with the sleeves pushed up. A large silver and turquoise medallion hung below her chest, and several bangles dangled from her wrist.

She looked beautiful.

And I was a fucking idiot.

I'd tried to rationalize walking off that stage a hundred times, but it always came back to the fact that if I was honest with myself, I couldn't. Yes, I'd become fed up with Eric's shit, but that was no excuse. I just didn't want to deal with it, simple as that.

What I'd done hit me in the car on the way back to the hotel that night in Denver. Not just leaving Eric while he was near death, which was bad enough in itself. I'd left Eva there with him. The girl I'd sworn was the love of my life, the girl I should've gone to any length to protect, who trusted and believed in me more than anyone.

After that, I almost decided to quit the music business altogether but fell into an A&R job and somehow worked my way up to head of the department. I'd seen Will and Keith in passing a few times over the years, but we'd never spoken, only exchanged awkward looks of recognition. I heard Matt had moved back to San Francisco. And Eric…Everyone knew about Eric Stratton. Somehow our paths hadn't managed to cross—I tried to make sure of that—but I never knew when they might. And that honestly scared the fuck out of me.

Now, here I was in the same damn restaurant as Eva. I sucked in a deep breath as I considered my options. Sit at the bar like the idiot I was and stare at her until maybe she noticed me? Pretend like I was walking to the bathroom and I just happened to see her?

Fuck it.

I swallowed the last of my bourbon and was about to stand when a man with dark hair entered the restaurant and walked toward the table. He was followed by two boys, one with the same brown hair, one blond, who were exchanging shoves. My stomach dropped as I watched the man place his hand on Eva's shoulder while the boys flopped into the chairs across from her.

I slowly sank back into my seat and scrubbed my hands along my face.

Of course, I thought to myself. *Of fucking course.*

"You all right?"

I slid my hands down to see Rain standing in front of me.

"Yeah," I lied. "Just tired, I guess."

She smiled and turned to grab the bottle of bourbon behind her.

"Hey, can I ask you a question?"

She rested a hand on her hip as she refilled my glass. "Go for it."

I sucked in a deep breath. "That woman, the one who waved to you when she came in…what's her name?"

She motioned toward the tables behind her. "That one over there?"

I nodded quickly.

"Oh, that's Eva. She used to come in here all the time, but this is the first I've seen her in a while." She tilted her head. "Why? You know her?"

I stared at the table across the bar. It didn't matter anymore. She wouldn't see me. She was too focused on her family.

Her family.

The words echoed in my brain.

"Hello?"

I shook my head and looked over to see Rain tapping her

fingers on the counter. "Oh, uh…no. She just looks like somebody I used to know."

I felt like someone had just stabbed me in the gut, but I managed a weak laugh as she winked and turned to greet the couple who'd settled in a few seats down from me. I sighed and downed the last of my drink, knowing I couldn't sit there and endure the twist of the knife as I watched the girl I'd let get away—twice—with someone else. I threw a hundred on the bar and headed toward the exit, stealing one last glance before pushing through the door.

CHAPTER FIFTY-ONE

OCTOBER 2008

From: Eva Mitchell
To: Denise Abbott
Date: October 24, 2008 1:03AM
Subject: UGH

It's one a.m., and I can't fucking sleep because I had to sit through the most painful fucking dinner earlier tonight. Miles begged Aaron to pick him up from school and for us to all have dinner together at his favorite restaurant for his birthday. Aaron's friend owns it, and we used to go there all the time. Maybe Miles thought it would magically put his family back together.

Anyway, Aaron agreed to it, and I wanted to evaporate into thin air the entire time, even though I smiled and laughed and pretended like everything was fine. It's hard for me to look at him, Denise. I just keep thinking about the fact that he was fucking someone nearly half my age before we even split up, and it pisses me off and hurts me and makes me wanna throw shit and cry 'til I can't fucking cry anymore.

I know I sound like a broken record, but I still can't help but think I did something wrong. Why wasn't I good enough for him? If I had just agreed to have another kid...if I'd been happier staying at home...would things have been different?

All right, I'm going to stop now. My mind is spiraling, and I should at least try to get some sleep so I don't look as haggard as I feel.

Love you.

———

From: Denise Abbott
To: Eva Mitchell
Date: October 24, 2008 11:08AM
Subject: Re: UGH

He's a motherfucker, Eva. MOTHERFUCKER. I swear to God I will fly out to Nashville and help you slash his tires. Waiting for the word "go."

You were too fucking good for him, babe. You hear me? Because if you don't, I'll say it over and over again 'til you do. You're an amazing woman, and he'll realize what he lost soon enough. What happened has nothing to do with you and everything to do with him. You are the same beautiful, independent person you've always been, and for some reason, he wanted to squash that. Chin up and tits out, sister. You're gonna come out of this stronger than you've ever been. Just gotta get that light he dimmed to shine bright again.

Call whenever you need me. I'm here.

Love you more.

———

From: Eva Mitchell
To: Denise Abbott
Date: October 25, 2008 9:05AM
Subject: Re: UGH

Thanks, babe. You always know what to say. And you're right. He is a motherfucker. But unfortunately, that motherfucker is the father of my children, so I don't know if I should slash his tires. I'll think about it. ;)

On another note, that reporter guy, Simon, from *Rolling Stone* emailed me and said the feature on Eric will be coming out next month. Anyway, I don't know how much he really used in the article, but I'm sort of nervous. What if I said something wrong? I don't want Eric to hate me anymore than he probably already does.But hell, what does it matter? That was so long ago, and we have completely different lives now. He's living it up in California, dating movie stars and driving fancy cars, while I'm in Tennessee, divorced and hauling two kids around. I mean, I said nice things about him. The best things about him. Because he was a good friend to me. Just wish I'd been a better one to him.

All right, I've gotta run. Aaron called and is allegedly working today (note: it is Saturday) and won't be able to take the boys like he promised. Shocking, I know.

Miss you.

———

From: Denise Abbott
To: Eva Mitchell
Date: October 25, 2008 6:29PM
Subject: Re: UGH

Again, I say: MOTHERFUCKER. Checking flights to Nashville right now. Make sure you have a knife sharp enough to cut through tire rubber.

You've got nothing to worry about with Eric. He wouldn't have told the reporter to call you if he didn't want what you had to say in the article. I can't wait to read it, honestly. Wonder what ever happened to Matt? ;)

XOXO

CHAPTER FIFTY-TWO
EVA

I hurried into the drugstore, flipping my sunglasses onto my head and mumbling a quick hello to the woman behind the counter who welcomed me to Walgreens. I almost left my glasses on, like I was on some sort of covert mission, but reminded myself I was just an average person buying a magazine. No one in the store knew my name was in it. And chances were high that no one I knew in town would ever read it.

I hoped.

Shit. What if they do? What if the parents at school see it?

Breaking News: Local Stay-at-Home Mom was Former Hollywood Wild Child. Details at Ten.

"Too late now," I muttered, taking a sharp right turn and heading past the greeting cards.

Shape. Glamour. Cosmo. I scanned the racks until I landed on Eric's face. My breath caught in my throat, and I slowly raised my hand to cover my mouth.

There were faint lines etched into his forehead, like the ones I saw when I looked in the mirror, and a lock of short dark-blond hair fell over them. His blue eyes were focused directly on the camera, and an invisible string tugged the corners of his mouth into a humble smile. A grateful smile, like the one I'd seen as he walked toward me in that rehab center nineteen years before.

I plucked the magazine off the shelf, then headed for the front of the store, grabbing a pack of gum and a Snickers at the checkout so it would look like I wasn't there just to buy the magazine. As if the cashier cared.

Back in my car, I immediately lit a cigarette, dangling my arm all the way out the window in the parking lot, while I flipped to the article and scanned it for my name.

Twice.

A sigh of relief found its way into the last stream of smoke I blew out before tossing my cig and starting my car. As far as I could tell, I hadn't been misquoted or said anything inane. But I still dashed through yellow lights and rolled through stop signs because I needed to get home where I could read the article in its entirety.

Which I did.

Twice.

I settled deeper into the couch, examining the pictures placed throughout the pages. I traced my finger over one of them, outlining my memory of that day on a particularly long stretch of road during the Black Widow Rising tour. Me and Eric on the bus, arms thrown around each other, singing what seemed like the entire KISS catalog using beer bottles as microphones.

Stratton and Eva (Holloway) Mitchell, who worked as part of Counting Backward's management team, somewhere in the middle of nowhere, 1989.

As I read the caption, a warm sensation traveled up through my body and settled into my smile. That was before I'd known how bad things were. And how much worse they were going to get. When days and nights of drinking and bumps of coke to keep the band going seemed like par for the course in the world of sex, drugs, and rock 'n' roll. Not like the problem they would become.

I wondered how Simon had gotten the photograph. Had

Eric saved it? I scanned the spread, taking in several other pictures of the band from that time period, sucking in a deep breath when I got to the one of Danny with a towel around his neck and his arm casually draped over Eric's shoulder backstage after a show. My eyes quickly darted to other photos of Eric as he progressed through his solo career.

Maybe Eric didn't hate me. He told Simon I'd saved his life. How good I'd been for the band. How good I'd been for *him*. I supposed the first part was true, that the CPR had kept him alive, but it was strange to see the words in print. As far as I knew, it was the first time I'd ever been mentioned publicly in connection with that night. But how could he say I'd been good for him when I'd vanished without a trace? When I'd abandoned him?

At least my part in the article felt like some small sort of redemption for what I'd done. I was able to tell the world what a beautiful person Eric was. That he'd suggested I take the job with the band and he had believed in me, appreciated me, and trusted me. I'd left out the part about disappearing on him, only saying we'd lost touch over the years. The shame was too much. I could name the reason: that I craved something stable and I'd left that world behind to find it. But I'd ultimately let a friendship go in the worst way possible. I hadn't even said goodbye.

All because…

I squeezed my eyes shut as the thought began to painfully claw its way to the front of my brain. I pressed my fingers into my forehead, pushing it back down into the shadowy tomb where it had lived for nearly two decades. But this time, the thought felt stronger and the grave shallower, leaving me wondering how much longer I could keep it buried.

CHAPTER FIFTY-THREE
EVA

"I don't understand why Santa is so mean to Rudolph," Miles announced, stretching across the couch in his plaid pajamas as a commercial popped on the TV screen.

Drew snorted from the other side of the sectional. "Santa's not even real, dork," he said, not bothering to look up from his phone.

"Drew! Do not say that to your brother!" I picked up a throw pillow and tossed it across the couch.

Drew flipped his long blond bangs out of his eyes, his thumbs furiously working the buttons on his cell. "It's true. Santa isn't real, and Miles *is* a dork."

"Call him that one more time and you lose your phone for a week."

"I'm just saying Santa's mean in this show," Miles explained. "I *know* he's not real."

I cocked my head. "You do?"

"Um, I'm *ten* now, Mom."

My eyes widened, and I nodded slowly. "Oh. Right. Of course."

"So you can ditch the different wrapping paper for our presents," Drew said, the glow of the phone illuminating his face as a wide grin spread across it. "We know they're all from you."

As Miles started giggling and rolled off the sofa onto the floor, I couldn't help but smile. If there was one thing my boys could agree on, it was how enjoyable it was to make fun of me.

Rudolph's flashing red nose reappeared on the screen, and Miles turned onto his stomach, chin in his hands, as the band of misfits made their way through a snowstorm. It was dark in the room, except for the television and the colorful display of Christmas tree lights dancing on the walls.

Where had the time gone? In less than three weeks we would celebrate our first Christmas without Aaron in the house. Some days that hit me harder than others. Grief was strange like that—never quite linear, no matter how much I wanted it to be. Sometimes the ache in my chest lifted, and it felt like years had passed since he'd left. Other times it was so heavy, I could've sworn he'd just told me yesterday he wanted a divorce.

The phone trilled from the kitchen. The home phone—the one I always forgot we had because I used my cell for every-thing. Sure it was someone trying to convince me to switch auto insurance companies, I decided to let it go to voicemail.

And then it rang again.

"Mom, are you gonna get that? It's super annoying," Drew said, still focused on his phone.

"Your mouth is going to get you grounded for the entire Christmas break," I warned as I pushed myself up from the couch and walked into the kitchen.

I flipped on the overhead light and plucked the cordless receiver off its base to see a 310 area code displayed on the screen.

Los Angeles? Could it be Denise…calling from some random number?

Oh God, I thought. *What if she's been taken for ransom and somehow managed to steal the kidnapper's phone and only knows my home number by heart and her fate hangs on whether or not I take this call?*

Somehow, this outrageous scenario managed to morph into reality, and I quickly pressed the talk button.

"Denise?" My voice was low and quiet, as if I were afraid her kidnapper might hear me.

There was a pause on the other end, and then the caller spoke. "Hello?"

The male voice sent a tingle of adrenaline up my spine. "Hello? Who's this?"

Another pause.

Fucking telemarketers. I rolled my eyes and was about to punch the button to disconnect the call when he spoke again.

"Wow, sorry. It's just so crazy hearing your voice." He paused. "It's, um…it's Danny."

The tingle in my spine spread throughout my entire body. I opened my mouth to speak several times, but all that came out were a few tiny squeaks from the back of my throat.

"Danny Kincaid," he continued, mistaking my silence for a simple memory lapse that could be remedied by stating his full name.

My silence, however, had nothing to do with my memory and everything to do with the fact that the only words my brain could process at the moment were *What. The. Fuck.*

"Eva? Are you there?"

Danny Kincaid.

The name spun like a tilt-a-whirl in my head. I leaned against the kitchen counter to steady myself, managing a few soft breaths, which signaled I was still on the line.

"Just don't hang up, okay? I…Fuck, this sounds crazy, but I read the *Rolling Stone* article, and I haven't been able to stop thinking about you since."

"How'd you get my number, Danny?" My voice was cold, clipped.

He cleared his throat. "I, um…I saw your new last name in the article and looked you up."

FOR EVA

There was more silence while he waited for my response. But I had nothing to say. After spending the better portion of a year rehearsing all the things I would say to Danny Kincaid after he broke my heart for the second time...*nothing*.

"I'm sorry to call you out of the blue like this. And I know it's insane, but the article got me thinking about everything that happened and how I never said I was sorry, and I guess I just wanted to say that. To say I'm sorry."

I took a deep breath and placed my hand over the phone's mouthpiece. "Boys, I need to talk to someone," I called as I hurried down the hall. "I'll be in my room."

I closed the door and sat at the end of my bed in the darkness, the only light a sliver of pale yellow from the house next door cutting through the window.

"Eva, are you there?"

I sighed and ran my fingers through my hair. "Yeah, Danny. I'm here. What do you want me to say? That I forgive you? Would that make you feel better?"

"No. I mean, yeah, I guess it would," he admitted. "But I don't expect that. I just needed to say it. And I want to know that you're happy. Because I saw you a few months ago in Nashville and—"

"You *what?*"

How the fuck did he see me?

"I was in town for work. I had no idea you live there. I was at this restaurant, and I saw you with your husband and kids." His voice faltered. "You waved at the bartender, and I asked her for your name because I couldn't believe it was you. But it was."

I swallowed hard, trying to dislodge the lump that formed in my throat at the mention of that horrific birthday dinner. That had to have been when he'd seen me.

"You looked so fucking beautiful," Danny continued. "And then the article came out and I...I just wanted to know if you're happy. Because you deserve to be, Eva."

I stared at the thin slice of light shining off the wood floor.

"Eva?"

"Yeah, well, my husband and I got divorced, Danny, so, you know…I've been better," I said, the words escaping before I could stop them.

He blew out a long breath. "Shit, Eva. I'm sorry."

I mumbled an involuntary "thanks," cursing myself for telling him something so personal…so painful.

"I, uh…I was kinda surprised you talked to the *Rolling Stone* guy," he said. "But I guess I didn't know—I mean, I *don't* know— what happened after…everything."

"Yeah, well, you don't know because you fucking took off, Danny. But I talked to the reporter because I owed it to Eric."

His breath shuddered at the mention of Eric's name.

"I was wrong to leave. There aren't words to tell you how sorry I am." He paused. "I'm not sure my saying any of this matters now."

I sighed, the tightness gripping my chest easing a bit. "I'm not sure, either. But thanks, I guess."

He sighed. "Fuck, I wish I'd never let you go. You wouldn't be going through all of this right now if I hadn't been so fucking stupid."

My eyes narrowed. "What did you just say?"

"I just meant if I hadn't left, maybe we'd, you know, still be together. And you wouldn't be in your, uh, situation."

I balled my left hand into a fist, nails digging into flesh. "*Fuck you*, Danny."

"Wha…what'd I say?"

A bitter laugh escaped from somewhere deep inside me. And then, when just moments before I'd thought I had nothing to say to Danny Kincaid, I realized I had plenty.

"You are un-fucking-believable," I spat into the receiver. "Somehow, after nearly twenty years of not seeing or talking to you, you've managed to make *my* pain all about *you*. Well, let me tell you, Danny—I'm grateful *every day* of my life that you left. I would go through all of this hurt a million times over, knowing

I would get to be a mother to the two most incredible kids in the world. But you'll never understand this because you'd need to have the ability to care about someone other than yourself. And you calling after what you did to me, Eric, and the band shows me once again how selfish you are, since I feel pretty damn confident this is all just an attempt to ease *your* conscience. But good fucking luck with that because I can assure you, your apology means *nothing* to me, Danny. *Fucking nothing.*"

I mashed my thumb into the button to end the call, throwing the phone on the bed and flopping back onto the mattress. I inhaled deeply, holding my breath until my body was ready to expel the anger that had settled somewhere deep inside of me all those years ago. Anger I hadn't realized was still there.

The phone rang again. I groaned and swiped the receiver off the bed.

3-1-fucking-0.

I picked up, determined to put an end to this bullshit.

"I want you to listen to me," I began, trying to keep my voice down. "I'm done. The conversation is over. So do not fucking call me *ever again.*"

I tried to hang up, but the off button was stuck from when I'd jabbed it earlier.

"Goddamnit," I muttered, beginning to dig at the edges of it with my nail when I heard the voice on the other end of the line.

"Hello? Do I…do I have the right number? Is this Eva?"

I cocked my head and looked at the digits on the screen. Definitely 310. But definitely *not* Danny.

I raised the phone back to my ear.

"This is Eva. Who's this?"

CHAPTER FIFTY-FOUR
ERIC

"Hi, I'm actually calling from the KISS Army headquarters. We were going through our records recently and noticed you haven't been active in the organization since 1979. Would you be interested in renewing your membership...Eva Holloway?"

I cupped my hand over the phone, stifling a laugh. I silently prayed she'd get the joke before hanging up on me. Once Simon told me he'd gotten in touch with her and all the things she'd said, I'd spent countless nights lying awake in bed wondering if I should try to contact her. And what I should say if I did. Starting with *Why'd you disappear on me?* seemed a bit harsh, even though I'd spent years wanting an answer to that exact question. Was it the last letter I'd written—the one that went unanswered when I told her I wanted to see her after the tour was over? Or had the song about our night in Cleveland scared her off? Did she know it was about her and didn't have the heart to tell me she didn't feel the same?

She was quiet for a moment, and the churning in my stomach quickened. But then I heard it. The most beautiful laugh in the world. God, I'd missed that laugh.

"Okay, who is this?" she managed to choke out. "Did Denise put you up to—"

She gasped. Then silence.

My body tensed, and the momentary relief turned to dread. *Fuck. Did she hang up?*

"Oh my God," she said, her voice softening. "Is this…Eric, is that you?"

"That depends. Is it okay that it's me?"

"Oh my…Yes! Yes, it's okay! I can't believe this. How… What…How…"

"Well, I was just sitting here, listing every KISS album in order of greatness, like normal people do, and I got stuck. Is *Love Gun* number four? Because obviously, *Destroyer* is number one, followed by the self-titled album, then *Creatures of the Night*… but after that, it gets tricky."

Eva cleared her throat, and I imagined her lips pressed together, trying to hide a smile. "I can see why you called, Eric. This is a very serious quandary. But before I can answer, I need to know if we're talking only studio recordings, or do live albums count, too? And what about the solo records? In or out?"

I grinned, lifting my bare feet off the wooden planks of the deck and onto the ottoman in front of me. "Fuck! I hadn't even thought about that. See, you've just blown the whole thing wide open."

She laughed again. Was she tossing her hair behind her shoulder? Was it still long and blond? Simon had told me she was living in Nashville, which explained why the last number I had for her in Chicago had been disconnected that final time I tried to reach her.

We both spoke at the same time.

"So I—"

"So what—"

She chuckled. "You first."

"Okay, but before I start, I need to know who you were yelling at when you picked up the phone," I said, taking a sip of water. The inside of my mouth felt like it was lined with cotton.

"Oh, that? That was nothing. Just, you know, something stupid. What *I* wanna know is, am I seriously talking to you right now? I'm not in some, like, parallel-universe-slash-*The Matrix* thing, am I?"

I looked out at the hazy swirl of orange and purple as the sun began to disappear into the ocean. "Sometimes I wonder that myself. But I'm pretty sure this reality is…real."

"So then—and I don't mean this in a why are you calling me way—but *why are you calling me?*" She giggled, and I detected a hint of nervousness in her voice, too. "I mean, I'm glad you're calling me. Was it the article? Did I say something wrong?"

I shook my head, as if she could see me through the phone. "Eva, the fact that you even took the time to talk to Simon…" I paused and cleared my throat as years of suppressed emotions rose up from my core. "I didn't know if you would. We hadn't talked in so long, and…well, if I'm being honest, part of the reason I mentioned your name was because I was hoping he would find you. Because then *I* could find you."

"So you don't…hate me?"

Her words pricked at my heart. She'd helped launch my career with the band. She'd helped catapult us to stardom. *She'd saved my life.*

"I could never hate you, Eva."

"But I…I know I kind of disappeared, and I'm so sorry, I just—"

"Hey. The past is the past. You don't have to explain it to me." No matter how badly I wanted to know what I'd done to make her disappear, there was only one thing that mattered. "The important thing is I found you."

"Yes, you did." Her voice radiated warmth all the way to the West Coast. "Did Simon give you my number?"

"Yeah," I admitted. "He's not technically supposed to do that, but he thought you wouldn't mind hearing from me. Actually, his exact words were, 'if you don't fucking call that fucking woman, you're mad as a cut snake, mate.'"

We both laughed at my weak attempt at an Australian accent.

"Well, he was right. If you can't tell, I'm really glad to hear your voice."

"Yeah?" I asked, running a hand through my hair as the breeze off the water picked up.

"Yeah. But hey, can you hang on a second?"

There was shuffling and a door opening. I couldn't make out exactly what she was saying, but there was another voice, then a creaking sound as the door shut.

"Sorry. One of my kids wanted a snack. And he's such a slick negotiator. Please note, he did not get that from me." She laughed, differently this time, but I couldn't put my finger on why. My brain was too busy processing one word.

Kids.

Tiny humans.

Eva is a…mom?

"Oh, wow. Kids, huh? That's…wow…that's great. How many?"

"Two boys. Ten and fifteen."

I pressed my hand into my chest. I knew from the article she'd changed her last name, so chances were good she was married and settled into the normal life she'd said she wanted, but it still stung to find out for certain. "So you're…married, I guess?"

She hesitated before answering. "Divorced. Kinda recently."

I know I'm a dick for thinking this, but thank you, God. Thank you.

"Oh, I'm…sorry?" I wasn't sure if she was happy or sad about the situation, so I gave her space to fill in the blanks.

"It's okay. I'm fine. I mean, I'm not, but I am. If that makes any sense."

"It makes perfect sense, actually."

"So enough about that," she insisted. "What about *you?* Making multiplatinum albums, selling out stadiums, dating movie stars and supermodels. Do you actually know how famous you are?"

"Ha! I can't win on this one. If I say yes, I sound like a pompous asshole. If I say no, it sounds like a humble brag."

She clicked her tongue against the roof of her mouth. "Okay, then. Tell me this. Where are you right now? Right this minute, where are you and what are you doing?"

I smiled, looking down at the beach as several couples strolled by. "You know, just...California."

"*Where* in California?"

"Malibu."

"*Where* in Malibu?"

"What do you mean *where* in Malibu?"

"You know what I mean by *where* in Malibu."

"Fine. My house in Malibu."

"And..."

I smiled and threw my head back. "And I'm sitting on the big deck of my big house looking out at the big ocean. Any more questions?"

Eva laughed. A laugh that sent me floating over the water in front of me. I'd always known I missed her. But I didn't truly understand just how much until that moment.

"Okay, then," I began. "My turn. Where are *you* right now, and what are *you* doing?"

"I'm sitting on my bed in my 2900-square-foot ranch house in Nashville. It was built in 1963. Try not to be jealous."

Not jealous, I wanted to say. More like wishing I was there.

"I'm curious how you ended up in Tennessee," I said instead.

"My husband—ex-husband—is from here. So you know... family, jobs...life just takes you places."

"Yeah, I, uh...I figured you'd moved when your number was disconnected." I chewed on my lip. "I did try to find you. Internet and all that. Borderline stalking. Which I obviously suck at."

"Yeah, I'm sorry about that. I...Well, you were getting all

famous then and probably didn't have time to keep up with me, anyway."

I watched the last bit of light fade into the ocean. Something told me there was more to the story, but I didn't press her. Nor did I tell her that all the fucking fame in the world couldn't have stopped me from wondering where she was or what I'd done to make her disappear.

"No, it's fine, I get it," I said, knowing for certain I didn't get it at all. But like I'd said, the past was the past. "I mean, I *did* have time to keep up with you, but yeah, life and all that." I took a deep breath and closed my eyes, trying to stop the automated recording telling me her number was no longer in service from playing in my head. "Anyway, speaking of life being crazy, I'm actually going to be in Nashville the week after Christmas. I've been helping produce an album for these kids out of Indiana, and they're heading down there to record some tracks. A little unusual to do it around the holidays, but I'm free right now, and studio time is cheap. Would you wanna, like, maybe get togeth—"

"Yes," she answered before I could finish my sentence. "Yes! When will you be here?"

The corners of my mouth turned so far upward I was sure my cheeks were going to explode. "The twenty-seventh through the thirty-first. Quick trip because I need to get back to LA for the opening of the counseling center, but I'd really love to see you."

"It's so amazing you're doing that, Eric. You're gonna help so many kids."

"I hope so. I really do."

"Well, while you're here, we'll do dinner, drinks, you name it. Shit. Not drinks. No drinks. I mean, you're still…Oh God, I feel like an idiot."

I laughed. "You're not an idiot. And yes, still sober."

"Well, I am an idiot, but whatever. I'm proud of you. And I can't wait to see you."

"Yeah. Me, too."

We sat in silence for a few seconds.

What is she thinking?

Is she thinking what I'm thinking?

What the fuck am I doing thinking what I'm thinking, anyway? We were just friends back then. And that's probably all we'll be now.

"So, um, I'm sure you have to get your kids to bed or, you know, whatever you do with kids. But I'll call you when I get to town."

"Yes. Please," she said before we exchanged cell numbers. "And don't forget about me. You're kind of my entire social life that week."

"I told you a long time ago I'd never forget you, Eva from Illinois."

"You did. I remember," she said, her voice softening. "I'll see you soon, Eric. Merry Christmas."

She sighed before the line went dead. I leaned back into the cushion of the chair, pressing the phone into my chest, as if that could keep us connected just a little bit longer.

CHAPTER FIFTY-FIVE

DECEMBER 2008

From: Eva Mitchell
To: Denise Abbott
Date: December 3, 2008 9:48PM
Subject: #@*($&@#$&@!!!

Denise. Denise, Denise, Denise!

You're never going to believe who just called me. Like, back to back crazy-ass phone calls. And before you yell at me for deeming this "phone-worthy news," I did try to call but got your voicemail at home and on your cell.

OK. So tonight I was watching TV with the boys and the phone rang. The landline. And I wouldn't normally answer a number I don't know, but it was a LA area code, and I thought you'd been kidnapped. Do not ever question my love for you.

I picked it up, and it wasn't you. Obviously it wasn't you because it was—are you ready for this?—DANNY KINCAID. Your eyes are not deceiving you. DANNY FUCKING KINCAID. He told me that he read the article in *Rolling Stone* and he saw me in Nashville when he was here for work and he hadn't been able to stop thinking about me since then and he was sorry for what he'd done to me.

WHAT THE FUCK.

Anyway, I ended up cussing him out (oh my God, it felt so good), and just after I hung up on him, the phone rang again. Another LA area code. So I answered and told him to never call me again, but it wasn't him, Denise. It wasn't him because it was Eric. Yes, that Eric.

He said he appreciated me doing an interview for the article and that he's coming to Nashville a couple days after Christmas, and he wants to see me. I said yes.

Was that right? Was that wrong? What am I doing, Denise? S.O.S.

———————

From: Denise Abbott
To: Eva Mitchell
Date: December 3, 2008 11:54PM
Subject: Re: #@*($&@#$&@!!!

OH. MY. GOD.

The only reason I'm not calling you right now is because it's nearly midnight there, and I don't want to disturb your beauty sleep because you need to look amazing when you see ERIC STRATTON.

Holy shit, Eva! You are 100% doing the right thing! Call me first thing tomorrow, and I'll tell you all the reasons why. Okay, I'll tell you one now. BECAUSE HE'S ERIC FUCKING STRATTON AND HE WAS IN LOVE WITH YOU BUT YOU COULD NEVER FUCKING ADMIT IT.

Also, Danny can go suck a dick.

Muah and call me.

———————

From: Eva Mitchell
To: Denise Abbott
Date: December 4, 2008 7:13AM
Subject: Re: #@*($&@#$&@!!!

FOR EVA

Stop with the whole "he was in love with you" thing. We were just good friends with a shared love of crab rangoon and KISS, and I ruined that by vanishing. For some reason, he's decided not to hate me for it. I'm not sure why, but maybe he'll tell me why when I see him.

Oh my God, I'm going to see him.

What if he just wants to meet me so he can yell at me in person? And tell me how horrible I am for disappearing on him?

Oh shit. Maybe I shouldn't go. I can't deal with that.

I'm calling you in exactly two hours. Or call me if you get this first.

Going to throw up now.

CHAPTER FIFTY-SIX
ERIC

DECEMBER 2008

"Just a black coffee." I handed the cashier a twenty and stuffed the change into the tip jar on the counter. As I stepped back to let the next customer order, I caught the woman to my right peering at me out of the corner of her eye and whispering to the man she was with before flashing me a nervous smile.

Shit, I thought, diverting my eyes. *Any other time. I swear, I wouldn't mind. Just not now when I can barely fucking function.*

"Hey, man, here you go," the barista said, placing my cup on the counter.

I muttered a quick "thanks," then headed to the back of the coffee shop, settling on a spot with a view of the door. I retrieved my cell from my pocket before draping my leather jacket over the chair and sitting down, my eyes darting between the entrance and the phone.

9:54 a.m.

Six minutes.

I was going to see Eva for the first time in nineteen years. From the way my leg bounced and my chest tightened every time the chime on the door rang, it was clear that my plan to have a moment of Zen before she arrived wasn't working. I'd actually gotten there later than intended and had lost all ability to remain calm about the situation.

The vibration of my phone against the table nearly sent me out of my skin. I scooped it up, relieved to see it was the manager of the band I was working with rather than Eva calling to tell me she'd decided she didn't want to see me.

"Hey, John, what's up?" I said, glancing at the door.

"Eric, hey, sorry to bother you, but I, uh, wanted to let you know the guys were out pretty late last night. I definitely don't want to inconvenience you or anything, but is there any way we could start an hour later in the studio today? It won't happen again. They're just excited, you know? This is the big city for them, and they may have…*overdone* things a bit."

"Fine. But tell them this is their one pass. I'm not making an album with a band that can't even show up to the studio on time," I said, adopting a serious tone even though I was laughing to myself thinking about how the years had caused the tables to turn.

"No, of course, I completely understand," he assured me, his voice quavering a bit. "It won't happen again."

He continued to apologize for the band, but the sound of clanging metal, followed by a vision of soft blond waves spilling over a gray scarf, rendered me completely uninterested in anything else he had to say.

"Yeah, it's fine, John. I gotta go."

Time slowed as I dropped my phone on the table and watched her turn to the left, scanning the faces in front of her. Her eyes moved past me, then shifted back and met mine. She tilted her head and a soft smile formed on her lips.

I rose from the chair as she made her way through the room, everything still moving in slow-motion. She stopped at the edge of the table, dropping her purse in the chair beside her, and before I knew what was happening, she'd wrapped her arms around me, the warm scent of vanilla filling my head as her hair brushed against my cheek.

I wanted so badly to pull her into my chest, to feel her

pressed against me, but I hesitated, worried I would make her uncomfortable. But while my mind was trying to figure out what to tell my body to do, she sank into me and rested her head on my shoulder. And that was all I needed. I breathed her in and held her so close that the years between us faded away.

Eva pulled back, her deep brown eyes brightening as her smile grew into a grin so full and beautiful it caused my stomach to flip.

"So not *The Matrix*, right?" She took my hands into hers, and though her skin was chilled from the cold day, my body turned warm. "You're here? This is really you?"

I chuckled, squeezing her hands. "It's really me. And you're really you?"

She laughed as she hung her purse on the back of her chair and slid into the seat. "It's me. Just a million years older."

"You look…" I paused and thought of all the ways I could describe her: absolutely stunning, still the most beautiful woman I'd ever laid eyes on, unbelievably fucking perfect in every way. I sucked in a breath, shaking my head as I sat across from her. "I know this is a thing people say sometimes to be nice, but *Jesus*—you look fucking incredible."

"Oh, wait, you obviously forgot your glasses. Here, you can borrow mine." She pretended to unzip her purse before turning her attention back to me with a wink.

But I could see her clearly. Very clearly. And it was like looking at a fucking angel.

"Eva, I'm serious, I—" I had to force myself to stop staring at her. "Well, just believe me when I say it's true."

Her cheeks pinked, and she dismissed me with a wave of her hand. "Ugh, whatever. But look at *you*. The short hair and this whole, like, stubble thing going on." She reached across the table and ran a finger along my jaw, sending a chill up my spine.

Was it just my imagination or was her hand trembling?

"You look good, Eric. Really good."

I managed a modest smile, still reeling from the electricity of her touch.

"But hey, you already know this," she added, unknotting her scarf and tossing it on the table. "Weren't you voted *Sexiest Man Alive* or something? Which, while one hundred percent accurate, is also one hundred percent hilarious."

"Oh God." I groaned. "I was a runner-up or something. I don't know. Can we never talk about this again?"

She giggled. "I dunno, I might need to bring it up at least one more time. But for now, I'm getting a coffee."

"Wait, let me get it," I said, my hand brushing against her ivory sweater as I reached out to stop her from getting up.

"No, no, no," she protested.

I began to stand up. "Eva, seriously, I want to."

"Oh my God, sit!" she insisted, laughing and squeezing my shoulder. "I've totally got it. Do you need anything?"

"Still stubborn, I see." I shot her a playful grin, then glanced over at my full cup. I hadn't even taken one sip. "But no, I'm good. Thank you."

I watched as she walked toward the counter, the heels of her boots clicking against the concrete floor. Her hips were fuller, and the way the dark blue denim of her jeans hugged them made me shift in my seat. Thank God I was sitting down. I felt like I was a freshman in high school staring at the chick who sat beside me in homeroom and never wore a bra.

Think about something else, Stratton. Think about something else.

I was on number eight in a countdown of my favorite guitarists in an attempt to calm things down when Eva returned to the table. She took a sip of her latte, licking the stray foam from her top lip.

Fuuuuuck.

David Gilmour. George Lynch. Frank Zappa.

"Hey, you okay?"

I blinked and shook my head. "What? Oh, yeah. Yeah, I'm fine. Just, you know, thinking about how good it is to see you again."

She smiled and rested her chin in her hand. "It is good, isn't it? A totally unexpected and amazing end to a really shitty fucking year."

"The, um…do you mean your…"

"Divorce?"

"Yeah. That." There was a sadness in her eyes, and I wished I could take away every ounce of pain she'd had to endure. "But we don't have to talk about it."

"I don't mind. Honestly, sometimes it helps to talk about it, you know? To just get it all out. I don't know if that makes sense."

I swallowed the lump that formed in my throat. I knew all too well that talking about your pain was ultimately the only way to make it stop.

"It does," I said. "You don't ever have to explain that to me."

The corners of her mouth turned up into a smile that reminded me both sorrow and hope could live within a person at the exact same time. "I know I don't."

Our eyes locked in understanding, and for a second, I thought I might tell her. Tell her I'd known since Jesse Trainor grabbed her at that party I'd do anything to protect her. That even if he'd managed to end our career that night, I would have done everything all over again. But it was about more than protecting her. I would've done anything to see her happy. I remembered the moments from our past. Singing on the bus till everyone told us to shut the fuck up. Eating Chinese on the rooftop in Cleveland. Fighting about whatever stupid shit I'd said or done during an interview. It was somewhere between all those little moments that I realized I loved her. I really fucking loved her.

She ran her nail along a small crack in the wood. "I just…I wasn't what he wanted in a wife. I tried to be. I quit my job. I ran carpools. I baked cookies for the kids and threw fancy dinner parties. But somewhere along the way I failed him, I guess. So, he found someone else."

I rested my hand on top of hers. "Actually, it sounds like *he* failed *you*."

Her eyes shifted to our hands, and I immediately pulled back, afraid I'd crossed a line. "What…what do you mean?"

"I mean, he asked you to be someone you're not. That's not what relationships are about. It's about loving the other person for who they are. Who they *truly* are, and not trying to change them into the person you want them to be."

She shrugged and sighed. "I guess that's true. I just keep wondering why I couldn't be what he wanted."

"Because you're *you*, Eva. And you're amazing, so you don't ever need to wonder that again." I pressed my lips together to keep the words I wanted to say from tumbling out.

"Thanks," she said, managing a smile.

"So," I began, tapping my knuckles on the table. "Besides being amazing, tell me what you've been up to for the last nineteen years."

She laughed, and I listened intently as she recounted her time in Chicago and moving to Nashville…about how she'd quit her job five years ago at her husband's urging but had often thought about starting back again. Her eyes gleamed with pride as she talked about her two boys, then crinkled with laughter as she explained how excited she'd been when they'd gone to their dad's the day before…only to find herself missing them this morning when there was no one asking her for Lucky Charms.

"What about *you*?" she asked. "I don't recall the article mentioning a wife or kids."

"Nah. I mean, I haven't ever been against having kids. I think it's more that I've been against having them with the people I've been in relationships with." I chuckled, finally taking a swig of my coffee, which was now lukewarm. "I don't know, just one of those things that never happened."

A mischievous smile formed on Eva's lips as she raised her brows. "So what *is* Eric Stratton's relationship status these days? It's been a while since I've seen any headlines about your love life, but I think I recall at one point you were with someone who may have just rolled off her parents' health insurance?"

"Not true," I insisted. "She'd been off for at least a year when we started dating."

We both burst into laughter.

"She *was* young," I admitted, clearing my throat. "And you're right. Turns out she was only looking for health insurance, so, you know, it didn't work out."

Eva's shoulders shook with laughter, and she covered her mouth. "Okay, okay. Tell me the real reason. I'll be serious if you will. Promise."

I sighed and ran my hand along my jaw. "You're talking about Christina, right?"

She traced her fingers around the rim of her latte. "If you mean the former Hollywood 'It' girl, then yes."

I nodded and chewed on my bottom lip. "Yeah. She's a great person, and I cared about her, obviously. But she wanted the wedding, the kids, the whole nine yards. And that wasn't where I was at. I figured if that was the case after six years, then I wasn't ever going to get there." I paused, taking another sip of my coffee. "Jesus. I sound like a total dick."

But at that moment, sounding like a dick seemed like a safer bet than telling her the truth.

It was because she wasn't you, Eva. No one could ever be you.

"No, you were just being honest with her and yourself," she said, reaching for her cup. "You think you'll want that eventually, though?"

Her tone wasn't judgmental, but her question ruffled me, and heat rose to my face as my leg started to bounce once again.

"Uh, I mean, I…I don't know," I answered, doing my best to make sure my eyes didn't meet hers for fear I might give myself away.

I wished for a minute she actually *would* see through me, but I knew that was selfish. The man she thought she was going to spend the rest of her life with had walked out on her, and she was obviously still hurting from it. This wasn't the right time. And honestly, I wasn't sure it ever would be.

"Uh-huh. Same ole Eric. Love 'em, leave 'em, kick 'em off the bus in the middle of Nebraska." She cocked her head and smirked. "It *was* Nebraska, right?"

I cringed. "*Not* my proudest moment."

She smiled. "Well, you have a lot to be proud of since then. All you've accomplished with your career and your sobriety. And now you're opening this counseling center."

"I've kinda had this dream for a while. Sometimes I look back and don't know how I made it through everything. I'm just hoping this will be a place kids can come and know someone gives a damn about them. That maybe telling my whole story will make them see they can survive whatever they're going through."

Eva reached for my hand. "That is so incredible, Eric. I mean it. All joking aside about shit that happened a million years ago. You completely turned your life around."

I nodded. "I did. And I hope you know you were a huge part of that."

She swallowed hard and sat back in her chair, her fingers trailing over my skin as she released my hand. "Maybe. When I was around. I really am sorry I sort of…vanished. I got caught up in life, I guess."

"It's okay, Eva. I'm just glad you're here now. That we're here now."

"Yeah. Me, too."

"And I'll be here all week, so we can do this again, right? Or maybe we could go to dinner? You probably already have plans for New Year's Eve, but if you don't, I'm free."

She lifted her eyes—staring through me or past me, I

couldn't tell—and my heart stopped.

Shit. Had I officially crossed a line this time? Was she going to say no?

"Yes," she answered, finally fixing her eyes on mine as a wide grin spread across her face. "I mean, no, I don't have plans, and yes, I'd love to go to dinner. Because I can't make up for nineteen years over one cup of coffee."

We may not have been able to make up for the lost time over a cup of coffee, but seeing the way she looked at me made up for every moment I'd spent missing her.

CHAPTER FIFTY-SEVEN
EVA

DECEMBER 2008

"Wait—Will and Angela have *how* many kids?" I took a sip of my wine and set the glass back on the wooden table.

Eric had pulled some strings and gotten a last-minute reservation at one of the quaintest restaurants in town for New Year's Eve, complete with candlelit tables and a fireplace. When I'd pushed the wine menu aside, he'd insisted I order whatever I wanted, assuring me his years of sobriety wouldn't be shattered by me drinking a couple of glasses of wine in his presence.

"Four," he said, cutting into his steak.

"Jesus. Was that on purpose?"

He chuckled. "I think so. Hard to believe, huh?"

"Incredibly. I hit my limit at two, but good for them. I always liked Will. And Angela. I'm glad they're happy."

"They liked you, too. I ran into them not too long after I talked to you on the phone and told them I was going to see you. They made me promise to say hello." He tipped his water glass at me and grinned. "So, hello, Eva."

"Well, please tell them hello back. And let them know how impressed I am that they deal with four children on a regular basis."

"I'll make sure to pass along the message. And maybe you

can see them if you ever come out to LA." He paused and cleared his throat, swiping a black cloth napkin over his mouth. "Do you, uh, ever do that?"

The warmth of the fire crackling across from us and the wine I'd just imbibed swirled with Eric's words, causing my chest to flush.

Did I ever visit LA? Of course, I did.

I'd been out to see Denise more times than I could count. But admitting that meant I'd been in the same city as Eric and deliberately decided not to see him. Even though he'd asked me to before we—I—lost touch. Before he'd climbed his way back up to rock star status. Before I let his last letter go unanswered, stuffed it away in a shoebox, and disconnected my phone.

I took the last sip of wine, thankful for the dimly-lit restaurant, as the flush spread to my cheeks. "I try to visit Denise from time to time. You remember her, right? My best friend... old roommate..."

"Right. Short brunette. I think she threatened to kick my ass once."

"Sounds accurate."

"Well, next time you're out, you have to let me know." His eyes held mine over the flickering candle in the middle of the table. "I don't want to lose touch again."

My eyes darted down to my plate, my face catching fire once again.

What do I say? How do I explain to him why I ended our friendship all those years ago when I can't explain it to myself? When I won't explain it to myself?

"I know I've said I'm sorry, but I really do owe you an apology, Eric," I said, finally looking up. "For disappearing on you. I think I was just afraid that...I mean, I think I was afraid you didn't need me around. That I was a reminder of your past."

Lies.

"Or maybe I got busy with my own life and was a shitty friend."

At least part of that is true.

"Either way, I'm sorry. I truly am."

He nodded, a soft smile appearing on his lips. "It's okay, Eva. Life happens. And now we have another chance."

Is he…Does he mean…

His eyes locked with mine, and my thoughts floated in the two glasses of wine I'd drunk, a canoe with no paddle to steer them one way or another.

Another chance at…

"Can I get you all anything else? Perhaps a look at the dessert menu?" Our server swept up to the table holding a piece of paper in her hand.

I startled and broke our stare.

"I'm stuffed, actually," I said, and Eric nodded in agreement, telling her we'd take the check whenever she had a moment.

As soon as it arrived, he insisted on paying, even though I protested.

"We really could've split the check." I slid into the passenger's seat as the valet opened the door to his rental car. "But thank you. Again."

"I've wanted to take you out to a nice dinner for a long time," he said, pulling away from the curb. "And I'm glad I found you again so I could do it."

"Chinese food on a rooftop isn't nice?" I laughed, then immediately pressed my lips together once I realized what I'd said.

Rooftop. His first solo album. Song number seven.

His Adam's apple bobbed in his throat. "It was actually very nice."

I nodded, gazing out the window, unsure what to say.

There were so many other girls. Hundreds of them. But what if…

"Until you stole the last crab rangoon, that is," he added, nudging my arm.

I laughed, his quip pulling me out of my head. "Turn left here. And I didn't steal it. I just ate it while you weren't looking."

"And *that* is what we call stealing, Eva Holloway."

My skin prickled at the mention of my maiden name. Nostalgia. Memories of a life lived years ago combined with a hint of the independence I'd once felt before Aaron had stripped it away.

I glanced over at Eric, the streetlights casting watery shadows over his face. "You're right. I mean, about that being nice. Not about me being a thief. Take a right at the light."

"I should refuse to take you home until you admit it. Drive aimlessly around this city and get us lost."

I smiled. "You can't get me lost in my own city, Eric."

He glanced over at me and grinned, flipping his blinker to the left, rather than the right. "I can try."

I elbowed his arm and he laughed, switching the blinker back.

"What a million girls wouldn't give for that. Getting lost with Eric Stratton."

"I'd wager most *men* wouldn't mind getting lost with *you.*"

Does he want to get lost with me? *Do I want to get lost with him?*

"Maybe once upon a time," I said with a wave of my hand. "But even if it *was* true, those days are long gone."

"Don't be so modest. You still turn heads, Eva."

It didn't escape me that he turned his own head toward me as he said those words.

"Okay, *Sexist Man Alive* runner-up." I pulled my scarf over my mouth to stifle my giggles. "Sorry, I said I might have to mention it one more time."

"Whatever. Admit you stole the last crab rangoon, woman."

Woman. A soft chuckle slipped through my lips, and my body tingled at the word, a bittersweet reminder of the past. *Chill out, woman. Calm down, woman.* It was nice to hear him say it sober.

"Never."

"All right, that's it. I'm not taking you home till you 'fess up."

He pretended he was going to turn onto a side street before straightening the wheel and continuing on.

I threw my hands over my face and laughed. "Are you really gonna kidnap a mother with two defenseless children at home?"

He sighed and shook his head. "I guess you're right. Can't do that to the kids. How are they, by the way?"

My heart fluttered.

He wants to know about my kids.

"I think they're doing okay," I said. "They were happy to spend time with their dad, even if it was just a few days."

"Do they not see him often?"

I sucked in a breath. "He's got a new girlfriend. Actually, not so new, really. She's the woman he left me for, and she's pregnant, so he's…*preoccupied.*"

"Jesus, Eva. Seriously?"

"Yeah. It's been interesting to navigate."

"Do you have the boys most of the time, then?"

I nodded. "I do. Which is fine because they're my world, you know? But it's not fair to them that Aaron's so focused on his new life. They need their dad."

"Can I say that he sounds like a complete asshole without offending you?"

"You can because he is." A remorseful laugh rose from deep inside me. "I dunno, maybe he'll see the error of his ways and step up. He was a good father while we were together, but things just…*changed.*"

"Well, you're a great mother, and your kids are lucky to have you," he said. "But I'm not surprised. You always kept us in line. I think Keith would still hire you in a heartbeat."

I directed him to turn at the next stop sign, where he'd find my house ahead on the right. "I've thought about going back to work. But trying to figure out the logistics with the kids and everything…sometimes it seems like it's too much."

"I get that, but don't let it stop you. You've got so much to offer, Eva. You made Counting Backward happen." He pulled into my driveway and cut the engine. "I know it didn't turn out the way we all imagined it would, but I wouldn't be where I am without you."

I opened my mouth to protest, but something in the way he looked at me made me believe him. Even if just a little bit. His face was softened by the warm glow from the lamppost outside the car, and I wondered how he'd managed to grow even more handsome than he'd been when we were young.

"I wish I didn't have to go back to LA," he said.

"I wish you didn't, either."

The words spilled out of my mouth before I had a chance to think about what they meant. I just knew I hadn't felt like anything but a divorced mother of two until I'd met Eric's gaze at the coffee shop. It was at that moment I finally felt like *Eva* again. And though I didn't want that feeling to end, I had no idea what to do but let him go.

"I, uh…I better get inside to make sure the kids aren't starting fires or killing each other. But it was good to see you, Eric." My hand trembled on the door handle. "And you have my phone numbers and email now, so we'll stay in—"

"Wait, I'll walk you to the door," he interrupted, and my body tingled.

"Oh. Okay. But you don't have to. I'm fine, really."

"I want to," he said, flashing me a smile.

He waited for me to walk around the car, then followed me up the brick sidewalk to the porch.

"So, like I was saying, you have my phone numbers and email now," I babbled on, nerves causing my stomach to churn. "And I have yours, so we'll stay in touch."

I turned around, my eyes dropping to where he'd placed his hand on my arm. It felt solid. Strong.

"You promise?" he asked.

A lump of shame formed in my throat.

"Yes," I managed. "I promise. And I'm sorry, Eric. I'm so sorry for disappearing back then. I won't…*it* won't…happen again."

I forced my eyes up to his, the porch lamp causing flickers of light to dance in their deep blue depths.

"Good. Because I've missed you, Eva." His hand trailed down my arm, stopping to grasp mine, and warmth flooded my body. "More than you know."

"I've missed you, too," I said, my voice so quiet I wasn't sure he heard me.

He nodded, his eyes holding mine captive, and I watched from somewhere outside my body as he tilted his head and moved closer.

Oh my God, what's going on, what's happening? I'm Mom, not Eva. But I want this. Do I want this? It's just the wine. Or maybe not. Holy shit, do something before—

I gasped and quickly unclasped our hands, throwing my arms around him. A soft sigh escaped his lips as he rested his chin on my head. I blinked slowly, coming back into myself, then released him, pushing my key into the lock.

"Don't forget to email me when you get back to LA," I said, patting his arm like he was one of my kids about to head off to summer camp.

Jesus, woman.

My heart squeezed.

Woman.

He nodded and stepped back as I entered the house. His wistful smile spoke a thousand words, but I refused to listen. "I won't forget, Eva. I promise."

CHAPTER FIFTY-EIGHT
EVA

JANUARY 2009

"What are you doing, Mom?" Miles asked, popping his head through the opening to the attic.

I was sitting cross-legged in the middle of the floor surrounded by storage tubs, frantically pulling out old photo albums and books that had been packed away since we'd moved to Nashville. I'd been so focused on the task at hand I hadn't heard him climb up the stairs.

"Nothing." I slapped a lid on one of the tubs, blushing like a child who'd been caught lying to her parents. "What do you need, buddy?"

"I was in the kitchen getting a Pop-Tart, and it kept ringing." He handed me my cell phone and grinned. "Can I have a Pop-Tart, by the way?"

"Thanks. And yes, but if you wait, I'll cook you break—"

Miles had already disappeared down the stairs before I could finish my sentence.

A chunk of hair fell from my ponytail, and I brushed it out of my face, my eyes searching the space for other possibilities. It had to be here somewhere. The shoebox that held the only tangible memories that remained from all those years ago. The one with my tour laminates and pictures. The one in which I'd buried Eric's last letter.

I sighed and looked down at my cell. Five missed calls and three text notifications, all from Denise. The screen lit up as I was about to call her back.

I held the phone to my ear and chuckled. "Are you dying or something?"

"Yes, I am, in fact," she said, not missing a beat. "Dying to fucking know what happened with you and Eric last night."

I shook my head at her, as if she could see me. "No Happy New Year? How are you doing? How are the boys?"

"Happy New Year, how are you and the boys?"

"We're—"

"Enough small talk. Tell me about *Eric!*"

"Okay, okay. Hold on." I pushed myself up and carefully climbed backward down the stairs, folding them up and shutting the hatch before padding down the hallway into my bedroom. I closed the door and propped myself against the headboard of my unmade bed. "All right, crazy lady. What do you wanna know?"

"Only fucking *everything*. What did you wear? I bet you looked hot. Did *he* look hot? Did you guys make out? Did you sleep together? Oh my God, you slept together, didn't you?"

I laughed and slapped my hand over my face, which turned warm at the thought. "*No*, we did *not* sleep together. What the hell? It was the second time I've seen him in almost twenty years. And I have two children in my house."

"You could've gone back to his hotel."

"Denise."

She sighed. "Okay, *fine*. No sex. But did you at least kiss?"

My cheeks flamed, the memory of his lips moving closer to mine flashing in my mind. "No. We didn't. But I…"

Shut up, Eva.

"But you what?"

"I think we almost did. I don't know."

Why, why, why did you say this?

"Eva! What do you mean you 'don't know'?"

I squeezed my eyes shut. "I think he was going to kiss me, and I kinda hugged him instead. Maybe he wasn't, though. I probably just imagined it. Why would he wanna kiss me when he could kiss some twenty-five-year-old with a hot body and no kids?"

I heard what sounded like a hand slapping a counter. "Probably because he's wanted to since you guys sat on a fucking rooftop in God-knows-where. You know, the time he wrote an entire hit song about?"

"We don't know if that song was about—"

"Oh, it totally was. And maybe one day he'll confess that to you. But for now, believe what you want and tell me about the rest of your date."

"It wasn't a date."

Was it a date?

"Fine. Tell me about the meal you ate with your *friend*."

I could almost see her eyes roll through the phone.

"It was good," I said, trying to remain stoic. But the images of us talking and laughing over the candlelit dinner and in the car on the way home tugged at the corners of my mouth so hard I had no choice but to give in. "Actually, it was more than good. It was *really* good."

She squealed, causing me to chuckle and hold the phone away from my ear.

I grabbed the throw pillow to my side, squeezing it against my chest. "I felt like my old self for the first time in forever, Denise."

"Oh, babe, I'm so glad. You deserve that. You deserve that so much."

"Thanks," I said. "The year did end better than it started."

Better than me sitting on the bed, tears streaming down my face, asking Aaron over and over again what I'd done to make him want to break our family apart.

"So," she began, dragging out the word. "When are you gonna see him again so you can make up for the hug you gave him when he was clearly trying to stick his tongue in your mouth?"

I pressed the heel of my hand against my forehead in an attempt to banish the awkward moment from my thoughts. "He didn't...*Fuck*. I don't know. I don't know what happened, and I don't know when I'll see him again. He had to go back to LA today."

She groaned.

"But honestly, Denise, we're friends. *Maybe* there was a lit-tle, I don't know...*spark* or something. But I'm sure it was just that whole feeling-young-again-when-you-see-someone-from-your-past sort of thing."

"Uh-huh."

"No, really," I insisted. "I think he got confused or some-thing. Or maybe *I* got confused."

"I know you were married for seventeen years, but I don't think you've forgotten what it looks like when someone's try-ing to make out with you."

"You know what? I should've never told you this. It was *nothing*, Denise. I'm sure of it."

Am I?

"Eva," she began. "Do you not realize you've been on cloud nine since the day that man called you?"

"Oh, it was just a little bit of excitement in my life. Famous rock star wants to see me. Doesn't hate me for being a terrible friend. It was a sort of...*closure* for us."

"Or *maybe* the beginning of something brand new."

"Please," I said, waving my hand in the air. "He'll probably go back to LA and find some model or actress and forget all about last night."

My chest tightened at the thought.

"You and Aaron have been separated for a year now, babe. It's okay to have feelings for someone else."

"I don't have *feelings* for him. We went through some really heavy things together. And we were close once. But..."

I thought about how I'd laid in bed the night before, tossing and turning, wondering what would've happened if I hadn't freaked out and pulled him into some stupid hug. How I'd snuck outside at 2 a.m. in my pajamas, my coat pulled tightly around me as I chain-smoked and recalled all the times I'd thought about him over the years—memories triggered by magazine covers or songs on the radio. How I'd popped out of bed that morning and rushed to the attic to try to find the shoebox. The letter.

"But what?" she asked.

"But nothing," I said, sighing. "We'll probably send the occasional *Hi, how are you?* email, and that'll be it."

"We'll see," Denise said. I pictured her staring at me through the phone with one raised brow.

"All right, I'll leave you and your imagination to run wild," I said, throwing my legs over the side of the bed. "I've got to go fix the kids' breakfast."

"Okay, just be sure to call me as soon as Eric sends that *I've loved you for nearly twenty years* email."

I smiled and shook my head. "You're insane."

She chuckled. "Love you."

"Love you, too."

I dropped the phone beside me and rubbed my lips together, staring at an invisible spot on the wall across from me.

Was that all there would be? The occasional friendly email? My insides ached at the possibility, while my pulse raced at the thought there could be something more. I closed my eyes and clasped my hands under my chin, allowing myself one last glimpse of the night before, of how good it felt to be *Eva.* Then I pushed myself off the bed and took in a deep breath, morphing back into *Mom.*

CHAPTER FIFTY-NINE

JANUARY 2009

From: Eric S
To: Eva Mitchell
Date: January 1, 2009 5:04PM
Subject: Back in La La Land

Eva,

Back in LA safe and sound. Had the driver stop by El Compadre so I could pick up takeout. I was thinking about that day when I asked Keith to hire you as what's-his-name's assistant, and I realized I hadn't been there in ages. Guess seeing you got me feeling all nostalgic. Either that or it got me craving chimichangas. ;)

Hope you and the boys are having a good New Year's Day. I'm about to listen to the tracks the kids from Indiana laid down while I was in Nashville. I tried to listen on the plane, but this lady sitting next me wouldn't stop talking about how I was such a "nice, handsome man" who would be perfect for her daughter. Even slipped a piece of paper with digits into my hand as I was getting off the plane.

Her daughter enjoys knitting and lives in Burbank with her six cats.

Whaddya think? Should I call her?

Love,
Eric

———————

From: Eva Mitchell
To: Eric S
Date: January 1, 2009 7:21PM
Subject: Re: Back in La La Land

Eric,
Oh, you should definitely call her. Don't forget to invite me to the wedding. ;)
New Year's Day has been a thrill a minute. The boys and I watched movies and ordered pizza. Correction: I watched movies while Drew played on his phone, and Miles whined about how he should have one, too. Then they got into a fight because Miles kept "accidentally" touching Drew's leg with his foot, so I left the room and am now emailing you. Such fun times around here!
Anyway, enough "mom shit." Tell me about some "music shit." Oh, and is everything ready for the opening of the counseling center? So excited for you!
Eva

———————

From: Eric S
To: Eva Mitchell
Date: January 2, 2009 11:10AM
Subject: Re: Back in La La Land

I actually love hearing about your kids. It's cool that you do "mom shit." Makes you even more amazing, especially with Drew being the age he is. Remember, I've been a fifteen-year-old boy, and—wait, I probably shouldn't tell you what it's like. ;)
Re: "music shit," the Indiana guys are gonna finish up record-

ing in Nashville, then a couple of them will fly out here while the album is being mixed. The tracks sounded great when I listened to them, so I'm excited about that. Then there's another new band Keith is managing, and he asked if I'd be interested in helping with their album. And yep, the counseling center opens on Monday. Once I feel like things are running smoothly there, maybe I can work on some of my own music. I don't know, I've had my time in the spotlight. I just feel so damn lucky, I wanna do what I can to give back.

But enough about me. It's a new year, woman. A whole new start. So, you should really think more about going back to work if it's something you wanna do. Which I think it is from the way your eyes lit up like a fucking Christmas tree when you talked about your old job. :)

From: Eva Mitchell
To: Eric S
Date: January 3, 2009 3:54PM
Subject: Re: Back in La La Land

OK, here's some "mom shit" for you. Miles busted his head open on the coffee table last night and we spent five hours in the ER waiting for him to get stitches. That was my wild Friday night. He couldn't even explain how it happened, but it clearly involved some sort of jumping off the couch action with his friend. Anyway, Drew had to stay home with the kid so his parents could come pick him up while I rushed Miles to the hospital. I'd be mad at him for getting blood all over my living room rug and car, but the poor little guy is so pitiful with his bandaged head that I've been letting him watch TV and eat cookies all day. I'm a sucker.

Your production work sounds exciting! I'd occasionally get to pop into the studio every now and again for the label I used to work with, and it always sent me back in time. Like it was

1988 all over again. Fuck, I guess I really do miss it. But I don't know…I've been out of the business for so long, and with me doing the majority of the stuff for the kids, I'm not sure it makes sense. But speaking of work, don't let your own stuff fall too far by the wayside. I read that *Rolling Stone* article. I know you've got ideas for a new album. The world is just waiting to hear it. :)

———

From: Eric S
To: Eva Mitchell
Date: January 3, 2009 11:23PM
Subject: Re: Back in La La Land

Just now getting this. I'd text you, but I'm sure you're asleep. Is Miles OK? Let me know how he's doing.

———

From: Eva Mitchell
To: Eric S
Date: January 4, 2009 8:54AM
Subject: Re: Back in La La Land

Miles is fine. In fact, I just caught him trying to jump off the couch again.

Boys. Why.

Thanks for checking on him. And good luck tomorrow with the opening of the center. You're gonna change so many lives, Eric.

CHAPTER SIXTY
EVA

FEBRUARY 2009

"Drew! Miles! Your mom's here!" Aaron closed the door behind me as I stepped into the house.

"Hang on, we gotta finish this game," Drew called from upstairs.

Aaron looked at me and raised his eyebrows.

"That's fine," I said, walking into the living room from the foyer.

"Do you, uh…do you want anything to drink?" he asked, motioning for me to have a seat.

"No, thanks." My phone vibrated, and I perched on the edge of the couch before retrieving it.

Eric: *A picture of the Sunset palms to make you smile.*

The corners of my mouth twitched as my fingers moved over the keyboard.

Me: *TY. Need a smile. Picking boys up from Aaron's. Ugh. To Aaron, not boys.*

Eric: *Major ugh. Abort mission. Come to LA immediately.*

I chuckled and sent back a wink.

"What's so funny?" Aaron asked, sitting in the chair across from me.

I looked up, my mind still on Eric. "Hmm?"

"Your phone," he said, pointing at it.

"Oh, nothing. Just a text."

He nodded. "So, um, how are you?"

"I'm good. How are you? How's—"

"We're good," he answered, cutting me off before I could say his girlfriend's name. It was something he'd done since he'd first told me about her. As if hearing her name coming from my mouth made him feel some sort of inexplicable culpability he didn't have time to think through. "She's out with her mom doing some last-minute shopping for the, uh…stuff."

"Right," I said, looking at my phone as it pinged again.

Eric: *How is pregnant girlfriend? Super pregnant?*

Me: *Out shopping for "stuff," which appears to be code for baby. He can't even say it. Oh, the guilt.*

Eric: *Make him say it. And take a picture so I can see his face when he does.*

"Ha!" I glanced up at Aaron's tilted head, then quickly coughed and patted my chest. "Sorry."

"Is that Denise?"

I shook my head and cleared my throat, trying not to laugh. "No. Just another…friend."

"Kate?"

I lifted my chin and narrowed my eyes at him. "Why does it matter?"

"It doesn't." He flicked his gaze away. "Anyway, it was such a nice day yesterday, and I asked Miles if he wanted to go outside and throw the ball around. But he told me he doesn't want to play baseball this year. Did he mention that to you?"

Another ping.

Eric: *Where's my picture, woman?*

I pressed my lips together in an attempt to hide my smile. "He did. I mean, he didn't say why, but I have an idea."

Aaron sat forward in his chair, elbows on his knees.

I sighed and slipped my phone into my purse. "He doesn't want to be the kid without his dad there. He's afraid you won't come to his practices or his games."

"I…" He opened his mouth, then closed it.

"You what?"

"I come to his practices and games."

"Aaron."

"I was there last year."

"At the beginning you were, but then there was always work or something with Olivia."

He flinched at the mention of his girlfriend's name.

"I had that huge case I was trying to settle, and then we found out she was…pregnant." He mumbled the last word. "I didn't mean to not be there. Things will be different this season."

"I think you should be telling Miles this, not me. That is, if you really mean it. Neither one of those boys needs any more disappointments."

He ran his hands through his short dark hair and sighed. "You say that like I purposely—"

He stopped himself at the sound of footsteps descending the stairs.

Miles slid into the living room with his duffel bag. Drew followed behind, lifting his hand in a casual wave.

"Hey, Mom," Miles said, plopping down on the couch beside me.

"Hey, buddy. Get your shoes on, and we'll head out."

"Okay. Bye, Dad." He pushed himself up, gave Aaron a quick hug, and headed for the foyer.

"Drew, go on out to the car. I'll be there in a minute."

Drew muttered a "bye" and shuffled after his brother. Once the door clicked, I stood, slinging my purse over my shoulder. "So you, um…you don't happen to remember seeing a box around the house with my old things in it, do you?"

Aaron cocked his head and rose to his feet. "Things?"

"Yeah, from when I lived out in LA."

His forehead wrinkled. "I don't think so."

"It was a shoebox. Like, a big one for boots. It had my pictures and—"

"Oh," he said, tapping his finger against his mouth. "We threw that away when we were cleaning out the garage. When the neighborhood had that yard sale a couple of years ago."

I grabbed my stomach, as if that could stop the ache from the punch he'd just delivered. "We *what?*"

"Threw it away. I'm sure I asked you about—"

"You did not, Aaron. I wouldn't have told you to throw that away."

"Okay, well, what's the big deal about it, anyway?"

"The big deal is that it was *mine.*"

"That stuff was so old, Eva. Why do you even care?"

"Because that was part of my *life*. And you just fucking tossed it."

"I told you I asked you."

"You didn't."

He scrubbed his hands down his face. "Look, I don't even remember. Maybe I didn't ask you, but I don't understand why you're freaking out over—"

"Never mind," I said, pushing past him. "Forget it. You're right, you don't understand, just like you never fucking understood *anything* about me."

"Eva, come on."

"You know what? It's fine." I held my hands up in front of me, signaling I was done talking. "I've gotta get the boys home so they can finish their homework before bed."

"All right. Tell them I love them."

I clenched my teeth and gripped the doorknob so hard my knuckles turned white. "Sure, Aaron. Whatever you say."

He closed the door, and I stood on the porch, taking in several deep breaths. The photographs. The postcards. The unanswered letter. Gone forever.

I pulled my phone from my purse and scrolled back to the photo Eric had sent. My pulse slowed as I took in the tall, thin trunks adorned with thick green fronds lining either side of

FOR EVA

the street. I held the phone close to my chest, knowing I had at least one picture Aaron couldn't throw away.

CHAPTER SIXTY-ONE

FEBRUARY 2009

From: Eva Mitchell
To: Eric S
Date: February 23, 2009 7:06PM
Subject: Crazy?

So I did something kind of crazy today. I reached out to my old boss and told him I was thinking about going back to work. I just kept thinking about how you said my face lit up when I talked about it and that I had a lot to offer, and I did it. Obviously, my old position is filled, but he promised I'd be the first person he'd call if anything opens up. Apparently, he's missed me and said things haven't been the same since I left. Who knew?! It's a smaller label, so not sure if there will be something for me, but it felt so good to actually take the step, you know? I think… well, I think Aaron made me believe it was wrong to want to be anything other than a wife and mother. Actually, I don't think that, I know that. And I'm angry at myself for letting him get into my head.

Which leads me to the next crazy thing I did today. I called and made a therapy appointment. I should've done that months ago, but I don't know…I think I sort of figured I could deal with it all myself. But I know you told me when we last talked how

FOR EVA

helpful therapy has been for you, and Denise has her therapist on speed dial, so… yeah. I think this is gonna be good. Just not sure if I'm gonna clam up and not say a word or completely vomit everything I've ever kept inside onto this poor woman. TBD. I'll keep you posted. ;)

———

From: Eric S
To: Eva Mitchell
Date: February 24, 2009 10:21AM
Subject: Re: Crazy?

FUCK YEAH. This is amazing! Forget crazy—do you realize how fucking brave you are? Both of these things are major, and do not think otherwise. And of course your old boss misses you—how could he not? I'm so happy for you. Truly.

About therapy…I remember being really scared of it—like, why would I wanna dig up things from the past when I could just try to forget about them and move on? The problem is, of course, you never really forget them. Things can haunt you for life if you don't talk about them with someone who can help you work through the feelings they bring up. I'm so damn proud of you, Eva. I know you don't need me to say that, but I have to because it's true. You're remembering who you are. And that's someone who can do anything she fucking puts her mind to.

Call me soon. Our last phone call/viewing of *KISS Meets the Phantom of the Park* was the most fun I've had since 1978. That movie is fucking phenomenal. Robot KISS fighting real KISS? Come on. That was Emmy material.

CHAPTER SIXTY-TWO
EVA

MARCH 2009

"Oh my God, Denise. Why did I agree to do this?" I brought my knees to my chest and rested my forehead on them. "What the hell was I thinking?"

"Because you have to get back out there, Eva," she said. "And this is just practice. For when you come out to visit me and see Eric again."

I imagined her lips twisting into a sly grin as I raised my head and flopped against the corner of the sectional. "For the ten *thousandth* time, Eric and I are just friends. And I don't need practice because I don't want to date anyone."

"Okay, fine. Then why *did* you agree to this?"

"I was conned into it. My friend Kate asked if I wanted to go to dinner, and I said yes. Then all of a sudden—*surprise!*—her husband and his coworker are joining us. So, I did *not* agree to this. I was duped."

Denise chuckled. "Kate sounds fun."

"Great. Then you should come out here and go to dinner with them."

"Sorry, babe," she said. "Considering your date's in two hours and the flight to Nashville is four, looks like it's gonna have to be you. Plus, my husband gets weird about me seeing other men."

333

I managed a half-hearted laugh.

"Maybe you'll end up liking the guy. He could be superhot. Have you seen a picture?"

I blew out a breath and ran a hand down my face. "She sent me the website for their company. He's the chief accounting something or other. Objectively good-looking, I guess, for a guy in a suit and tie who spends his days talking about numbers."

"As opposed to a guy in a T-shirt and jeans who spends his days writing songs about how much he loves you?"

"You're never gonna let that go, are you?"

"No. I'm not."

"Fine, whatever," I said, pushing myself up from the couch. "I've got to get in the shower so I can go sit through dinner, pretend I'm having fun, and then never see this guy again."

"Just picture Eric's face while you're fucking him."

"Denise!"

She tried to stifle her giggles. "Okay, okay, I'll let you go get ready. Tell me all about it after you get home…tomorrow morning."

"I'm hanging up."

"Love you, babe."

"Love you, too."

I trudged down the hallway into my bedroom, tossing my phone on the bed before I opened the closet to see if I had anything remotely suitable to wear that evening. As I flipped through the hangers, my cell rang.

Oh! Maybe it's Kate calling to cancel. Or maybe it's Aaron calling to say one of the boys is sick and needs to come home so he won't infect the rest of the house. They have a new baby now and simply can't risk it. The perfect excuse to bail. Kate will understand.

I squealed at the possibility of Miles or Drew having the flu and hurried to the bed, ready to tell Aaron I'd be right over. The name that appeared on the screen wasn't his, but I wasn't disappointed.

I smiled as I walked back over to the closet. "Hey, you."

"Hey, back," Eric said, a smile in his voice. "What are you up to?"

"Oh, I'm just…" I trailed off, wondering if I should tell him the truth.

Is this weird? Why do I feel weird? If we're just friends, it's not weird. Which we are…just friends.

"I'm getting ready to go to dinner."

Mostly true.

"In that case, call me tomorrow. I'll be around."

I glanced over at the alarm clock on my nightstand. An hour and forty-five minutes before I had to leave to meet Kate, her husband, and my mystery date at the restaurant.

"No, it's fine," I said, padding back to the bed. "I can talk for a little while. How's Hollywood? What glamorous events will you be attending later tonight?"

"Trying to decide between dinner at Brad and Angelina's or sitting here on my deck eating pizza. What do you think?"

"Oh, Brad did Jennifer Aniston so wrong, Eric. I vote for pizza."

"Good, because I don't really know Brad *or* Angelina, so it would've been awkward showing up there."

I laughed and settled into the pillows resting against the headboard. "So what kind of pizza?"

"Pepperoni," we said in unison.

"Is there any other kind?" he asked.

"Absolutely not. Pizza without pepperoni is an abomination."

"You speak the truth. So who are you going to dinner with?"

I paused, a shot of adrenaline rushing from my head to my feet.

"That's not my business, is it? That was…Sorry."

"No, it's fine," I assured him, picking at the fabric pilling on my comforter. "It's just…I kinda got conned into going on a date." My chest tightened as soon as I said the words. "But I don't wanna go."

Eric cleared his throat. "Why, um…why don't you wanna go?"

"Because my friend Kate asked me to go to dinner and then sprang it on me that her husband and his coworker were coming, too. I was tricked. Hoodwinked. *Bamboozled.*"

"Hmm…sounds like you need an excuse, then. You could tell her you have to talk to me? That I don't like to eat alone? My name might still carry a little weight in certain circles, right?"

I flicked my eyes back to the clock, my brain pulsing in time with the colon between the five and the forty-five, my heart tugging at the sound of his laughter. "I mean, maybe I can think of something, but I…actually, hang on a second."

I quickly flipped through my contacts, found Kate's number, and pressed the button to send a text.

Me: *Just started my period and am dying. In bed with heating pad. No way I can make it to dinner. So sorry!*

I placed my phone back to my ear. "Text sent. Now you have to entertain me."

"Wait—did you seriously bail on your date?"

My phone pinged, and I glanced at Kate's response telling me she understood and we'd do it another time.

"Well, I bailed on Kate, who will have to tell said date I won't be coming. So, yeah, I guess I did."

"How did you—"

"Never mind," I answered, chuckling. "Now, what are we talking about?"

"Well, I actually called because this guy I know who used to work at my record label is starting his own label. But he doesn't wanna base it in LA, so he's decided on none other than Music City. I was kinda thinking you two should chat."

"Are you serious? He wants to come to Nashville?"

"Dead serious. With your marketing experience, you'd probably have some great ideas for him, and I'm sure he'd be looking for someone to lead that team."

"Oh my God, Eric…this is amazing. I don't expect you to vouch for me, you don't know my work, but—"

"You think I don't know your work, Eva? You *saved* my band. Remember the fucking tiger?"

I laughed as the original Counting Backward album artwork flashed in my mind. "I *do* remember the fucking tiger."

"I can't guarantee anything, but I may have mentioned I know someone who could probably help him out, and he was psyched about it. I hope you don't mind."

"Of course I don't mind! Thank you so much. I'd love to talk to him."

"Good," he said. "Now that's settled…how's the weather out there?"

"Too fucking cold for late March." I scoffed. "I hate this month. It makes you think winter's over, then decides to fucking spit ice in your face. How's the weather there?"

"Oh, you know. Sixty-five. Sunny. Really sucky."

"Send me a picture of the ocean."

"Okay, hang on."

He went silent, then my phone pinged. "How's that?"

"Oh, so nice of you to send one with your face in it for the extra jealousy factor."

"Now you have to send one of you."

I pulled a pillow over my face and held my phone above it.

"Not fair," he protested.

"Ugh, fine." I snapped another photo, making sure to slap a huge cheesy grin on my face. "Better?"

"Much."

"I made sure to take it at a skinny angle."

"Please, Eva. You don't need to worry about that. You're a fucking ten."

"Ha! *Maybe* I can wear a twelve if I don't eat carbs for a week."

He chuckled. "What are you talking about?"

I opened my mouth to explain, but snapped it shut when I

realized I was also confused. "Wait, what are you talking about?"

"I'm saying you're, you know…a *ten*." He paused, his words settling into my brain. "You're beautiful."

"Oh."

"Was that…weird?"

I swallowed the lump in my throat.

Did Eric Stratton just tell me I'm beautiful? Did I hear him correctly? Do I understand the English language? Do I know how to speak it?

"Sorry, I didn't mean to be—"

"No," I interrupted. "Thank you. For saying that. It's a real compliment coming from the second *Sexiest Man Alive*."

"I swear to God, woman, if you mention that again I will hang up."

I laughed and pulled the comforter over my legs. "Don't hang up. I'm just getting cozy. And I really don't want you to have to eat alone."

CHAPTER SIXTY-THREE
EVA

MARCH 2009

"Finally," Denise began, emphasizing the word. "I was beginning to think you may have eloped with your date from last night. That I was gonna get a midnight call to meet you in Vegas."

"I bailed," I confessed, dropping my keys on the counter. "I just got back from taking Miles to his friend's house."

"I thought the boys were at Aaron's?"

"Oh, they are. But Aaron couldn't be bothered because he's a new dad, you know? He's very busy nursing the baby." I rolled my eyes. "I swear, sometimes I feel sorry for what's-her-name."

"She's young and knows not what she's done. So what'd you do last night instead of having sex? Lifetime movies and chamomile tea?"

"Are you making fun of me?"

"Yes."

"I can't believe I've put up with you as long as I have." I walked to the living room and sank into the couch. "But no, I...I actually ended up talking to Eric."

"Ooh. So *phone* sex instead of *actual* sex?"

"Denise, I swear to God."

She laughed. "Okay, okay. So you talked to Eric. How's he doing?"

"Good. He knows this guy starting a record label out here, and he wants to put us in touch. Like, maybe I could work for him."

"That's incredible!"

"Yeah, and then he, uh…Denise, you have to promise you won't get all *whatever* on me. Because I'm starting to wonder…I mean, I'm starting to think…"

"I promise, babe. What's going on?" she asked, concern creeping into her voice.

"He told me I was beautiful."

Denise was silent. No quips. No sex references.

"Are you still there?"

"Does that surprise you?" she finally asked.

"What?"

"That he said that."

"I don't know. I mean, we talked for *four* hours. We ate fucking *dinner* together on the phone. And I don't know, am I crazy to think…" I massaged my forehead. "Fuck, I don't know what to think."

"All right, Eva," Denise said. "I'm going to be serious here. No song jokes or sex jokes or any of that. I've told you time and time again he's in love with you. He was your biggest fucking champion in that job with Keith. He wrote you postcards and letters after you moved back to Chicago. Nearly twenty years later, he told the *Rolling Stone* reporter to find you and talk to you for the article. And then he called you himself and came to see you, and now you guys talk on the phone and email and text probably more than we do."

"But I—"

She squashed my attempt to protest. "I'm not done. He's also encouraged you to think about going back to work—to do something you love and you're so fucking good at. *And* he's supported you going to therapy so you can unravel all the things Aaron told you over the years that got you tangled up about who you are."

I took a shaky breath and ran a finger below my eyelid to catch the liquid that spilled over. "But I can't…Everything that happened with Danny, that can't happen again, Denise."

"Just because Eric's a musician doesn't mean he's Danny. Danny was a selfish asshole who loved himself and who he *wanted* you to be. And even though Aaron dressed things up in a suit and tie, he's the same fucking person. Eric loves you for who you *are,* Eva. And I honestly don't know how many other ways he can show it."

The teardrops became too many to catch, so I let them roll down my cheeks.

"You still there?" she asked.

I swallowed and nodded as if she could see me, then closed my eyes and imagined my heart was a puzzle. I'd tried to put it back together after Danny had taken it apart, but I'd thrown away the piece that would make it whole for one that never quite fit. I couldn't undo what I'd done, nor would I want to. Without Aaron, there would be no Drew, no Miles. But even though I had discarded the missing piece all those years ago, it had found *me.* And I didn't want to lose it again.

"Eva?"

"I love him, Denise."

"I know you do."

"I need to come out there."

She chuckled softly, and I felt her smile through the phone, wrapping me up in warmth. "I know you do."

CHAPTER SIXTY-FOUR
EVA

APRIL 2009

"But I don't understand why we can't come," Miles said, the words garbled around a mouthful of cinnamon bagel. "I wanna go on that *Jurassic Park* ride again."

"Sweetie, I told you, this isn't that type of trip." I sighed as I rummaged through my purse to confirm that my phone and wallet were located safely inside. The last thing I needed was to arrive at the airport without them; I was frazzled enough as it was, and Miles's inability to accept the fact that he would not be going to California wasn't helping. "I've got to go do some… mom stuff. But we'll all go back out there together soon. Universal, Disneyland, whatever you want."

"I don't know why you wanna go on that ride, Miles," Drew said. "All you did last time was close your eyes and hold on to Mom."

"Shut up, Drew!" Miles hopped out of his seat and darted across the room, attempting to shove his brother. Drew grabbed his arm before it landed and laughed as Miles struggled to break free.

I ran my hands along my face. "Can we please not do this right now?"

Drew let go of Miles, who managed to sneak in a quick punch to Drew's forearm before retreating back to his barstool.

Drew's mouth flew open as he pointed at me. "Did you see that?"

I tightened my jaw and shot him a look to convey not only how fed up I was with the fighting but also how desperate I was for a mere five minutes of tranquility before I left for my trip. He threw his hands in the air, pleading innocence, but I sharpened my stare and motioned toward Miles.

He rolled his eyes, but nevertheless walked over to the island and mussed Miles's hair. "Sorry, buddy. You were little. I would've been scared, too. I'll make it up to you and play *Mario Kart* when we get to Dad's."

Miles jerked his head away and narrowed his eyes as he looked up at his older brother. "Ten races."

"Two," Drew countered, kicking off the bargaining that concluded when they finally agreed on five.

"Okay, good, glad we're all friends again," I said. "But now we gotta go, so shove the rest of that in your mouth, Miles, and both of you go grab your stuff."

"Fine. But I still wanna come," Miles reminded me for the five hundredth time as he swiped his bagel off the counter and dragged himself out of the kitchen.

I clenched my fists and squeezed my eyes shut, pleading for a higher power to keep me from completely losing my shit.

"Sorry, Mom."

I startled and opened my eyes to see Drew leaning against the counter beside me.

"I know things have been…I know you've been doing a lot. And maybe Dad hasn't been the best dad. Sorry to cause more problems."

I stared at him for a minute. So tall and grown up. But still needing his father so badly. He'd never been the affectionate kid, his arms remaining stick-straight whenever he sensed one of us might go in for a hug, but I wanted to wrap him up more than anything at that moment.

FOR EVA

"You're fine, sweetie. And your dad loves you, he just…" I paused, knowing damn well Drew was too old to buy any excuses I could come up with. "Well, just know he loves you."

"I know. And thanks, Mom." He threw his arms around me. I let out a tiny gasp, a smile slowly spreading across my face as I hugged him back. "For everything."

———

"Bye, boys," I called from the bottom of the porch steps as they filed into Aaron's house. "Love you!"

"Hey, Eva, wait a sec." Aaron hurried outside, shutting the door behind him.

I groaned. "What, Aaron? I have to get to the airport."

"Did you see my text?"

"No, my phone's in my purse."

"I just wanted you to know I talked to my sister, and she might keep the boys a couple of days this week," he said. "You know, with the new baby and everything, we're kinda worn out, so—"

I cocked my head to the side. "You're too worn out to raise your kids?"

He huffed. "I didn't say that. We're just so exhausted. The baby isn't sleeping, and Olivia's having to feed him all the time, and—"

"Oh, wow, you said her name."

"Huh?"

"Never mind." I sucked in a deep breath and clenched my fists before starting toward my car. "Fine. Send the kids to Laura's house. They'll probably have a better time there since she actually pays attention to them."

"Oh, come on. Don't you remember what it's like to have a newborn?"

His words stopped me in my tracks, and I turned on my heels. "Oh, I remember, Aaron. *Very* well. And I'm also reminded every day that those two newborns *we* once had are now ten and fifteen and need their fucking father."

"Why do you act like I'm not there for them?"

"Because you're fucking *not*. We're supposed to have fifty-fifty custody. That's what *you* said you wanted. But if you've changed your mind, let's make it official. We can go ahead and set a court date because I'm beyond done with you making everything else a priority over those boys."

"It's just hard right now."

"Step the fuck up, Aaron," I said, pointing my finger at him before yanking open my car door. "I'm over these constantly shifting plans of yours. It makes them feel like shit, and they deserve much better than the father they've had for the past year."

"You know I love them, Eva."

I folded myself into the SUV. "Then fucking act like it or I *will* call my attorn—"

"Okay. I don't want that and neither do you." Aaron held his hands up. "You're right. I'll do better."

"I hope so."

I shut my door and started the engine, gripping the steering wheel and taking a few deep breaths to settle the anger Aaron had ignited in me. The attorney wasn't an impulsive threat, but it also wasn't something I'd wanted to bring up on my way out of town.

I relaxed my hands and dug my phone out of my purse, quickly bypassing Aaron's text.

Denise: *Get your ass here ASAP. The Veuve is chilling!*

I chuckled and scrolled to the next message.

Eric: *Can't wait to see you tonight. Pick you up from Denise's at 6:30.*

My anger subsided as a tingle of nervous excitement caused my skin to pebble. I was at the top of that first hill on a roller coaster, staring down at the ground far below me, ready to take the plunge. Ready to admit to Eric why I'd disappeared all those years ago. Ready to finally tell him that I loved him.

FOR EVA

I arrived at the airport with an hour to spare. It was Saturday morning, meaning most travelers had already departed for their weekend jaunts, allowing me to breeze through security. My nerves had killed my appetite, but I knew pretzels would be my only form of sustenance on the plane, so I found a fast-food joint and forced down a breakfast sandwich and a Diet Coke.

As the announcement that my plane would begin boarding soon echoed throughout the terminal, I headed across the walkway to grab as many magazines as I could to distract myself during the flight. I scanned the rows of glossy covers and plucked thick copies of *Vanity Fair, Vogue*, and *Harper's Bazaar* off the shelf before moving over to the celebrity gossip rags. I grabbed several of them without much consideration since I was sure they all contained the same stories.

The cashier had just finished swiping my card when the call came for first-class passengers, so I scooped up my purchases and hurried toward the gate. I didn't normally spring for first-class, but it was either that or a middle seat in coach, and I couldn't deal with being squished between two people for four hours. Not when I was already on edge.

I settled into the leather seat and wedged all but one of the magazines into the pocket in front of me. I offered a quick smile and nod to the man next to me, then flipped open the magazine on my lap, perusing the table of contents. Nothing particularly shocking like the headlines always promised. *Hollywood's Secret Diets, Twilight Stars' Real-Life Romance, Eric Stratton's Mystery Woman…*

Wait, what?

"Ma'am?"

WHAT?

"Um, ma'am?"

"WHAT?"

I jerked my head up, startled by my own voice yelling at the flight attendant who was working the first-class cabin.

"I was just wondering if you'd like something to drink before our departure?" Her voice was small as she shrunk back into the aisle, her eyes locked on me like a frightened animal staring down the barrel of a shotgun.

My entire world was going up in flames, and she was asking what I wanted to drink? My eyes darted around the plane, searching for the nearest exit. I had to get out. A fire engulfed me, the smoke stinging my eyes and filling my lungs. I was choking, suffocating.

"Ma'am, are you okay?" The flight attendant's face was blanketed with concern.

Say something, Eva. Say something.

"I'm so sorry," I managed, my mouth thick and dry. "I, uh… I'm just a nervous flier."

The older man next to me took that as his cue to touch my hand and offer up the usual statistics on dying in a car accident versus a plane crash.

I gave him a weak smile and moved my trembling hand away as I closed the magazine. "I'll be fine once we get in the air."

"Maybe some water would help?" she asked, her expression still troubled.

"*Water?*" My aisle mate scoffed. "Get her a glass of champagne. It'll help the nerves. And I'll take a scotch."

The attendant's wide eyes moved between us like a metronome.

"Water, please," I insisted.

The man balked, and I wanted to kick him…punch him… anything to make him hurt half as badly as I did. Instead, I opened the magazine, my heartbeat pulsing in my fingertips as I turned to page twenty-one.

Who's that Girl?

*Twice in one week! Singer Eric Stratton, 44, was
spotted cozying up to an unidentified woman at a
West Hollywood Starbucks on Monday, March 30th.*

FOR EVA

*The two were seen holding hands in a secluded booth
before heading outside, where Stratton hugged the
mystery woman as they parted. Later that week, they
dined at James' Beach in Venice with friends, after
which they appeared to leave together. Could it be the
beginning of a new romance for the sexy bachelor?*

There were several pictures of them—her smiling as he held her hand across the table, his arms around her slight frame, the two of them laughing at dinner. She was young and petite, with long auburn hair and a sleeve of tattoos.

Would it hurt less if she was blond…if she was my age…if she had two kids at home?

He didn't love me after all. At least not like I loved him. Maybe he *had*, but I'd been too afraid to admit what I was feeling, and he'd moved on. He thought I was just flying to LA to visit Denise, and we'd have a friendly dinner where maybe he'd tell me about his new relationship. And could I blame him? The last time I'd seen him, I'd sent him off with a hug and a pat on the arm.

Stupid. I've been so stupid.

I let the pages fall back into place, stuffed the magazine behind the others in the seat pocket, and pressed my head against the window. My tears blurred the outside world as it sank into the very core of me that I'd lost the missing piece of my puzzle once again.

———

"Hi," Denise sang as she opened the front door and flung her arms around me before I even had a chance to enter the house. I tried to lift my own arms to hug her, but they fell limply at my sides.

She stepped back and squeezed my hands, her smile dissolving as she studied my face. I didn't have to look into a mirror to know it was blotchy and streaked with mascara.

I'd somehow managed to hold it together on the plane,

allowing a few tears to escape once the man sitting beside me finally passed out from his multiple scotches. But I'd spent the forty-five minute drive to Denise's curled up in the third row of the black Suburban, using my purse to muffle my sobs in hopes the car service driver wouldn't think I was in danger of having a complete mental breakdown in the middle of the 405. Based on the sympathetic smiles he gave me as he retrieved my luggage from the trunk, I hadn't fooled him.

"Hi," I choked out, flipping my sunglasses on top of my head.

Denise released my hands, allowing me to trudge inside with my suitcase. I dropped both it and my purse beside me and stood like a zombie in the middle of the foyer.

"What's going on, Eva?" Denise's chipper tone quickly turned panicked as she shut the door and scurried over to me. "What happened?"

"Can I sit?" I asked, my voice soft and slow.

Without hesitation, Denise nodded and started toward the living room, motioning for me to follow. But I had already taken a seat in the middle of the floor.

"Jesus Christ." She hurried back to me after she realized I wasn't going to make it to the sofa and sat down cross-legged in front of me. "I'm freaking out here, Eva. You have to tell me what's going on."

I sniffed and pulled the magazine out of my purse, placing it on the floor between us.

Denise's forehead wrinkled as she picked it up. "What's this?"

"Turn to page twenty-one."

She hesitated but did as I asked. "Okay, let's see. It says here that Jennifer Aniston may never find love again." She narrowed her eyes at me. "*This* is why you're upset?"

I shook my head. "Farther down."

She scanned the page, her eyes widening as she lifted her gaze to me. "But I don't...It can't..."

I cleared my throat in an attempt to speak, but ended up sputtering words even I couldn't make sense of as tears cascaded over my lids once again. She reached for me, and I collapsed into her, my head resting on her shoulder as she stroked the back of my hair.

"I fucked up, Denise," I finally managed. "I fucked up so bad."

"No, babe, you didn't fuck up."

"I did. It was so stupid not to tell him how I felt when I had the chance." I lifted my head, and Denise's hands slid to my cheeks. "I waited too long, and now *this*."

She wiped at my tears with her thumbs. "Maybe this isn't what we think. Maybe it's not serious. Like, if he sees you and you tell him how you feel, that girl won't matter anymore. *If* she even matters *now*."

"He was holding her hand, Denise. And the way he was hugging her... You don't hug people like that who don't matter to you. You don't drive to Venice fucking Beach to eat fish tacos with people who don't matter to you."

My phone pinged from my purse. "Shit. What if that's him?"

She nodded toward my bag, and I sighed and pulled my cell from it.

Eric: *Did you make it to Denise's?*

"He wants to know if I made it here. Oh God, Denise. What do I say? What do I *do*? I can't go to dinner with him. I just can't."

Sobs racked my body once again, and I buried my face in my hands.

"It's okay, babe," she assured me. "We'll figure it out. Maybe you can tell him you're not feeling well. See if he can go tomorrow night after you've had time to—"

"I can't, Denise."

"Hey, Eva, look at me." Denise squeezed my knee. "You don't have to see him. We can figure something out. But I think you should. And I think you should still tell him how you feel."

"And *humiliate* myself?"

"It's not humiliating. It's brave. You cut him out of your life nineteen years ago because you were afraid. I don't want you to do that again and live with regret for the next nineteen."

Her words settled into my brain, where a picture of my future formed. I was alone, or maybe not, but always wondering *what-if.* The pain that gripped my heart thinking about it was almost worse than the pain of seeing him with the girl in the magazine. And even if he did tell me it was too late for us, did I want to lose him as a friend? A friend who encouraged me and believed in me. A friend who saw amazing things in me when I couldn't see them myself.

A friend whom I'd lost once before and been lucky enough to find again.

No. He was too important to me. Much too important.

But I couldn't tell him at dinner. Not in public.

"What are you thinking, babe?" Denise asked.

"You're right...I have to go see him," I answered, slowly nodding my head. "I have to see him now. Before I lose my nerve."

"Really?"

I ran my hands along my cheeks and sucked in a deep breath. "Really."

"Do you have his address?"

I nodded.

Denise's eyes glittered with hope as they met mine. "I'll get you my car keys."

No what-ifs, Eva. No what-ifs.

The words played on a loop in my head as I turned off the PCH and headed toward Point Dume. Eric's house was barely a mile off the highway, and I slowed as several gated entrances came into view, waiting for the GPS to tell me I'd reached my destination.

I pulled the car into his driveway lined with tall toyon

shrubs, then flipped down the visor, lamenting my red puffy eyes. I'd quickly splashed water on my face at Denise's but didn't reapply my makeup. The longer I waited to get in the car, the more time I'd have to talk myself out of seeing him.

And I *had* to see him.

After one final deep breath, I stepped out onto the stamped concrete. My hand trembled as I pressed the button on the call box, then leaned against Denise's car, the warmth of the black steel seeping through my sundress. I tipped my head back and closed my eyes, the steady pounding of my heartbeat pulsating in every part of my body.

And I waited.

And waited.

After several minutes, I pressed the button again, my eyes squarely focused on the speaker, holding my breath and praying to hear Eric's voice.

But there was nothing.

No voice.

No buzz signaling the opening of the gate.

Nothing but the squawks of a few seagulls circling overhead before flying off toward the beach.

I stared at the call box for another minute or two.

Should I call him? Text him?

I dismissed the thought as an image of him lying in bed with the girl from the magazine crept into my head. She was draped over him, listening to the crashing of the waves while he stroked her hair. He'd pull himself away from her in a few hours, explaining that an old friend was in town whom he felt obligated to meet for dinner.

I rubbed my eyes with the heels of my palms, blurring the sequence that played in my brain, and resigned myself to the fact that all I could do was to head back to Denise's. I opened the car door and sank into the tan leather seat.

Maybe I should let him come to Denise's and tell him there.

Maybe I should text him and tell him I'm sick.

Maybe I should've gotten off the plane in Nashville.

Maybe there's a car blocking me and I can't even get out of the damn driveway.

I blinked before looking into the rearview mirror again to see a silver Porsche idling behind me with Eric inside, leaning forward, trying to figure out exactly who the hell was parked at the entrance to his house. Worried that flinging open the door and running toward him like a lunatic might send him peeling out of the driveway, I did the only thing I could think to do. I twisted my body in the seat and stuck my head out the open window as far as it could go—not entirely avoiding the whole lunatic scenario.

"Eric, don't leave! It's me! It's—"

"Eva?" He leaned out his own window and removed his sunglasses before cutting the engine and stepping out onto the driveway.

I got out of the car and watched him walk toward me, amazed at how he could turn an old T-shirt and jeans into the sexiest outfit on earth. Beads of sweat formed on my forehead, and I steadied myself against the car door, afraid I might fall into a heap on the ground.

He stopped in front of me, his eyes catching the sun like a pair of blue crystals as he smiled. "What are you doing here? I said I'd come pick you up."

My pulse throbbed in my neck as I searched for the right words.

"Are you okay?" he asked, studying my face. "Have you been crying?"

I'd rehearsed what I was going to say on the drive, but he was so beautiful—his hair a little longer, the beginnings of a beard tracing his jaw and upper lip—that I couldn't look at him and formulate any sort of intelligible words.

"I know this seems kinda crazy…or weird…or both. But I came because I had to tell you I was afraid." I paused, tightening my fists in frustration because I was already fucking this up.

"Afraid of…"

"You," I continued, finally looking up at him. "All those years ago, when I stopped answering your letters and phone calls, I was scared. And I guess I'm still scared now, but I don't want to live with what-ifs." I groaned and squeezed my eyes shut. "Fuck, I'm not making any sense."

"What's going on?" he asked, touching my arm. "Do you wanna come inside and sit down?"

"No, I need to get this out." I swallowed and pressed on. "What I'm trying to say is I think I missed my chance. And it's fine if I have. I don't want to lose our friendship, it's too important to me, so if—"

"Wait." Eric placed his hand on my arm to stop my rambling, and I allowed my gaze to settle on him. "What do you mean you missed your chance?"

"Because of that girl. The girl you were with in that magazine."

He let his hand fall away and narrowed his eyes. "What girl? What magazine?"

A pit formed in my stomach as the vision of them tangled up in bed flashed in my mind. "The girl you're dating. But it doesn't matter because it's okay. I get it. I waited too long to admit to myself how I feel about you and how you maybe used to feel about me. And so I missed my chance. But I don't want to lose you as a friend. I just couldn't tell you at dinner. It's all too—"

"*Used* to feel about you?"

I nodded, looking down as my eyes began to water. "I knew this was a possibility, but I had to let you know…Wait, what?"

My brows turned inward as I jerked my head up to find him smiling at me.

"You haven't missed anything, Eva."

"But the girl…You were hugging her outside Starbucks… You were in Venice Beach. Auburn hair. Tattoos."

Eric sighed and threw his head back. "Fuck."

My body tensed. "Why 'fuck'?"

"Eva. That's Ruby."

"Ruby?" The name was familiar, but the only Ruby I could think of was—

I gasped. "You're dating Keith's daughter? The one who was born when we were on tour?"

He laughed and shook his head. "No, Eva. I'm actually *not* dating someone who graduated from high school two years ago, but thank you for thinking so highly of me."

I cupped my hands together over my nose and mouth. "So it wasn't…She's not…Oh my God, Eric, I'm so sorry."

"I'm not dating her, but I *am* helping her band record a demo. The band she plays in with her boyfriend. She's been down about the possibility of never making it, and I've just been trying to encourage her to keep going."

I let my hands fall away, though I would have preferred to hide until my cheeks ceased turning five hundred shades of red. "I didn't think…I was already on the plane coming here, and I saw the pictures, and I just…"

"My publicist mentioned some photos, but I wasn't even paying attention," he explained. "I don't think twice about that shit anymore. Regardless, I can assure you Ruby would be horrified if anyone thought for a second she was dating a forty-four-year-old—especially her Uncle Eric. So, maybe I do need to shut that story down."

I pressed my palm to my heart. "I…I don't know what to say."

"I think starting with how you feel about me is good." He smiled and cupped my cheek in his hand.

Warmth traveled down my body, and I wanted to close my eyes and melt into him. But I took in a deep breath and steadied myself. I had to tell him what I'd come here to say.

"I disappeared all those years ago because I was afraid, Eric," I said, holding his gaze. "Afraid I was falling in love with you. After what happened with Danny, I thought I was broken, and I needed someone to fix me. And I thought maybe you were broken, too, so how could we ever fix each other? But I was wrong. Because now, I'm standing here wondering how I ever managed to keep my feelings from you because I'm so absolutely, completely in love with you that I—"

Eric pulled me into him, his lips crashing into mine. Bursts of white light exploded behind my lids, his kiss so intense that my knees buckled and I fell into him, his arms the only thing holding me up. I regained my balance as his lips brushed over mine once more before finding their way to my forehead.

"I love you, too, Eva. More than you could ever fucking imagine." He chuckled softly, his hands smoothing the hair that fluttered against my face in the ocean breeze. "Do you have any idea how long I've been waiting to say that?"

I nodded, my head still hazy from our kiss. "I think I do."

"I wrote you a letter once, asking you to come to LA when I finished that first solo tour. I wanted to tell you how I felt in person. But I never heard back, so I thought I'd missed *my* chance."

Oh my God. The letter.

"I...I didn't read it. But I tried to find it and—"

He shook his head and placed his thumb over my lip. "It doesn't matter, Eva. You're here now."

"I am. And I have a question, actually."

"Shoot, woman."

A smile crept over my lips. "Did you ever sit on a rooftop with any other girl?"

His lips twisted as he looked up to the sky. "Hmm...not sure." He grabbed my hips and pulled me closer, bringing his gaze back down to mine. "But I do know there's only one I ever wrote a song about."

EPILOGUE
DANNY

SEPTEMBER 2010

"**C**an you get the Chunky Monkey? And the Chocolate Chip Cookie Dough. Oh, and cheese puffs! *Not* Cheetos. Make sure they're the puffy kind."

I stood in the threshold of the front door, one hand on the doorknob, the other pressed to my forehead in an attempt to ease the dull ache enveloping my brain.

"Anything else?" I asked, wondering for a second if driving off a cliff generally resulted in a quick and painless death.

Jade smiled at me in a way that made me think she was enjoying sending me out on a snack expedition at 11 p.m. way too much. Her black hair was piled into a bun, and she was stretched across the sofa with her feet propped up on pillows. A package of Oreos rested on her stomach while she watched some horrible show about New Jersey housewives.

"Nope, that's it. Thanks, sweetie," she chirped before spraying a shot of Reddi-wip directly in her mouth.

I closed the door and sighed, gazing up at the hazy night sky, the lights from the city below casting their yellow glow upon it. I stood there for a minute, unsure if I was asking the universe to tell me how I'd gotten into this situation or how to get out of it. Maybe it was a little bit of both, though I knew the latter wasn't an option. I may not have been the most stand-up guy in the world, but I wasn't gonna leave the mother of my kid when she was seven months pregnant. Even if she *had* forgotten to bring her birth control pills to her modeling gig in Hawaii and thought it'd be fine to miss a week.

A week that just happened to fall during a time when we were *on* in our on-again, off-again whatever it was.

I clicked the key fob and trudged to my car, opening the door and sliding into the seat. As soon as I started the engine, Justin Timberlake's falsetto began blaring from the speakers.

"For fuck's sake, Jade." I quickly pressed the display to change the station, then pulled onto the street as a Guns N' Roses tune faded out and the DJ introduced the next song.

"So does anyone remember when these guys were supposed to take over the world? They had that one *massive* album. *Everyone* had that album, man. Of course, we all know their singer, Eric Stratton, went on to do a ton of solo stuff. And their drummer played with Center of Fear. But the other two guys…maybe working desk jobs these days? Who knows. Anyway, here's some Counting Backward for ya."

"Fuuuck you," I groaned, jabbing the off button.

I drove in silence the rest of the way, half-pissed at the DJ for being a dick and half-pissed he was right in that I technically *did* have a desk.

I pulled into the parking lot where only a few cars sat under the dim glow of the metal light poles. As I headed into the store, I quickly snatched up a basket and set about searching for Jade's requests, grabbing a six pack of Lagunitas along the way for myself.

There was a single cashier working, so I took my place in line behind the one person in all of West Hollywood who'd decided to do her weekly grocery shopping at eleven thirty on a Saturday night.

I sighed and placed my basket on the floor, settling in for a wait while the midnight shopper unloaded the contents of her cart. My eyes wandered to the magazine rack to my left filled with covers promising "exclusive" celebrity news. I was about to pull my phone out of my pocket and check emails when a cover line on one of the magazines stopped me in my tracks. Not trusting my tired eyes, I plucked it from the rack.

OFF THE MARKET:
Eric Stratton Engaged!

Seriously? Does the universe have a fucking hit out on me tonight?

I quickly flipped through the pages until I found the blurb with his picture above it. He was walking down a city sidewalk in jeans and a T-shirt, holding the hand of a woman who was similarly dressed. Her hair was pulled back into a ponytail, a few loose blond strands wisping into her face. Two boys were on either side of them—the taller one with the same blond hair walking alongside the woman, the other with dark hair beside Eric, who had his arm around the boy's shoulders. There was a close-up shot set within the larger photo showcasing a ring on the woman's left hand.

I looked up to make sure the person in front of me was still checking out, then started to read:

> *After years of being touted as one of the music*
> *industry's most eligible bachelors, a publicist for Eric*
> *Stratton confirmed there are indeed wedding bells in*
> *the future for the singer-songwriter and his girlfriend,*
> *Eva Mitchell. While the couple has managed to keep*
> *their relationship out of the spotlight, sources reveal*
> *that Mitchell is a marketing exec with an indepen-*
> *dent record label in Nashville, and previously worked*
> *with the band Counting Backward, for whom Stratton*
> *served as front man in the mid to late '80s. She also*
> *has two children from a former marriage, which will*
> *make four-time Grammy winner Stratton a stepdad.*

I stared at the glossy page until the words started to blur. With one last look at the picture, I closed the magazine and returned it to the rack. I blew out a breath, picked up the basket,

FOR EVA

and stepped forward with my ice cream, cheese puffs, and beer.

As I unloaded the groceries onto the belt, I shook my head and sighed, the beginnings of a smile tugging at the corners of my mouth.

Eric Stratton.

That motherfucker.

ACKNOWLEDGMENTS

Though I do have a flair for the dramatic, you have to believe me when I say this book simply would not exist without **MELISSA GRACE**. For *three whole years*, she encouraged me and read every word I wrote—multiple times. An accomplished author in her own right, she helped me every step of the way on this journey and to say I am eternally grateful doesn't seem to suffice. But since I'm sick of looking up synonyms, that will have to do. And though I won't go into all the details, I'll just say that she believed in Eva and Eric before I did, and this could've been a very different story had I not listened to some very solid advice.

To **KATE**, my treasured alpha reader and friend, who is always honest with me in the kindest way possible because that's just who she is. She's been with me since the beginning, and I hope she stays forever.

To my editor, **CHRIS WHEARY** a lovely human and master grammarian who mostly leaves my dialogue alone (bless you).

To **P.L. HERNANDEZ,** an incredible author and kind soul, who came to the rescue of some random chick she met on Instagram and helped turn a Word document into a book.

To **KAYLA**, my alpha/beta reader and hype woman.

To **REAH, ELISE, ALLIE, BROOKE,** and **CHRISTANA,** my amazing beta readers who gave me the confidence I needed to see this through to the end.

To my husband, **RYAN**, who might just be the best man

ever to walk the face of the earth.

To **MY DAUGHTER**—you're Rizz, bro.

To **ITTY**, my perfect-in-every-way angel kitty. Also, he is a lil orange lamb and a baby bear.

To **BETHEL** and **SARAH**, aka Table 45, please, thank you, please.

To **BOBBY, MEGAN,** and **BETH**, my college ride-or-dies. They know things.

To **ANNE**, the woman who walked into a pie shop and became one of my best friends.

To **KIM**, the woman I stalked at preschool because I knew we were meant to be.

To **ROSE**, who always sees right fucking through me (damn it).

To **BECCA**, who asked me about this book every time she saw me.

To **CINDY, ALLYSON,** and **JAMIE**, who threw me the best book-themed birthday party (along with Kim, Rose, and Becca).

To **LISA** and **ELISSA**, my GN'R girls (and so much more)— just fucking look at what Twitter did.

To **DIVYA**, who also gets weak over men who look like Johnny Thunders.

To the Hearthstone Hotties: **LAURA, MEGGAN, AN-DREA, ANGIE, CLAIRE, ERICA,** and **SUSAN.**

To **AMANDA** and **DAWN**, the women I can always count on to help me with all the mom things.

To **MICHAEL**, for answering all my questions about how a label launches a band.

To **JEFF**, my dear friend, who also happens to be an amazing attorney.

To **NICOLE** and **OLIVER**, two wonderful medical professionals who helped me with the hard stuff.

To **ROMI, SUMI, ANNIE,** and **MARA**, the lovelies who helped me get the Italian right.

To the Australians I harassed, **STEVE** and **PRU.**

JEN DAVIS

To **GIANNA, PHIL**, and **JEAN**, the people who remind me it's okay to not be okay.

To **MY MOM, DAD, SISTER, AUNTS, IN-LAWS**, and the rest of my family who encourage and support me.

To **PAUL, GENE, ACE,** and **PETER**, who taught a five-year-old girl the meaning of rock 'n' roll.

To **IZZY STRADLIN**, my forever crush.

And to all the bands who ruled the Strip in the '80s—a million, trillion thanks for creating the soundtrack not just to my youth, but my entire life. There would be no book without you.